Pelican Coast

**Center Point
Large Print**

**This Large Print Book carries the
Seal of Approval of N.A.V.H.**

Pelican Coast

Alan Le May

Center Point Publishing
Thorndike, Maine

This Center Point Large Print edition
is published in the year 2004 by arrangement with
Golden West Literary Agency.

The text of this Large Print edition is unabridged. In other
aspects, this book may vary from the original edition. Printed in
Thailand. Set in 16-point Times New Roman type by
Bill Coskrey and Gary Socquet.

ISBN 1-58547-385-5

Library of Congress Cataloging-in-Publication Data

Le May, Alan, 1899-1964.
  Pelican coast / Alan Le May.--Center Point large print ed.
    p. cm.
  ISBN 1-58547-385-5 (lib. bdg. : alk. paper)
    1. Lafitte, Jean--Fiction. 2. Mexico, Gulf of--Fiction. 3. Privateering--Fiction.
  4. Louisiana--Fiction. 5. Pirates--Fiction. 6. Large type books. I. Title.

PS3523.E513P45 2004
813'.52--dc22

2003060278

Chapter I

1

OHE LITTLE LUGGER moved but slowly over the surface of the bayou; her patched canvas hardly filled under the impulse of a breeze so faint that it whispered only dimly in the tangle of the cypress. She was barely four fathoms long, no more than a rowboat with a rag up; yet she seemed to fill the narrow ribbon of water completely, so that the gray sail moved like a tall ghost between trees. It was as if a vessel long dead glided through jungle that had once been sea, retraversing tracks from which the sea had long since gone.

The young Frenchman in the bow stirred, his patience yielding.

"Here," he demanded, "what's those old planks there, on the starboard beach? Ain't that the De Verniat landing?"

The ancient Spaniard in the stern answered in a husky still voice from which all energy seemed to have been sapped by the hungry years. *"Sí, señor."*

"Put in there, and wait for me."

"Sí." The tiller swung.

Jacques Durossac sprang to the landing and sauntered up the path. The long beards of Spanish moss, drooping low from the arms of the cypress, waved faintly for a moment after he disappeared. The sail of the little lugger rattled down, and she lay at rest, as quiet on the

5

still water as if she would never move again; and over her settled the silence of the Louisiana swamp, the hush of perpetually suspended activity.

Jacques Durossac's first call upon the widowed Madame de Verniat was inspired by a mistaken idea that her plantation was some kind if public stable. The journey from Barataria Bay, where the irregular privateers dropped anchor, to New Orleans, which received their smuggled spoils, was a sixty-mile drag through the swamp country by lake and bayou; and in this case the privateersman had grown tired of sitting still.

He knew that Jean Lafitte, boss of Louisiana smugglers, always abandoned his lugger at this point and proceeded on horseback. The Mississippi River was four miles away, and New Orleans six miles down stream, so that the time saved by keeping a mount at the De Verniat plantation was material. Durossac was not himself inclined to favour the saddle, associating it with certain unpleasant experiences; and since most of his trips to New Orleans involved the incidental transportation of contraband he had not before investigated the short cut.

Upon this simple fortuity the first meeting of Durossac and Madelon de Verniat was based.

2

OHE PLANTATION of Madame de Verniat and her daughter was a tongue of soggy ground a mile long and a few hundred yards wide, thrust into the swamp from the higher ground beside the Mississippi. Through it, splitting it lengthwise, ran the trickle of water that had built that tongue of soil from its own muck—the Bayou des Familles, the last thread in the snarled skein of bayous that gave the Baratarian smugglers a hidden way to New Orleans from the sea. It was land that by all rights belonged to the swamp; even at that time Madame de Verniat's overseer was making only a losing struggle against the seeping brown waters which every spring seemed to well up through the soil itself, mocking the levees. In the end the jealous swamp reclaimed its own. To-day cabbage palms with boles as thick as a man's body grow in furrows that can still be seen trailing off into tangle; and only a couple of ruined brick pilings are left of the house that Jules de Verniat built.

But in 1811, on the morning that Jacques Durossac went swaggering up from the lugger landing, the buildings still retained an air of comfortable means and pleasant leisured hospitality. After he had got through the fifty yards or so of jungle tangle beside the bayou he could make out beyond the trees the broad square house, low-roofed, painted white by the violent sunshine. It was girdled by broad galleries, raised high off the ground on pillars of plastered brick; and in general effect was so much more impressive than anything Durossac had expected that he hesitated; and then, nonchalantly, turned off on a side path that he could see led to the stables.

It was characteristic of Jacques Durossac that neither his incongruous appearance here, nor the fact that he had as yet spent but little time on Louisiana soil, could make him appear anything but at his ease, as if he were upon familiar ground. He was, as a matter of fact, as much at home here as he could have been upon any soil. Durossac was one of that score of French privateersmen who, when the British took Guadeloupe, lost their last friendly port, yet now continued to sail, portless, uncommissioned, and without benefit of admiralty, but—by their own declaration—privateersmen still. Without a friendly base in the Western world, and with their prizes changed to contraband overnight, the French privateers had the year before, in 1810, made a rendezvous of Barataria Bay, sixty miles west of the Mississippi delta on the forlorn Louisiana coast. And Jacques Durossac, commander of his own one-gun schooner, had come with the rest to put his business interests into the hands of the master smuggler, Jean Lafitte.

At the De Verniat stable he was met by a small humpbacked negro.

"Here, you—get a horse out here!" Durossac shouted. "What am I waiting for? Have I got all day?"

A gibbering of gumbo French came tumbling, after a frightened pause, from the little negro's lips. Durossac, who understood no more than half, yet gathered that there was no horse for hire; none for sale; none to borrow for miles around.

"Oh," said Durossac.

He accepted his mistake in good part; and, there being no breeze, set about a general inspection to see what manner of show they had got here, anyway. Entirely unconscious of being in any sense an intruder,

Durossac unofficially checked over the resources of the stable; tickled Lafitte's hammer-headed mare with a stick, and hurriedly withdrew when she promptly kicked a board out of the wall beside him; picked some green peaches from a runty little tree with the vague notion of having somebody cook them for him; hoisted the stable boy up to the gable of the barn with the hay tackle to see how it worked; and presently let the boy down again because he could think of nothing to do with the end of the rope. There was little activity within Durossac's head, but he liked to keep his hands busy at this or that.

Passing on, he strolled through a weedy grove toward the house, and thus unexpectedly he came upon Madelon de Verniat.

Durossac's mouth sagged open. Mademoiselle de Verniat sat in the fork of a live oak, watching him, round-eyed, like a treed cat. She was at that time no more than sixteen years old, but, being bred in a climate in which women mature early, she was by no means a child. Her small triangular face had a certain look of fragility, made the more noticeable by her heavily lashed dark eyes. She was tanned almost as thoroughly as Durossac, which was not to his taste. Still—his surprise dissolved in a friendly grin.

"Eh là, bon jour!" he offered.

Madelon had watched Durossac's exploit with the stable boy and the hay derrick with alarm. When he entered the grove she would have dropped to the ground and fled, but a momentary paralysis of fright had made her too late, and she had sat still, her ankles tucked up under her, in hope that he might pass unnoticing.

The privateersman presented an uncommon figure. He wore the whacked-off dungarees in which he went to sea, for he kept his lugger not very clean. But his shoes were low cut of fine leather, with enormous buckles of tarnished ormolu; and his shirt, open at the throat, was freshly white, starched rigid. In one ear he wore a gold ring an inch and a half across; it was an ornament he always wore to New Orleans, not so much because it was common among seamen as because he believed it to be the *dernier cri* among the elegants of Paris. He was newly shaved.

Before his bland smile Madelon de Verniat's fright subsided. The peculiar talent for murder that earned Durossac his living was an innate one, born into his character; it did not show in any wastage of perverted or broken character in his face. He was but twenty-two years old; his mentality remained that of a child, and the spirit of the man, simple and untroubled by self-doubt, was no older. His face, without the distortion of action, was a boy's face. It had got him into trouble more than once; it was serviceable to him now. Madelon, still speechless, smiled back.

Durossac leaped into the air, caught the branch upon which she sat in a hand like a steel hook, and swung up beside her, scaring her half out of her wits again. Leisurely he drew out a frog-green peach, crunched it in two with his teeth, and found it so savagely sour that it might as well have bitten him in return. He urged a bite upon Madelon, pretending it was good; and when her face puckered up he laughed at her immoderately. Presently she began to laugh with him, nervously, high keyed by the excitement of the unaccustomed adventure.

"You live here?"

"Yes."

"Well, that's nice. I'm from Barataria. I'm a captain."

"Oh, do you know Captain Lafitte?"

"*Mister* Lafitte? Oh, sure. Why? Do you?"

"Oh, yes. He stops by to see my mother."

"He stops to see your mother, does he?" Durossac sucked his teeth wryly as he talked.

"Yes, often."

"To see your *mother?* To see you, you mean."

"Oh, no. Mother gives him coffee."

"Oh." Durossac was exulting inwardly at turning up an affair which would be a great joke to tell on Jean Lafitte. The uncomplicated but direct mind of Durossac already perceived things that Lafitte would have wished undiscovered.

Conversation flagged, but Durossac saw that Madelon was in no great hurry to run away. Taking his time about his love-making, as he took his time about everything but his fighting, Durossac essayed to divert Madelon by a feat of strength. He let himself tip backward off the limb, skinned the cat, and very slowly reversed, his good shoulder muscles hunching in great swells that slit the linen of his shirt halfway down his back. He came up onto the limb again very bright-eyed and red in the face from the suspension, and examined the injury with some concern. It would not show with his coat on, he decided; and thought nothing more of it. Madelon, he conceived, looked impressed.

One of Madelon's hands lay idle upon the rough bark of the limb. Durossac casually covered it with his own.

A great screech from the house snapped Durossac into fixed attention, like a dog. "MadelO-O-ON!"

"That's my mother," she told him.

"Oh?"

She clambered to the ground, and he swung down after her.

"Good-bye."

"Good-bye."

She went toward the house reluctantly, turning her head once to smile at him over her shoulder; and he leaned against the tree watching her departure sadly, impervious to the shocked stare of the fussy little lady who had called Madelon away.

3

DUROSSAC'S CALL was not over, quite. A hurried conference took place between mother and daughter immediately within the threshold of the house.

"Madelon! I'm astounded! Who was that man?"

"Why, Mother, that man is a friend of Captain Lafitte's. One of Captain Lafitte's *best* friends. And he is a captain himself—a very important man at Grand Isle. I think—"

"Well, why didn't you bring him in? I'm scandalized! My own daughter up a tree with a—"

"Captain Lafitte is going to be terribly offended—

you'll see. He'll—"

But Madame de Verniat was ahead of her. For this particular gentle-lady, Lafitte's name was enough. "Jezebel! Jeze-BE-EL! Run after the captain—there he goes toward the landing. Tell him I desire him to have coffee. At once!"

Thus Jacques Durossac was surprised to find himself pursued by a leggy negress, insistent with the news that it was necessary for him to have coffee—at once. Always confident, unfearful, and willing to try anything, Durossac cheerfully about-faced and went back.

He was received upon the gallery, where there were chairs; it was easier for people to live on galleries in the drenched heat of Louisiana summer than in the airless rooms inside. Madame's vague greeting—they knew him only as "the Captain"—he accepted with reticence, but passably enough. Madame was made uneasy by his dungarees and his lack of coat and stock; but she supposed she would have to overlook such seaman's eccentricities, under the circumstances, and in view of his connection with Lafitte. Durossac was, after all, a very handsome young man. While Jezebel delayed the bringing of coffee, Madame de Verniat attempted to inveigle him into conversation.

"I've heard so much about you brave captains of Barataria," she began, simpering

"Oh?" said Durossac.

Behind Madame de Verniat, embodied in her class and race, was an advanced culture, shallow and superficial perhaps in some of its phases, but nevertheless singularly rich, intricate, and closely defined. This background was invisible to Durossac; even if he had perceived it, he would have been unimpressed. That man was one who thought well of himself. He was uneducated and of undistinguished birth; yet he never thought of himself as a common man.

"Do tell me about some of the others," she urged. "I'm so interested!"

"Who?" said Durossac, badly off his course and promising to founder.

"I've heard Captain Lafitte mention so many interesting names," Madame de Verniat rushed on. She felt patronizing, putting this quaint fellow at his ease. "Nez Coupé, for instance. What does he look like?"

"Who, Nose-Off?"

"Yes— M'sieu Coupé."

Durossac meditated, amenably trying to think of an answer. He started to draw a peach from his pocket, but thrust it back.

"Like the after end of a cow," he offered.

A great gasp escaped Madame de Verniat. "Oh! Oh!" She had never been so shocked in her life! "Oh! Madelon! Smelling salts!"

Durossac was alarmed; he thought the old lady was going into a fit. Madelon, red faced and bursting with suppressed laughter, was motioning him to leave. He got up with a sort of sad dignity and started for the stair.

As he imprudently turned his back the tear in his shirt was revealed; it had now grown to a long rip from neckband to belt, laying bare the tanned skin. Madame de Verniat, to whom the shirt appeared utterly backless, was overcome. A brief shriek startled Durossac into nimbly leaping the rail. He paused for a moment to peer curiously around a pillar at the hysterical lady, then set off toward the landing, walking briskly.

Chapter II

1

$\mathcal{D}$UROSSAC slowed to a stroll as he neared the bayou. A second small boat was now moored short to the landing in the black shadow cut into the sunlight by the cypress, and its crew of half-naked blacks and mulattos were clambering stiffly to the wharf. Job Northrup, young, tall, and unmistakably Yankee, was striding up the path through alternate bars of sunlight and shadow that gave his face the appearance of being lighted by successive gunpowder flashes.

"Hi, Jacques," said Northrup.

"Hello, you," said Durossac. He noted the drench of sweat upon the heavy bare arms of the oarsman, and immediately leaped to the conclusion that some emergency had arisen of which the Yankee brought word. "You come after me?" he asked with annoyance.

"No, not me. I'm going to New Orleans, is all."

"You seem to be in a hurry," Durossac commented. The Yankee did not see what he was talking about. "I never hurry," he averred.

Durossac had seen this man for the first time but two days before. Northrup had appeared at Grand Isle in search of Jean Lafitte; and, with the catlike watchfulness of the privateersmen, Durossac had taken pains to nose out his exact business. The Yankee had announced that he had come to the Mississippi as mate of the brig *Charles*, now lying for sale in the river before the town; and that he was seeking a new berth, on which question he wished to consult Lafitte. The simplicity of this statement told Durossac nothing. He retained a faint instinctive hostility for the gaunt young Northerner, whom he found too coolly abrupt, and too hurried, for his liking.

"You still looking for Lafitte?"

Northrup grinned. "I'll catch up with him yet."

"You could have saved the niggers," Durossac told him. "Didn't you know he was due back at Grand Isle Thursday night? You're a good one! First you chase out of New Orleans just as Lafitte comes in; now you chase yourself back to town just as he's about to come back to the coast. If you'd ask me—"

"If I catch him in New Orleans," said Northup, "and get no berth, I'll have saved a day. No use waiting at Grand Isle if I'm moving on anyway."

"Saved a day for what?"

The Yankee looked blank. He didn't know for what. "Well—I'd save it." He started up the path in long strides.

Durossac stepped in front of him. "Here, you—where you going?"

"Lafitte hires a horse along here somewhere, doesn't he? I'm sick of these mosquito creeks." A sudden thought struck him. "Look—that gunny sack on a stick won't take you any place. Tell you what I'll do. If I get

16

a horse I'll make you a good price on the use of them blacks. They're costing me—"

"You'll get no horse here," declared Durossac.

"Well—I'll try it. Wait for me if you want the crew." He started to turn away, but the other caught his arm.

"I wouldn't go up there if I was you." A faint hint of menace tinged Durossac's tone.

"What's the reason?" The big Yankee casually dropped an arm across Durossac's half-clad shoulders, turned him, and carried him along as he ambled on. He inclined his ear with an air of grave attention. This highly friendly and reasonable move took Durossac by surprise; he was annoyed, but not ready for open hostilities yet.

"I found out that it's a damned poor place to go," he answered.

"Dogs?" asked Northrup, twisting his neck to eye the privateersman's linen.

"That may be, too."

"Well—I get along all right with dogs."

"That ain't it, exactly," Durossac told him. "The thing is, there's a crazy woman up there."

"Crazy?"

"Crazier than a saw fish. She threw a fit just now. I wouldn't put anything past her."

The Yankee took this as a good point at which to break away. He let out an explosive chuckle, but Durossac's quick eye found his face a mask. "Much obliged, Jacques. I'll keep my shirt out of her reach."

Durossac stood looking sideways after him as he went striding away; he was half minded to send a knife after the tall Northerner, but he could not decide between the knife and a hail, and while he hesitated the Yankee disappeared around the turn of the path. Durossac turned back to his boat.

"Yankee son of a bitch," he muttered under his breath.

2

THE SCENE that Madame de Verniat was creating over the unhappy call of Durossac was interrupted by a knocking at the front of the house. She was not sorry. She felt the swamp years bearing heavily upon her in spite of herself, and she could not throw energy into hysterics as she had once been able. Madelon in the last year or two had become rather callous to her mother's tantrums, and the lack of sympathy made them a little flat. Madame de Verniat now sat bolt upright, searching for her handkerchief and trying with her fingers to repair the effects of tears upon her complexion.

Madelon went through the house to the door, and partly opened it.

The Yankee stood before her, immensely tall, thin, and erect. His costume represented a sort of slop-chest potpourri, featuring a coat that was a cross between a light peajacket and a long-tailed frock. His shirt showed traces of having been at some time dyed butternut, and his stock appeared to have been improvised from a crumpled handkerchief. Yet upon his spare frame these miserable garments hung with a loose ease, a certain careless implication of elegance, as if the character of the clothes did not matter upon this man.

"I came," he said, "to apologize for the intrusion of my man."

His bow to Madelon was from the shoulders, like a Northerner's, instead of from the waist like a Creole's; it was poised and deferential, but at the same time, far from its own setting, suggestive of a vague austerity that was not intended, nor indeed a part of it. Madelon stared, starting to speak, but at a loss what to say; her complete inexperience made every human contact a fresh problem, with no guiding customs or dependable conventions.

"He had no right to come busting up here," the man continued in English; then immediately translated into French that happened to be weaker but more formal in sound.

Like Durossac, he was recently shaved; the razor had left the skin fresh and clear, untroubled by the dark underlying bristle common to older or swarthier men. It was the innate gravity of his expression and the weather-creased lines in his cheeks that made him look older than he was. These things to Madelon made him seem impressive, a person of distinguished conse-quence. Unlike Durossac's, his hands were clean.

She must answer him, yet could find nothing to say. After some hesitation she decided to seek counsel. Returning to the rear gallery she found her mother quite bright and composed. The astonishing transfor-mations of which her mother was capable still could give the girl a queer sense of unreality, as if what had gone before had been illusion; it was only a little while ago that Madelon had begun to understand what sort of mental make-up made that volatility possible. Madame de Verniat was stirred to curiosity by the Yankee's baritone voice; she expressed the opinion, with an airy tilt of the head, that the stranger should be admitted.

"You are welcome to my house," said Madame de Verniat with dignity as he appeared on the rear gallery. "We are always glad to see—one of Captain Lafitte's friends. You are Captain—"

"Job Northrup," the Yankee supplied. "Not Captain. I am a seaman. I feel honoured, Madame de Vormiac."

"De Verniat," Madame informed him.

"How?"

"De Verniat!"—with some asperity. Madame was disappointed in his declared status. "Was that creature who was here a captain?"

"Possibly," said Northrup gravely.

"Possibly? I don't understand. He said he was a captain of Barataria, one of Jean Lafitte's captains."

"He should know best, madame."

"And you are—uh—"

"An able seaman, madame."

An awkward silence fell. Though Northrup was speaking an approximation of Madame de Verniat's own language, his language of tone, of gesture and attitude, were strange to her; not unintelligible, but grossly misleading. It was the meeting of two different cultures, not at the time adjusted to each other. What the Yankee thought was an attitude of deference transmitted itself to Madame de Verniat as barren effrontery.

Yet she did not know where to place this man. Neither

she nor her daughter believed that the Yankee was what he pretended to be. Had he announced himself as a person of distinction, Madame de Verniat, at least, would have discredited him. As it was, she thought him no seaman, but perhaps something more. She was the victim of a passionately detested isolation; it made her forgetful that once, in better days, she would have considered the rejection of a dozen acceptable people preferable to the entertainment of one of dubious standing.

"Won't you," she suggested hesitantly, "won't you have a cup of coffee?"

Her guest seated himself leisurely, without further invitation. Inwardly, Northrup was in a state of uneasiness very rare to him. He was incapable of the rushing excitements of the Creoles, which sent them into rapid speech and gesturings of quick hands. But he was subject to the compressed intensities of his own race, which created havoc enough in their way. Since his presentation to Madame de Verniat his face had remained unexpressive, as still and stiff as if it had been made of hardened cowhide. He did not look at Madelon, yet he was keenly aware of her; conscious of her to the exclusion of Madame de Verniat, to the exclusion of the articles of utility that commonly took precedence, in his attention, over living people. Northrup was in that phase of sensitivity experienced by all seafaring men during the first days ashore after a protracted cruise. He had but recently made port; and he had been a long time in the loneliness of the sea.

"You are from the North, I assume?" Madame suggested. "What is it like there? Is it much the same as here?"

"Not one bit," said the Yankee.

"But how is it different?"

"Well—" the Yankee's eyes screwed up, and he tore off a strip of fingernail with his teeth; then suddenly he went on with unexpected coherence—"there are low mountains near the coast; they are black with pines. The coast is made up of huge rocks."

"As big as a pillow?"

"Many of them as big as a house."

Madame de Verniat turned cool, faintly insulted. She felt that he might have compromised with her guess instead of correcting her so radically. There was a slight disciplining pause before she politely continued her examination. "And in the winter it is full of ice," she offered, wishing to show her knowledge of geography.

"Yes, madame."

"And you were a mariner there?"

"A whaler, madame."

The dull tenor of inquiry was broken by Madelon's sudden exclamation.

"A whaler!"

"Harpooner, on the barque *Justice*." He let himself turn his eyes to her, now, and was struck by the quick interest in her face.

"Oh, tell us about whaling!"

He explained, readily enough, that such-and-such a proportion of the New England population were dependent upon whaling; that about so many vessels whaled out of Salem and New Bedford, and so many out of

Gloucester; that Boston in a typical year received so many barrels of oil at a cost of approximately . . .

"How are whales apprehended?" asked Madame de Verniat with a minimum of interest.

"Well," said the Yankee, turning to Madelon again, as if it had been her question, "when you are in whaling waters you keep a lookout in the crow's nest. When he yells 'Thar she blows!' you sail near the whale, then you lower a boat and harpoon the whale, and when he is exhausted you lance him and bring up the ship and begin trying out the blubber. See?"

There was a vague silence. "I thought whales were extremely large," offered Madame de Verniat.

"Pretty big," he agreed.

"Then," said she, "what keeps them from breaking out of the net?"

For an instant Northrup glimpsed the great gulf that separated him from these people of another race. The tools of their fathers' hands, the artifacts they had set about them, the scenes that had shaped their minds— not among all these was there one common connecting link. The very savour of the cold salt air that had in his cradle saturated body and soul made him incomprehensible here.

At this point Jezebel brought among them the coffee that had been meant for Durossac; about the preparation of it she had distinctly taken her time. Her jaw dropped at the sight of Northrup: the substitution was unexpected to her; it made her feel guilty, as if people had been coming and going all day, while she was dripping the coffee.

Her advent freed Northrup from the necessity of answering Madame de Verniat's amazing question. He sat brooding upon the ignorance of Louisiana people and wondering if there were any chance of talking to the girl alone.

"Tell us how it is done," Madelon urged.

Northrup had to keep reminding himself to turn to Madame de Verniat once in a while. His eyes were perpetually on the girl; he could no more keep the mother in mind than as if he and Madelon had been alone, sole living creatures in a world gone blank. The Creole women of New Orleans, of whose beauty he had heard so much, had failed to impress him. He thought their faces a trifle hard; and they had a knack of looking both plump and hungry, as if the satisfactions of life were too brief for their needs. That same Creole hunger was in the face of Madelon de Verniat; but the plumpness was not there, nor the hardness about the mouth. An inherent fragility, rather, from which he could not turn his eyes.

"Well," he began again, "first you lower a boat." He paused, rubbing his upper lip with a finger, while he waited to see if Madame seemed to get this.

"Oh, yes; I know about lowering boats." Madame de Verniat, who really had heard of this manœuvre before, visualized a boatload of men sliding down a steep chute into the water.

"Well, then, the boat is rowed close to the whale, and the harpooner lets drive."

Madame de Verniat badly missed the gestures that should have accompanied her visitor's narrative. Her mind persisted in wandering just enough to lose the thread. "Oh, yes, yes, I see," she exclaimed vaguely.

Northrup, perceiving her confusions, esteemed it appropriate to illustrate. He picked up a pointed bread knife, and balanced it in his hand for throwing.

"I'm standing in the bow," he explained. "I raise my harpoon like this."

Madame de Verniat found herself in line with the knife blade, as if she were impersonating the whale. This was not, she was thinking, a man one could depend on. The startled look on her face the Yankee took to represent increased interest.

"When the boat pulls alongside the whale, I let him have it. Zam!" At the last instant he diverted the knife from Madame de Verniat, and impaled a roll that lay upon the table, not noticing that he sunk the blade a good inch into the wood beneath.

"The whale rushes off," he continued. He wrenched knife and roll free of the table, and picking up a second roll gave a mid-air demonstration of how the whale towed the boat this way and that.

Madame de Verniat, who had not understood that the harpoon was attached to a rope, got a curious picture of the furiously rowed boat pursuing the dodging leviathan nose to tail at incredible speed, much as one rooster chases another in the hen yard. She not only thought that the Yankee was the most monstrous liar she had ever seen, but that his methods of narration were the most unpleasantly extraordinary.

Madelon had got a more accurate picture—a very fair one, except for a considerably exaggerated idea of the animal's size. She could imagine that unearthly vast body slowly bulging out of the sea, the brine streaming from its back; and the tossing boat, with the Yankee tall and set-faced in the bow, balancing the harpoon that was to hitch his boat to the monster.

Unlike her mother, whose childhood had been spent far from the track of smugglers and privateers, Madelon thought of the fighting seamen of Barataria as uninteresting ruffians. But the whalers, the men of the far frozen seas who fought sea beasts bigger than ships—there was colour, there was romance!

"Really," said Madame, "you don't mean to tell me. And how do you get the whale into the boat?"

3

LATER, when Northrup found that his boat had disappeared from the landing, he immediately suspected that Durossac had sent it away: a suspicion afterward confirmed by the negro boat crew, and adhered to by them under the whip. The Yankee was more angered than inconvenienced, the only result being that the De Verniat overseer was forced to lend him Lafitte's mare; and thus Northrup reached New Orleans considerably sooner than he might otherwise have expected.

Now, it so happened that the Yankee did not make the ride alone.

There was at that time in Barataria a small Capuchin friar, a middle-aged personage with a straggly gray beard and more piety than wit. He was known by the name of Père Miguel.

For seven years Père Miguel had been almost as homeless as the early founders of his order had meant that friars should be. In 1804 that anomalous Spaniard, Father Walsh, had resurrected in New Orleans the ancient struggle between the monastic brotherhoods and the secular clergy, and had won for the latter a partial success that, while it left the masterful Franciscan, Père Antoine de Sedella, triumphant in the St. Louis Cathedral, had effectively routed the lesser friars out of the back-country parishes. Thus Père Miguel had lost his humble but pleasant station as priest of an obscure parish, and found himself set afoot in an only partially appreciative land.

This man arrived at the De Verniats' just as the Yankee was about to leave. He had, he let it be known, poled his way there in a pirogue under the belief that this was a suitable mode of self-castigation. Having said a Mass which the Yankee could not get out of attending, the little friar insisted on borrowing nothing better than a field mule; and, thus mounted, accompanied Northrup onward.

They rode slowly, very uncomfortable in the sun-slashed steaminess under the cypresses. The Yankee, who did not know the way, had to keep sawing at the mare's mouth to keep her pace down to the jog of the lop-eared plough mule on which the friar jiggled erratically. A brief attempt at conversation fell to the ground; and presently Miguel began telling his beads.

A deer fly followed Northrup persistently, lighting about his ears to bite, darting up again in time to avoid the rider's vicious slap; it buzzed in interminable spirals, never more than six inches from his head. His war upon the fly being futile, the Yankee unconsciously began to turn his annoyance upon the friar.

"Hey!" boomed the Yankee at last. "Can you get on faster?"

"Eh?" said the friar, returning from another world.

"CAN YOU RIDE ANY FASTER?"

"Oh, yes! Surely! I am sorry I have seemed slow."

The friar kicked the mule's barrel, and for six strides was jolted a little more roughly as the beast hurried on. Then the animal returned to his former gait: Père Miguel had already returned to his prayers.

The Yankee's irritation grew toward fury. He suddenly began to sing in a great rude voice that made Miguel's ears ring. The song was one out of the Yankee hell ships: a blatant yelling song that once grew of its own accord to accompany heaving backs and stamping feet; a song urging to great labouring rhythmic effort, yet sneering at that effort, and the men who made it, and the scant pleasures for which they lived; a leering, fighting song that had made itself:

"And this gal was a sturdy craft—
PULL for wormy biscuits!
Broad in the beam and slopin' aft—
HAVE another cockroach!"

The friar turned a pained gaze upon him. "You disturb my thoughts," he suggested faintly.

"Well, you disturb mine!" shouted the Yankee. "What d'you mean, setting there mumbling? You draw flies, that's what you do!" He gave himself a ringing box on the ear, and this time the neat gray fly dropped away, broken.

"Excuse me," said the friar. "I am sorry."

He covertly studied the Yankee with a new and favourable interest. It was almost the little man's goal in life to be abused. The rebellious breath of heresy that had brought on his semi-exile had exhausted completely what little spirit of combativeness there was in him. The abject penitential attitude suggested by his religion accorded comfortably with his natural instincts. He made himself as miserable as possible, and by this means found a sort of happiness and a hope for eternity.

Until the Yankee had pounced upon him for making annoying sounds, Père Miguel had been aware of him only externally, as an object. Now that the man had trampled upon him, however, Miguel conceived that the Yankee must be a somebody. He glanced at Northrup covertly, then, finding that the Yankee was staring dourly ahead, he studied him sidelong. He noticed for the first time the Yankee's comparatively great height, the rugged set of his head and shoulders, the long strength of his spare frame. And especially he was impressed with the Yankee's blondness; the lank hay-coloured hair looked, in comparison with the dark growths with which Miguel was more familiar, like a halo of gold.

A sincere pity for the Yankee came into him, a regret that such an uncommon figure of a man should be consigned to damnation, kindled into hell fire at the stroke of death. The urge of his vocation pressed him toward some attempt to rescue the fellow's soul. He essayed conversation.

"See how beautiful the day is," he remarked, successfully divorcing his contemplation from the prickly heat that was tormenting him. "Surely God is smiling upon us!"

"What was he doing yesterday," demanded the Yankee, "snivelling?"

The friar recoiled into himself from that blasphemy; a little shiver ran over him in the midst of the bludgeoning heat. The mental shock, coming on top of his over-exertion of the morning, toppled his physical equilibrium, so that he felt ill. He was one at home in cloisters; he often longed for an Old World monastery where from a narrow cell deep within stone he could look up to a night star through a slit in the wall and pour out his soul in racked prayer.

The Baratarian seamen, with whom he had lately been thrown, were blasphemous and turbulent men, but they did not specifically flout God. He believed that most of them hoped for salvation by repentance in the end; they slurred over their sins of lust and blood, telling themselves that they were no worse than the rest of the world.

"My son," he said presently, his voice quavering slightly over the incongruous appellation, "did you ever consider giving your soul to God?"

There was a considerable silence. The mule's tail switched as it jogged. The Yankee was annoyed, and confused by the little man's interest in his welfare, so that he did not know how to reply. "My people were pious folk," he said queerly.

"Catholic?" asked the priest eagerly.

"No."

Miguel sighed. Poor, misled soul, he was thinking, cast upon the wastes of the sea unarmoured, without faith; never, probably, having been shown the way to that faith which was his own shield and support, and a glorifying light to men oppressed of earth. He found himself longing to save this hard case; it always stirred his imagination to think of the cloister reaching out over land and sea to rescue the brutalized men who went where Miguel himself would have been too timorous to go. He thought of himself as the only hope that remained to this great towering figure of a man. In the Yankee's young face he could read the strenuous labours that had been required of him by the sea; he gazed appalled at the picture he conceived of those labours, reading into them horrors of hardship that would have astonished the Yankee. All that wasted, thought the friar, unless he could think of a way.

For a long time he searched his mind; and, since he was of a race not without its foxes, he eventually hit upon a means that he thought would serve. He nerved himself for an effort of boldness.

"I noticed," he said, "that while I said prayers your eyes were on Mademoiselle Madelon."

The Yankee turned upon him with a jerk. Slapped in the face by the personal observation, he failed to deduce that the friar's eyes must have been wandering also. "Well, what about it?" he demanded harshly.

31

"I would say," said the friar, "that you are not entirely blind. No, far from it. There is hope for a man whose eyes can see. Mademoiselle is a most remarkable young woman. I know of no other as beautiful, as talented, as well born, as fervent."

"Fervent?"

"In devotion."

The Yankee slowly relaxed.

"Well," he said, "I expect you're right."

His voice sounded unnatural and hesitant, so that Miguel looked at him quickly. The materials, the friar decided, were ready to his hand. He knew that he should not attempt to rush his plan, but his eagerness to see how it would work sent him forward headlong.

"My son," he said, "would you give your soul to God for the sake of this girl?"

The Yankee, who did not immediately reply, was surprised to find himself brooding sombrely. He laughed drily. "Hell, man, I'd give my soul to the devil!"

The priest was only half satisfied, but that was enough. His mind went swarming over the possibilities of his scheme. A lost soul recovered would be a jewel in his crown—in this case a singularly blazing one; he felt himself in need of such, for as an evangelist he had not met with much success. The mule slowed down and stopped, as it had been attempting to do at every hundred yards; and this time the engrossed friar did not urge it on. Northrup, having ridden a couple of rods farther, stopped the mare and looked back.

"Well, what's the matter now?"

The friar hesitated. Now that he was sure of his object

he was in a fever to push the thing through. He made a hasty decision.

"I have to go back," he called. "Just take the right-hand path, at the fork."

Chapter III

1

UNDER THE VOICES, under the sound of the night surf, lay the stillness. The twelve or fourteen men who lounged in Lafitte's main room talked several at once; the voices of some were loud, and their laughter boisterous. You sensed, rather than heard, the perpetual sibilant voice of the Gulf of Mexico, piling its low combers onto five miles of beach, drawing back into itself long hissing runners of foam. It was like a continuous heavy wind whisper; you forgot that it was there.

Minutely fretting the moan of the beach, the mass chant of the negroes on the adjacent Isle of Oaks rose and fell. The high male voices vaulted in flamboyant arpeggios, ringing faintly across the flats. Yet beneath these sounds the stillness managed to lie untouched, just as the warm ground-dark of Barataria lay undisturbed by the stars. The Louisiana coast had a way of absorbing all sound and all movement into its own salt marshes, so that even the surf drone became an undertone to its silence.

Jean Lafitte was perhaps the only one there who was aware of that stillness, that odd unyielding silence;

unless it were Père Miguel, the Capuchin friar, who was by no means one of them, but a curiosity half explained. Lafitte's considerable frame sprawled languidly all over a chair by the rear door. His brocaded vest was open, but he still wore his silver-buttoned blue coat in spite of the mild warmth of the night; and he had not, as Dominique You had done hours ago, unwound his stock. Beluche, sitting on a stool opposite, kept eyeing Lafitte's clothes: the fawn-coloured pantaloons, too fleckless, too well pressed, seemed to bother him most. Lafitte thought that Beluche was envying his ability to look like a gentleman.

One or two noticed that Lafitte was becoming terse and rather unnaturally courteous. The excellent Cuban rum, mingling with Lafitte's smooth wines, was taking effect upon them all. Lafitte was mentally contrasting his roomful of harsh-faced seamen with other scenes that persisted in rebuilding with a sort of dark sentimentality in his mind. That unnatural silence beneath the scurl of surface sound was taking a vague underhold on him. The Old World village, placidly asleep in a fold of its mountains, where he was born; Bordeaux, mellow and old like its own wine, which nearly twenty years before had been his last touch of East Hemisphere—these were other worlds, now permanently lost.

"Once as I sat naked," Dominique You said, "writing my memoirs, the tide came up, and began swashing around my legs—"

"Memoirs?" bellowed someone with a great guffaw. "You must have been drunk!"

"Why, certainly," Dominique agreed. "Nobody

except a puffed-up jackass would sit down and write his memoirs sober."

Lafitte, who had begun his that morning, stirred uneasily. He was trying to concentrate on things more nearly aligned with his interests, at that time wavering in the balance. That concentration pressed back older and more bitter thoughts that the liquor sometimes brought into his head, as sunset brought the swamp mists up through the arms of the cypress.

The men about him, as it happened, were at once his tools, his opponents, and his allies. Three years before, in 1808, the American embargo had shown Lafitte an opportunity that he had been able to grasp only through the medium of such men. The United States, new in Louisiana, had in that year put pressure upon England by starving her West Indian colonies; the measure for that purpose provided that no American ship might clear for a foreign port, and no foreign ship leave an American port, except under ballast. In thoroughness, the coastwise trade, also, was all but throttled.

This experiment not only threw the West Indian negroes into famine, but gripped Louisiana by the throat. Indigo, cotton, rice, tobacco, corn, and crude sugar accumulated in immense quantities, but there was an immediate shortage of everything else, and, most especially, of money.

In French-speaking New Orleans, public feeling swelled in a fretting tide against the nation of which the Creoles found themselves an unwilling part. Idle men and hulls were for the asking. New Orleans was bankrupt, but there was still capital available through discreet channels for Louisiana's profitable relief. Louisiana had food; the Indies had money and the transhipped foreign products that New Orleans was without. Adventurers were stared in the face by such an opportunity for two-way smuggling as the world had never seen before.

There was a sudden upsurge in the fortunes of Jean Lafitte. Before 1810 he was perhaps Louisiana's richest man.

The world was changing now. In the shifting moil of events Lafitte thought he saw the supreme opportunity for which he had prepared. Yet it found him partly unready. He was like a man in a crucial chess game who finds himself one move too late.

René Beluche, easily the most influential of Baratarian privateer captains, hitched a chair close to Lafitte, and began talking in his ear.

"Who's this big Yankee?" he demanded, speaking in French. "I don't like his looks."

Lafitte, as it happened, did not know the answer. Northrup had caught up with the boss of Barataria only that evening, and had found opportunity to state no more than his name. However, Lafitte chose to dissimulate.

"Who, Job Northrup?" said he. "What's the matter with him? Seems like a nice fellow to me."

"Oh, Jesus," said Beluche, as if aside. He pressed his whacked-off moustache with a forefinger, then scowled at the finger as if he had stuck himself. "That man's a spy of some kind, that's what's the matter. It sticks out all over him. He stands around where people are, listening to what they say. He never asks any questions; that's always a bad sign. He pretends he pays no attention to anything, but all the time you see him listening. All right, then, he's a spy. Now, who's spy is he?"

"Not mine," Lafitte said good-humouredly.

"Maybe the government's."

"That's silly. Silly of the government, I mean," he added hurriedly. "They know perfectly well we don't always pay our import duties. What would they want a spy for? What they need is twenty or thirty gunboats. I could tell them right where to put them to do the most good."

"It would be about like you," Beluche grumbled.

"All right," said Lafitte, "he isn't a custom-house spy. Whose then?"

"Maybe Governor Claiborne's," said Beluche. "You know what that one wants to hang on our outfit here."

"What?"

"Piracy, that's what!"

"I'm surprised," said Lafitte. "Well, let him spy, then. Do him good."

"Let him spy?"

"Why, certainly. Everything is perfectly legal here. That is, practically legal."

"Oh, yes!" Beluche agreed without humour.

"The true law, in this country," said Lafitte sententiously, "is the will of the people. Some of the statutes are a little out of line—that's all."

"Oh, sure," Beluche agreed. "We only want to do what the people want. And if they send a spy down here, I'll have somebody cut the throat of the son of a bitch, that's where *I* stand."

Lafitte smiled as he lighted a cigar. He knew Beluche to be his active, if clandestine, enemy; yet he admired and valued the man. "Well," he broke the pause, "what's the question?"

"I just wanted to know if he's a man of yours, that's all."

Lafitte turned his eyes to the end of the room. Job Northrup stood there against the wall, his thumbs hooked into his four-inch belt. The tall Yankee was peering into the corners, trying, evidently, to estimate the value of the furnishings. They were worth valuing. Tapestry, silver, fine brass, and Chinese silks made the edges of the room a bright clutter. The trinkets of a hundred cargoes—choice bits that had caught Jean's fancy while the merchandise passed through his hands—were in that room.

Northrup was newly shaved, so that the lower half of his face was oddly pale, as if he had received a terrific slap from a cupped hand. There was no one there, with the exception of Lafitte, who looked so intrinsically clean of body, and yet so little conscious of the increasing litter underfoot, of the airless choke of smoke, of the reek of those who set no store on bathing—unaware of these things, as a man who has known ships' forecastles for a long time.

"Very well, then. I mean to keep him."

"That's all right, too," said Beluche. "If you keep him you'll have to answer for him."

Lafitte's small gray eye ran over Beluche with leisure.

"Oh, I'm only telling you for your own information," said Beluche. "If he's your man you want to make him solid, that's all."

A grin was coming to Beluche's face under Lafitte's stare. It brought again to Lafitte the acrid sense of insecurity that had been growing upon him in the weeks now past. It was as if the walls around him were becoming saturated with unease. Barataria was slipping slowly out of his grasp; other men knew things that he did not, predicted happenings that he could not foresee.

2

GAMBIO, the Italian sea bully, was ridiculing the heavy armament that was coming into fashion for privateering vessels. His chesty, buzzing voice battered down the comments of those nearest. What did a privateer need? Speed. What were the guns for? To clip the gear of the prize with chain shot, so she could be overhauled. Bite the grappling hooks into her, that's what he wanted. Then:

"Come on, you lousy swabs! Swarm her over!"

His voice rose to a great bellow, and his arms waved. From a lolling seated position he was trying to act out the taking of a ship.

Gambio had a great blurred nose in a face of padded leather; his jaws were heavy, his mouth big and loose; the lust of life burned hotly in his eyes. Physically he was rather small and lightly muscled, so that masked he would have been an unimpressive figure. But that big ugly face, swung low, as if borne down by the heft of

39

power in the jaws, so dominated his appearance that most of his fellows thought of him as a powerful man. He was in a windy mood, flushed with alcohol, half belligerent in his opinions, half desirous of comradely support.

"Ain't I right?" he demanded, turning to Beluche.

Beluche said nothing, but Gambio thought that he perceived a slight nod. He assumed that he had obtained whole-hearted agreement.

"Why-y-y, sure!" blared his deep voice, powerful and loose, like his mouth.

The turn of the conversation had reminded Nez Coupé of an anecdote. Coupé, a compatriot of Gambio's, was small and quick, like the little fighting schooner he commanded. A sabre slash had clipped off the tip of his nose, leaving it with a grotesque turned-up look, from which he got his name. His eyebrows usually strained upward in a speciously innocent, willing-to-learn expression; but this solemnity was perpetually breaking down into a slack, liquid grin, a peculiarly personal, ridiculing grin that seemed to be trying to conceal itself, as if the alert eyes had discovered vulnerable indecencies in the affairs of those around him.

Now that he was drunk, all things had become comical to him. He was thinking about a time when he had seen a gang of seamen walk the plank. The curious device of the plank had no root in expedience—chucking 'em over was quicker—but the plank put an element of humour into it. The ship rolled, the plank jounced and teetered; the victim skittered out onto the plank, assisted by hanger points behind; hovered for a while halfway, struggling with wild silly gestures to keep his balance; lost it, and fell awkwardly, corner-wise, with shrieks.

Nez Coupé was trying to relate such an incident now, though no one was aware of it. He would get out the first few words, bubbling but intelligible: "He went to work an'—" The laughter came piling up through his speech, so that he seethed off into inane giggles. Presently he would simmer down enough to try again; and again the first sentence would be too much for him, and he would double up, giggling hysterically, face red and contorted. It happened over and over, until everybody around him was laughing at him; so that when Coupé finally gave it up, weak and watery-eyed, he could not remember whether he had told the story or not, but only thought it had been a great hit.

Gambio had stopped talking to laugh at Coupé with the others. Now that the diversion had subsided, he could not remember what he had been talking about. He sat rocking on his haunches, grinning vacantly, and rubbing his knee caps with heavy-nailed hands. Then he chanced to meet Lafitte's gray-green eye, which was lying indifferently upon him, and gradually he stopped rocking.

For as long as he could remember—thirty years, at least—organized society had been Gambio's enemy. He instinctively recognized no rights but those of force, and other expediencies were hard to explain to him. He had no name for any god, but he had some sense of a malignant destiny which needed cheating. By living each day for itself Gambio eluded both the stupidities of society and the devices of that formless, malignant god. Unconsciously he preferred to possess what he could take by strength or cunning rather than what he could gain by compromise with the peoples leagued in law.

In his conflict with society Gambio had been successful. The associates he sought or tolerated were like himself, without the standards and notions he despised. Among them he was among friends; he overbore them, bullied them, was accepted almost at sight as boss. The putting down of rivals was his keenest amusement.

Jean Lafitte had somehow the faculty of cutting from around Gambio this animal world that he had built for himself. When the British took Guadeloupe, closing it to the French privateers, Gambio had put into Barataria with certain vague plans that Lafitte, without open opposition, had somehow contrived to frustrate. By an obscure chain of events, Gambio had temporarily become a slave runner for Lafitte. Sober, Gambio explained this to himself; drunk, he could not remember the reason.

He sat staring back at Lafitte's quiet gray eye through the golden cigar smoke, weaving a little from side to side in an effort to get a better view. To Gambio, Lafitte looked out of place there, like a naval officer or a spy. Lafitte's flat, square chin looked like a piece of stone. A man too quiet, too self-possessed, too well-shaved. The gray eyes looked at Gambio without animus, as if they brooded unseeing upon a casual object. Or they were the eyes of a man coolly watching a hostile dog, speculating as to whether the dog was going to leap upon him and get shot. Gambio *felt* like the dog, half baffled, angering under that gray gaze.

Gambio stopped weaving. The blood was welling into his bulldog head, forced up by a deepening, unreasoning hate. The other figures in the room blurred out into a drunken golden haze. As if he and Lafitte were alone. Man to man. Man to dog. The man barring the dog's way with that steady calculating gaze. No dog of spirit can stand it. He has to spring; he has no choice. One of Gambio's feet moved unsteadily under his chair, taking a brace.

Lafitte's eyes flicked away indifferently, as if they had not been conscious of the contact. He became one figure in a roomful again. Nez Coupé was offering Gambio a drink.

3

PÈRE MIGUEL hiccoughed solemnly. The little friar had seen not much to laugh at in Nez Coupé's hysterical exhibition. Not that he was scandalized; it was mercly that very few things struck him as funny. He was seated on a bench in a thick knot of four or five French captains, and it was becoming very stuffy there. His rusty brown robe, with its heavy cowl, muffled warmly about his neck, making him sweat. It never occurred to him to blame his robe for the heat—it was the room that was hot.

Père Miguel was sojourning at Grand Isle in the hope of recovering one or two of the souls now Napoleonically lost, and, incidentally, to gather a few choice bits of information that would interest certain Spanish connections of his in town.

It was said, by some who had no reason to know much about it, that Père Miguel was a powerful and accomplished man, a man of mystery who sat high in the councils of Spain, perhaps directing far-reaching movements and conspiracies that would alter the map of the New World. This, of course, was almost unadulterated bosh. It was true that the little fellow was used from time to time by Père Antoine de Sedella, and one or two other Louisiana friends of Spain, for errands of a confidential nature. It was also true that he reported regularly to Père Antoine whatever he could learn in the Baratarian strongholds of interest to those in Spain's pay. Jean Lafitte had, in fact, found this out, and with a malicious humour had used Père Miguel as a post box into which he stuffed such items of misinformation as it amused him to contrive.

Sometimes the errands of Père Antoine sustained Miguel in a condition of comfort for an interval. But he always returned before very long to his rather aimless wanderings up and down the Mississippi levees. His peripatetics sometimes carried him as far north as Natchez and as far south as the Balize; but his favourite haunt was the Baratarian fastness, where he timidly held himself available as a sort of missionary to outlaws and chaplain to privateers. Here he solemnly buried ruffians that had slit each other's throats, nursed those who had contracted disease, shut his mouth when he was told he had preached enough, and ate or drank what was given him—which was always plenty.

What Père Miguel would have been sorry to realize was that he had enjoyed Jean Lafitte's dinner perhaps more appreciatively than any of the others, most of whom are inclined to gulp. He had, in fact, eaten until his belly was as taut as a little balloon. This was in line of duty, however. Whom the Lord loveth, He chasteneth. Père Miguel had had to eat some of everything to show he did not feel himself above these fellows.

The dinner had been in Lafitte's best style, comparing favourably with dinners in leading houses in New Orleans. The meal had started off with terrapin soup, singularly rich and highly seasoned, of the kind that cannot be made in less than four days. Next came a bisque of soft-shelled crabs and oysters thickened with rice and sharpened with sherry. Then green trout from the bayous, fried a crisp golden brown in cornmeal. Then sheepshead from the lake, simmered in a rich, hot Spanish sauce and garnished with cress and sorrel; then roast wild turkey with spiced stuffing, sugared yams, and butter beans. Then high snipe and papabotse broiled on charcoal, with asparagus and broccoli. Finally cheese, guava jelly, and quince preserves. Miguel blamed the quince preserves for his slight feeling of unrest.

He was thinking, as he pressed down that increasing uneasiness in his middle, that these were stupid men; that if he had entered their profession, instead of his Orders, he would have outdone them; or would have, that is, if he could ever have got the hang of standing up and shouting at a man. There was a born humility in Miguel's bearing that his calling increased. When he spoke among these loud-voiced men, his own voice sounded ingratiating, and so faint that they had to ask him to repeat.

The heat bedewed the scraggle of his whitening beard. Small details, too distinct through the smoky haze, were beginning to annoy him excessively. It irritated him that there was gravy on the vest of La Maison, that Gambio had kicked off his shoes, that Beluche had hairy ears. He tried to picture what it was that made these men captains of that other larger rabble on Grand Isle: what they did efficiently that gave them success, and drew them together here.

Then, as his eyes drifted over the varied faces, there came upon him the sudden realization of what it was these men did well. Having caught the key to it, his humourless imagination swiftly unrolled a great surging picture, appallingly complete.

In his fancy he heard the clank and bite of grappling hooks as two ships ground together on the heave of a gray sea. Along the rail of the attacking ship showed the faces of the men that were about him now, no longer genial with wine, but savagely transfigured, with eyes like knives. They leaped over the rail; there was steel in their hands, they bellowed and cheered as they leaped. And each was the cutting point of a great thrust of men, a yelling pack of nondescripts, yellow, oyster-white, and brown, made momentarily invincible by the fanatic energy of these leaders among whom he sat.

In a sudden irrepressible nausea, Père Miguel stumbled up and reeled toward the outer air.

4

Dominique You, a wiry little Frenchman, was draped over a corner of the table, the fine linen of which was now smeared with gravies and spilled wine. He was one of those men secretly dissatisfied with their faces; so that he constantly repeated the experiment of growing a moustache and shaving it off again. Just now the moustache was off, revealing a short upper lip that drew up from his teeth when he smiled.

Until a few minutes before Dominique You had been in a genial mood, reminiscent and expansive. He had that genius for long-winded conversation that makes a man either a delight or a distress, according to the quality of his imagination. For an hour he had managed to disregard Gambio, relying upon his own wit to retain a circle of listeners against Gambio's bellowings. Especially he had avoided being drawn into the arguments the Italian captain would not refrain from starting. But Gambio was too loud, too importunate, too violently gesticulating, and Dominique You was getting tired of being shouted down.

Gambio, recovered sufficiently from his black alcoholic sulk to be vocal again, was arguing the merits of the United States navy.

"I don't want trouble, mind you. And I don't want interference with my business, either. What are these here Jefferson gunboats? Wallowing rowboats, with a big jackass of a gun in the middle fit to turn them over. There's your bastardly United States navy! You,

Dominique," he roared, "what about it?"

"Everybody knows those gunboats are no good," said Dominique.

"Why-y-y, sure!" blared Gambio's heavy bass.

"And if you think," said Dominique, "that you can stir up the United States and have nothing fly out at you but a couple of gunboats you're a soft-headed fool!"

"Wha'!" Gambio shouted; he had caught nothing but the last clause, and it set him back on his heels.

"Don't you yell at me," Dominique said. "I'm not deaf. Go out and shout at some niggers, if you want to holler. You want to listen when I talk: you'll learn somethin'."

Lafitte stirred and spoke rapidly to Dominique You in an obscure dialect. He was cautioning Dominique against bringing on a quarrel, but Gambio was mystified and took exception.

"What's this here?" he demanded. "Talkin' about me behind my back, are you? Say——"

Dominique's short upper lip drew up in a nasty little smile to show his front teeth like a rising moon. His voice was hard and ugly.

"Don't you bother yourself about what he's talkin' about. You want to watch where you're goin' if you're goin' to stay around here, my short friend!"

The room fell into a hush; the violence that always lurked under the surface of Baratarian assemblies was rising again into visibility. Men exchanged glances. The Yankee, relaxed and smiling faintly, let his eyes roam; they selected a bottle on the table before him, picked a solid spot in the table's edge where he could smash the bottle into jagged points, and estimated the comparative nearness of other hands that might snatch for the same tool. Then the hush broke, and half a dozen men were trying to divert the attention of Dominique and of Gambio.

The Italian, momentarily wavering, took an attitude of abused righteousness. "I say gunboats are no good, an' he jumps at me. Why-y, that . . ." Cursing, he half-heartedly tried to rise under the restraining hands of his friends.

Dominique You said, "Let him come if he wants." But it was lost in the buzz of voices. Dominique waited a minute, motionless, observing the group about Gambio with keen eyes, both amused and watchful. Then he smiled again, a trace of his geniality reappearing to supplant some of the ugliness in that smile. He rose, stretched, and sauntered out by the rear door.

The tautness within the room melted away into the golden cigar smoke. The groups talked and laughed. The quarrel had blurred out, leaving the gathering as it had been before.

Gambio brooded, his eyes on Lafitte again. Lafitte was tilting back in his chair, his head against the wall; his face was turned to talk to Captain Marco, who leaned against the wall at his side.

As Gambio stared unsteadily at the profile of Lafitte's head the crowd once more faded out into the yellow, so that only Lafitte was distinct. Gambio was weaving again, trying to see Lafitte more clearly, though he already saw him too well. The hate welled up, dizzying him, trying to burst his head.

49

Suddenly his hand went to the back of his neck, scrabbling for the hilt of the knife that he had not brought along.

Lafitte turned that cool gray eye on him again. "Fleas, Gambio?"

The tobacco smoke might have been swirling cannon fumes for all Gambio knew. He tottered in his seat, breathing hoarsely through that big vague nose.

Chapter IV

1

LAFITTE'S EYES, grayly urbane, ran leisurely over the captains who had eaten his dinner. Of the nearly two dozen privateers using Grand Isle as a base these were the leading spirits, men who showed the way for the rest. Not often, under the exigencies of their trade, were so many of this group to be found together in port; fortuity was to be thanked for their presence now. But though chance had brought them to the anchorage at the same time, it was for a definite purpose that Lafitte had called them to his house.

In 1809, after the lifting of President Jefferson's embargo had made smuggling unprofitable, Lafitte had for a time engaged in the illicit slave traffic; but within a year the fall of Guadeloupe, the last French port in American waters, had opened new possibilities. The French privateersmen of the Gulf and Caribbean—men of many nations, but one flag—no longer had available any court of admiralty for the condemnation of their prizes. Their loot instantly became contraband, acceptable in no Western port. Morally they were French privateersmen as before; technically their commissions had lost all validity. Jean Lafitte's efficient smuggling system proved to be just what the portless privateers desperately needed. Within a year more than a score of unauthorized fighting ships had made Barataria their rendezvous, and Lafitte their receiving and distributing agent.

This arrangement, unfortunately, did not work out acceptably to everyone. The trouble was that little money, after all, was to be made in privateering. Most of the captain owners no more than paid expenses; they hung on morosely, hoping, each cruise, to throw hooks into the supreme capture that would make them rich men. On the other hand, Lafitte, taking a cut of every captured cargo, found their efforts lucrative in the extreme. He did as well for them as he could without reducing himself to the margins of a legitimate trader; but nothing could conceal that the privateering business was being conducted mainly for the benefit of Jean Lafitte.

It was now the summer of 1811. The quarrel that for months had been developing between Lafitte and these young sea captains was irrepressible; even in the first days of his relationship with them he had perceived the conflict to be one he could postpone but not evade. His intention now was to force that strengthening dispute, bringing it to an immediate climax that would serve his ends. All evening that necessity had hung over him, an edgy threat, like a blade that he must presently grasp with his bare hands; but he had delayed, reluctant to make the first move. He saw now that his procrastination had saved him trouble: the subject was opening itself, without effort of his own.

He leaned his head back against the wall and closed his eyes that he might more easily sort out from the maze of shuttling voices those of Jean Ducoing and Dominique You.

"Look here," Dominique was demanding. "This is the best rendezvous left in Western waters: a fine unvisited anchorage, only sixty miles from New Orleans by the swamp bayous. And what hold have we got on it? We haven't any. This is United States territory. Nothing on earth keeps us in Barataria but the grace of God and Jean Lafitte. . . ."

Dominique You and Lafitte had shared more than one borderline project before the rest had come. They were well fitted to understand each other, these two, halfway, two thirds of the way. They even looked something alike, in a truer sense indeed than Jean and Pierre Lafitte looked alike; for whereas Pierre showed Jean's lineaments made faintly grotesque by an unfamiliar character behind, Dominique resembled Jean in substance, in the essence of spirit itself, expressed through dissimilar features.

Lafitte was waiting to hear Ducoing's reply. He had reason to know what its tone would be.

"Lafitte's got organization," Dominique hammered on. "Lafitte's got influence. He's got the people of Louisiana with him. I doubt—"

"Lafitte, Lafitte!" Ducoing exploded, careless of the fact that he sat in Jean's house, of the probability that he was heard by Jean himself. "Who is this Lafitte? What ship did he captain? Who did he whip? I doubt if he ever went to sea in his life. You talk like Lafitte was God almighty. I'm sick of hearing about this Lafitte!"

Jean still reclined in his tilted chair, his eyes closed so that he seemed asleep; but perhaps he was watching through his lashes. He spoke unexpectedly in a strong voice:

"Just what is it you want, Ducoing?"

There was a momentary lull as everyone glanced at Jean, except La Maison, who stared out the high window, and De Verge, who sprawled belly up on a bench, smoking.

Ducoing's voice raised to quarter-deck timbre. "I want a decent price," he answered. "You know damned well what I want. I go pounding up and down the sea. Sixty men sail three months, I come in full of Spanish cloth and leather. What comes of it? Sixty men swearing they'll have my liver. Go out and explain to them where the money went!"

Lafitte opened his eyes to look at Ducoing. The privateersman's head was not ordinarily ugly, though marked by a mouth broad beneath its moustache, and by eyes too deep set; but now it looked as if it had been badly made in the dark, with a life breathed in afterward to make the best it could of the circumstance. This was a very earnest young man and not impervious to rum.

"We're coming into the summer months," said Lafitte. "You know trade is slack in the summer. It's not my fault if you're not prepared to hold for the market."

This was so close to the truth that Lafitte momentarily regretted having spoken it.

"In the meantime," he continued, "we have the slave trade, where we're fairly well fixed. If you fellows would take your ships and—"

"Are we stinking blackbirders?" growled a man called Spanish Dick. He had merry eyes above a shapeless black beard that covered his entire face.

Lafitte shrugged deprecatingly. "What can I do? Pierre and I do the best that conditions permit."

Ducoing fumbled at the problem for a few minutes, staring smokily at the floor.

"This is beside the point," he decided. "What I want to know is, is there going to be money or not?"

"There is," said Lafitte.

"When?"

"I don't know."

De Verge suddenly sat up. His saffron face, broad cheek-boned like a sleepy cat's, was perfectly expressionless, even to the surface-lighted eyes; so that he resembled a corpse jerked upright by a rope.

"That's you!" he declared. "That's you all over! I'm another that's tired of your shilly-shally. Either there'll be a new deal here pretty quick or, by God, I'll find means of my own."

Lafitte had hoped to adopt a reasonable pose, making them seem to force the issue against his will. This method he now perceived to be closed to him. He was among men who held in respect only those who gave promise of exploding in their hands. They were too ready to forget that they were in Lafitte's house, that they had often been in his debt.

"No," Lafitte answered De Verge, "not you, because you haven't the brains."

"Because *what?*" said De Verge after a moment's strained pause.

"Because you're a fool," said Lafitte distinctly.

De Verge's eyes burned in his yellow mask; yet he seemed less angered than astonished. "What's to prevent me shootin' you where you sit?" he asked in a curious voice.

"The fact that you have no pistol," said Lafitte.

Beluche broke in, changing the drift. "The point is this," he said, speaking slowly and heavily. "If you don't want to serve our purpose, we'll get somebody who will. You have a nice little ring built up, and you can make yourself useful if you want to. But if you don't we can go outside your ring, and you're through."

Here, said Lafitte to himself, is the crux of the whole thing, in this one man. He studied Beluche impartially.

2

RENÉ BELUCHE was older than the rest, nearing forty in a game in which men rapidly grew old. He had a strong, jutting nose, its ridge parallel to the line of his cheek, as if it were a narrow block stuck onto his face by main force and hammering. Under that wooden nose he wore a thin black line of moustache—thin by necessity, since the nose had not left much room for upper lip. His jaws were broad and muscular, shaping into a chin like a walnut; and his mouth was perpetually broadened by a grimly sardonic smile, giving him an air of covert superiority.

He was thinking these days that it was time for him to make his stake and quit; and he took it very hard that this younger man should, without hardship or great effort, reap most of the profits. Beluche was not a man of many words, or indeed of many ideas; his constant preaching boiled down to a single refrain: "We have the goods, we have the niggers; nobody can meet our price. Lafitte is taking all the money out of this business. To hell with this Lafitte! Do you think New Orleans buyers will go broke to please him?" He did not emphasize the obvious—that he was available to serve in Lafitte's place.

That Beluche would inevitably fail in the distribution of prize goods Lafitte was confident. They were well into the bankrupt summer months; the money from Louisiana's fall and winter crops was spent, the new crops a long way off. If matters drifted, Beluche would use the scarcity of summer money to further his opposition; and if Lafitte was overthrown in the autumn, it might turn out that Beluche would be able, after all, to deliver as he promised. Everything pointed to the wisdom of giving the privateers a bellyful of Beluche before the rich days of fall.

And yet—Lafitte hesitated, unwilling to take the step that might, if he had misjudged, put the control of Barataria permanently beyond his grasp.

"I want to be fair," said Beluche, his voice deliberate. "He was here before I was. But other men were here before him. Barataria has been a rendezvous for a hundred years. It always will be a rendezvous, and if Lafitte—"

"The United States," Dominique interrupted.

"The United States!" echoed Ducoing. "Where's its navy? There ain't any. And there ain't any British navy, or Spanish, or French, that I can't outrun, outfight, and outsmart. Not in these waters. I'm sick of this silly talk."

"You don't know what you are talking about," said Lafitte.

"And what's it to you?" Ducoing demanded.

"Plenty," said Lafitte. He could see no reason for affecting disinterest. "I'm in this up to the hilt. The day Barataria is closed I'm wiped out."

"Don't figure that you're big enough to cripple the best rendezvous that's left," said La Maison without turning from the window. His dry bitter voice seemed directed to the outer night.

"You must see that, M'sieu Jean," said Beluche. He wanted to sound amiable, but a suggestion of irony crept into the "M'sieu" in spite of him. "Here's you, making more out of our prizes than we make ourselves. I'm ready to tell you something on my own account: you and your brother can run back and forth as our go-betweens just as long as we like it and not an hour longer; and when we decide that you're in the way you're through."

A load seemed to pass from Lafitte's shoulders; he drew a deep breath and sat up. Their faces told him that there was no longer any possibility of turning back. It only remained to make the breach decisive.

He said, "You ought to be glad anybody takes over your pirate prizes at all."

"Piracy, is it?" cried Beluche. "What piracy?" As if by main strength he forced his voice down again. "Everyone knows we have no commissions, and everyone knows why: because there is no French port in the New World since Guadeloupe. The French will come back, and we privateersmen will be confirmed."

"One of you," said Lafitte, "has taken an American ship. No French court in the world will justify that. I've told you a thousand times what that sort of thing means to us here."

Beluche angered; his hammered block of a nose stood out shiny and gray, lighter than the red of his face. He shot a furious glance at Jacques Durossac, whom they all knew to have whelmed and scuttled a small American brig, marooning her crew on a coral reef near Havana. Durossac, buoyant and almost childishly carefree, looked interested; but if Durossac was willing to hear that subject hashed over again Beluche was not. He obstinately clung to his subject.

"That's nothing to do with the question," he declared. "What I say is this: we have the goods, we have the niggers. Look at the New Orleans price! If your ring doesn't want to play our game we'll go outside the ring, that's all."

"Outside the ring," Lafitte repeated in an uncomplimentary voice. "Who's outside that's any good to us? John K. West? Bourdin? Sauvinet? Have you seen their money?"

"For that matter," suggested La Maison, "we can see

what Lafitte's ring has to say."

"Every dollar in the New Orleans ring rests upon my word or my brother's," said Lafitte. "If we say run for cover not a picayune will show its head."

"Oh," said La Maison sourly, "I imagine there are ways—"

"You imagine there are ways?" echoed Lafitte. "Well, you'll find those ways take time to build up. What when you have a million dollars in piled-up goods, and no powder, no grub, no money? Stuff stacked ready for a revenue raid, and a thousand niggers eating their heads off? All supply and no demand, and you don't get the price of your chain shot." He was merely prophesying for them now, salting them down with facts he hoped they would have reason to recall.

"We have the goods, we have the niggers," droned Beluche stubbornly. Even in his anger he remained a man of one idea, set upon holding the others against Jean's bombardment. "I guess there'll be buyers, all right. One thing is certain: the Lafittes have been getting us damned little money."

"You don't see the New Orleans side of it," said Lafitte. "Every townsman or trader that buys from me is wide open to prosecution for aiding and abetting smuggling; he relies on me to protect him from that, because he knows I can. Niggers are contraband; and not a prize you bring in has the stamp of any court of admiralty. On top of that your commissions are no good. What have you got? A man who pays De Verge a dollar is liable for procuring piracy, for abetting murder on the high seas. Naturally he can't pay market price.

"I'll tell you something else. About one more fool capture like Durossac's and you'll have the United States on you like a thousand of brick. Who's going to—"

"Give 'em Barataria," offered Spanish Dick. "We'll take to the Sabine River. Give 'em the Sabine—we'll ship to Snake Island. I say—"

" 'The Sabine,' " Lafitte quoted. "Nothing bigger than a rowboat can come within thirty miles of it. Row in, and you've got a creek in a jungle, three hundred miles from even a trading post. I suppose you'll portage three hundred miles and then try to get some money out of West!"

"The American navy," La Maison said, "couldn't down two determined men in a washtub. All this is bilge."

"One cutter," said Lafitte, "can stand off the coast with a long nine and bash your boats as they come out. One boat sunk in the pass and you're through. Do you think you can catch and board a Baltimore-built cutter between here and the Balize?"

"This gets—" began Beluche.

Lafitte's voice battered through; his eye looked little and ugly, and his rushing words blurred. "The next thing they grab our guns on Grand Terre, and that's the end of Barataria. Who stands it off? Who built the New Orleans ring? Who pulls strings in the legislature itself? You know all that! What you don't know is what's good for you. You've got an easy thing here. You want it easier. All right. Sit tight and you'll get it."

Ducoing was frothing. "Whose opinion is this? I'll

tell you whose! A merchant's, for God's sake! A damned merchant!"

Beluche said, "I can catch, and I can whip, any damned cutter—"

Lafitte's voice cut him down: "What if you could? One cutter down means ten up and at you. The likes of you want none of that! Hit and run, that's you. You never tackled even odds in your life. I know you. I know you inside out. Whisky and gunpowder to get your blood up. One day's fighting and six weeks' drunk!"

There was an immediate struck silence, such as follows physical concussions. Dominique imperceptibly adjusted his belt; his eyes flicked from the motionless figure of Beluche to Ducoing, to De Verge, to Durossac, and back to Beluche, where they held. Lafitte tilted against the wall, his eyes sultry. There was not a man in that stuffy narrow room that did not expect instant action there, pistol, knife, or hanger, clash of metal, and the acrid smoke of gunpowder above the sickly smell of hurt flesh. And each was glad the smash had come; yet each waited motionless for the explosion, counting on Beluche.

So there was silence, for perhaps as long as it takes a man to breathe four times. Then Beluche chose the unexpected course. He spread out his hands extravagantly and shot out his face at one and another of them: "See? See? See?"

As if Lafitte had humiliated all except Beluche, who could now show them where they had brought it on themselves.

3

After that there was nothing more to be said. No written agreement could have told them as clearly that trade with Lafitte on the old basis was over; a phase of Antillean privateering that they would not see again had passed as they sat there that night.

Beluche and Boquierre slowly got up and went out, and by ones and twos the others followed. Dominique You left with the rest, after exchanging an unreadable glance with Lafitte. Spanish Dick and Durossac returned for a moment to carry away the drunken Gambio; and when this was done Lafitte was left alone with an underfoot clutter of snipe bones, bread crusts, and the saturated butts of cigars.

Only—the Yankee waited until the rest were gone. He stood by the open door, one hand leaning against the wall, and grinned.

"Well," said Lafitte, "what the hell do you want?"

"I'm a navigator," said the Yankee.

"Well—I had gathered that."

"I thought you might need a man."

Lafitte surveyed him. "You understood what took place here to-night?"

The Yankee nodded.

"Yet you wish to ally yourself with me?"

"You understand me," said Northrup.

"Then you're a fool," said Lafitte shortly.

"That's my affair," said the Yankee without angering.

"You have money?" Lafitte asked.

"Not a cent in the world."

"Then why do you come to me?"

"That," said Northrup, "is exactly why."

"You want to place yourself under my orders, do you?"

"If," said the Yankee, "it pays me."

Lafitte studied the Northerner speculatively. He gained his knowledge of a man by watching him and trying him; not by asking questions. Yet he asked one more question now.

"What reason have I to think," he said, "that you can be of any use to me?"

"That's your worry," Northrup told him.

"Fifty dollars a month," said Lafitte after an interval, "with such duties as I shall choose."

"A hundred," said Northrup.

"Sixty," said Lafitte.

"A hundred," said the Yankee again.

"You are expensive, my friend."

"Sure I am."

The night had left Lafitte in no mood for bargaining; he wished to be alone. "I'll give you an answer in the morning," he said at last.

But he had already made up his mind that this man was to be of use.

Chapter V

1

MADAME DE VERNIAT, looking into her mirror, was seeing her reflection in terms of the way she had looked at one time. Thus the favourable lineaments were strong and familiar, while the changes time had made, having crept upon her by easy stages, remained mercifully obscure. The spherical contour of her face was reflected as a rather piquant oval; and her large dark eyes, which by harsher lights might have seemed singularly bleak and woeful, were shown as having retained the sweetly sad, somewhat languishing appeal that she had cultivated in her youth.

After all, she was not so old as she looked, even to others; the difficult climate, hot and steeped in semitropic damp, had made a mature woman of her at fourteen and had continued the ageing process relentlessly through every hour of the years thereafter. That she had physically declined under the pressure of time, she knew; she carefully nurtured forty or fifty engrossing ailments that were more and more becoming her chief interest in life. What she could not comprehend was that a youthful appearance was incompatible with these things.

Thus the dressing table before her carried a great contradictory clutter. The pathological phase was represented by eight or nine bottles of villainous-looking pills and fluids, the most impressive of which bore an American label recommending it for man or beast; but principally by a collection of mystic charms—curiously knotted cords, a large glass marble, the carved tooth of an ox, oddly shaped bits of root, and, since she believed in taking the best from every civilization, a buck eye from Indiana, to ward off rheumatism.

Mingling with this mob of nostrums, in democratic caucus, swarmed such aids to beauty as were then available in Louisiana. Their range of ingenuity was smaller than that of the nostrums, but they included creams and powders imported from France, hair dye from Bermuda, and pomade laboriously contrived on a suet base by the negroes in the De Verniat kitchen. It was a battlefield of stratagems, courageous and pathetic, against age. All manner of folly lived on that dressing table, together with desperation, superstitious faith, and a gallant hope.

The room was dimming in the autumn twilight, so that behind Madame de Verniat the massive bed seemed to swell indistinctly in shadows as soft as dark cotton. Its four heavy posts reached upward toward the sixteen-foot ceiling like trunks of Druid trees. She shivered and turned to the tri-paned French window.

Westward, seen beyond the columns of the gallery, the gray sky showed a strip of dull colour, as if brushed with a long smear of orange chalk. Beneath it, set into the dark cypress brakes, a small sheet of water gleamed white, like a scar. That was Smuggler's Bight. Across it the boat of Jean Lafitte had to pass on the way from Barataria to New Orleans.

Customarily Lafitte paused for coffee with Madame de Verniat and her daughter while his mare was being saddled at the stable. These brief visits constituted the high lights in Madame de Verniat's plantation life.

To Madame de Verniat, Lafitte was a hero, an ideal, the embodiment of romance. The inevitable poverty that had followed the death of Jules de Verniat had constrained her to close her small house in New Orleans and retire to the more economical seclusion of her plantation. She was a victim of mental anæmia; deprived of her social functions, she found herself quite incapable of her own entertainment. But that saddle mare of Lafitte's—it was her connecting link with the living world.

She anticipated his coming for days on end, repeatedly going to her window to see if his boat might not be crossing Smuggler's Bight, always tormented by a twinge of fretful disappointment when it was not. She could tell the cut of his lug sail two miles away, and could even guess by the stroke of the sweeps whether or not the master was really aboard. If by chance he passed by, failing to change to his mare, she was thrown into such a fever of annoyance that the house became uninhabitable.

But Lafitte was more in her estimation than a romantic figure: he had a financial significance as well. Lately he had accepted small sums from her for investment; the returns ran into many hundred per cent., leading her to hope that she might yet gain the fortune that Louisiana had once promised.

Under Madame de Verniat's admiration Lafitte

remained meticulously formal. His constraint increased, if anything, with her increasing efforts to make him feel at home; and invariably he was in a hurry to get away.

To-day no boat was crossing Smuggler's Bight. She chewed her lips in desolate annoyance.

2

THE STEALTHY STEP of a servant sounded through the door, and Madame de Verniat jerked away from the window. As the latch clicked stealthily, she snatched a riding crop from an open drawer and concealed it in a fold of her skirt. Into the room, with long tiptoeing strides, came a lean mulatto girl.

"Jezebel!"

"M-a-m?" like the questioning bleat of a sheep.

"Come here!" Madame de Verniat indicated the exact spot she wished occupied, and the yellow girl took position warily.

"Where is my coffee?" Madame de Verniat's voice quivered with wrath; she might have been asking, "Why have you burned down the house?"

"Ah thought—"

Madame de Verniat's dumpy little figure jerked upright, and Jezebel retreated a step. A trilling splutter of French burst staccato from Madame de Verniat's lips. "What is the meaning of this? How many times have I told you? What is necessary here?" With a bound forward Madame de Verniat caught at Jezebel's sleeve, slashing at the yellow face with her whip.

The move failed. The mulatto girl agilely put a table between them.

"You come here! You come here!" Madame de Verniat jiggled futilely back and forth behind the barrier.

"Captain Lafitte gwine hear you, you shout so."

"Captain—" Madame gasped with shock. A name taken in vain! "What—"

"He jus' come fo' his hoss."

"What—why didn't you say so?" Madame de Verniat collapsed into her chair and leaned back panting. "Quick! My silk dress! Where is the pomade? Why aren't you changing my shoes?"

3

THROUGH ALL HER CHILDHOOD Madelon de Verniat had loved the swamp land. Something was lacking in it now.

To the little girl it had been a world of beauty and mystery; very still, but vivid with life. She had a little tippy pirogue, with which she had explored the cypress brakes that stretched dense greedy arms into the hard-won tillage. With that uncertain craft she threaded paths of quiet water hardly more than alligator trails through jungle. Even when she lost herself she had no fear of the brooding tangle; to her it had been a mystery mothering and gentle.

Under the drooping shades lush flowers, of colours like the plaintive minor notes of a violin, bloomed hidden for half a day and were gone. Lizards no bigger than her finger ran with a minute whispering patter over the leaves; sometimes they even ran across the surface of the water, so swift and light were their feet. If she whistled at them while they skimmed the surface they hesitated and sank, and had to be fished out, helpless; the small frightened life within her fingers was softly cool, faintly struggling, like a handful of water drops.

She liked to sit listening to songs of unseen birds that she knew only by names the negroes gave them— Whee-tee, Li'l Jenny, Bushloo—and she would think: "Just within reach of my paddle a hundred things are living. In a minute I shall see one." Sometimes it would be a swimming snake like a bit of green ribbon; or perhaps only a scooter bug on top of the motionless water, his legs denting the surface so that six circles of sunlight, big as picayunes, followed along on the leafy bottom just below. . . .

It was impractical to tell her mother of these explorations. Madame de Verniat feared and hated the swamp. She considered it full not only of fevers, but of other nameless and more ominous evils that made her draw close the curtains of her bed at night. When Madelon was gone for hours at a time Madame de Verniat became nervous, and troubled that she could not keep in better touch with her daughter.

"Madelon Céleste! Where *have* you been? Your poor mother is distracted!"

"Playing, Mother."

That, if not a complete answer, was sufficient to stump Madame de Verniat. She resented this daughter, who seemed so queer and quiet when not flaring up in one of her father's own tempers. To satisfy herself that she was raising Madelon properly, she gave her elaborate tasks of needlework, while the child's fingers were yet hardly apt at handling knife and fork. These stints were performed secretly by Boojoo, Madelon's negro mammy. The withering negress hated sewing, but she preferred it to watching Madelon scolded for leaving it undone; that was too much like having a stranger slap your baby.

Madelon's childhood had been both free and furtive, like a timid young animal's; not lonely, but peculiarly companioned.

But the swamp had now subtly changed. Madelon was sixteen, and under the whip of the Louisiana sun she was already a woman. Many of the Creole girls were mature, marriageable, at fourteen. From a brown-faced elfin child Madelon had turned, almost overnight, to something beautiful and new. She had a little triangular face, very quick and fervent, with the luxuriant hair common to Creoles. Her eyes were big and dark, with lashes like a veiling shadow. They were eyes that saw without looking; or rather they seemed to look abstractly through, and beyond, as if she were more listening than seeing. Into them had come a new glow, half eager, half sulkily tormented. With the metamorphosis from girl to woman a new nameless hunger had developed.

Madelon had grown swiftly aware of an indefinable restlessness that for weeks impelled her to paddle the furtive pirogue across new reaches, seeking out new small bayous lost in the swamp, rethreading the old. She could not remember a time when she had not felt the lure of the bends, the silent calling of the undiscovered a little way beyond; but the lure had been a quiet and dreamy one, as if the hidden things had been there forever, could wait while she rested her paddle, and became better by the waiting. But they were no longer quiet; they clamoured uncertainly, with voices not quite heard. Sometimes it seemed to be a small thing unprotected and lost; but mostly it was an expectant mystery, sometimes mocking, sometimes appealing, always elusive, lovely, and unknown. Something half suspected waiting in the cypress brakes, something dearer than her life. She hunted everywhere for it and found only the fecund mud-and-water creatures, which she had always loved, but which would not serve her now.

Madame de Verniat, inattentive to changes about her, accidentally ended it by planning a week in New Orleans for her daughter. The most elaborate scheming was necessary to make the visit possible. It is no good to live in a place where soup can be made for a picayune if you have no picayune at all. But clothes, not soup, were the difficulty. Such a cargo of French lawns, velvets, silk laces, silver filets, and assorted spangles were necessary to Madame de Verniat's proper advent to New Orleans as taxed her financial ingenuity to the utmost. A young girl like Madelon might get along with one or two simple gowns, but Madame de Verniat had her position to keep up—which, to her, meant that she must take along three times as much stuff as she would have any chance to wear. With long scheming, however, she had contrived it.

So Madelon came at last to the huddled Creole city by

the levee, the city of narrow streets and close-hanging iron-lace balconies, of great arches and vaulted carriageways, of mud, and flowered courtyards, gay music, and odd smells.

The result of the single turgid week in New Orleans had been an entirely new view of life for Madelon. The music, the rhythms of the dances for which her mother had drilled her, the great unaccustomed number of faces, made a profound impression. But it was the attention of the young men that had affected her most. She returned, with her head full of candlelight, faces, and whispered words, to a swamp land that had become empty and meaningless. Bits of ephemeral New Orleans gossip stuck permanently in her head, sketchily delineating the Outer World. The glorious Bernard Marigny had fought a duel. Ma'm'selle du Bois was to have a six-horse coach just like those of Paris. Twelve young men had serenaded Micaela Lausanne. . . .

Unfortunately, the eyes of the Creole dandies had perceived only a brown-armed little country girl, plainly dressed, tongue-tied, and abashed, in tow of an overdressed and simpering old woman. However, someone had serenaded Madelon on her last night in New Orleans. He had sung under her window a song from Gascony, one that she had known all her life; but the caressing tones of his voice had given it unsuspected meanings. . . .

Then that ridiculous mother of hers had crashed open a shutter and flung out a great gawky poinsettia spray—in lieu of a rose, no doubt.

At breakfast her mother had said, with some pleasurable excitement that she tried hard to conceal: "That outrageous Nicolas Odesse serenaded me last night. Silly fellow! That is what one must put up with in New Orleans!" Her eyes shone like a terrier's.

"I noticed it," said Madelon coolly. "You threw something at him. The limb of a tree?"

"Why! Madelon! What can you be thinking of!" her mother expostulated, blushing furiously. "I did no such thing! And what if I had? It is most customary to fling a flower—most customary. Limb of a tree! *Dieu!* Insulting! I suppose a poinsettia . . ."

Madelon thought her mother obscene.

She and her mother had little in common. She did not, for example, share Madame de Verniat's excitement over Jean Lafitte. Madelon considered him a rather stuffy, middle-aged man.

4

LAFITTE strode directly to the stable through the twilight, slapping his roll-top leather boots with a short whip. The crippled negro boy came hobbling out to meet him.

"Yas, Capum! Yas, Capum!" His dog eyes shone with pleasurable fright. To him Lafitte was the grandest and therefore the most terrifying figure in the known world. That hammer-headed dun mare was the one animal on the plantation whose hide was always rag-polished.

"Where's my mount?"

"Yas, Capum!" The boy produced the saddled mare instantly. He had seen Lafitte coming long ago.

"Is Ma'm'selle at the house?"

"No, Capum. She watch wuk." The boy spoke a gumbo French that Lafitte could hardly understand. "Down dah!" the boy added, as Lafitte scowled. He indicated a deep muddy track trailing off through undergrowth toward the only cotton field that the swamp had not already regained.

"I show!" he started to run ahead down the path, but Lafitte stopped him.

"Never mind." He clambered not too expertly into the saddle and hauled the mare's mouth around with a heavy hand, so that her eyes rolled.

Madelon's horse stood drowsily on the low mud levee that kept the bayou out of the cotton. It was a shaggy, worthless brute with a great sagging paunch. She sat lightly, gracefully, on a side-saddle strapped about the brute's immense girth; so that the great lump of a horse made her look unexpectedly small and delicately made.

Jean Lafitte came galloping up with a levee-shaking hammer of hoofs that brought curses to the lips of the overseer who bossed the slave gang in the field below. He made an impressive figure, heavy shouldered, rigidly straight, and tall, the silver buttons glinting on the blue of his coat even in the gathering dusk.

The dark beard showed in his shaved cheeks, as if the under side of the skin were faintly dusted with charcoal. His eyes were bright as he gustily saluted Madelon.

"Eh, pardee! You're looking better every day. How you're growing up, child!" The negroes stopped work to stare at him, which the overseer failed to notice because he was staring, too; but Lafitte paid no more attention to the lot of them than as if they had been so many cattle.

Madelon's eyes were vivid; visitors were scarce at the De Verniats', and even the most uninteresting found a welcome here. "Oh, it's you! I'm so glad you came. Mother will be so glad to see you."

"Oh, she will, will she? Well, aren't you glad to see me?"

"Why, of course I am."

"How is the cotton?"

"Poorly. It always is."

"Yes, I suppose so. I can't tell you," he said contemplatively, "how pretty you are."

Madelon unhurriedly looked Lafitte in the eyes, like a boy. Then, unlike a boy, she turned her face away. Behind the decorous courtesy of his glance she sensed an intimate searching estimation. It gave her an unpleasant tremulant uneasiness. Her fingers went to her throat, drawing her dress closer about her neck.

"Prettier every day," he added slowly, heavily, almost.

There was a pause. Lafitte sat pondering, staring out across the ragged cotton rows to the encroaching swamp jungle beyond; yet she remained clear before his eyes, many times more clear than the far brush, like blown rabbit fur, in which his eyes rested. Her cheeks were colourless except for the olive tint toasted into them by indirect sun, cool and clear. Her right knee was hooked over the horn of the side-saddle, so that the light unstarched skirt revealed the rondure of her thigh. She seemed to Lafitte a thing utterly fresh and new, completely untouched. A dismal twinge of inferiority whispered to him that so far as he was concerned she would always remain so.

Jean Lafitte's ultimate ambition was a thing which remained undefined. Sometimes he thought in terms of a vast plantation estate; once for a little while he had let his mind dream upon the governorship of Louisiana. His nature was the combined result of an overmastering pride and an inadequate childhood. Coming with the early years of the century to Louisiana he had found a liberal democratic spirit prevalent; a tolerant spirit of mutual friendliness among these exiled French, permitting his conception of his possible future to leap all previous restraints.

But he was a penniless adventurer, seeking sustenance where sustenance offered. When, in an idle interval, he plunged into the illegal, and hence immensely profitable, slave trade, he unconsciously established his social position forever. The dim mark of the pariah was upon him, unerasable. He could not have gone back, even had other means to the power he sought been opened. Though without genius for friendship himself, he made strong friends of others; some of these made extravagant efforts to make him their social equal in the stratified life of New Orleans. It was of no use. At best he was a character of the borderland, liked, admired, believed in, supported, but still stigmatized, held off as a man apart.

This discrimination, which he had unwittingly brought upon himself, was a ceaseless lash to Lafitte's pride, driving him with perpetually renewed energies in the search of power.

Now in Lafitte's ears the world was humming like a nest of young rattlesnakes—of whom he, perhaps, was one. Up the gulf with every south-cleared ship were coming rumours of vast revolt; the destinies of provinces greater than the whole of Europe were shaking under the impact of bold young men, hard-fighting adventurers hardly any of whom were as much as thirty years old. Lafitte's sympathy was with these rebels, these youngsters who meant to remake the Western world to suit themselves. Certainly his opportunities lay with them.

Yet his own ultimate purposes remained unclear. Throughout the whole of his tumultuous career, full of contradictions and cross-purposes, it is doubtful if he ever was sure of his goal for very long. One thing he knew—he was for Lafitte. He could tolerate no situation in which Lafitte was second to anyone. He must be boss, first, last, and always, accepted and acknowledged. This, perhaps, was in itself his goal, the unconscious purpose that lured him in pursuit of vast wealth, urging him to gain dominance over fleets of men and ships for which he had no clearly defined use when he had mastered them. No man ever satirized Jean's ideals better than the disgruntled privateersman who paraded Grand Isle chanting drunkenly: "Great God Lafitte! Great God Lafitte!"

Upon this man Madelon de Verniat had an unsuspected effect. He was less in love with her than taunted by her inaccessibility. In her presence the lash fell upon him mercilessly. He always left her with his ambitions in an angry, sullen fever. He would not concede his defeat. He had thought that wealth would mean his acceptance everywhere as a gentleman in this new land. But the considerable wealth he had already attained, chiefly in the single year of the embargo, had not been sufficient. Still believing in his ultimate invincibility, he was at this time gambling it all in pursuit of resources many times as great.

He said suddenly, "How would you like to go to school in France?"

She did not understand him at first; but when she comprehended her eyes filled with a quick despair.

"Oh, there's no use thinking about anything like that."

"Perhaps there is. I am going into certain new projects. By turning your mother's investments into new channels it might very well be possible."

"Do you mean it?"

"Of course. Why should I tease you?"

"But do you think—do you suppose—" She faltered and stopped.

"That she would send you if she had the money?"

Madelon hesitated, then nodded faintly.

"Well, I'll talk to her about it."

A sudden rush of gratitude, wholly unexpected, overwhelmed Madelon. "You've helped us so much—almost as if you were my father!"

Lafitte's face showed no reaction; his smile was politely pleasant. She had no key to his mind. She thought he looked like a kindly middle-aged courtier, on a horse that he made appear a size too small. Her face was alive with a new impersonal interest.

"Will you talk to her now?"

"Not now. I must go on."

"But you'll at least stop for coffee?"

"Impossible," he said. His voice remained suave. "I'll try to stop on my way back, for a moment. *Au revoir.*"

"Au revoir!" she cried after him; and over his shoulder, as he jerked the mare around, he managed a quick bright smile, almost as if he had been twenty years younger.

Disappearing around the bend of the path the mare's tail gave a great switch, like a jerked flag, as the vicious slash of Lafitte's whip put a bloody welt on the beast's flank.

By the time that Lafitte was out of sight, Madelon was no longer thinking about Lafitte. It was curious that the thought of going away, thrilling as it was to her, should bring the Yankee into her mind. She was thinking that wherever she went, whatever she did, she would forever remember that tall strange man, the fighter of sea beasts, the explorer of far frozen seas. She could feel yet the quiet penetrating thrust of his green eyes into her own; and in the mist that was rising from the swamp dusk she was seeing the strong angular striding of his gaunt frame and the glint of sunlight on his blond hair.

Chapter VI

1

$\mathcal{J}$EAN LAFITTE was in New Orleans no longer than was necessary to familiarize his brother Pierre with their altered situation.

Between Jean Lafitte and his elder brother there was an instantly noticeable resemblance; but it was a resemblance limited to form and line. Pierre had Jean's height, his breadth of shoulder, and the long spade chin suggestive of Gascony; but Pierre, the elder, was gaunt, bony, gangling, with a terrific hard power of wrist and thigh but an awkward lurching stride.

Behind the mask of superficial resemblance Pierre but poorly concealed a nature so dissimilar to Jean's that the brothers could not be reckoned as of the same type. He had none of the foxiness, the indirection, and the subtle devious diplomacy that made the frontal assault of a problem impossible to Jean. He was a natural exponent of the direct attack; and his routine of approach to any subject was that which he had learned in his early privateering experience upon the sea: all sail and long guns, close quarters and the carronades, then grappling hooks, cutlasses, and the short savage carry by the board.

Pierre was cross-eyed. It is hard to know what figure Pierre Lafitte might have presented had it not been for this single eccentricity of feature that, in his own mind, set him apart from other men. The affliction added a touch of humour to his otherwise rather grim appearance; and at the same time induced in him a surly ugliness of temper which gave that humorous touch an aspect sardonically bizarre.

This was the man who in New Orleans upheld all the interests of the Lafittes. Jean had placed him there when his divided affairs at Grand Isle and in the city had become too demanding and too complicated for handling by himself alone. He did not serve the purpose as well as Jean could have wished; but there were few men whom Jean wished to trust, and Pierre had to be made to do. The two brothers quarrelled energetically and continually; but at bottom they counted upon each other to an extent that their friends never would have believed.

The disagreement following Jean's break with the privateer captains was particularly violent. Pierre paced up and down the main room of their little house on the Rue Bourbon, chewing a cigar to a pulp and shooting sparks in two discordant directions from his small green eyes.

"You fool, you little fool," he snarled as he paced; "after all my work; after all my planning; after all—ah, you fool, fool . . ." If there had been a tail attached to Pierre he would have lashed himself with it.

Jean's huge form lounged luxuriantly upon a spindly legged gilt chair that looked entirely incapable of supporting his balanced weight. He smoked fastidiously and smiled at the ash of his cigar.

Pierre was becoming incoherent, as he always did in

his moments of high pressure. "I told you twenty times. I told you forty times. You wouldn't listen. No, you had ways of your own. Now where are we? We're in the street. You with your smart ideas, you've got us in the street! This is what comes out of your stubbornness. You never fought a ship in your life. You know nothing about men and the world's ways. You . . ."

Jean snickered. It sounded arrestingly idiotic, coming from that powerful body and the grave, imposing face with the spade chin. Pierre was infuriated. He whirled and stood before his comfortably sprawled brother with his strong fingers jerking tentatively as he wondered whether or not he had better take Jean by the throat.

Jean Lafitte stared upward into his brother's one straight eye. His eye could not put down Pierre's, for there was the same fibre behind both; but Jean could divert his brother's attention that way, so that Pierre's thoughts slowed up, and what he was about came to nothing.

Pierre remained standing there for several moments. Jean had closed the tall French windows at the beginning of the interview, and a couple of big blue flies were buzzing against the panes.

"Well," said Pierre finally, in a new tone, "what d'you think we're to do now?"

Jean told him exactly what they were to do. Pierre must at all costs fend off and divert all speculators who wished to invest in Baratarian goods. Such materials as the Lafittes themselves held were to be let out in dribbles, to satiate the market to a certain extent; or to break the price, suddenly, upon any commodity which the rebel privateers seemed about to make some money on. The same policy applied to the goods of Dominique You, and any other friendly captains—if there were to be any others remaining loyal to the Lafitte régime.

Those passive measures alone, Jean pointed out, would presently reduce the hotheads to a state of effective poverty.

"And what are you going to be doing?" Pierre wanted to know. "You, I suppose you'll go fishing, hanh?"

"I'm going down to the Temple for a while. I mean to keep this new Yankee bucko standing by. Just now he's having my stuff moved from Grand Isle—such of it as I'll need at the Temple."

"Me," said Pierre, "I don't like the looks of that damned Yank."

"You'll like him less," Jean predicted, "when you know him better."

"Why?"

"Because," said Jean, "he's too much like yourself."

Pierre had not the curiosity to probe that. "Those bully boys," he prophesied, "will rout you out of the Temple in three days."

"Have it your way," said Jean.

2

JEAN was not, however, routed out of the Temple as immediately as Pierre had predicted. For one thing Jean Ducoing, Nez Coupé, and Beluche were the only captains who had not once more taken the sea. Even the ship of Beluche was out, under his second in command.

Masselier, of the *Two Brothers*, of course remained; but that ship was the Lafittes' own.

The Temple was not the mysterious and impressive thing its name implied. Deep down in the mangrove tangles west of the Mississippi, twenty miles south of the point at which the tortuous unmoving Bayou des Familles touched the Mississippi levee, a small island humped its back out of the jungled muck. It was perhaps twice the size of the New Orleans Place d'Armes; and its only distinguishing features (other than the substantial footing it provided) were three huge looming mounds of shells marking the spot where forgotten aborigines had once for a long time dined on clams. The shell heaps rose vague and gray behind the trees, great unexpected mineral extuberances upon the muck.

Baratarian slaves had here built a straggling half circle of shanties for the convenience of the captains, two or three patched-together warehouses for smuggled goods, and a long flimsy shed that served as a barracoon for transient blacks. These handiworks sprawled sketchily under the trees at the foot of the gray shell heaps, looking indifferent to themselves and to each other, as if to-morrow might find them fallen in. The island and the mounds seemed to have a detachment from the works of man; no roistering mob of drunken privateers could make that spot seem anything more than a temporary stopping place, and nobody, probably, ever thought of it as anything else. Meanwhile, it was a convenient rendezvous for illicit slave auctions and the transfer of illegal goods.

Seven miles south of the Temple the fresh water-mangrove and cypress feathered off into the wastes of salt marsh that lay in a belt thirty miles wide along the shore of the Gulf. Across the gray flats a man could see ten miles without finding any mark to tell him where he was. The bayous here were shallow salt tracks between ten thousand islands of sedge and muck. They crossed each other, circled, doubled, led off into blind alleys. No one of them looked any different from any other. A boat that missed its turning could poke about for days without finding the way out until some other boat, seen far across the flats, showed the true way through. Of this desolation of brackish mud no survey existed. Today the map of that waste shows a mottle of muck and water more intricate than the pattern of a turtle shell, or the skin of a frog.

The last ten miles of the way to Grand Isle were through the waters of Barataria Bay, to which the narrow strait called Grand Pass gave the privateers access from the sea.

Lafitte now moved from Grand Isle nearly everything he had there of value, including fourteen slaves, and three lugger loads of assorted loot which he had previously purchased from various of the privateers. He left only his cordage and ship chandlery under the Grand Terre guns. And, concentrating upon the island in the swamp, he set up a very temporary establishment of his own.

Here Job Northrup joined him, coming up from Grand Isle with the last boatload of loot. A half-dozen nondescript characters, who always seemed to trail disconsolately after Lafitte like lost dogs, presently followed him there, instinctively gathering themselves about the man who was their only means of support; but for all practical purposes Northrup and Lafitte now found themselves alone.

The days dragged by slowly, three days, five days, a week. Lafitte sat against the wall of his shanty, his chair tilted back, hardly ever moving except to flick away the flies with a switch; or else paced the rotting planks of the fifty-foot lugger landing beside the Bayou des Familles.

Sometimes he questioned Job Northrup, foxily seeking to lead out the tall Yankee's past. He was holding Northrup there for the present on captain's pay, for reasons that he had not seen fit to divulge; and Northrup, on his own suggestion, was using the slaves to clean and recondition a considerable muddle of assorted weapons that he had dug up in Lafitte's warehouse. He had also at his own initiative instigated and carried out a complete inventory of Lafitte's stuff. Both of these enterprises, Lafitte could see, were motivated by no desire to make himself useful, but were merely the efforts of an active man to keep himself entertained in idleness.

Lafitte came to the conclusion that the Yankee's restless energy must derive from some desperate concealed worry. Few people in Louisiana moved about much in the summer heat if sitting still would do. He tried to find out what the irritant was, but failed because his hypothesis had been incorrect. Nor was he much more successful in learning what had been the Yankee's past. Northrup was never a man easily stimulated to speech;

and the brevity of his replies made him seem to Lafitte taciturn and secretive.

"You seem to know weapons," Lafitte would suggest. "I should imagine you have been an armourer or a gunsmith."

No reply from the Yankee. He never understood a question that was merely implied, however broadly. Irritated, Lafitte would lower his manners and try to pin the Yankee down. "Am I right?"

"Not exactly."

"Might I ask," Lafitte bore down, "where you got your schooling in firearms?"

"Different places. On the north coast and on ships."

"Oh, I see," exclaimed Lafitte. "On land and sea!"

"That's it." The Yankee sucked at a pipe; and so far as Lafitte could see the sarcasm was wasted.

Sometimes, however, Lafitte settled a point of consequence to him.

"This thing of carrying a ship by the board is a peculiar thing," he suggested. "Often—but then, I suppose you know more of all that than I."

"No," said the Yankee.

"My experience is limited, I assure you."

"As for me," said Northrup unexpectedly, "I never attacked a merchant ship in my life."

"You mean—"

"No occasion for it ever come up."

Lafitte's instinct was to assume at once that the man lied. Yet for some reason he found himself forced to believe this Northerner whom he so little understood.

A dull weapon, Lafitte told himself; but a hard-edged

one, and one that would not be likely to turn in the hand. . . . He started to suggest to Northrup that he say nothing to the privateers of his inexperience, but he stopped himself with a smile. To counsel the Yankee to silence would have been like suggesting to Gambio that he stand up for his rights, or advising Durossac to familiarize himself with arms.

Meantime, as Lafitte doubtless was aware, Northrup was coolly measuring this man with whom, for the present, he had chosen to associate his fortunes. The continued idleness irked him; yet he thought he detected in the air some hint of approaching action, some manner of stir-up and boil-over that might conceivably bring his own interests to the top. He understood, better than Lafitte supposed, what had happened the night of the gathering at Lafitte's house on Grand Isle; and he was undeceived by the Temple's atmosphere of desolated peace.

"Doesn't this inaction annoy you?" Lafitte asked.

The Yankee shrugged. "Someone's going to get sheared off at the hips before long."

"Who?"

"Who knows?"

"I've promised you little or nothing here," said Lafitte, pressing his advantage. "At any time you wish to leave you are free to do so."

"If I want to leave, I'll leave, all right," the Yankee assured him.

This was the sort of man Lafitte believed he knew how to use. The Yankee had that rigidity of character which the planner thought useful in the construction of schemes.

Lafitte saw the Yankee at least in part for what he was: a fortune hunter from a Northern land, an ambitious man and a hard one, striking out toward his goal through such channels as offered themselves. It was even apparent to the Baratarian that the Yankee was stirred by that same world restlessness to which Lafitte himself responded. An upstart Corsican had smashed the map of Europe; Burr and Wilkinson had attempted a Southwestern empire as big as Europe, and, as far as Lafitte could see, had not missed it by very much; a handful of Yankees on a storm-swept coast had set up a nation of their own, thrashed England, and sent their frontiers westward like rushing waters to cover the better half of a continent. The world was on the melt; nothing was impossible, no ambition too arrogant. Lafitte could understand that to the Northern son of a seafaring race the call of the adventurous times should come from the sea. The Baratarian, also, chose to seek his opportunity in the political fogs and perpetual turbulence of the sea frontiers.

As for the Yankee, studying the man with whom he had voluntarily cast his lot, he was at first displeased, and then reconciled in ways that he had not anticipated. Northrup's ultimate plans were incomplete. In common with Lafitte, he believed that wherever there were violence, uncertainty, and disorder, there opportunity stood concealed from common minds by the fog of action itself. He had sought the Lafittes because he had reason to believe that no one was turning the disorganization of the sea frontiers to such good profit as they.

Three years before, Job Northrup had sailed south

from New Haven in the old tub of a brig, the *Charles*, which had been his principle heritage from his father. The austere New England top layer, whom he liked to call the codfish aristocracy, he affected to hold in disdain; but he meant to become one of them nonetheless. For three years, up and down the latitudes, the Yankee and his brig had pursued an undefined opportunity that remained just beyond the rim of the world.

A succession of fortuities had kept Northrup out of the harbour of New Orleans until the day when he came looking for Jean Lafitte, who, he had been told, knew how to make money faster than any other adventurer on the pelican coast. He came ready for any undertaking; yet, with a sort of conservative providence that never quite left him, he had concealed his ownership of the old slow *Charles* lest in some hazardous speculation he should be led to lose the brig, and with her his means of egress.

Now, at last, he was in a position to study the man whom he had been at such pains to seek.

Lafitte's appearance he had found unprepossessing. He had come expecting to find a man "six feet two inches tall," a bully "always ready for a fight with any weapon," a commander who "put men down with his eye." This mythological figure had not materialized. Instead he found Jean Lafitte a trifle under six feet tall—not quite so tall as the Yankee himself; a rather placid-looking, courteous-spoken man, with a small, mild gray eye and an unusually well-kept moustache. In dress Lafitte commonly looked like all other men who tried to keep in the fashion, with possibly the slight distinction that the expensive quality of his clothes appeared a little too much stressed. Northrup thought he looked like a prosperous shop keeper; he could imagine Lafitte being cross with his clerks. And he was not long in learning that Jean Lafitte had never commanded a fighting ship in his life. So this was the boss of outlaw Barataria, the king smuggler, the pirate of the Gulf!

Yet he knew that this Lafitte must possess some practical and profit-reaping quality that common men did not; and he remained, trying, for his own use, to find out what this attribute might be.

His first insight into the hidden abilities of Jean Lafitte was provided upon the third day of their sojourn at the Temple.

3

Down the bayou through the swamp came a boat—well-rowed, the Yankee noticed, for no negro was long in that country of much water without getting his bellyful of practice at the sweeps. The blacks chanted as they rowed, giving notice of their approach from a long way off; and presently Lafitte was courteously receiving at the landing a pair of quick-speaking and rather fussily dressed gentlemen.

They were Creoles, Northrup saw at once; people of that transplanted race of pure Spanish and French blood that carried itself so proudly upon the new world soil, looking down upon the rough flatboatmen from the North, and still bitterly resenting the destiny that had left Louisiana under the domination of the Anglo-Americans. Beside those short wiry men Lafitte looked more like the towering figure Northrup had heard described. That the two were merchants from New Orleans on an errand of speculative purchasing became immediately apparent.

What was no less apparent was that Lafitte wished to confer with them alone. Northrup discreetly retired, but not to such a distance that he could not overhear part of what was said.

Lafitte, Northrup could see, was apologizing, deprecating, offering them wine. He could see those speculators, at first displeased, melting under the jests and liqueurs of Lafitte. The Baratarian was explaining affably why he had so little material for them to take away.

"Beluche's silk? Yes, you're right, there is a great deal of it; so much that it isn't going to bring very much, I'm afraid. . . . Personally, I have at hand only a little of it— to tell you the truth, M'sieu Beluche has been arrogant about the price and let me have only this bit to tide over his immediate expense. Here is a sample. . . . I'll have to ask you forty dollars for the lot; I paid only twenty-five, but I think it's worth forty, don't you?"

"Sold," said the quicker of the Creoles. "Have it thrown in the boat. Damnation! Beluche is asking three times that for an inferior pattern!"

Lafitte shrugged and smiled.

The second speculator drew a cigar from an elaborate and paunchy vest. "D'you know what Beluche is saying, M'sieu Jean? That you have broken with the privateers; that Baratarian—importations are going to be available only through him."

Again Lafitte's slow smile. "That old story again?"

"I'd never heard it before," said one.

"M'sieu has perhaps been considered less easy to dupe than some of the others, that they should try you with it last. Believe me, there is hardly a—merchant in New Orleans who has not been cheated by that old lie. You'd hardly believe it. The captains try it over and over, nearly every cruise. Like children. Me, I won't stand for their ridiculous demands, and they know it. I have to protect my New Orleans people. You fancy Beluche's silk, m'sieu? Trust me, you shall have it. I'll let you know, just you two, when the price is best for you. . . ."

Seven times in the next four days Northrup watched Lafitte turning speculators back from the Temple with deprecations, with assurances—and, in each case, with some trifling handful of merchandise pressed upon them at a price that left them speechless. Men that had come to bargain and haggle to the last picayune more than once found that Lafitte's first price undercut what they had intended to pay by half.

Northrup, at first at a loss, accidentally learned that those trifles that Lafitte let go so cheaply were indeed from the cargoes of the rebelling privateers—and that in each case Lafitte had paid, in New Orleans, three or four times the price at which he sold. Indirectly, through devious channels the very circumspection of which was expensive, Lafitte had obtained samples of the various goods that Beluche was offering for sale on behalf of the privateers, and now tossed them, at a ridiculous reduction, to those purchasers so eager for wares as to brave the tiresome journey to the source at Grand Isle.

"This price is more like it, eh, m'sieu? A price that a man can do something with. But rest assured, m'sieu, I'm taking a profit I'm ashamed of. The truth of the matter is that soon prices will be much lower even than this. I would not wish that generally known, m'sieu— you can understand that; but, if you wish, I will send you private word . . ."

Suddenly Northrup perceived the character of Lafitte's game, and he chuckled to himself. What chance had the blunt Beluche and his hairy-fisted allies against a plausibility like that of the boss they sought to deny? Northrup pictured with glee the situation at Grand Isle, where Nez Coupé and Jean Ducoing sat on their stacks of unliquidated loot, waiting for the purchasers that had always come in a steady stream to Lafitte but now reached Grand Isle no more. It was questionable, of course, if Pierre Lafitte was holding his ground against Beluche in New Orleans; but the Yankee could not evade the belief that Jean had somehow stacked the cards there, also.

A day of reckoning, the Yankee knew, was bound to come. He wondered how long it would be before Ducoing and Nez Coupé learned of Lafitte's trickery and came boiling up into the swamp to clean him out. The sense of impending action now transmuted itself to a more definite prediction. Northrup looked forward with elation to the day when the pack at Grand Isle would be deceived no more.

Chapter VII

1

IF PÈRE MIGUEL had any outstanding talent other than a certain gift of duplicity, or any other merit than a blind faith in what had been taught him, that old chess master Antoine had been unable to find it out. Homeless as a lost ghost, always fatuously unctuous, mild eyed, and neatly shabby, he wandered the bayous, arriving unnoticed and leaving the same way. No one knew his age, or cared a whoop either; but the truth was he was not so ancient as he appeared. An unfriendly climate, fever, and a congenital tendency toward worry had aged him rather before his time, turning him bald and rather wizened, with a scraggly gray beard. For the most part the ruffians of Barataria treated him with kindly mocking tolerance, as if he were a foolish old dog for whom there was no longer any practical use.

Such was Père Miguel's condition at the moment when Lafitte made his ill-timed suggestion that Madelon be sent to school in France. Miguel, appearing at the De Verniats' shortly thereafter, found himself impressed not at all against his will as a tutor for Madelon. Miguel's life now assumed an outwardly placid stability. Though unpaid, he was provided at the De Verniats' with food and shelter; and for the time his wanderings ceased.

If Miguel's situation was outwardly placid, however, inwardly the man was restless and disturbed. His daily close association with Madelon de Verniat filled him with an ambitious fervour for which there was no obvious outlet. Whatever Miguel's youth may have been, it is certain that for a long time he had been as strictly celibate as required by the Franciscan vows. Years had passed since he had last been moved to think of a woman as attainable by himself. He did not so think of Madelon now. In justice to the old muddle-head it must be granted that he probably never recognized the true nature of the unrest with which Madelon inspired him. Long training enabled him to repudiate and to forget, with admirable mental discipline, any flash of insight that threatened to illuminate the undesirable.

His code permitted him, however, to attempt such adjustments in the lives about him as seemed advantageous. It was in line with his calling to save the Yankee's soul if he could. And with Madelon's slender figure haunting him he was able to convince himself that the matching of Job and Madelon would be in several ways salutary.

For the tall blond man of action Miguel held an immense instinctive admiration which was increased by the pleasurable sense of humility induced in him by the Yankee's rough manner. Yet, even while he told himself that his primary aim was the salvation of Job Northrup's soul, it was the girl that possessed his mind. He thought he perceived in Madelon's rather wistful face something reminiscent of the Madonna; and thus was able to cast a gratuitous aura of holiness about his intense preoccupation with it. Rapidly, in the course of days spent within sight of Madelon and nights spent mostly in what passed for meditation, Miguel had nursed his vicarious project into an all-absorbing obsession.

He was annoyed and alarmed by the Yankee's failure to return to the De Verniats'. Believing unequivocally in a fatalistic providence, he yet esteemed himself an instrument of that providence; some failure of his own, he conceived, might be holding up the game. He studied again his memory of every word that had passed between the Yankee and the girl upon the occasion of Northrup's only visit. And presently he concluded that Madelon had not done herself justice; had, in fact, presented too wooden an appearance, evidently failing to recognize the Northrup qualities that stirred Miguel to admiration.

Here was an unforseen deficiency in his plans. He set his wits to work and swiftly devised a suitable remedy.

2

"YOU SEEM SAD, Père Miguel," Madelon suggested on the fourth morning of her tutelage.

Père Miguel's eyes wandered in a blurred gaze that seemed to look beyond the walls, beyond the fields, beyond the cypress jungles, as if he surveyed a suffering world. It was a touch of theatrics that he had learned in the pulpit; it gave him time to collect his thoughts—and, in this case, served the secondary purpose of assuring the friar that Madame de Verniat was not within range. That lady had a disconcerting way of wandering in and out of the room.

"Ah, mademoiselle," replied the little Franciscan, "I have recently witnessed a heartrending sight! A young man, struggling for the salvation of his immortal soul." He paused; and added in a dramatic, vibrant voice: "And losing out. . . ."

"Eh, pardee!" exclaimed Madelon interestedly.

With his eyes out the window the friar proceeded to supply selected details. His language was imaginative, his sentences round and measured.

"Picture to yourself a tall young man, handsome of figure as the peculiar pagan notion of a god; a young man with a clear gray eye, full of light and spirit; a young man with hair like a golden cloud. . . . He is of great strength and no less intelligence. No achievement might have been beyond him. Yet, I must tell you—and do you wonder that I am sad?—this young man is an infidel."

"A Turkish young man?" Madelon suggested.

"Do Turks have golden hair?" Miguel demanded peevishly. He turned sharply upon Madelon, taken aback by what he conceived to be her idiocy. Yet, as he studied her for a brief moment, it seemed to him that he had never seen the girl's face more beautiful. The sunlight from the tall French windows turned her skin so radiantly golden that it seemed to possess a delicate translucence. Her hair was a dark mist, and her naturally sombre eyes were upon his face. Miguel was inspired to new grandiloquence of misstatement.

"No," he told her more gently, "he is an American. A man of mystery, in part; he is without friends or family, having as a little child been thrown upon the world. What a man he has made of himself, in the face of everything!"

"Can nothing be done for him?"

"I am doing what I can," Miguel told her sadly. "I am in constant touch with him and in his confidence. Indeed, I may say that perhaps I alone, of all men, am in his confidence. Yet there is little I can do. There is an obstruction, a great sorrow in his life."

"What kind of sorrow, Père Miguel?"

"Ah, my child—I am not at liberty to tell you. I can only say," he declared musingly, "that it is very real. I cannot believe that you have not seen it in his eyes."

"I have seen him then?" cried Madelon.

"Quietly, quietly," urged Miguel. "Ah, I see I have said too much. I might have known you would guess at once to what young man I referred."

He paused and looked at Madelon, waiting for her to speak Job Northrup's name. He was annoyed to find that her expression was perfectly blank. He sighed.

"Yes," he admitted, as if further concealment were futile; "it is M'sieu Northrup. What a wrong I have done him to speak of his misfortunes! Yet, somehow I feel that if he wished anyone but myself to know of his trouble, it would be you, Mademoiselle Madelaine."

Looking at Madelon again he saw that his last shot had gone wild. A peculiar expression of perplexity suffused Madelon's face. The fact was that Père Miguel's florid description had not suggested the big Yankee to her at all. To think of Northrup's hair, like bent hay, as a "golden cloud," required practice, no doubt.

"But—" Madelon began.

The nervous tap of Madame de Verniat's step interrupted them.

"Ah, well, we will take this lesson over again tomorrow," said Miguel ambiguously. "I do not wonder that you have trouble with the latter letters of the alphabet. But learn to search your mind, my child, and do not be dismayed."

As the friar had hoped, it was Madelon who opened the subject next day.

"I'm so worried about M'sieu Northrup. Isn't there anything we can do?"

Père Miguel was silent for some time. He bowed his chin upon his breast, apparently lost in thought. Finally, as he slowly shook his head, his short grizzled beard scraped audibly back and forth across a fold of his coarse gray robe. Yet—the old fraud somehow managed to present a convincing picture of a devout and sorrowing man, old in the wisdom of the world. Older heads than Madelon's had time and again listened soberly to that man's words.

"He will die young. He is without fear and completely reckless in his despair. That is the danger: that he will die before he finds the light. . . . What can one say to a young man who is lost in the despair of a hopeless love?"

Suddenly he glanced up at Madelon with an expression shocked and appalled. "What have I done?" he exclaimed. Then, appearing sadly to compose himself:

"Yet, after all, I have told you nothing that you did not already apprehend—or else would surely have learned. From a woman such things cannot be concealed. I can console myself that you read the whole story, long ago, in his eyes. After all, why should he not love you? In a different way, you are as admirable as he."

The puzzlement in Madelon's face when he stole a glance at her again was stronger than before; but there was a curious illumination in her eyes that he could not, at the moment, accurately read. For a brief span he was assailed with doubt as to the legitimacy of his methods. For one passing moment the little old fraud was touched by an unfamiliar sense of shame.

"Are you certain—of what you have told me—about M'sieu?"

There was a quaver in Madelon's voice that Miguel did not pause to define. Vigorously he put doubt behind him. That man was practised in the ways of faith; almost he could convince himself that all he had said was true.

He ignored her question. "I beg of you," he said, "that you try to think but kindly of this poor young man. If, by any chance, a mention of his devotion to you should be—wrung from his lips, repulse him but gently; remember always, there is involved the salvation of a human soul."

Père Miguel had at one time read—the better to combat their influence—a number of proscribed romances; they were of assistance to him now.

"Let us remember," he adjured her, "that after all, in spite of his rough exterior, for all his great strength and competence in the world of men, at heart this poor young man is but a helpless lamb; he often makes me think of a little wandering child—a dove lost upon the face of the waters."

The trick was turned. It was a push-over, a slaughter. He had outdone himself. So completely had he convinced himself of his righteousness that not even his acrobatic description of the big Yank as an infant and a bird occasioned him any sense of the inappropriate.

"Ah, well. Perhaps we shall see him no more. Such is the world's way. We will certainly speak of the matter no more."

And late in an afternoon, three days later, the big Yankee himself came striding up from the landing, wondering if he would be remembered by the girl he had seen but once in his life, wondering, in fact, if he correctly remembered her name.

Chapter VIII

1

Walking up the path from his lugger, Northrup came abruptly upon Père Miguel. The little Capuchin friar, looking no bigger from the point of view of the Yankee's height than a waggle-beard gnome, was pacing among the trees, his hands clasped at the back of his robe. He had been mumbling, apparently, to the toes of his sandals; but at the sight of Job Northrup he checked with a startled jerk and stood staring with a hardly justified bewilderment.

"Hello, Pa," said the big Yank.

Père Miguel glanced over his shoulder at the house; then suddenly came forward, both hands extended.

"Ah, M'sieu Northrup! How happy I am to see you again!"

Northrup was taken aback. "The devil you say," said Northrup. He was thinking of a call the friar had made at the Temple a few days before. Since the little Capuchin had made almost no impression upon him at all, Northrup had failed to recognize Miguel at first; and, perhaps in return, the friar had instantly subdued his cordial greeting, and pretended to mistake Northrup for another man.

What obscure convulsion of the friar's mind now caused him delight the Yankee could not imagine. Northrup let the friar have his hand, and Miguel shook it slowly, speaking politenesses, and studying the Yankee's face with his vague eyes. This went on for so long that Northrup became nervous.

"I thought maybe I could get a cup of coffee here," he suggested.

"I'm sure of it, my captain; I'm certain that Madame will be delighted to see you!"

They walked slowly toward the house, Père Miguel delaying Northrup's stride by an affectionate grip upon his arm.

"In a way, I'm established here now, for a little while," Miguel confided. "I am acting as tutor of Ma'm'selle Madelon. Without remuneration, of course. It's a great privilege to me. Such a beautiful, innocent mind, so thirsty for the riches of learning!"

"That's nice," said the Yankee. He thought of the friar impatiently as a harmless old fool. Still, he had no desire to have Madelon's tutor speak disparagingly of him. "You're just the man for it," he offered.

"Ah, my captain, you do an old man too much honour!"

Beyond question, thought Northrup, Madelon was completely hemmed in by idiocies. He dreaded unreasonably the twittering impact of Madame de Verniat; and he was not set at his ease by the fact that there was a considerable delay. Madame was taking a siesta; almost forty-five minutes elapsed before she honoured him with her appearance upon the gallery.

"I'm pleased to see you, Captain Northrup," she told him; and he was surprised that her manner of address was less fluttery than he had remembered. He was surprised, too, that for the moment she seemed but freshly middle-aged, when he had recalled her as an aging, if not aged, woman. He could not like her; but at least he thought her, upon this second consideration, a rather handsome matron.

"You are welcome here," she went on. "I am always glad to see the friends of Captain Lafitte. He has spoken very highly of you, by the way. Bring coffee, Jezebel."

"Is it possible?" said Northrup woodenly. When they had seated themselves he attempted a few propitiatory statements.

"I'm much struck with your country here," he told her. "I think it has magnificent possibilities, both agricultural and commercial. You Louisianans are most fortunately placed, madame, if I may say so."

An appreciative, almost eager gleam lighted Madame's face. Northrup had chosen the second-best approach to the esteem of a lonely middle-aged woman whose pitifully small competence was tied up in a bog.

"Do you really think so?" she said. "We here have always had faith. Only sometimes—it seems the good days are a long time coming."

"It's only a matter of a little time," he assured her, lying readily. He proceeded to outline a short view of Louisiana as the centre of the universe. He was stiff, and limited in expression; but he was not stupid. Upon occasion his mind could click metallically through conceptions that the minds of the dreamy-eyed Creoles only skirted. He talked on, and thought well of himself, not fully realizing that whatever he might say or do, Madame de Verniat inevitably held broad reservations, based on the recollection that Northrup was, after all, only a boorish Yankee.

Fifteen minutes passed, while he waited with an increasing hidden impatience for Madelon to appear.

Then suddenly she was standing in the doorway behind her mother's chair. She had appeared there silently, so that when he looked up and found her eyes upon him he wondered how long she had been looking at him without his knowledge. Madelon half-curtsied, with a slow movement and without inclining her head; and Northrup, getting to his feet, executed his stiff shallow bow, his eyes upon her face.

As he watched her face a quick flush mounted to her eyes; yet, surprisingly, she showed no other suggestion of embarrassment, and her eyes did not drop from his. Then, out of that flush she smiled at him, so merrily, so sympathetically, that he was nonplussed. He had not seen the same contradiction of expressions before; or, if he had seen anything approaching it, he at least found it unexpected here.

"Mademoiselle," he mumbled.

She seemed to him more like a woman than before, and less like a child. She seated herself at one side, where she went to embroidering with a not too practised hand; but a touch of colour remained in her cheeks, and a certain half-readable brightness in her eyes that was only partly concealed by her long lashes. There was a quiet, even latent vivacity in her bearing where only subtropic languor had been perceivable upon his first visit.

"Captain Northrup has been saying," Madame de Verniat told her daughter, "that within a few years these lands will be quite priceless."

Madelon nodded inattentively, as if the statement had been trivial, beside the point.

To himself Northrup was saying, "Now, just what the hell . . ." Aloud he said, "This is the garden spot of America. If I could be at home anywhere but upon the sea, I would wish this to be my country, here in the South. Do you think I could make a good Louisianan, madame?"

He waited to see if Madelon would say anything to that, but she did not look up.

Madame de Verniat side-stepped. "After all, if it were not for you men of the sea we would have no country."

The situation was much better in Madame de Verniat's hands than upon his previous visit, for which, in all justice, Durossac had provided a preparatory devastation comparable to an advance bombardment by artillery. The Frenchwoman was conversationally his master; she turned the big Yankee's remarks into whatever channels she wished, as if it were a game of skill. Thus Northrup was presently led into a prolonged lecture on herring fisheries. The dissertation bored Madame no less than Northrup himself; but she assumed that it was edifying, and it passed the time.

An hour passed, while Northrup talked jerkily, his conversation herded along by the deft efforts of Madame. The long shadows of the sunset blurred out and were lost in the interminable fogging twilight of the swamp. With the impalpable swamp vapours rose the mosquitoes, making the gallery almost untenantable; and still Northrup stayed on.

From time to time, glancing aside at the girl, Northrup found her watching him beneath her lashes. He could see that she was studying him speculatively; once or twice he thought her eyes showed a profound pity, and it annoyed him that he could not define its occasion. He tried to tell himself that the pity he perceived in her eyes was for herself, not him; but he could not convince himself that, even if this were partly true, the pity was for herself alone.

Madame de Verniat, not letting pass unnoticed the unaccustomed flicker in Madelon's eyes, told herself that here was an affair that needed choking off. And the Yankee, puzzled, not at all sure that he correctly understood all he saw, told himself that if anything was indicated it was that he was becoming too deeply involved in the lives of people with whom he had nothing in common. He told himself: "This is no place for me." Yet he stayed on and on, ignoring—or unconscious of—Madame's evident desire that he take his leave; until at last Madame could stand the mosquitoes no more and was forced to ask him inside.

"Jezebel, have set another place. The Captain is dining with us, I am sure."

They ate in a dining room that was a long high hall, vastly more spacious, more cavernous, it seemed to the Yankee, than the hall of an ancient and deserted inn. The two candles which provided the only light showed a long reach of fine but threadbare linen, and gleamed upon the sparse De Verniat silver, so little of which now remained; but the feeble yellow flicker of the tallow could touch only dimly the high damp-stained walls, up which the shadows of the three towered majestically and still, as if dark looming forms watched unwholesomely over their destinies here.

Northrup never forgot that dim-lit table. Before him a plate of Louisiana gumbo had been set, upon which the twin candles seemed to concentrate their yellow glow, as if it were a shrine. The plate among other things contained a great intact crab, as is the custom yet; and out of the deep soupy gravy of the gumbo the legs of the crab groped upward grotesquely, gaunt, hooked, and gnarled, like a clutching skeleton hand. The tall French windows were tight shut to exclude the night mists; yet the swamp was in the room, all about them, its damp breath seeming to cloud, with an invisible vapour, the candles' little light.

For the Yankee it was a depressing and wholly unaccustomed environment. The damp was clammily chill, and the swamp silence morbid. An all-pervading odour of mustiness gave a fictitious effect of great antiquity. Only—even in the candlelight Madelon's face was bright, glowing with life. The contrast of the looming shadows gave her appearance a touch of fay, as if she were no part of the close-pressing bog in which she was yet completely at home.

They ate for the most part in silence. When the meal was over the Yankee told himself again what he had known before: "The best thing for me is to get out of this—and stay out." Yet he did not go.

He was probably never aware of the duel of silences with which, thereafter, Madame de Verniat sought to eject him. The poor fidgety lady had little chance of overcoming the Yankee in any such contest as that. She could never understand that while she was becoming acutely self-conscious in the silences, Northrup was welcoming them as a relief from the necessity of speech.

He was waiting, as they sat in a living room no better lighted than the dining room had been, for one more opportunity to read what was in the eyes of the girl. Perhaps in his ignorance of Creole manners he even hoped for a word with Madelon alone. But for the present she met his eyes no more, and the evening dragged on.

Madame de Verniat was driven at last to something near desperation by Northrup's unconscious tenacity.

She opened a creaky little parlour organ and sang a number of bright-measured songs, to the instrument's melancholy wail. Her voice was thin, cracked, and gusty; but the Northerner praised her singing immeasurably, to the temporary abatement of her hostility. Fatuously he considered, with some satisfaction, that he was pretty well taken into the family, by now.

"Please go on, madame! A real treat for a man from the sea." Accustomed to the long night watches of the ships he had no idea of how long his welcome had been outstayed.

"No more to-night," said Madame. "Some other time, perhaps."

She did not sit down, but stood waiting rather pointedly for him to take his leave. The man's inability to remove himself scandalized and infuriated her. There was a silence, a very awkward one; and poor Madame once more broke under the weight of it before Northrup had realized that a silence was on.

"Perhaps," she suggested ironically, "you will allow us to put you up for the night?"

"You are extremely kind," she heard the incomprehensible Northerner reply. "Fourteen miles through the night mosquitoes is no joke. Thank you; I expected no such kindness, I assure you. It is more than appreciated."

Madame de Verniat paled. The impossible bucko from the Northern seas, the man of whales and Gargantuan lies, the *Yanqu' perdu*—he was staying for the night!

Northrup congratulated himself on the courtly and

correct grace with which he had conducted himself under novel conditions.

2

JOB NORTHRUP found himself, lighted by a single candle, in a great square room on the second floor. The furniture here was not of the type that furnished the downstairs. It was crudely made, apparently by the little-skilled labour of slaves, and but roughly finished. Yet, in spite of its ill proportion and lack of polish, it had a rounded, curving quality of line that made it utterly different from New England furniture of like makeshift. The square-set ruggedness of Northern handicraft was lacking, and in its place was something else that Northrup felt indefinite and spineless, in spite of its massy weight.

There was a washstand with rudely carved legs, a tall armoire, a dresser with a stickily varnished top, and the usual enormously towering four-posted bed. Two windows, extending from the high ceiling almost to the floor, had neither sashes nor glass, but were boarded shut by unventilated battens. The air within was musty and close, as if long disused and dead. He forced open one of the swollen shutters with shoulder and boot. Into the room flowed the cool wet odour of the Baratarian night, swampy as water grass, but sweet in comparison to the fustiness within. A handful of mosquitoes rode in with that air, and as their tuning-fork notes hummed past his ears he closed the shutter again with a grunt.

He pulled off his boots in preparation for sleep; but

instead of undressing he sat on the edge of the bed looking at the great bare room about him, moodily pondering the novelty of his situation. A great restlessness was upon him, and he knew that sleep was far away. He was a man who only yielded to sleep through exhaustion; he never courted it, nor lay restless in his bed. He had no desire to lie down now. He sat for a long time with square-planted legs and folded arms, like a man waiting for something which he could not have named.

It seemed to him that some sort of madness was upon these people in the swamp. Père Miguel, at least, he was sure was quite fiddle-headed and unaccountable. Madame de Verniat appeared merely fussy and silly, only a little off. But it was the girl who was uppermost in his mind. She had been trying to tell him something with her eyes; of that he was certain. Ordinarily, he would have leaped to conclusions readily enough, but in this case he was puzzled and in some manner restrained.

He could see, more clearly in memory than he could in her presence, that she was hardly more than a child; and that her life had been immured, almost cloistered, he knew from what little Creole gossip he had heard. The women to whom he was accustomed in the New England climate matured much later; and even in maturity seemed by comparison coolly armoured, less impetuous, and at the same time less wise. . . .

In sheer restlessness he rose and paced the room; then, taking up his candle, softly unlatched the door and went out into the upper hall. There was a water cooler of porous earthenware on a table there. It was his intention to get himself a drink.

Madelon was standing by the water cooler, a slim white figure behind which one of those enormous grotesque shadows that haunted this house rose up as his candle came into play. She was clad in her night-gown and a white robe of some coarse stuff. Her knitted slippers concealed no more than the toes of her white blue-veined feet. He stopped, and stared awkwardly, for the turn of the hall had brought him abruptly upon her.

She smiled faintly and offered him the glass of water that she had drawn. Afterward, in recalling that unex-pected scene, he concluded that she had far greater sophistication of breeding than he had supposed. For them to stand there, somewhat less than formally clad, alone in the sleeping house, was grossly immoral by the canons of the day. Yet he could not recall that she had made any gesture of embarrassment or that she had car-ried herself other than naturally, as if they had met on the street.

He accepted the glass and tossed it off.

She said, "You are not sleeping well, m'sieu?"

"Not a wink."

"There is something about certain nights. . . . Spirits in the air, the negroes say."

So, he thought, she had not been able to sleep either. He drew another glass of water from the slow-trickling spigot of the cooler and handed it to her. It was curious that the things she wore, which made her as shapeless as a gallery column, should seem infinitely more revealing than the gown she had worn earlier in the twi-light. As she drank he watched her solemnly, head down, with a puzzled stare like a baffled bull. Across the rim of the glass she returned his gaze curiously, in her eyes a certain mistiness, as if by this time she should have been asleep.

He said, "You are the most beautiful woman in Louisiana."

She smiled faintly as she set the tumbler down slowly, meticulously. Suddenly she made a curious little gesture toward him and as if she had started to reach out and touch him and then drawn back her hand.

"Listen," she said, her voice husky, near a whisper. "Listen: You must not think the things you think. It is impossible. You are harming yourself." Suddenly her eyes raised and met his squarely; but he could not read what was in them. "I understand," she told him. "I understand and I'm sorry. . . . More sorry than you know. But it is beyond reason."

"Beyond reason?" he repeated stupidly. He was thinking slowly and heavily, completely at a loss.

"Impossible," she repeated, "now, or ever."

As he stared at her idiotically her face changed, so that he thought she looked as if she might be going to cry. Then she turned and left him. Before he could collect his wits he was standing there alone, gazing open-mouthed down the long empty reach of the hall.

He turned and made his way uncertainly to his room, in the grip of a complete astonishment. Racking his brain, he could think of no other explanation for her unexpected advice than that she had read his mind, divining, with an assured accuracy, the physical desire with which she inspired him. This apparently inevitable assumption appalled him, set him back upon his heels. He had prided himself that he was as stoic of feature, as difficult to see into, as a north-coast rock; yet this back-bayou girl, without worldly experience of any kind, had read him far more easily than she could have deciphered a printed page. . . . He was humiliated, in so far as the tough fibre of his character permitted humiliation at all; and he was shocked into an instant awed respect of the girl's astuteness.

Nor was it less astonishing that, having read his mind to his discredit, Mademoiselle de Verniat had not been offended. He had thought, with vigorous Northern assumptiveness, that he understood Louisiana manners and morals; he thought he comprehended both the motives and limitations of the religion and the way of life of this transplanted people. He had thought, too, that he had understood the exact position of the De Verniats as to ethics as well as to social status. That the girl should read his mind without taking offense was as impossible as that she should have read it at all. Northrup was forced to conclude that he knew no more of the mental methods of these people than he had known of their abilities.

She was wise, he pondered, incredibly wise. Also, he decided—partly under the influence of his fearsome respect for her penetration—she was incredibly straight in principle; for in her recalled gestures, voice, and expressions he could find nothing of the coquette. Wiser than a witch—looking through him in the first moment of their meeting on the veranda and forced to blush at what she saw there. She had, he thought, been laughing at him all afternoon; covertly mocking him, keeping the joke all to herself. For God's sake, he asked himself, what devil did the Baratarian swamp put into these women?

And yet—she had not been so very much displeased: sympathetic, rather, understanding—as no woman had any right to understand—the hidden forces that stirred him. Picturing to himself the childlike quality of Madelon's face, he found this concept grotesque. Yet she had said that she was sorry. Without knowledge of the devious devices of Père Miguel he could but put one construction on this: that, having recognized his desire, she was sorry that she could do nothing to assuage it. Sorry, more sorry than he could know, sorry enough to look as if she were going to cry.

He could no more settle himself for sleep in that unfriendly and unnatural room than if there had been more skeleton hands about him, thrusting out of the corner shadows that were thick as gumbo itself. He went to the window and again forced open the batten shutter, oblivious to the thin twang of the mosquitoes.

On the sea it was perhaps moonlight; but here, deep in the mangrove and cypress, the fog pressed in, not itself utterly black, but making the night impenetrable to the eye. He could see the columns of the gallery upon which the window opened, and the great crooked arm of a live oak curving beside the gallery rail out of nowhere. Beyond that, nothingness. Along the floor of the room he could almost see the long tentacles of the mist reaching past his ankles toward the candlelight in low-rolling curls. He shivered slightly, leaning against the window jamb between the candlelight and the fog.

He wondered if Madelon were asleep; or whether—the thought banged against him like the recoil of a musket—whether she was sitting on the edge of her bed as he had sat on his. That slender girl form might be expected to tremble in the knees if her thoughts were similar to his own. His own muscles were tough and rigid. There was not a quiver in him; but there was no sleep in him, either.

His mental confusion was not clearing or promising to clear. He was not without experience with women; but for once he was finding himself in a situation he was unable to define. If he knew one thing it was that this was a hell of a way to spend a night. Once more he told himself, and now for the last time: "The quicker I get out of this, and stay out, the better I'll be fixed. . . ."

When he had retrieved his stock and boots he stepped out through the window and tiptoed across the mist-wet gallery. Down through the boughs of the live oak he swung hand over hand, as if it were the rigging of a ship; and went fuming off toward his lugger, walking like a blown-over storm.

Chapter IX

1

JEAN LAFITTE returned to the Temple two days later. Northrup went to meet the boss of Barataria as he walked quickly up the path from the lugger in which he had come; and the Yankee was struck again with the incongruity of Lafitte's immaculate figure against the rude decaying shanties, the gray shell heaps, and the swamp. The Baratarian was wearing one of the silver-buttoned blue coats that were his particular affectation; and his white ruffled stock did not seem to have been affected by the long journey through the bayous.

More interesting to the Yankee than these trivialities was the repressed intensity which he immediately perceived in Jean's manner.

"What busted?" Northrup demanded.

Lafitte looked at him blankly for a moment. "Plenty," he admitted. "Where have you been? I had expected to see you in New Orleans."

"I didn't go there," said Northrup. "I changed my mind."

For a moment Lafitte looked at him sharply, while the gleam of an emotion that might have been jealousy crossed behind his eyes. He had a fairly accurate idea, no doubt, of where the Yankee had preferred to spend his time.

"At any rate," he told Northrup, "I'm glad to find you here. There's work for you, at last. Do you know my light schooner, the *Two Brothers*? Have you ever examined her, I mean?"

"I looked her over when I was at Grand Isle."

"Is she in shape to take the sea as a fast-running ship? What would you say she needs?"

"Careening," said Northrup instantly.

"I'm forced to agree," said Lafitte. "I'm afraid there's no doubt that her bottom is pretty foul. Well, fortunately, it's not her time, quite yet. What else?"

"A new suit of sail," Northrup suggested. "Her canvas is a bunch of bags."

"I think she has very good canvas," said Lafitte impatiently.

"Well, I don't."

Lafitte shrugged. "I suppose," he said, "new sails can be fitted to her while she runs, if it comes to that. What do you know about careening?"

"What does any sailor know? The whole story is the weather and a proper beach. Generally you have to unstep the lower masts, which is awkward as hell; and that's about all there is about it, unless she likes to trick her ballast."

"Her lower masts are nothing but stubs," said Lafitte.

"So I noticed."

They went into Lafitte's shanty. Jean, having seated himself and helped himself to a drink, motioned to Northrup to pull up something to sit on.

"I will lay my cards on the table," Lafitte said gravely; and mentally the Yankee put up his guard. "I am forced to tell you," he went on frankly, "that it may be necessary for me to put the *Two Brothers* on the sea at a moment's notice. It may be at once, or it may be a matter of weeks, even months. In any case, we will take time now to put her in shape as rapidly as may be.

"The *Two Brothers*, as you know, is at present in the command of Charles Masselier. He is a good captain; I have been fortunate to hold him for so long, considering the schooner's inactivity. Unfortunately, he's not a man well adapted for the direction of such routine labours as that of careening. He is a fair navigator and a master at fighting a ship. But he has the fault of many of these privateers: he is slouchy in the care of his vessel."

Northrup wondered what a ship's officer might be good for who was not competent to careen, but he remained silent.

"I've come to the conclusion," Lafitte went on, "that you are the man to careen and refit the *Two Brothers*. For that matter, Masselier at present lacks a first mate; that we will consider later, and separately. I'm going to send you to Grand Isle, to careen. I assume you want to undertake this project?"

"All right," said Northrup.

"For all I care," said Lafitte, "Masselier can go on leave until this is done. You are the man responsible for this work, remember that. You can have twenty negroes from among those we have here; more, if you like. The important thing is speed—I can't emphasize that too much. Now, as to materials . . ."

He rapidly sketched the layout of the flimsy warehouses at Grand Isle, showing where Northrup might find the various items of ship chandlery that Lafitte had accumulated there.

"Nez Coupé and Ducoing have a mob of idle hands down there. It may be you will find that no provisions remain. Provision the *Two Brothers* if you can. Otherwise we will make other arrangements. Pironeau, the second mate, is little better than any bosun, but he will be of help to you; more so, no doubt, than Masselier. The question is, of course, if you can handle these men." He had meant, "Can you get along with these men?" But afterward he was able to recall that his phrasing had perhaps been ambiguous.

"Well," said Northrup, "we'll see."

There was a great deal more in the way of explicit instructions: Lafitte directed, for one thing, that the *Two Brothers* be taken to Cat Island, some leagues west of Grand Isle, for the work, in order that no more of the *Two Brothers*' crew be disaffected by the malcontents under Coupé and Ducoing.

"I don't want you to misunderstand me about Masselier," Lafitte concluded. "Charles Masselier is an indomitable leader and a great fighting man. Few can match him in single fight. He wouldn't care, I suppose, to face Durossac, who is the best swordsman of all; and there are perhaps one or two others that might turn out to be his master. But outside of Durossac I doubt that there are three men in the Mexican Gulf that could stand against him in a weapon pass. I don't advise you to mix it with him, certainly, under any circumstances. A good man. . . . But speed is the essential. Choose your negroes, thirty, if you wish; and leave as soon as you can."

"I've left," said Northrup shortly.

2

BARATARIA BAY was coppery under the flat slant of a late afternoon sun when Northrup, having travelled since long before daylight, hailed the *Two Brothers* and climbed aboard.

A small swarthy man whom Northrup knew to be Antoine Pironeau threw off an air of dejection to grin at Northrup merrily enough and extend a wiry hand.

"Masselier here?"

Pironeau took a confidential turn. "Very much; too damned much." The mate of the *Two Brothers* was young and lean, with hard prominent eyes above a thin hook of a nose. "This no fighting puts the devil into the Old Man. I don't know why he stays. But maybe he don't want anything different, who knows?"

"How many men have you?"

"There's a dozen here, that's all. They stay on because they're broke. As scurvy a lot as ever you saw, m'sieu. Ah, well, better days." His conversational voice broke off and was replaced by a low casual rumble of obscenity.

"Masselier's below, is he?" Northrup asked. "I'll talk to him."

"As you please, m'sieu. Personally I would as soon talk to hell's lions. . . . You are heavily manned, m'sieu."

"We've got work to do," Northrup told him. Pironeau made no move to announce him to his superior, so Northrup swung down the ladder alone.

Charles Masselier lay sprawled upon a filthy and disordered bunk. He seemed asleep; and the Yankee idled for a moment or two before waking him, studying the evil derangement of the cabin, the unscrubbed woodwork, the littered floor, where, to mark the grease spots, bluebottle flies crawled over each other in clots. When he looked at Masselier again the man's eyes were open and regarding him sidelong. Suddenly the captain of the *Two Brothers* swung down his feet and sat upright with a movement unexpectedly agile.

"Well, what the devil do *you* want?"

"Damned little," said the Yankee without expression. He handed Masselier his note of introduction from Lafitte.

The man on the bunk verified the signature and scratched his unshaved jaw with the knuckles of his fist. Then he crumpled the bit of paper, set his hands on his knees, and regarded Northrup with red-eyed malevolence.

"Well?"

"I have instructions for you from Lafitte," Northrup began, his voice unpropitiatory.

"Well?"

"To begin with, you weigh immediately for Cat Island; there to careen." He paused while this soaked in.

"Careen, is it?" said Masselier at last. "I know when I need to careen! Go back and ask that fathead who's captain here. Go back and tell him I'm damned if I'll careen. Who has the running of this ship? I, by the good God! And while I do I'll careen when I see fit."

"I came down here to careen this ship," Northrup told him. "Count on it: when I go back this ship will have been careened."

He turned and went up the ladder, leisurely and careless of step. Pironeau was grinning on the skylight.

"What's the matter with him?" Northrup asked.

The mate shrugged. "He's too much himself. Just now he's been drunk for four days. To-day he's getting over it. If it weren't that, it would be something else maybe. That man is hard to get along with. That you will soon learn, m'sieu."

Northrup stood for a minute or two by the taffrail, his eyes wandering over the live oaks and shanties of Grand Isle, over the flat marsh lands of Grand Terre, where the low, square-cut gun revetments lay black and lonely under the eastern counterglow of the setting sun. A cool inshore breeze was bringing in the perpetual roar and hiss of the Gulf of Mexico upon the desolate Louisiana beach; and in from the sea with that breeze a long flight of pelicans was drifting on great wings silent and slow.

Northrup turned suddenly to find Pironeau's prominent eyes regarding him shrewdly. The mate grinned, and Northrup answered with a crooked smile.

"When are you going back?" Pironeau asked.

"When my work is done," Northrup told him.

"God help you," said Pironeau.

Beside the small lugger in which Northrup had come a porpoise rolled, his hide black and wet gold in the reddening light. The Yankee swung over the side, and the thick mass of the thirty negroes that bore the lugger down almost gunwale to the water shifted silently to give him room.

"Port oars," said Northrup. "Now, then, smartly: All hands!"

The black chanteyman took up the wordless song he had used all day, pacing the sweeps: "Ee-e-e-ay, hi-ho-ah-ah, ah!" barging the overladen lugger slowly over the last half mile of water to the beach.

ᴍORE THAN A SCORE of idlers gathered on the beach of the Smuggler's Anchorage to watch Northrup disembark. These were the mal-assorted privateersmen of the crews of Nez Coupé and Jean Ducoing; among them were the faces of men of no less than five nations, and as many shades of colour, ranging from the satin-skinned black of Bantu freedmen to the fish-belly yellow of wharf scum that the subtropic sun could scorch but not turn to bronze. He knew that none of the men of these crews remained at Grand Isle who had any means of sustenance elsewhere; yet, by the yellow glow of lights among the shanties of the Baratarian village, by the smoke of cooking fires, and by the movement of figures here and there far down the island from the beach, Northrup judged that more than a hundred men must be so stranded here.

A hurried computation filled him with what amounted almost to a sense of awe. Those that had sailed must return; certainly they could not sail again without disposing of some of the loot that, for want of Lafitte's offices, already lay unliquidated at Grand Isle. Yet there were more Baratarian ships on the sea than these; at least a dozen captains, he knew, were still cruising without knowledge of what had happened at the rendezvous. Unless the privateers could work out a new salvation through Beluche, a thousand, more than a thousand, idle ruffians would accumulate unpaid and unfed upon the shores of Barataria Bay. This was the lethal fighting mass that Jean Lafitte was now setting out to master and subdue, once and for all, one man of wits against a fighting power fit to defend a nation! Yet, more than ever, the Yankee believed that he had allied himself with the right man. . . .

He marched his thirty blacks to the abandoned house of Lafitte, the one solid and substantial building among all those flimsy shelters of wattles and mud; and there he quartered his slaves in the long sheds behind. They carried with them sacks of cornmeal and rice, rations enough to sustain them for several weeks. In the few pots that were their only utensils they could boil with their rice the crabs that were abundant on the inner beach, and so sustain themselves at a trivial cost. Northrup put them in the charge of the black chanteyman, himself a slave. Then, having selected a cook from among them for his own service, he left them to themselves.

When the Yankee had eaten he was favoured by a call from Nez Coupé; and half an hour later the sardonic Ducoing joined them. Nez Coupé, the Yankee thought, seemed sour and subdued. There was a hard black mood concealed behind the grotesquerie of the sabre-clipped face; yet he was friendly, even cordial, in so far as he knew how to be. Nez Coupé was a reasonable man.

"I was surprised that you flung in with Lafitte," he told Northrup as he drank the Yankee's wine. "Still and all, a man has to look out for himself these days. I hold that against no man, except the old son of a bitch himself, that holds out on honest sailormen—better than him, so Jesus help me. . . . Well, you and me may find ourselves on the same side of the mast one of these days, like as not. . . . Here's how, and better days."

Jean Ducoing was less friendly. Few words, and those non-committal, broke their way out of the broad frog-like mouth under his moustache. Though he was shaved and Nez Coupé was not, Ducoing somehow appeared the worse conditioned of the two; as if ill times and adverse circumstance were an accustomed habitat of Coupé's, whereas Ducoing might be out of place and unable to thrive. More than once Northrup caught Ducoing's deep-set eyes watching him with a steady shadowed disaffection, as if he would have welcomed a good reason for eliminating the Yankee.

"Hell, times are slow here," said Nez Coupé, pouring himself another drink. "If this Beluche would come and take this stuff off my hands I'd ship rations and take a chance on the sea. A fine sweet bunch of sea lawyers I'd have to ship, with the divisions not made, but what the hell? I try to get Jean here to keep an eye on my stuff while I go out, but damned if he will. Well, in a little while there won't be no rations."

"I'll be lucky if I don't get a knife in the back as it is," growled Ducoing, reaching for a fresh bottle.

The two rebel captains left at last, when the wine that Northrup had set out had all been drunk. But the information that they had come for, they went away without.

4

THE NEXT MORNING Northrup ate a leisurely breakfast contrived of such materials as were at hand and, after a salt bath and a shave, once more rowed out to the *Two Brothers*.

Masselier, he was surprised to find, was not only on deck but was standing naked in the waist, having himself doused with buckets of cold Barataria Bay. The captain of the *Two Brothers* had trimmed his moustache, and with his untended whiskers slicked down by the sticky salt water he had a considerably more respectable appearance.

"Well, what do you want now?" he asked disinterestedly.

"My orders from the owner," Northrup told him again, without tact, "are to see to the careening of this ship."

"Oh, you're to see to it, are you?"

"Lafitte's instructions," Northrup went on, "are that you can take a leave in the meantime, if you so choose."

"I don't choose," said Masselier.

"You mean you won't careen?"

"I have nothing to do with it," said Masselier illogically.

"Am I permitted to go ahead with it?"

"I don't give a goddam what you do."

Masselier's self-possessed indifference puzzled the Yankee.

"We'll have to get some chandlery aboard here," he suggested, uncertain of what he was up against.

The red eyes of Charles Masselier lay upon Northrup with an expression malignant but peculiarly abstruse.

"I have nothing for you," he said.

Northrup studied the naked figure of Masselier. The

man was thickening in the waist, but his body was strongly muscled and finely poised. It was apparent, he decided, that Masselier had as yet no intention of carrying out Lafitte's orders.

"I presume," he said ironically, "you won't object if I get the necessary materials aboard?"

"Do I care what you do?" said Masselier impassively.

Northrup, still puzzled, decided to give him another hour to think it over. He went ashore again, and set about finding out what stores were available to him in the warehouses of Lafitte.

Nez Coupé joined him as he strolled from one to another of the makeshift shelters to which Lafitte had directed him. The little man with the clipped nose had acquired a leering grouch since the night before. Nevertheless, he maintained a show of congenial helpfulness. He joined the Yankee uninvited and stumped along at his side while Northrup made his tour. A half-dozen surly-eyed hangdog loafers followed along at a little distance and in silence; but for the most part the stranded crews remained little in evidence.

In the first warehouse, where Lafitte had instructed him to find cordage, sail, and pitch, Northrup was disturbed to find nothing but a litter of rubbish and broken crates. He went striding ahead, taciturn, and sphinx-faced; but when the second and third storehouses yielded nothing better he eyed Nez Coupé grimly, bit off a chew from a twist he had found, and leaned against a wall to think.

"Oh," said Nez Coupé; "you looking for that stuff?"

The Yankee waited.

"Masselier," Coupé told him, "took it aboard his schoon'."

"No," Northrup lied, "I wasn't looking for that."

Nez Coupé turned away to hide, partly, one of his sudden loose leering grins. Northrup walked on, making a show of checking the clearance of the other sheds, while he nursed the red anger that had swept upon him. Then he went steaming down to the inner beach, whistled his black oarsmen into his boat, and rowed out to the *Two Brothers* again.

Masselier was eating breakfast under a tattered awning on the flush deck poop. Northrup instantly perceived that a naked hanger—the short, nearly straight naval cutlass of the day—lay beside the captain's greasy tin of fried food.

"You, Masselier," said Northrup in a loud voice, "why didn't you say you had that stuff aboard?"

The black-jowled face darkened. "Do you know who you're talking to?"

"You think I don't?"

"Why, you damned Yankee swine!" snarled Masselier; he levelled an arm at Northrup, and his voice quivered as he sought, for some instinctive reason, to hold it beneath a roar. "You come here and stand up to me? You get your bloody carcass off of this ship before, by God, I—"

"I'll see you in hell first," said Northrup.

Masselier's congested throat relaxed, and a new light came into his eyes. He turned to Pironeau. "Give this bastard a weapon," he said.

With a quick anticipatory grin the swarthy mate of the

130

Two Brothers whipped his hanger from his sash and handed it to Northrup. Slowly, delicately almost, Masselier's hand closed over the grip of his own hanger, where it lay on the table before him. Then suddenly his knee knocked the table upward and to one side, and the steel of the hangers slithered together as the Yankee's blade came up.

Half a dozen men that had been lounging in the bow came running barefoot; in a moment there were more, piling up from the forecastle companion. They were bleary-faced and filthy, a miserable handful of the dregs of Barataria, with a slink in their faces and a slink in their stride. Some sprang agilely into the rigging, and out of the galley came a scabrous mulatto cook who leaped upon the skylight and there crouched like an eager ape.

For a long moment those watchers saw the Yankee and the Baratarian swordsman stand almost rigid, their blades together, each watching the other's point, testing the strength of the other's wrist. And to those men out of the scum of the sea the tall tawny man from the North looked awkward, stilt-legged, in comparison to the compact balanced man that he faced. They should have known; if there was an ideal among them it was one of lethal skill, and if they were no judges of a weapon pass then they were judges of nothing on the face of the sea. A yell broke from them as Masselier disengaged his blade, feinted twice, and thrust with a long lunge in three motions as swift as one.

It was time already for Masselier's opponent to crumple up, cough blood, and let his hanger rattle from his grasp; but instead the big Yank leaped back, parried, and his long step carried him in again with a savage counter. Once more they rested an instant, blade against blade, Northrup waiting, the Baratarian angered by the strength and great reach of the Yankee's arm.

Among the seamen of the *Two Brothers* a few nudged each other and grinned, relishing each moment that the fight might be prolonged before the inevitable end.

Another coughing yell burst instinctively from the watchers as Masselier again attacked. The offensive was more complicated now: the blade of the Baratarian flashed and darted, and his booted right foot stamped the planking as he followed the retreating Yank in a passage of prolonged and bewildering intricacy. Pironeau's eyes were starting from his head; he had thought no man, other than the redoubtable Durossac, could stand against the brilliance of Masselier's attack. Yet at the end Northrup again stepped in with his fast vicious counter, forcing Masselier back two steps to the Yankee's one.

Masselier was red with fury. This time there was no pause. The Baratarian slid in, his point flickering, steel hissing along steel. No one saw what happened then. There was a click and swirl of the weapons, quick as the shimmer of light; a grating oath burst from Masselier's lips; and the Baratarian's hanger sung whirling over the rail into the sea. An astonished howl went up from the rigging, the skylight, the rails. There was a twisted grin on Northrup's face as he flung his own cutlass into the scuppers and rushed.

The first blow of Northrup's bony fist drove Masselier against the mainmast, where the back of his head cracked hard against the wood; yet the big Yank, driving in, was fast enough to smash the slackened jaw three times more—right, left, right—as the man slid limp to the deck.

"This ship got a boat in the water?" Northrup demanded of Pironeau.

"A dory," said Pironeau, "and two rotten pirogues at the stern."

Northrup turned on the watching seamen. "Get that carcass over into the worst," he ordered.

"Better the dory," Pironeau suggested detachedly. "When he comes out of it he'll overset and drown himself in a pirogue."

"Good," said Northrup. "Get a loop on him and lower him over. Dump two buckets of water on top and cast adrift!"

Shamefacedly, a little reluctant to manhandle Masselier even in his battered unconsciousness, they unceremoniously dumped the master of the *Two Brothers* over the side. Masselier lay in the wet bottom of the pirogue in a slack sprawl, a trickle of blood oozing from between his lips. Under the water Northrup had ordered thrown on him he did not revive.

Chapter X

1

TWO WEEKS of strenuous effort were all that Northrup spent at Cat Island. Some said afterward that the self-elected Yankee skipper did not, in the proper sense of the term, careen the *Two Brothers* at all, but only scraped her bottom sketchily by sending slaves with ax blades over the side. The fact was that he drove the schooner aground in an inlet at three-quarters tide, so that the ebb daily half-careened her, after a fashion, in the muck. There was no truth in the report that Northrup's negroes were clouted on the head by a bosun with an oar if they floundered too often to the surface for air.

Whether Northrup's careening was a good job or not, he at least drove his men through enough motions in the time he allowed himself. Of the fifteen privateersmen that went with the *Two Brothers* on that trip seven deserted before the two weeks were up, returning to Grand Isle afoot along the beach. And an eighth, of more spirit but less ambition, found himself in irons on bread and water. By the time the *Two Brothers* again tacked, sailing smartly, into Barataria Bay, the rest were bound to Northrup by that hatred accorded all of the more efficient Baratarian captains by their men.

Northrup entered Barataria Bay with his remounted swivels shotted with grape; and for two hours after dropping the hook he held his meagre crew of privateersmen (supplemented by his thirty negroes) ready to hoist nets and repel boarders. He was by no means certain what manner of reception awaited him. Masselier he did not fear: a badly thrashed and marooned commander was not likely to attract many enthusiastic supporters. He was, however, doubtful of what to expect from Jean Ducoing and Nez Coupé.

The *Two Brothers*, as was known to everyone, was carrying almost all the salt pork and flour that remained in Barataria south of the Temple itself. If the more than a hundred fighting men under Coupé and Ducoing were now out of provisions—which seemed altogether likely—their first anticipation would be that the *Two Brothers* would divide her stores. This Northrup had no intention of doing.

A light brig, low and slender under immensely tall fish-pole masts, now lay at anchor half a mile up the bay, between the vessels of Coupé and Ducoing.

"Bill Cochrane's ship," Pironeau told him.

But what puzzled Northrup was that the shanty village on Grand Isle showed no sign of life. He swept the island with his long glass; but though every grass blade was distinct in the early afternoon light, he could make out but little evidence of present habitation. Filled with a suspicion of some illogical treachery, he for the time being remained aboard.

When the *Two Brothers* had been nearly three hours at anchor a single boatload of men put out from the inner beach and came alongside. Northrup let Pironeau answer the hail.

"Can we come aboard, sir?"

"No," said Pironeau. "Come aboard, in Christ's name! What business has the likes of you aboard? Stand off before I drop an anchor through your bottom!"

"We be out of Bill Cochrane's crew," came the answer from the boat. "Slit me, what's happened to the bloody island? We dropped hook two days ago, and not a soul do we find on the damned sandspit, nor a cracker. There ain't a drop of grog on the island, nor a nigger wench on the Isle of Oaks!"

"How many are you?"

"Us and five more; and down to the last of the hard-tack and salt horse from the sea grub, will you believe me? We might as well have not come to port."

"Where's the rest?"

"Gone up the bayou. We're the bleeding ship guard. If you'll but lend us a bit of grub, sir—"

"Give 'em cornmeal and pork, and damned little," said Northrup.

When the scant stores allotted the stranded men had been lowered over Northrup walked to the rail. He was wearing a blue sea cap with a patent-leather visor, a clean shirt, and a double-breasted coat; and the half dozen in the boat stared.

"You had a good cruise?" asked the Yankee.

A burly man in the stern of the boat looked at the dole and turned Northrup a slow, hostile eye. "And who might you be?"

"No damned charity station," said the Yankee.

"You look like a bloody naval officer to me," said the steersman. "And act like one, too, with your fistful of weevilly meal!"

Northrup, grinning, half turned and shouted to an imaginary porter by the galley: "Put back that case of rum. I've changed my mind!"

A yell of apology and a great tumble of oaths went up from the boat as Northrup walked away.

When they stood alone again by the taffrail Northrup

and Pironeau looked at each other.

"What the devil!" said Pironeau. "What's happening here?"

"That's easy," said Northrup. "Coupé and Ducoing have moved to the Temple with their stuff." He chuckled as he thought of the thickening perplexities of Lafitte; yet he could not believe that the rebels, under any circumstances, would find the boss of Barataria at a loss.

"It's just as well," he added. "Hold half the port watch here to-night. Give the balance a keg of rum and send 'em ashore."

2

NORTHRUP HAD INTENDED to start northward through the bayous with the dawn; but the first light of morning showed them a sail coming in fast from over the rim of the sea, and Northrup delayed to find out who she might be.

By mid-morning he was able to ascertain that the newcomer was Durossac's small schooner *Culebra*, which had sailed in company with Gambio's *Lucia*, a fast three-master, just before Northrup's clash with Masselier at Grand Isle. And so swiftly was the little privateer bearing in that in another two hours she tacked under flat fore sheets and three-reefed mainsail through Grand Pass and lay to in the Smuggler's Anchorage only a few hundred yards beyond.

Northrup felt that in his peculiar and rather precarious position the part of wisdom was to display as little interest in the newcomer as possible. The handling of trouble was a type of work that he understood and enjoyed; but the embarrassments of diplomatic relations were something else. He therefore remained in Lafitte's cabin for the present. The crew of the *Two Brothers* was on the beach, and Pironeau rushed out to join it as the *Culebra*'s boats lowered away; but Northrup lighted himself a long cigar and complacently sat down to wait for news.

In half an hour Pironeau was back, bringing with him a tall privateersman whom he introduced as one Manault. This man, who, Pironeau explained, had been a former comrade-at-arms and lately first mate to Vincent Gambio, was bony and of gangling proportions, but the thick cords in his wrists suggested that his muscles might be of good metal, nevertheless. He had a direct eye and harsh features of an expression at once stoic and alert. His moustache was drooping and stringy, and on his head he wore, to bind down his shag of black hair, the knotted handkerchief esteemed by the privateers.

"The *Lucia* has wrecked!" Pironeau declared. "She ran hard aground on the Cayman Shoal and pounded herself into a basket before she could be got off!" His ax-like face was further sharpened by the unconcealed excitement of the news he bore.

"Nothing was saved," he went on, "not a quadrant, nor a chart, nor a jolt of rum. Gambio is a ruined man except for what little goods he has unsold at the Temple to-day."

"Sit down and have a drink," said Northrup.

Pironeau half sat on a table, swinging his foot; but Manault accepted the liquor standing, too restively strung for the present to sit down.

"Durossac's *Culebra* brings back a hundred and ten *Lucia* men," Pironeau continued. "The *Culebra* can feed them for a little while, but how long? She's light, and with forty men of her own she needs her stores. Who's to feed these men? A fine mess there will be in Barataria!"

"How does Gambio take this?" Northrup asked.

"Crazy mad," said Manault, speaking for the first time. He spoke a thickly dialectic French that Northrup could hardly understand. "The *Culebra* stands in and passes a line. Finally we get the *Lucia* over, she's in free water again. There in deep water she goes down, fast, by the head. Gambio, he goes mad. He has it he will beach his ship and save her. The *Culebra* is standing off and on to take the *Lucia* men, but Gambio says no, there is to be no abandoning the ship. Crazy mad, he doesn't know what he does."

The words piled out of him, quick and bitter, in a smother of almost unintelligible French. "I see he is crazy, yet I do all I can. Under me I have the gunners and the seamen of the port watch. Only a handful in that more than a hundred men, not a half, not a quarter of the crew. But these men that have been under me I can control. In those few minutes that the *Lucia* floats we jettison the long bow gun and the port and starboard carronades, and with loose fore sheets we try to hold up her head.

"But the rest of the men—*Dieu,* m'sieu, there is in

139

them the fear of death. The bosuns are as bad as they—worse than the men they are out of hand. That second mate Leblanc, he is no fool, but he is arguing with Gambio, and Gambio knocks him down. There is no more holding those men, it is mutiny, they are lowering the boats. Two mad Portuguese and a great gawk of a Swede seize the Old Man from behind and throw his pistols into the sea. I have done what I can; but not even my own men can I any longer control. The ship is empty. They are crammed into the boats, they are in the boats of the *Culebra* that have come alongside, they are in the water.

"Me, I am last to go. Gambio is swearing by the dear God he will sail the ship by himself. I bring him down with a belaying pin and sling him over my shoulder. Leblanc comes close by the lee rail at the risk of his boat, for it is God's truth, m'sieu, that rail is already awash in the sea. I heave Gambio in, and they are so loaded they are almost capsized by that one more bulk of a man. Me, I swim with the sharks. Pretty soon the *Culebra* picks us up, me and the rest that are in the sea. Two drown, that is all that are lost of the hundred and ten men.

"It is not three minutes, m'sieu, when the *Lucia* ups stern and goes down. I swear I felt the suck of her as I swam, as if she tried to take the whole sea under with her, that ship. And she is down in more than two hundred fathoms, though hardly off the Cayman Shoal."

"And now, mind you," said Pironeau, "Gambio blames Manault more than any other man. And this Durossac takes Gambio's part. I know Gambio, and

Durossac, too; and I can tell you, my captain, it is a wonder this man stands here to-day."

"Those men of the port watch," said Manault, "and my crazy fool cannoneers: I suppose they would like nothing better than to play ball with my head. Yet Gambio has reason to know I could put those men into a fight, and they can fight like wild men, m'sieu. That is what made the home voyage quiet. Maybe you do not see what I mean, but I can tell you it is true."

"I know this man," declared Pironeau. "And I can tell you one thing: this man with his handful of seamen and cannoneers could have made a shambles of that ship."

The three fell silent. Manault, in some part relaxed perhaps, by the tumble of words he had let run out off him, leaned against the wall, moodily studying his glass. Pironeau fidgeted. And Northrup stared out through the open door, on his face a shadow of the twisted smile with which he had fought Masselier.

Outside the door, in the narrow lane between the shanties, the subtropic sunlight struck down in a blinding sheet. At first the brilliance of the glare was almost as impervious to the eye as a wall; then, as the eye accustomed itself, the details of the outer scene slowly became minutely distinct. Every grain of the trampled sand, every irregularity of the opposite shanty's wattled mud stood as clear as if it had been no more than a foot before his eyes. Through an opening between the huts he could see the glittering blue of the Mexican gulf; and on the far horizon a long cloud of the ubiquitous nigger geese, a muddy drifting imperfection upon the brilliance of the sky.

He was thinking that within a few days the crews of Gambio and Durossac would add themselves to the malcontents at the Temple under Coupé, Cochrane, and Ducoing: nearly three hundred and fifty idle men—this time with no affluent Baratarian boss at hand to feed the penniless, reprovision the unsuccessful, turn captured drygoods to hard cash, and shunt them back onto the sea for more. Riot, assassination, rapine, lay latent in that mob of idle scum. He would not have wished to be in the shoes of Beluche.

"I thought there was going to be a fight on the beach," said Pironeau. "Before I knew anything about this business, I could see the trouble storming up. We haven't seen the end of this thing."

"Hardly the beginning," the Yankee agreed.

They said no more. A peculiar silence was upon Grand Isle; a silence, perhaps, such as the rendezvous had never known to follow so closely upon the return of a vessel from a cruise. In the midday stillness they heard the quick light step of Durossac upon the island sand almost thirty paces before he appeared, lounging gracefully, in the door.

3

THE CAPTAIN of the *Culebra* appeared less dandified than when Northrup had last seen him. His dungarees were whacked off raggedly just below the knees, exposing shins as dirty as if cinnamon had been thrown upon them; and his low-cut shoes were cracked and broken by the scour of salt water. He was in need of a haircut; but he had waxed his moustache and shaved, and he still wore the wide gold ring in his ear that had caught Madelon's eye. At his waist hung slack the three-inch belt that carried his sheathed hanger.

Nobody spoke. In the quiet, Durossac's eyes rested upon Manault, flicked to the Yankee, and came back to Manault again, where they lay insolently.

"Well, my pretty mutineer," he said slowly; "wallowing with the Lafittes, hanh?"

The Yankee came up onto his feet, so tall and bony that he must have looked to Durossac like a horse rearing. "Maybe you don't like that name, Lafitte?"

Durossac surveyed him with leisure. "I wouldn't," he said, "wipe my knife on it."

Northrup's slow-paced anger was beaten to the mark by Manault. There was a man, that tall Frenchman, who was always easily tempted by trouble. He exploded now.

Manault's hanger slipped out. "Come on, you little bastard!"

"Garde," said Durossac in a flat voice, as if his mind were not on it. He drew his cutlass mechanically and presented it with an accustomed, unhurried movement, as a man might point at something with a stick.

"Wait!" cried Pironeau. "Outside where there is fair room—"

Manault had already rushed in, trying as he lunged so to engage Durossac's blade that the strength of his shoulder might bear down the weapon of the smaller man. It seemed that Durossac hardly moved; yet Northrup saw the swordsman's face tighten with a

143

spasm of effort the instant before the blades engaged. There was a ringing crack, and Manault sprang backward, in his hand nothing but his weapon's useless hilt. There had been some flaw, perhaps, in Manault's blade; for the unexpected hard snap that Durossac had in his wrist had broken off his opponent's hanger at the guard.

For an instant Manault stared dismayed; then hurled himself forward, flinging the hilt in Durossac's face.

It was the effort of a man mad with rage; yet it succeeded, in part. As Durossac ducked Manault's thrown hilt the attacker was able to strike his enemy's blade aside and drive into a clinch. Manault's shoulder smashed Durossac backward against the wall; Manault's arms, with a sinew-cracking strength, bound Durossac's sword arm to his side. One of his hands strained upward over Durossac's shoulder, trying to get a throat hold from behind.

Durossac stood calmly, Northrup thought, pinned against the wall in Manault's hard-locked embrace. He blocked Manault's throat grip with his jaw. For a moment they struggled there, Manault trying to force back Durossac's head, and the muscles of the neck and arm shook with their opposed tension.

Then slowly, with a writhing hunch of beautiful muscles, Durossac began to draw his weapon arm upward out of Manault's body grip. Northrup would not have believed the move possible; nor could he now see how it was done. It seemed almost as if Durossac had turned his arm boneless and pulled it out of the lock like a rope or a snake.

As the cutlass came free its point flicked upward in an

arc, nicking a beam; then Durossac brought the ball of the hilt down on Manault's skull back of the ear, and the tall man dropped.

For a moment Northrup stood silent. He was, as a matter of fact, swept to a cold admiration. He had heard of the mad fury of Durossac's assault in action; but he was amazed by the unhurried, workmanlike way in which he had met Manault's attack. So this, he was thinking, was the first swordsman of Barataria, the man in a class by himself, whose name was always made an exception when comparisons were drawn. . . .

Job Northrup cast about him for a weapon. It never occurred to him that anything was possible but to go on with the fight where Manault had left off. For once Pironeau's hanger was not at his side. As an alternate resource Northrup lifted a heavy chair, smashed it upon the puncheoned floor, and from the wreckage got himself a substantial club.

"Come on again!"

Durossac looked faintly surprised. He considered Northrup and his peculiar weapon at some length; and the truth was that he did not know just what to expect of a man with a piece of wood in his hands. Not that he doubted that he could kill Northrup out of hand; but he found himself uneager to cut down a man as good as unarmed. The fall of Manault had left him better-humoured than before.

"No," he decided, "I've no quarrel with you, so I'm not going to fight you."

"The hell you're not," said Northrup, advancing.

"Impossible," Durossac told him. With a small smile

he examined the uncoiling wrap of his hilt, where the cord had been burst by some illogical strain of the blow.

"Why?" Northrup demanded.

"Wounded," Durossac grinned, exhibiting a fresh cut on his hand. He was being as propitiatory as he knew how to be toward a man threatening to attack. Durossac was a man who could afford to preserve enemies; he did not, in truth, want to excite this one into running onto his ready hanger and thus get no fight and no glory out of the tall Northerner at all.

"Get a weapon and practise yourself," Durossac advised. "I hear you disarmed Masselier. And now you want to fight with a piece of a chair. By God, my friend, there would be some satisfaction in sticking the steel into a set of guts like yours. Maybe there'll be chance soon, who knows?"

"There's no better time than now," the Yankee persisted.

"Nothing to it," said Durossac. He sheathed his hanger and turned his back squarely upon Northrup as he strolled out.

In a fit of temper Northrup flung his club to the floor; and to his amazement the wood had hardly bounded before Durossac had leaped to the middle of the street and whirled with his cutlass once more in his hand.

The Yankee burst into laughter.

"Big bastard," Durossac muttered and, sheathing his hanger once more, went stumping off.

Pironeau was urging wine between the lips of Manault.

Chapter XI

1

LAFITTE STAYED at the Temple for something over two weeks more. Not long after the Yankee's departure for Grand Isle Charles Masselier turned up at the Temple with his tale of woe; Jean laughed in his face, and, after a spasm of bitter threats, Masselier went his way.

Next luggers began appearing with the loot and men of Jean Ducoing and Nez Coupé. Day after day the bayou boats brought their goods to the Temple, repeatedly turning back for more. A small mountain of unsold goods filled the warehouse sheds and spilled across the island in tarpaulin-covered piles. With the luggers Nez Coupé came and went, taciturn and surly. Last of all came Jean Ducoing, and the removal from Grand Isle to the Temple was complete. More than a hundred men were now upon the island in the swamp. They loafed and wrangled, or shuttled back and forth between the Temple and New Orleans upon aimless and futile trips.

A day or two later came Durossac with thirty or forty men; and Gambio was close in his wake with nearly a hundred more. Nearly three hundred men now made the Temple their headquarters. By inquiries subtle and discreet, Lafitte learned of the wreck of the *Lucia* and of the exact status of the returned captains. To such privateersmen as applied to him Lafitte doled out a thin trickle of rations and rum and small quantities of coin. With these bread-line charities he offered an unvarying sympathetic plaint: "I wish I could do more, but I am destitute. I am given nothing to sell, and what can I do?" It was not apparent that either of these measures accomplished anything. Many of the men were bitter toward their leaders, as was to be expected under all circumstances whatsoever; but the captains themselves remained silent and very strictly aloof.

In the second week a new straggle of human flotsam began to arrive. By recognition of certain of these newcomers Lafitte knew that Bill Cochrane was back. Not much later he learned that Cochrane returned without loot, having been badly defeated upon the sea. Ninety more fighting men were added to the accumulation at the Temple by this arrival.

Lafitte waited until Cochrane himself at last came stumping up from the landing. If he had hoped that misfortune had made Cochrane amenable he was badly disappointed, for the raider was in furious and combative mood. Lafitte stayed at the Temple yet a few days more, principally for the purpose of showing that he was unimpressed by the physical dangers of being mobbed; then merrily made his way to New Orleans.

As he stood on the New Orleans levee he raised his arms over his head to stretch luxuriously. He felt that he had been a long time away from home. He gazed across the Place d'Armes, where leisured people strolled under the live oak and chinaberry trees; a flashily varnished carriage was promenading on the mud road circling the Place, and in sunlight and shadow moved negresses in bright cottons, with trays on their heads from which they peddled little cakes. His eye ran caressingly over the façade of the St. Louis Cathedral beyond the trees, and the massive arched Cabildo with its balconies of delicately traced iron; and he found it good to be back again with a whole hide.

2

PIERRE LAFITTE entered the little brick-paved court-yard through the side gate, which opened directly on the banquette. Whenever practicable he avoided coming in through the cinder heaps and iron-burned air of the blacksmith shop in front, which he considered unsuitable environment for a man of affairs and a seaman. Still, he had to look into the place once in a while. There was no one else to run the smithy; and it was a good thing, the Lafittes thought, to pretend to be in some other business than they really were, even if no one on earth should be fooled.

Within the courtyard's high walls the sun blazed white, except where, beneath the extended roof of the shop, the brick pavement lay damp and dimly cool and moss made green rims for every brick. There were a pair of tables of old carved mahogany, red as frosted persimmons, broken and rudely repaired; and some very passable chairs. Through the office, at the rear of the smithy, sounded the noises of the forge, the bouncing ring of hammers, and the duller thudding smash of the sledge on hot iron; but these sounds of shock came pleasantly diminished to the court behind, so that the clear stemware on the shaded tables remained unvibrant and cool.

Jean Lafitte was already seated, looking amiable and leisurely in the act of filling a pair of these glasses from a long-necked bottle.

"What's this?" said Jean. "No ice?"

"Blood of God," said Pierre disgustedly, wiping the sweat from his eyes with his finger tips. "It's time you were getting here! Ice? Why should there be ice? There hasn't been a cargo of ice since the first of May. Do you realize you're three days behind your time?"

It was already September; more than a month had passed since Jean's break with the privateers. For Pierre Lafitte it had been a bad month, full of anxiety, and the need for a type of subterfuge that he despised. It had also included moments of mystification which infuriated him. He was the elder brother; it was necessary that he maintain a show of leadership—a hard thing to do, considering that Jean was the one with the more commanding appearance, the greater confidence, and most of the brains. Pierre persuaded himself, however, that he upheld his position with fair success; and Jean found it desirable to encourage this belief by diplomacy and dissimulation. Yet times arrived when the truth could not economically be concealed, even from Pierre.

From certain angles Pierre Lafitte looked like a subtle satire upon his younger brother. He was as tall as Jean; they were indeed made from the same pattern, but Pierre, the first-born, had the appearance of an experiment. Compared with Jean he was too lean in the chest, too gangling, with that spadelike chin too long, the cheek bones too prominent, the forehead too gaunt and lumpy. And when his crossed eyes came into view the satire lost its subtlety; he became a sad caricature of the Jean Lafitte who made himself boss of privateers.

"Well," said Jean good-humouredly, "when I do get here, where are you? I have to send a boy hunting all over town."

"You've been gone two weeks," said Pierre harshly, "leaving me holding the sack."

"I would have come yesterday," Jean assured him, "but I was waiting to see a man from Grand Isle."

"That Yankee, I suppose. Didn't see him, did you? Well, he's in New Orleans."

"Who, Northrup?" said Jean. "Well, now, how the devil—"

"He rowed past the Temple in the night, with the idea you were here. There's a crew killer, if ever I saw one. Rowing all night through a mosquito swamp. Crazier than—"

"Where is he now?"

"In the Exchange Coffee House, I suppose, or some like bar."

Jean moistened his lips with wine and leaned forward with a tentative gleam in his eyes. "Pierre, I suppose you've heard the news from Cartagena?"

"What news? The town is full of nothing but heat, flies, and news from Cartagena. I got nothing else all afternoon from Leclerc, who gathers it up to put in his paper, then can't sort it out."

"I have definite word," said Jean softly, "that the declaration of independence has been drawn up. Torices now has enough men—"

Pierre set down his glass with a click and wiped his mouth with the back of his hand. "Cartagena! What I want is news from Barataria. The sooner you get your mind out of Cartagena and into New Orleans the better it will be for both of us. When do you have to go back?"

"Except for an occasional visit," said Jean, "I shan't have to go back."

"What the devil is this?"

"Your plan," said Jean, "worked perfectly—while it lasted." He glanced up to see if his brother was deceived by the suggestion that the plan had been Pierre's, instead of Jean's own. Pierre's face satisfied him that the desired confusion had once more been achieved.

"I took up my position at the Temple," Jean went on, "as you suggested. There I've waited ever since. I managed to intercept and turn back some half-dozen prospective buyers of contraband; otherwise my time was mostly lost."

Pierre allowed himself a one-sided twist of the mouth as for a moment he enjoyed a mental picture of Jean roosting among the shell heaps, twiddling his thumbs.

"Marsont and Villorme were at the Temple," Pierre said, "trying to buy silks. What did they say?"

"How did you know?" Jean demanded.

"Oh, I have ways of knowing."

"By God," said Jean, "I believe you sent them yourself."

"Of course I sent them! And if I did I had good reasons. You want to remember that."

"You took a very pretty chance," said Jean, "I must say. Suppose I'd missed them? They could have bought their stuff in a minute if Nez Coupé had been there—and cheaper than they expected, at that. Why the devil there should be such a sweat to buy at this time of year I can't imagine."

"Some fools," Pierre said, "have a notion of chartering a vessel and sending a cargo of the loot around to New York."

Jean stirred impatiently. "If there's going to be export, we'll attend to it. In any case, it's out of the question now. It's a damned funny thing you'd send them down there knowing what the situation is."

"What would I do? Have them in the calabozo?"

"A minute ago," Jean reminded him, "you sent them."

"Well—"

"Let it go. Beluche in New Orleans?"

"Naturally."

"Sold anything?"

"Very little." Pierre fidgeted irritably. "What's the reason you're not going back? I'll have something to say about that. Can I—"

"Ducoing and Nez Coupé are at the Temple. So is Durossac, and Gambio. I sent you word about the *Lucia* and all that. And now Bill Cochrane is back with his buckoes—empty handed and well whipped."

"Cochrane!" Pierre was ready to blow up. "Oh, hell! Of all men, it had to be him! Ninety men more, absolutely certain to go with Beluche. This is a sweet kettle of fish you've stewed up down there! The trouble with you is you can't get along with anybody. I can't be everywhere. If I didn't have to be in New Orleans I'd go down there and run that works myself!"

"Tut, tut!" said Jean amiably; but he sighed. They had jangled each other from childhood. It was a continuous irritation to Pierre that he was even partly dependent upon the wits and force of his younger brother. His own crossed eyes destroyed his confidence in himself at the root; he habitually expected to be abused, mocked behind his back, defeated. But he was one man whom Jean could not impress. After all, Pierre, by right of his seniority, was head of the Lafittes, and the Lafittes were promising to amount to something these days.

"I don't know how this damned thing is going to end," pursued Pierre gloomily. "Already more than three hundred idle at the Temple—shell backs, cut-throats, and common scum—"

"Three hundred hearty eaters," said Jean.

Pierre looked at him a moment and went on: "I suppose it's true, as I hear, that Beluche has sent his own vessel out again? That gets a hundred and twenty-five men out of there, but, good God, man—"

"They won't be gone long," said Jean. "They're underprovisioned. He'll have them back before he can turn around."

Pierre stared at him blankly. "Romain Very is due back any time, and so is Henrico Marco. That will make between three hundred and four hundred men."

"Durossac is about to sail, but of the others I doubt," said Jean, "if a one can cruise again without cashing his prizes—if he's got any prizes."

Pierre said, "That rabble will swarm into New

Orleans like a—like a—"

"Well, they can swarm back again," Jean countered. "There is no free food in New Orleans. They'll have to eat at the Temple at the expense of our friend Beluche. How long can that last?"

"We'll be broke before—"

"During the last slack season," Jean said, "we kept those men on the sea, and a pretty penny it cost. Now they've nearly doubled in number—and the expense will be to Beluche!"

Pierre remained appalled. "How long can this go on? Do you realize, if this lasts until all the crews are in, there'll be nearly a thousand men in that swamp?"

"More than that," Jean exulted. "It means the whip hand."

"And Beluche with the whip!"

"Nonsense! This is an eating contest, not a war, Pierre."

"Good God, Jean—the size of the thing!"

"They'll drop into our hands. It's a godsend, Pierre. We're going to run this to suit ourselves from here out. By manipulating the market we can keep them hoping, stringing along, as long as we like—long enough to give them a burning they'll never forget. I tell you, there's going to be tearing of hair next time the Lafittes turn their backs on Barataria!"

Pierre's eyes were blank in a grim face. "A thousand men," he muttered obscurely. "Enough to sack any port on the tropic seas. . . ."

Better than Pierre, Jean could visualize that uncontrollable swarm of armed men of all nations and colours, incoherently seething down there among the mangroves like insects in an ant trap; he saw them as a half-savage riff-raff, made dangerous no less by their stupidities than by their lusts and greeds. He was glad, under the circumstances, to be out of contact with them for a while. At the same time the explosive elements of the situation delighted him. Dissimulating his strength, even to Pierre, he remained master of the situation, he thought. The hazard, even more than the prospect of great gain, lifted him up on an exhilaration like the upward thrust of a cold salt wave.

He was eager now to see the Yankee; but first, for the sake of neatness in his plans, he wished to draw a new mandate from Pierre.

"What we ought to have," he began, "is a little something to toss to the buyers now and then. Nobody must get the idea that it's really feasible to trade with Beluche. That's our weak spot. After all, Pierre, we have no place in this except as we produce a little money now and then to tide the privateers over. Even in that there are speculators who'd be glad to step into our shoes. If we only had a few incoming prizes of our own—"

He was touching now upon Pierre's pet hobby, the one theory from which the elder brother was never long diverted. Pierre had been a privateersman himself before being manoeuvred by Jean into more lucrative projects.

"That's the trouble here," Pierre responded with some heat. "We should have had our own ships on the sea these fifteen months. I ought to be cruising now. This nigger trade has led us up a blind alley; I saw it a year ago, but your damned pig-headedness—you would be told nothing! And now—!"

"Well, I thought . . ." Jean put in, as if with hesitance. With a pleasure peculiarly ironic he let his voice trail off, and Pierre went plunging ahead in the way Jean had tricked him, striking aside the opposition that Jean offered as bait.

"The *Two Brothers* is fast enough for any such work," Pierre declared. "She's too good to be sneaking about with her belly full of blacks, and if you had any honest-to-God experience in this business you could see it. She should be over in the Narrow Seas. Half a dozen like her would make us independent of this mob. I told you last year—"

"Of course," said Jean, "it's too late, now—"

"Of course it's not too late," Pierre contradicted, his voice rising. "I suppose she's fouling her bottom at Cat Island. She is? Just as I thought. All right. She's got to sail. Send—"

"She can't, Pierre."

"By God, she will, though!"

"She has no legal commission to cruise."

"She can cruise as legally as anybody else. I'm tired of your stubbornness. I'm tired of being crossed by fool prejudices, and notions, and shilly-shally delays! I—"

"Oh, well," said Jean at last with an affectation of gloom. "I suppose it's up to you. . . ."

ᒫET ME TELL YOU," said the Yankee earnestly, "anything can happen there."

Northrup and Jean Lafitte sat in one of the small
upper rooms of the Exchange Coffee House. A window
like a pair of doors stood open beside their table, giving
the place a look of airiness; but they nevertheless owed
their privacy to the extreme heat of that room, for the
more cellarlike lower rooms of the coffee house were
already thronged by the late afternoon crowd. Outside
that tall window a little balcony of curly iron overhung
the Mississippi levee; through the dusty foliage of the
chinaberry trees they could see the tall masts and furled
canvas of anchored craft.

Lafitte turned his eyes from Northrup and looked out
at the river, flowing smooth and brown beyond the
chinaberry trees. The Yankee was continuing with his
report.

"I soon saw what a dirty mob there was going to be at
Grand Isle, even before Gambio wrecked. So I used my
own judgment. Before I careened the *Two Brothers*
instead of afterward, like you said, I loaded the coils of
line, the pipes of salt meat—where did that bear meat
come from, for God's sake? The rum, rice, cornmeal—
all that stuff you listed. I did better than that. I lifted
everything you had there loose that a vessel could use.
My own judgment, under the conditions. I took it to Cat
Island to keep it under my eye."

Lafitte frowned slightly, studying the big Yank. He

was seeing a singularly rangy but tight-knit young man, hard and brown of face, so that his weathered hair was lighter than the skin, and the green eyes looked like crystal set in ruddy leather. Northrup was very close shaved, so that his jaw was drily shiny; and the whole man looked dry and cleaned, as if he were so desiccated by the sun that the honest sweat of ordinary men was unknown to him. Jean tried to picture the Yankee in the dirty and littered cabin of the *Two Brothers*, with on deck a ragtag and bobtailed crew of all colours, shaggy and filthy, without discipline: but he could not. Sometimes it was impossible for Lafitte to look at this man so entirely different from himself without an instinctive hostility. He looked like something out of a navy—that was it.

"Gambio came around, wanting to know what I was about," the Yankee went on; "and I gave him a cock-and-bull yarn about going after a smuggle of niggers. He said as far as he was concerned, if ever he stowed another nigger he hoped he died full of salt water. 'Such a stink of blacks,' says he"—the Yankee imitated Gambio's buzzing bass so well that Lafitte started— " 'I've scrubbed the *Lucia* twenty times with lime,' says he, 'an' she can stink a buzzard off a gut-pile four miles down wind!' "

Northrup chuckled, evidently tickled by Gambio's unexpected sensitivity. "Not that it matters now," Northrup added. "Gambio was half drunk and kept forgetting the *Lucia* was bashed. Every now and then he'd remember and curse fit to cut his own throat. Well, for that matter—" his mind reverted to smells—"the *Two*

Brothers is no violet."

"You went to Cat Island to careen?"

"Aye. We careened and scraped in five days—"

"Five days! A fine job you must—"

"Well, the weather was favourable. The blacks swarmed over that hull night and day; you couldn't see the sheathing for niggers. They're good workers, those blacks."

"First I'd heard of it," commented Lafitte, sucking at his cigar. "But go on."

"The rigging was another matter. We've got it so it'll hold, at last."

"She's ready, then?"

"Watered, even."

"That's good," said Lafitte. "That's damned good." He was deriving a salt refreshment from this man. In the Yankee's blunt methods he found a stimulating contrast to the limber, weaving diplomacy that was his own reliance.

Northrup went on to describe the details of his preparations. They had been sufficiently thorough, by his own account; considering, as he mentioned without subterfuge, that he had been given no definite idea of the mission for which *Two Brothers* was preparing.

"In case you have no man in mind for mate," said the Yankee, brassily assuming that he was to have command of the ship he had refitted, "Manault has quarrelled with Gambio. There's a good man, if I know one. I sounded him out; he'll take the berth. Though of course I assured him of nothing without consulting you."

"I should hope not," said Lafitte; and the Yankee looked at him sharply.

Northrup had finished. Lafitte asked a perfunctory question or two, his eyes on the masts. He mouthed his cigar, half dropping his eyelids, enjoying himself immeasurably. The town had never seemed more pleasant to him than upon that hot afternoon as he had walked from the forge to the levee. Under the July sun the alleylike streets brimmed with melting heat through which a flat stale odour rose from the open gutter sewers; but these things affected him not at all.

He was feeling that he was at the crossroads of the New World. From the north the great river was bringing a constant stream of trade; at the south, almost at Louisiana's door, lay those tropic provinces out of which the world's boldest adventurers were moulding empires to suit their tastes. West of New Orleans, with a frontier in that day unbelievably near, spread a country undeveloped, its possibilities not half explored; and at the city's elbow lay the sea, the road to all the world. A new town in a new land, where one man was as good as another, and riches offered themselves to all. . . .

Yet in spite of its freshness of spirit and its outpost nearness to the world frontiers New Orleans had a distinction of another sort. That other character—a touch of the Old World, perhaps—was embodied in the laced iron galleries and the whitewashed walls of plastered brick that brightened the alleylike streets; in the arched carriage gates that opened directly from the banquettes in the galleries' shade; in the glimpses of gardened courtyards that those vaulted carriageways sometimes allowed. It was even in the drowsy buzz of conversation in Tremoulet's Exchange Coffee House. Tremoulet's, greatly frequented by those interested in shipping, was perhaps the most excitably conversational spot in the South. Through its tobacco smoke floated extraordinary speculations, distorted rumours, and wisps of unlikely news; but beneath remained an undertone typical of New Orleans: a suggestion of pleasant leisure and an appreciation of the uses of that leisure. That town had a talent for rolling the savours of life slowly over its tongues. . . .

Lafitte removed his cigar and leaned toward the Yankee. Job Northrup was staring at the levee in such motionless repose that he might have been asleep with his eyes open; but he turned his face attentively.

"It was a fast careen," Lafitte admitted. "I must tell you, however, that there is a thing or two you have done that I don't care for. You take matters too readily into your own hands, my friend. I did not, for instance, send you there to thrash and maroon my Captain Masselier; and I did not—"

"I thought you wanted me to careen," said Northrup. "Was I to come running back blabbing that Masselier wouldn't let me?"

"I am willing to let it pass," said Lafitte; "but it leaves me short of officers, none the less. I suppose next I will hear that you have cut Pironeau's throat."

"Pironeau is a fair second mate," said Northrup, "and a reasonable man. For first mate, you could not do better than Manault; and there is this: Manault could bring with him fifteen good sizeable men from Gambio."

"You seem to assume that you are to be master of this ship," said Lafitte drily.

"I am on master's pay," the Yankee shrugged.

"Well, you're right. Sign this Manault, if you want him. That gives you some thirty men, with what Pironeau has picked up? Well, I'll give you a list of twenty more that I wish shipped on this cruise. If, as you say, you're ready to sail you should be able to ship your crew and weigh anchor within five days."

"Three," said Northrup.

"So much the better. Now I will tell you what not a dozen men in New Orleans know. By the time you sail Cartagena will be in revolt. This to my definite knowledge." His eyes glowed as he leaned toward Northrup over the table; and he paused until his statement was acknowledged by a cool green answering gleam in the eyes of the Yankee.

"You will sail directly to Aux Cayes, on the south coast of Haiti; Manault knows those waters and that harbour as he knows the palm of his hand. There you will find a man named Gutierrez, by this time an agent of Cartagena. He is younger than you, but treat him with respect. Such respect as you can," he added, as he studied Northrup's face. "By means of letters that I shall give you, you will obtain from him a sheaf of commissions in blank, authorizing privateers to cruise under the flag of Cartagena. As to what you shall say to this man, I have written instructions for you, as well as upon several other matters. Swear in your crew in the presence of Gutierrez. Incidentally, secure for the *Two Brothers* the new flag of Cartagena. Then return immediately. Is that clear?"

"Aye," said Northrup.

"Speed means everything," Lafitte continued. "You are to crowd the *Two Brothers* for every knot she is worth. Attack no ship, however fair a prize, because that means delay. I am convinced you are a good navigator. We shall now see. Do you understand?"

"Why these fifty men?" asked Northrup. "If I'm to repel hostile cruisers, it will be a matter of the long nines and a close haul."

"I meant to warn you. The twenty men whose names I will give you will be trouble makers, undisciplined, even worse than you now have. It is a part of your duty to keep them in order."

The Yankee nodded with a sort of slow contempt, conveying the intimation that he knew his job without being coached. "Why am I favoured with these rats?" he insisted.

"I have reasons of my own."

Northrup raised his eyebrows almost imperceptibly.

"You are to come to my house at eight to-night; at that time I will give you such letters and papers as you require, together with the necessary money. But others may be there, and if anything is to be explained, it must be brought up now. Of course, continued secrecy is expected of you in every detail."

Job Northrup slowly untangled his legs and squared himself to the table. There was a mass of detail to be gone into here. The Yankee combed over it slowly; and

Lafitte could see that in this man there was confidence always in himself but never in results. He wondered why he had thought Northrup looked young. An hour passed while they talked.

"One thing more," said Northrup, as they at last rose. "What do I get out of this?"

"You will be taken care of—trust that. I am accustomed to have men depend on me."

"I'll take a chance."

"Four days?"

"Three."

Chapter XII

❧

S HE RIDES HIGH," Manault insisted; "too high, sir, if you ask me. Another hundred sacks of—"

"You may be right," Northrup conceded. His dungaree-clad figure sprawled relaxed behind a table of spread charts; yet he looked neither at rest nor ready for action, but only propped about angularly, like a jointed marionette.

"We had no air on the Cat Island run," Northrup continued. "I'll try this way, though. It may cost us time in the end, but I think not."

"If a sou'wester leaps on us we're like to lose more than time," said Manault. He had sleepy eyes in a lean weathered face; and a trailing moustache, one end of which he kept frazzled by constant chewing. He studied his Yankee captain speculatively. "Those sou'westers jump like hell. I know."

"Rubbish," said Northrup impatiently. "You French carry no sail, that's the trouble. I'll show you how to set her through like she was jerked by the head."

Manault shrugged and relaxed. He enjoyed command, and action was a necessity of his life; but in matters of decision he preferred to lie in the hands of fate or of a better man.

There was a small thud against the vessel's counter, and Manault stepped to a porthole. "Nobody but that friar, sir," he grumbled. He was in a state of uncommon alertness, eager for the ship to be on her way. His narrowed gaze roamed with a specious drowsiness over the racks of muskets and hangers that made the cabin an arsenal; then wandered up the ladder to twitch at the partly visible tarpaulin beneath which the main swivel gun crouched like an animal bound down.

"I want you to go ashore, now," said Northrup. "Keep a general eye on the men. I want no one leaving Grand Isle. The place to stop that is at Grand Isle; I want no chasing after drunkards in boats. We'll weigh on tomorrow's tide, whether those fourteen men get here from the Temple or not. And if Mendez doesn't get back from Cat Island we'll go after him."

"Aye, sir."

Père Miguel, the little friar of the bald head and scraggly beard, had come part way down the ladder while Northrup spoke and now flattened himself against the bulkhead to let the mate pass.

"Go forward to the galley," said Manault roughly, "if you want something to eat."

"Let him alone," said Job Northrup. "Stay here,

Father; I want to talk to you."

Northrup stared idly through the open porthole. Beyond the low gun revetments of Grand Terre the blue waters of the Mexican Gulf flashed with needle rays of pure light. Farther yet, on the horizon of the sea, a vast flock of niggcr geese, the guano birds of that coast, drifted like an endless low cloud, hardly more distinct than smoke.

"You know these De Verniats?" said Northrup suddenly when Manault was gone.

Père Miguel started. "Of course, m'sieu. For more than a year, now, up and down this forsaken country, on foot, or in only the most humble craft—"

"Can you carry a letter there?"

The friar hesitated before he answered, "Gladly, m'sieu."

"You know Mademoiselle de Verniat?" Northrup began rhetorically.

Miguel was gazing through the porthole to where, in the dazzle of the sky, a pelican sailed, first a flash of floating silver, then a gray wisp of lost dust. He spoke dreamily, as if he found the syllables pretty, and delicately fingered them: "Madelaine Françoise Céleste de Verniat. . . . There is a—"

"Oh, that's her name, is it?"

"But yes."

"Madelaine Françoise Cé—what was that, now?"

"Céleste," said the friar. He mooned at the little disk of sky, apparently lost in unhappy rumination. Then a second great gaunt pelican, with a head like a doorknob and a face like an umbrella, shot downward just outside the port; and the crash of the bird's descent upon the water seemed to bring Père Miguel to earth.

"From time to time," he told Northrup, "I am her tutor."

"Well," said the Yankee with irritation, "I know it." He rummaged among the charts for a piece of paper and a quill. "This letter must be given to her."

"To her mother," Miguel corrected him.

"Certainly not. To Ma'm'selle and no one else."

"I cannot do it, m'sieu. You do not understand."

Job Northrup's hard green stare locked for a moment with Miguel's mild regard and the Yankee skipper saw clearly enough that the little man could not be made to serve. "All right," he growled; "then that'll be all. I'll get somebody else." He ducked his head over his papers with a jerk, as if he would plunge into furious scribbling, but immediately became motionless, quill poised, baulked by the baffling requirements of composition.

"Let me say a word, m'sieu," said the friar foxily. "Let me urge you not to do anything of that sort."

Northrup snapped down the pen. "Let you—*what?*"

Miguel gazed abstractly out the port, not caring for another contest with the Yankee's eye, and did not immediately answer.

In the silence Northrup sat staring at him. The ragged nerves from which he had lately been suffering worried the Yankee, making him seem unfamiliar to himself. He had been on the sea since childhood, deck-raised by his widowed father; and in that life of travel he had early become indifferent to strange places. Harbours moved toward him, engulfed him, receded into distant tininess again and disappeared, leaving Job Northrup unchanged. But it was now a great while, it seemed to him, since he had felt an icy sea; and for the first time in his life he found his fibre yielding under the influence of a place.

The Yankee was not a contemplative man. He had but a brief philosophy, and that a practical one. In this world, he conceived, men are set down with no understanding of where they are from or where they are going; but here they are, and—the wise man makes himself at home. He was accustomed to know what he wanted and to walk patiently toward it by the shortest apparent route. In his natural cold-sea habitat internal cross-purposes had been unknown to him.

Yet even this cold-weather habit of mind could not conceal from him that the three years he had now spent in tropic waters had impaired the fabric of his intent. The distinctness of his purpose was fading; and for the first time in his life he was doubting that his own efforts were worth while.

The command of the *Two Brothers*, with its promise of unusual reward without extraordinary risk, was a timely bit of luck, for he was at the moment short of money. He was glad, too, of an opportunity to get away from the land again. The dull drone of the beach had an insidious cumulative effect, relaxing and faintly stupefying, like the hot damp. Behind Grand Isle the interminable marsh lay as still and dead under its gray salt sedges as a foreshore at low tide, a foreshore thirty miles deep, featureless and desolate; and the spirits of the Northerner bogged down in its mud.

To this state of futility the heat itself added that irritation of desire in all its forms that is peculiar to hot countries: that stimulus that causes tropic peoples to overeat, to scorch their foods with pepper, to take many women, forever seeking new whips for senses that become more hungry as they become more jaded.

Job Northrup, who thought only weaklings were affected by climate, wondered what was the matter with him. He was stupidly revolving the problem in his mind when the Capuchin spoke again.

"It would be even better, m'sieu," said Miguel, "everything considered, if you were not to go there any more."

The angry flush that started to rise to the Yankee's face died away, and he sat scratching with the quill at a margin of the chart. "Why do you say that?" he asked at last, his voice repressed.

"M'sieu Northrup," began the friar; and then seemed to check himself. "No good can come of it," he trailed off weakly.

"Why?" Northrup insisted.

Père Miguel hesitated. He did not know how to read this man, or in what terms to appeal to him. He chose to stand at the angle of the Yankee's commercial relations. "You wish to do business with Jean Lafitte?"

"I am connected with him, at the present."

"It will be profitable for you if that relationship persists? Perhaps for a considerable time?"

"It may prove so," the Yankee admitted, his green stare hard upon the friar's face. He could see that there was something in the mind of the little gray-robed man which he was now determined to draw out.

"If," said Père Miguel, fumbling over his choice of words, "M'sieu Lafitte perceives that your eyes are upon Ma'm'selle de Verniat, you and he have come to the end."

"What do you mean? Out with it, now!"

Père Miguel considered for nearly a minute. "That is a man of ambition," said he at last. "You know what that means to those French. A family, an establishment, about which to gather the possessions of this world. It is well known here, a matter of common talk, that Jean Lafitte has found Mademoiselle de Verniat necessary to his plans."

Northrup's face remained blank; the friar's surreptitious glance found the Yankee's eyes apparently uncomprehending. But under the pressing cup of the heat, which seemed to hold him motionless beneath its weight, a heavy unpleasant emotion had stirred within the Yankee.

He was eager to feel the lift and fall of deep water, to watch a solid green sea pile roaring over a ship's deck. An icy sea would have suited him better; a tepid one would do.

And yet—Louisiana, through Madelon de Verniat's dark eyes, had gained a hold upon him that he found himself reluctant to break. There had been too many long hours upon his hands during his month at Grand Isle, and too little with which to engage his brain. In that endless wasting idleness he had often thought of Madelon, at first only because his recollection of her was fresh and clear. He had called at the De Verniats' a second time, and a third; and then no more—but the three visits had already created a focus for his unrest.

He had believed himself armoured against a restricting attachment for any woman. But Madelon, being of a type foreign to his experience, had roused his curiosity; and the long days and interminable warm nights of Grand Isle had rusted his armour away. He was always remembering the peculiar depth of her eyes as they lay upon his, carrying a message not to be ignored. When he had recalled that contact of her eyes often enough, he got to thinking that she already belonged to him, that he possessed her in a relationship of frustration not to be endured. Often, alone with the surf drone and the tepid waters, he felt her compelling presence, as if she were thinking of him far away. The fancy made him savagely irritable, and he longed to be on the sea; yet it took no introspection upon his part to know that once at sea he would be equally impatient to return.

And now the little Capuchin was telling him that Madelon was held in option by Lafitte!

"Why, that old rake," the Yankee exclaimed suddenly, "he's old enough to be her father! How can she bring herself to— Look here: is that what she wants?"

It surprised Père Miguel to note how young the man looked, how unsophisticated could be the tone of his voice.

"In this world," said the friar, not without a certain sadness, "what women want is not always considered. And that, perhaps, is just as well. You realize, of course, that matters of a young woman's welfare are for her parents to decide; mature experience—"

"But will Madame de Verniat—is she crazy?"

Père Miguel sighed. "I do not like to speak of these things. There are wheels within wheels."

"What was it you started to say?" Northrup demanded. He had an eye that could chop like an ax. An impulse was upon him to seize and shake the friar, so that something would tumble out of the little old man to clear his own befuddled wits.

Père Miguel seemed to flinch, and his voice came muffled, as if unwilling to let itself be heard. "It is a matter of common knowledge, and I violate no confidence in mentioning it, though I should not like to be quoted: but Madame de Verniat is a woman of no resources in this world. It is believed she is heavily in M'sieu Lafitte's debt."

A powerful protective urge, instinctively felt for a face he thought lovely, swayed the Yankee with unaccustomed force. He could see Madelon's little triangular face, in which he thought he had perceived something obscurely tragic, something sensitively passionate and imprisoned; and he imagined an acute hurting emotion in this girl, this fragilely made little creature, broken-hearted and lost, as if something were twisting a frame too delicate to withstand. . . .

And now the little old fraud conceived that the time had come to play his final card.

"Listen!" he demanded, leaning suddenly forward as if an impulse had overwhelmed him. "Listen! I will tell you why I say that you must go there no more. Over you, this—this girl is distraught."

"What—" began the Yankee confusedly.

"She has had the misfortune to fall desperately in love with you," Miguel declared.

The friar dropped back in his seat in something of a tremor, and his eyes turned out the porthole. Now that his work was done he had hardly the temerity, he found, to observe what manner of havoc his lies had effected. For the greater part of a minute there was silence in the cabin. Then the Yankee stirred himself.

He reached across the table, gripped the breast of Miguel's frock in a big hand, and jerked him forward so that he could peer into the friar's face. "Listen!" he commanded with a sort of confused savagery. "Are you lying to me?"

Père Miguel, thus abruptly confronted by Northrup's glare, was frightened half out of his wits. He had expected to turn presently to see a lovelorn young man, dazed a little perhaps, but looking emotionalized and sheepish. Instead he was jerked around to confront a face that seemed, in contrast to what he had expected, that of a murderer. For an interminable moment he was unable to reply at all.

"No, no," he said at last; and though his voice quavered faintly its tone was composed. "Why should I deceive you? I am one of the Brotherhood. I wish all people well. I—"

Northrup let him drop like a sack, and Père Miguel's voice stopped suddenly, as if the words had been wrung out of him by the big man's hand. Northrup made a gesture of exasperation and slumped back into his seat. His mind was in a swirling drift, as if his rudder had carried away and he were falling off helplessly before wind and sea. He was trying to find a mental anchor, and there was none to his hand.

Out of his fuddled chaos the need for action slowly emerged, as a ship lifts its head through the last of an all but overpowering sea. He knew that he must go to this girl who seemed to need him, that he must go at once, somehow making the distance to the plantation and back again before he sailed. What he was to do when he again stood in Madelon's presence he had not the least idea; nor did he later evolve any sort of plan. Yet it seemed necessary to him that he go.

"Come along here!" he said suddenly, getting to his feet.

Miguel had been about to speak, but he was now jerked upright by a grip that bruised his spindly arm as if it were caught in a twist of chain. Northrup went surging up the ladder, hauling Miguel after him so that the little man stumbled and ran, his robe tangling about his knees.

"You, bosun! Leave no one come aboard until an officer arrives! Here," he said to Miguel, "I'm going ashore to find Manault and get a boat and crew. You paddle to Grand Terre and find Antoine Pironeau and tell him—"

"But, m'sieu—if you mean to go to De Verniats', you will never be able to get back in time for to-morrow's tide."

"Sailing date set ahead one day. Find—"

"If you must go there, let me go with you!"

"Catch me on the beach, then. Find Pironeau, I say! And tell him . . ."

Chapter XIII

1

THEY SAT on the gallery of Madame de Verniat's house drinking milk coffee embittered by chicory and sweetened with syrupy black sugar that tasted of the cane. Madame de Verniat and the Capuchin friar chattered continuously; but Job Northrup and the girl sat silent, inwardly strung to the ringing point and most ill at ease. They were waiting, and knew that they were waiting; though for what, was not clear.

Northrup's first five strides after he had touched the De Verniat landing had been long and swift; the sixth had slackened. Through the fifty yards of jungle between the lugger landing and the clearing he had walked slowly, head down and feet dragging.

Père Miguel, plodding at his elbow, had noted Northrup's hesitation. "Do nothing foolish, my son," he begged.

"*Will* you shut up?" the Yankee mumbled. He took a brace and went stumping ahead, breaking into the clearing like a harassed ox coming out of the water.

Madame de Verniat had at this hour but just arisen and was taking coffee in the darkened dining room at the rear of the house. The emergency of receiving visitors found her attired in curling papers, bedroom mules without stockings, and a sleazy green wrapper. Some time had therefore elapsed while Madame got herself suitably overdressed.

The interval was a trying one for Northrup, who had paced the gallery nervously, with a heavy tread. Trying also for Madelon, who awaited her mother at the foot of the stair, listening meanwhile to that quick hard tramping of the Yankee, up and down, up and down, picturing to herself as best she could his mental state. In this way she had contrived to make herself so nervous that she was ready to flee to her pirogue by the time her mother came down. But it was over at last, and—there they sat.

Externally, in spite of his inward perturbation, the Yank was like clay, as cool, as drab, as unexpressive. He watched with some distaste the conversational efforts of Père Miguel, who vivaciously produced a great many words with a minimum of meaning; the friar appeared to be proud of the finesse with which he was ameliorating an otherwise hopeless situation.

Behind the Yankee lay unforgotten shadows of a night in which he had hardly slept, a long parade of hours spent cramped in a longboat while the negroes rowed steadily and doggedly to the unceasing chunk of the oars against thole pins, with little help from a lazy breeze.

A slow narcotic swamp madness was enveloping him. Some part of him fought against it, longing for the clean salt sweep of the sea. Here were stagnations, ancient things, the reek of vegetable decay; yet in the heavy vapours was a vibration of teeming life, like a deep resonance; the swamp itself was a tangle of primitive life, immutably fecund, forcing upon everything within it the necessity of fructification. It bore upon the man impalpably, until he was tormented by a warring inner chaos to which he could give no name.

Now the eleven-o'clock sun was pouring down in sheets of heat; it struck through cypress and palmetto in bars that were invisible until they struck fronds or trunks; so that oddly carved masses of growth stood out in sudden gold against the muddy velvet of the shade. In this sun glare the reality of the girl disconcerted him. Her starchless faded muslin dress, clean but limp and worn-looking, the heat-dampened wisps of hair at her temples, the delicate but visible grain of the skin of her tanned hands—she was of as authentic substance as a sail or a spar. And yet her dark eyes, deep and elusive of surface as the seal-brown water under the mangrove roots, brought back the swamp mood of the night; as if she were the embodiment of the living fecund swamp, of the deep-rooted tangle of life that perpetually bred life.

Northrup sat fumbling with his cup, wondering what it was he had come to say or do. As he studied Madelon's half-averted face it seemed to him that there was apparent in her an excitation she tried to repress. Almost her skin glowed with it; but its nature he could not define. Sometimes, when her eyes briefly met his, he thought that he saw in them puzzlement, fatalism, and the faintest discernible hint of a fear. It was as if she, like the Yankee, was being drawn toward something she had not the power to evade.

At first, while Madame de Verniat was pouring the coffee, the Northerner had seemed to Madelon as thoroughly a stranger as if she had never seen him before. During the month since first he had knocked upon their door she had called up her memory of him a hundred times, a thousand times; and each time the image had been a shade less true, so that the Yankee now appeared an inaccurate representation of himself.

In some ways she found him more presentable than she had remembered or dared to hope. Northrup had stopped that morning at Lafitte's hut by the shell heaps, and had there shaved and reattired himself as best he could. He had got hold of a fresh silk stock and a long steel-gray coat with pewter buttons, cracked out of a case of them that had never reached the port to which it had been consigned. In contrast to the rusty Capuchin the seaman looked cleanly gaunt and cool, his eyes as lucid as water over sand. There never was anything moiled or turbid about the exterior of that man.

He seemed younger than she had remembered him, and less harsh. In the coolness of his face there showed the puzzlement of an animal uncertain of itself and of its surroundings. Only, as he looked at her his eyes seemed to be trying to conceal that he knew her better than she knew herself.

Thus each one read erroneously the other's eyes; so that presently, complete strangers as they were, they fell under the illusion of having known each other untold years.

2

MORE COFFEE WAS POURED, and before the last of the milk was cold Madame de Verniat had worried herself into a state of fretful anxiety. No glance between Madelon and Job Northrup had escaped her observation, and each had added to her accumulating alarm until she could almost have brought herself to order the Yankee from the premises. She adjudged Northrup to be a mere hireling of the sea, of a class no better than menial. The man had no gesture or phrase that did not incur her dislike. His lack of any sense of leisure made her imagine him to be scheming malignantly, ready at any moment to burst into some unaccountable action. The possessive look in his eyes as they rested upon her daughter seemed to Madame de Verniat insulting. Worst of all was his evident effect upon the girl; it raised the intruder to the importance of a menace, one that must be repulsed at all costs.

She addressed her daughter coldly.

"If you have finished your coffee, Madelaine, I am sure Father Miguel and—Captain Northrup—will excuse you. Your tasks are waiting, I think."

Madelon made a single dismayed effort to stand her ground.

"Tasks, Mother? What tasks?"

"Madelaine—your mother has spoken!"

With the girl out of harm's way Madame delayed her further subterfuge but briefly.

"And now, M'sieu the Captain," she said, rising, "I

am sure you will excuse us; I wish Père Miguel to examine for me certain papers—important matters concerning the church. . . ."

She had expected that he would thereupon take himself off, but Northrup showed no inclination to leave, and she was forced to add, "Taking only a moment, my *dear* Captain."

Madame de Verniat switched furiously through the door, drawing the confused friar in her wake, and the Yankee found himself alone.

3

JOB NORTHRUP was at a loss. "Louisiana hospitality," he remarked drily, aloud. Being as yet unaware that Madame de Verniat considered him less a person than a threat, he could not understand why Madelon had been withdrawn; and he was irritated that Madame could so far ignore his personal importance as to venture a direct affront.

That was a minor thing, though. What made him writhe was the intolerable suspension of activity. His immediate purposes were now no clearer in his mind than they had been when he left Grand Isle the morning before; and he was harried by the knowledge that time pressed, that even at that moment he ought to have been far away, aboard his command.

He leaped up and paced the gallery, flayed by a sense of loss now that Madelon was again out of his sight, and made furious by that loss. Successively his anger turned against the friar, against Madame, against the inopportune exigencies of Lafitte. And yet he could not make up his mind what to do, or admit to himself what it was he desired to accomplish. He knew only that he was exasperated beyond all measure, and that pity was due the next man or thing that crossed him.

An impulse came upon him to go plunging off to his boat, to start back on that twelve-hour pull to the ship he should never have left. Reason told him that this was the only sensible move remaining to him—and perhaps also the only safe one; for he recognized in Madelon a danger of captivity that he feared and dreaded. Yet he did not go, but paced and fumed, his heels stinging the mist-corrupted wood.

Then presently, as he paced, he glanced through one of the French windows that rose tall from the gallery floor. The room into which he looked was dark except for the bright rectangle of a second window in the far end; but in that block of light Madelon stood, her profile distinct against the green and gold beyond. She rested one shoulder against the frame and stared out into the trees, and her hands were folded before her in an attitude weary and sad, in the lassitude of a small creature hopeless of escape.

The Yank's pacing stopped, and he stood leaning a hand on either side of the window, his gaze across the room upon the girl. It did not occur to him that he was taking advantage of her by watching her unawares, or that she might be startled if she should turn and find him lowering through the glass. He was thinking, "That girl, that girl I'm looking at, she as good as belongs to me."

He knew that he was looking into danger, the danger of an entrapment; but such defensive instinct as the man possessed was unserviceable to him now. Northrup's self-protective strategy in the presence of any mysterious threat was that of the rhinoceros, which rushes head down directly at the centre of the alarm. The Yankee felt that he must talk to this girl, conceiving vaguely that some further decision could be made when he had got that far.

The windows upon the gallery were closed against the heat and the flies, as they had been closed all night against the damp; the door, too, was closed to him—he had ironically noted the click of the hook when Madame de Verniat had taken herself inside. It was characteristic of Northrup that he did not think of signalling Madelon that he wished to be let in. If he had not a before-the-mast mob under him he thought only in terms of what he could do himself. He laid a hand upon the double sash and pushed. The screws drew almost noiselessly from the rotten wood, and brown dust powdered the back of the Yankee's hand as he stepped inside.

4

ONCE CLOSETED with Madame de Verniat in the still-disordered dining room, Père Miguel lost no time in coming to the point. He was haunted by the notion that the Yankee might at any moment rush off to his longboat and be at sea before the friar could again get all the materials of the situation into his hands.

"Madame de Verniat," he began at once, "I have proposals of the greatest gravity, and also, if I may say so, of the greatest desirability."

Madame, whose jaw had dropped a little at the dolorous tone of the friar's voice, immediately leaned forward, agog.

Since the first inception of his fantastic project to save the Yankee's soul Père Miguel had felt shaky, thrilled by uncertainty. Here, however, he felt himself upon sure ground. It was not that he failed to realize the importance of Madame de Verniat to his plans; she indeed was the key to the situation. Madame, not her daughter, had the decision as to her daughter's marriage. The careful and effective handling of the Yankee of course had been a primary essential. The attitude of the girl, on the other hand, since she had nothing to say about the matter, had been of negligible importance, and indeed could have been ignored had it not been necessary to create in her some sort of disturbance which would lend colour to what he told the Yankee. With Northrup well in hand only Madame remained to be arranged—a task, he felt, well within his talents.

"I wish to speak," he continued, "on a matter of no less importance than that of marriage, and of the marriage of a person of no less importance to you than your daughter herself."

At this point Père Miguel was puzzled to notice a faint cooling of Madame de Verniat's expression, as if she had been disappointed in something of which she had momentarily been permitted a faint hope. For an instant the friar tried to analyze this suggestion of a

184

frustration in the woman who would not concede that her youth was gone. But he had to push on in search of fitting expressions for the conveyance of his message; and in the next moment Madame de Verniat's complete interest had returned.

"You must understand," the friar said with a great air of imparting a confidence, "that I am not fully empowered to represent the gentleman whom I represent. Rather let us put it that I wish to apprise you of a situation most favourable to all parties concerned. Of course, of course there is no question in my mind as to the wishes of the young man. Oh, no; of that, I feel I can assure you, I know all. It is only that, if you understand me, the young man is hesitant, he doubts himself, he needs, that is to say, a breath of assurance, from me, for example, in whom, I am certain, without wishing to exaggerate my—my position of trust, the young man places, if I may say so, the utmost—"

"Who is it?" demanded Madame de Verniat.

"A young man of most unusual integrity and ability," said the friar, well aware of the necessity to hedge a bit. "A young man who, if I am not mistaken—and there are many who will tell you, I feel sure, that I am not often mistaken in these things—a young man, as I say, who will go very far. An honour to the finest of Louisiana families, from the viewpoint of those, of course, who see into the heart of things, who can penetrate to essentials, like yourself, Madame de Verniat. An honour, that is to say, to the Louisiana family with whom he shall ally himself—for I must say at this point, and I hope you will not leap to a not wholly favourable conclusion because of it, and I am sure you will not, this young man is not, strictly speaking, a Creole."

"A French—" began Madame de Verniat, delighted.

"Well, no—not French. He—"

"Ah! Spanish, then—"

"No, not Spanish either, in fact, quite not—I mean—"

Madame de Verniat looked exceedingly stupid, and Père Miguel perceived that he was being rushed into disclosures without sufficient preparation.

"After all, madame," he assured her, returning to his air of confidence, "the important thing is not the nationality of a man—" he was astonished to hear himself utter such an absurdity, but he felt it was required—"but his character, his soul, I may even add his—material well being, his general desirability in a family. Take, for example, the Irish, in themselves an uncouth race, in which one is surprised to find the true faith. And yet, in the best Spanish families there is quite a strain of Irish blood—"

"An Irishman?" asked Madame dubiously.

"No. He is, in point of fact"—this with great frankness—"that is, he may be roughly described as—an American."

Madame abruptly jerked backward half a foot, as if he had snapped his fingers in her face.

"Père Miguel!" she exploded, instantly almost beside herself with disappointed shock. "How could you! The very suggestion! An American! *Un Yanqu' perdu!* My daughter! *My* daughter! My own daughter in such a connection! An American! No better than an infidel! A—"

"I assure you," said Miguel with his deepest slow dignity, "I would never countenance a union outside the faith."

"Who—" Madame blew her nose and managed to calm herself a little thereby—"who is this man, this outrageous *Yanqu'*?"

"An outrageous *Yanqu'*? Surely, madame, such a splendid specimen of manhood as Captain Northrup—"

Madame squealed. "Captain Northrup! That boor, that great brute—"

Miguel took as stern a tone as he was able.

"My good woman," he said harshly, "compose yourself! Listen to me!" And so astonished was she by his tone that intermittently she actually did so.

Père Miguel flung himself at his task in a great torrent of words which only his feeling of surreptitious activity kept low in tone. He felt more like shouting as to a multitude, had he not known very well that this would have brought the Yankee crashing upon him, if the Northerner heard enough to gather what was going on. In a small compressed voice he exhorted, he laid down the law, he pleaded; he pointed out the salubrities of the Yankee's character, his excellent commercial prospects (of which, until he extolled them, he had not before heard), the necessity of Northern alliances, the political and social advantages. On and on, in a masterly display of forensics.

Excitable, highly strung up by his own words and his

own effort, it seemed to Père Miguel that he was making the verbal struggle of his life. He fully believed, in that half hour, that he was battling with the devil for the Yankee's soul. Yet it meant more to him even than that; he was talking to save not a single soul nor a simple project, but an obsession. "You fail in everything," Père Antoine had told him; and Miguel fought to wipe out the past. In a peculiar sense Miguel felt as if he were fighting not so much for the Yankee's soul as for his own. The perspiration appeared upon his forehead; his scraggly beard was flecked with foam.

Then suddenly he realized that the faint hypnotized expression that was appearing upon Madame de Verniat's face was not induced by his eloquence but by the growing suspicion that the friar's raised voice could be overheard. And when that had become clear to him Miguel's voice fell away almost in mid-sentence, and for a moment he utterly despaired. All his work, his cherished plans, were stopped abruptly just short of fruition; stopped by a stupid and obstinate woman who was inured to his pleadings because she was armoured against comprehension. The irresistible had met the immovable; and Miguel was hung up on a snag.

But he could not quite yet give up. Drawing himself together he tried a final hold—administering extreme unction, as it were, to his cause. He lowered his voice to a tone of the deepest gravity.

"There are things of greater importance than our trivial ambitions here below," he began. "Mind you I do not say that worldly ambition is not served by this match—it is served supremely, could you but see it. But even were it in every way humiliating, yet there are reasons for it supremely to be desired."

From there—Madame de Verniat, who was always reading surprising implications into his hints, was again according her complete attention—the friar went on to speak of the value of a human soul; of the necessity, sometimes, of tempering the wind to the shorn in order that they might be saved; of the hazard now surrounding the Yankee's soul; of the extreme gravity of shutting a groping soul away from that light of happiness, which was in this case, as he put it, the soul's only chance of salvation.

"I don't believe," said Madame with a snort of conviction, "that Yankees *have* souls."

The little friar sat back nonplussed. It gave his face an inane look, so blank that even in the stress of the conflict Madame de Verniat tittered. The objectionable sound came to the friar as an insult in defeat. He was crushed beneath his disappointment, aghast at the definite frustration of what had become his pet obsession. And now this silly giggle—he was burned with fury. He sprang up and went stamping to the door.

"We shall see, we shall see!" he stammered, fully aware that he had already seen more than enough; and his hand, snatching at the doorknob, missed it twice.

Then, as he got the door partly open, he suddenly checked, and for a moment stood staring, as if temporarily paralyzed by what he saw; then softly he shut the door again, without going through it, and turned to lean his back against the jamb. And Madame de Verniat perceived with curiosity that Miguel had become swiftly composed. A beatific smile slowly appeared upon his face, anomalously decorating features in which the angry flush still glowed.

But he only said: "Think over what I have said, madame, and try earnestly and piously to accord your heart with the will of God."

He shook the latch with ostentation and went out, followed by the mystified Madame de Verniat.

5

NORTHRUP'S IDEA that the girl had been unconscious of him was wrong. Instinctively she knew why he was there, perhaps better than Northrup knew himself. On the gallery she had read bafflement in his eyes, as he had read it in her own. When she had been sent indoors she had been rebellious against a disappointment that she could not have defined. Then, after Madame de Verniat and the friar had likewise retired, Madelon had been possessed by an impulse, in defiance of convention and of her mother, to return to the gallery where the Yankee waited alone. She had lifted her hand to the gallery latch before the purpose was lost, not in fear of her mother, but of the Yankee himself.

So Madelon had retreated, at last, to a far window, and there stood staring moodily out at nothing. And she was pitying herself; for the conventions of the times were not so rigid, nor her own isolation so great, that they could modify for her the angry caged panic that the young feel in the grip of a distasteful restraint. In her ears sounded the hammering of the Yankee's heels as he paced the gallery, his boots bruising the wood. She could sense the faint tremor of the floor under the shock of his stride; it conveyed to her a consciousness of the tall bone-and-muscle mass of this man who she knew desired her, and from whom she was barred, so that she gathered from it a desolate thrill.

Then she heard his pacing stop by the window, and knew as well as if she had turned her eyes that he was looking at her; and she was filled with such a quick fright that she was unable to move. Any human society was an adventure to her, full of unaccustomed panics and forebodings. But as for this strange outlander, whose tall frame and cool eyes disturbed her in ways half understood, the impact of his personality was an experience for which society could only partly have prepared her; yet she was not even this far prepared.

Then the latch burst, and the Yankee stepped into the room; and she turned a white scared face upon him, with her hand at her throat.

If he noticed that he had frightened her he thought it was only the sudden sound of the sprung latch; more likely he did not notice at all. Now that he was within the room his direction left him again. He advanced uncertainly, his face curiously baffled. His eyes did not meet hers, but wandered vaguely about the room, half seeing.

In the middle of the room he hesitated, leaned on the back of a chair, and forced himself to look at her.

"Hello," he said inanely.

It was not until then that Madelon realized the truth— that this man was afraid. The realization was like a sudden flood of light, astonishing her, but bringing with it such a relief as was akin to delight. Immediately, in that instant, she knew that she was not afraid of him, perhaps would never be afraid of him again.

She smiled; and, when he saw that, he came and stood beside her, leaning against the jamb on the opposite side of the window; and this gave her a chance to look at him. This time she was satisfied with what she saw.

Presently he turned to her, making her eyes evade him. He noticed again how fragile she seemed, with, in her face, that suggestion of a hunger. He was close to her for the first time, so close that he could see the delicate blue veining in the lids of her eyes. He was able to decide now what he had better do; for it came over him that had he rushed off to his longboat he would have been a fool.

The Yankee said obscurely, "It seems it has been a long time."

She answered, "Yes," without any notion of what he had meant.

He told her that he was going to sea. "I ought to be aboard now, only I felt as if I'd got to see you before I went. I may be gone a long while, but I'll be back. Don't let 'em tell you I won't be back."

She was silent, and he hesitated. From behind the dining-room door came the steady insistent mutter of the friar's arguing voice, like a fretting sea, cut now and then by the shriller complaints of Madame. Northrup caught the words *"Yanqu' perdu"* and *"cochon du Nord, Américain,"* and a hard spark came into his eye.

"Don't let 'em tell you different," he repeated. "Don't

let 'em tell you anything." He was speaking in poor French, fluent enough, but somehow endowed with a Yankee tang, as if the speech were pure American, even while the words were French. "I'll be back. And if you want me by that time, or anything I can get you, it's yours. You count on me, then, or any time. I go the whole hog or none, that's me. Don't let 'em tell you different."

The sunshine gave her skin the radiance of translucent porcelain; so that although her face was sombre in expression, it seemed alive with light. Her fingers went to her forehead, brushing away a wisp of hair. He caught her hand and held it, cramping the small fingers so that they hurt, as if he did not know they were in his grip.

"You don't know me," he went on. He was talking quickly and volubly—for him. "I'm a tough customer. I'm not used to ladies—people of your sort. At sea I'm all right. Nothing special, none too good. But an owner doesn't need to worry about his hull if I'm master of her and she's at sea. I'm no dancing gentleman. Maybe you won't like me when you get to know that. But that's what it is. And if you don't like me then, that's all right, too. You don't have to worry about that. But if you do—count on me, that's all."

She looked up at him with such bewilderment that he was disconcerted. "Maybe I talk too much," he said. "But, anyway, I guess you understand. I guess both of us know things we haven't said."

She nodded, with her head down; but suddenly she lifted it and looked him squarely in the eyes. All this time he had gripped her hand, hurting it, though it was not true that he had forgotten it was there. As they held each other's eyes he knew without question where he stood, what he wished to do, and what was expected of him now. He dropped the hand and took the girl in his arms. Her own arms hung limp at her sides, but she raised her face; and the Yankee kissed her mouth.

"Count on me. What you want I'll get for you or split wide open. I'll be back. And I'll be thinking about you when I'm gone. Listen. Every night at sea I stand watching the canvas. That's my watch, out on the sea. Hours at a time in the night, watching the canvas. And I'll be thinking about you then. Every night, you think that: I'm standing somewhere back of the wheel and thinking about you during my watch. . . ."

When a door in the side of the room was jerked open by the friar, the girl started violently, but the Yankee did not drop his arms. He would have felt it belittling to jump away as if caught at something of which he was ashamed. Instead, he turned his head with such deliberation that by the time his eyes reached the door it was again closed.

Chapter XIV

1

WHEN THE YANKEE HAD DEPARTED on his mission in the armed schooner *Two Brothers* time passed slowly for Jean Lafitte. He had spent three years in building a

New Orleans ring of speculators who were not only willing, but many of them eager, to pay cash for the irregular Baratarian importations. The clientele that he had developed included many of the most powerful and respected citizens in New Orleans of that day. Southern Louisiana had learned to look to the business acquaintances of Lafitte for no small part of the mercantile luxuries then available.

It was now Lafitte's task to hold in check that ring of buyers whom he had trained to his ways. Only complete failure as agent for the Baratarian smugglers would eliminate Beluche. If Beluche proved successful there was no longer place for the Lafittes in Barataria, and the rich income that they had derived from the traffic of the illegal privateers would be diverted to other hands.

Daily, as the bankrupt days of summer receded, and cooler weather reminded New Orleans of the crops ahead, those business acquaintances of Lafitte became more importunate, more insistently desirous of the cheap merchandise that Jean continued to promise but could not supply. Lafitte's supply of miscellaneous goods, with which he at first was able to appease the more avid, was exhausted. Dominique You, who stood by Jean through thick and thin, had sailed long ago, but had not returned with the loot for which Lafitte prayed. The Captains Marco and Romain Very, whom Jean also hoped to hold against Beluche, had not been in port since before the split at Grand Isle, and for all anybody knew were lost at sea. Men were beginning to believe Beluche's story that the goods of the Baratarians were never again to pass through the hands of the Lafittes.

In those days Jean accomplished miracles of obstructionism. Beluche had the ability to make immediate deliveries; and his prices were unquestionably lower than those of the Lafittes had ever been. Pierre by himself would have been beaten by Beluche in a matter of days. Only the extreme plausibility of the younger brother held the situation against all odds. Men studied his suave confidence and believed what he said against every tangible evidence.

It could not, of course, last for long. After Job Northrup sailed southward, on that errand with which not even his mates were acquainted, a week dragged by; two weeks; three. Almost two months had passed since the night of the quarrel at Grand Isle. The cords of mercantile intrigue were slipping out of Jean's hands, and with them a fortune, a little empire in the subtropic world.

But if Lafitte was in difficulty Beluche was having his troubles also.

2

THE BELUCHE that tramped down the Rue Royale in the morning sunshine of October was no longer a seaman with boots on his lean legs and a handkerchief knotted about his head. The privateer captain now dressed—in New Orleans, at least—in a black suit of plain severity. His coat was not too well fitting; his beaver hat rode a little too far back on his head, and he was inclined to wear his linen one day too long.

Nothing could disguise, of course, his seaman's gait or the weathered and battered bronze of his face; but in the main he was not conspicuously different in appearance from many a Louisianan whose background had never known the turbulence that had made itself a part of Beluche.

On this morning Lafitte was making his way to the shop of one of New Orleans's most successful merchants. The face of that shop was a weathered gray, its windows were little checker-paned bays, and it was marked by no more than a quaintly lettered little shingle. In these things the shop of M. Collard was like its competitors. It differed from most others, however, in that the proprietor was of most aristocratic family; hardly a leading family in New Orleans could evade, even if it had so desired, more or less distinct relationship to the merchant Collard.

Upon this shop Beluche marched determinedly; yet, at its door he wavered, hesitated, and passed on. A half-grown girl—a mulatto probably, though Beluche could not see her face—was bargaining there with a clerk; and on this slender excuse Beluche allowed himself to walk past. There was no aspect of his new calling from which the grim-faced privateersman did not instinctively shrink. With a hanger in his hand he feared no man; yet he could hardly bring himself to open a business conversation or to knock upon a merchant's door. Three times Beluche passed that shop before he forced himself to go stumping in—hoping to the last that M. Collard would not be there.

Collard, however, walked forward to receive him.

The merchant was of thin and distinguished feature, very sharp in the eyes, and with about his mouth a polite unsmiling hardness that Beluche in no way understood. Hardness was known to him; but politeness was full of mysteries. Yet, he was a man who could readily learn.

Grimly Beluche drew from his pocket a scrap of cloth and extended it to Collard without comment. The merchant rubbed it between thumb and finger and held it up to the light. Then he led Beluche into a small room at the rear of the store.

"What cloth is this, m'sieu?" Collard asked. He spoke quickly and nervously by habit, with his words cleanly clipped.

"I wanted your opinion on it," said Beluche. "You are a far better judge of materials than I."

"It is a very good grade of yellow nankeen," said Collard. "It is much used."

"What is it worth in quantity?" Beluche demanded.

"But I am not in need of it, m'sieu."

"I know. I am not trying to sell it to you. I ask your opinion only."

"Ah—as to that I could not say." Without opening the question he wished to convey that a Baratarian price was different from one for goods obtained through more regular channels. "Goods are worth what one can get for them. It varies greatly. I often—"

"Would you say twenty cents a yard was too much for that cloth?"

"Too much—no," said Collard nervously. "That certainly could not be called exorbitant. In certain conditions I have purchased similar cloth for less; in certain conditions I have paid more. In general I would say the price is certainly fair; but I can assure you that I am not at present in need of—"

Collard was troubled. He was reluctant to become involved in dealings with Beluche, fearful both that he might, by deviating from the channels Lafitte had established, ultimately cheat himself, and that he might in some way become openly compromised with an illegal transaction. Lafitte was circumspect in these matters. Yet Collard suffered exquisitely from the thought that others might take profit from him if he failed to keep his ears open or turned Beluche too definitely away.

The privateersman interrupted him. "Then," said Beluche softly, "if twenty cents is fair for nankeen, maybe you'll give me twenty-five for this." From another pocket he drew a piece of paper which he unfolded to reveal a little square of rose-coloured satin.

Monsieur Collard's left eyebrow flicked once up and down, as quick as the snap of a finger or the dart of a thought. In the reflected sunlight from a cobwebby window the bit of cloth shimmered and glowed, rich as translucent wine. Beluche had wits.

"How—how much of this is there?" Collard wanted to know. His voice, trained to ten thousand dickerings, carried a cool indifference, and his gesture as he took the sample in his fingers was disparaging.

"Perhaps five hundred yards," said Beluche.

"I could," said Collard doubtfully, though even Beluche could see that it was not in the man to refuse;

"I could perhaps take a hundred yards, providing a discount could be arranged for."

"All or none," said Beluche bluntly; "a gift, at twenty-five cents."

"But, m'sieu—"

Beluche angered. "My God, Collard! The lives of eight men are in that cloth, two of them honest French privateers! Bear in mind that cloth does not come here without bitter fighting and the smashing of a good ship, Spaniard though she was. There was blood on the decks of that ship when she struck, you can take my word. She bore the best goods out of Marseilles—I can give you her name."

These things were certainly the last that Monsieur Collard wished to learn. He reddened a little. "No, no! I do not impose upon your confidence, m'sieu. The price and the material is all that concerns us here, is it not?" He wished Beluche out of his shop—but the scrap of satin shone like a fabric of jewels. "Well, I will give you twenty cents and take the lot. It is my last word."

Beluche wavered. The final cut in price embittered him, but the actual sales he had closed had been extremely few. He pictured to himself the throng at the Temple. Nearly six hundred privateersmen were now in port. His own three-masted ship was back again, with but little to show except a hundred and twenty-nine men that must somehow be fed; and Captain Marco was back, with nearly as many more. Marco had chosen to swing with Beluche—more of an embarrassment, for the present, than an aid; and La Maison had returned, furious cnough to find no money waiting him. Only Durossac's little *Culebra* had sailed. The rest remained.

Those six hundred were noticeable in the thickened swarms of riffraff on the New Orleans water front, in the knots of loafers in the Place d'Armes, in the conspicuously frequent brawls in the levee grog shops. Yet two thirds of them were always at the Temple, clamouring with an ugly surly insistence for news, for money, for food. Cochrane, Ducoing, and La Maison had sought him for three days, and finally, having cornered him at last, had returned gloomily to the Temple with nothing but promises in their hands. There stood clearly in Beluche's mind a scene he had observed upon his last visit to the island in the swamp: a group of seamen cursing over a meal of soup made of fish heads and the boiled feet of ducks.

"It is positively all I can pay," Collard was telling him.

"All right," growled Beluche. "If you will send a cart to the lower levee road . . ."

3

JEAN LAFITTE called on Monsieur Collard late that day. He joked with the clerks, praised the white beaver hats that were on display, and purchased some trivial trinket in the way of a shirt stud. Collard spoke to him cordially and asked him to the rear of the shop to join him in a touch of wine.

"I could use some really pretty satin," said Collard, shrewdly seeking news that would confirm the astuteness of his purchase.

"There is some very nice red stuff that I know of," Lafitte told him. "It might be just what you want. Unfortunately, a good bit of it is stained by salt water—a loose hatch maybe, who knows?—but I imagine there are a few bolts of it that might perhaps be made to serve if it caught your fancy."

"A satin?" asked Collard; and the peculiar sharpness of Collard's eye told Lafitte that the sale had been made by Beluche.

"Yes," said Lafitte. "I am not handling it. It can be obtained, I think, if you care for it, from this Captain Beluche that you have seen around; I can point him out—but I remember now, we have spoken of him before."

The complete indifference of Lafitte to his Baratarian rival perturbed Monsieur Collard. "I had hoped," said the merchant, "that perhaps you or your brother would be able . . . Our dealings have been satisfactory, M'sieu Lafitte; one likes to deal with those he knows. . . . Could you obtain none of this satin, m'sieu?"

Lafitte glanced keenly at Collard, uncertain for a moment as to what the sharp-visaged Creole was about. He decided that his first guess had been correct and that Collard had already all the red satin he would require. It was Lafitte's position that was being sounded out.

Slowly Lafitte considered, while moodily he studied his glass. For the hundredth time he was estimating the time that Northrup was probably making in the schooner *Two Brothers*; wondering again how soon his envoy could be expected to return, and whether, after all, it was possible for the tall Yankee to be successful.

It was time, he decided, for him to play his final card, gambling everything on Job Northrup's success. It was a matter on which he had not consulted Pierre. Once the step was taken it would not be easy to retrace. Yet, he esteemed that the time had come.

"Could you obtain none of this satin, m'sieu?" Collard insisted. The delicate inflections of his voice eliminated the direct bluntness for which he retained an instinctive distaste.

Lafitte drew a deep breath. "I had a considerable amount of it, m'sieu," he said; and it was pure lying, for no red satin had in any way come into Lafitte's hands.

"But—of course, if other purchasers—I had thought—"

"I sold it to no one, m'sicu," said Lafitte gravely. "That part of the red satin which I owned I burned, in a hidden place in the swamp."

Collard's eyebrow went up and down. "But surely—"

"M'sieu," said Lafitte, "these are secret things. You will understand what I have said if I say no more."

Collard's eyes glittered with a self-protective curiosity. He hastily poured Lafitte another drink. Still, for a little while there was silence between them.

"M'sieu," Lafitte said at last, "I have tried always to be fair with you, and you have been my friend. I am going to tell you what I would tell no other man in New Orleans to-day. . . ."

Before night Lafitte was to tell at least two others the same story, with almost the same words as he cautioned them to secrecy. Yet no one could have detected insincerity in his grave mask now.

"You perhaps know, m'sieu," said Lafitte with a faint smile, "that I have sometimes evaded the United States customs laws: because those laws have been harshly unfair to Creole Louisiana. I look forward to the day when those imperfections in the laws will be ironed out. In the meantime, I have done what little I could that Louisiana should not suffer. That you know.

"You know also perhaps that I have tried to make it possible for the Louisiana French to aid those privateers of France who have been cut off from the waters of the Old World. This, I think, is justice, m'sieu. It is not right that the United States should receive the prizes of Spain, condemned at Havana, yet refuse harbour to the prizes of our France, because no French court of admiralty is available in Western waters. We have never spoken of this; but I think most people have known— including yourself, m'sieu, perhaps. Some of us still, though under a new government, remain patriots of France, as well as of Louisiana. . . ."

Thus, by blurred expressions and an acrobatic point of view, Jean Lafitte contrived to make his operations as a smuggler for pirates and a fence for sea robbers look like services of a double patriotism. His voice grew confidential. "What is little known here, m'sieu, is that almost the last of the French privateer commissions has expired in these waters. It is no longer a question of prizes condemned or uncondemned. Capture without a privateer's commission is piracy, m'sieu. Morally it is the same. But, legally, piracy is an ugly word."

"But—the morality being much the same, m'sieu—

surely the legal machinery—" Collard was not sure just what he was trying to say. "Claiborne has attacked you before now. Some of us remember and appreciate that in those cases you have stood alone, involving nobody for whom it might be—awkward. Louisiana believes in you, M'sieu Lafitte. Surely—the will of Louisiana—"

Lafitte slowly shook his head. He leaned forward and spoke in an even lower voice as he launched upon his great new lie.

"The national government no longer chooses to shut its eyes, m'sieu. I have but just learned that there are investigators in New Orleans to-day, and in places where they are least suspected. The United States has not the power to sweep its waters, nor even the strength of arms to take from us Barataria Bay. Hence they are approaching the matter from an even more regrettable angle. The man who possesses goods illegally captured at sea is liable to indictment as a procurer of piracy, m'sieu."

"Procurer of piracy!" Collard exclaimed.

"Thus, m'sieu, by closing the trade, they hope to make destitute the privateers of our France. . . . Now you know, m'sieu, why I would have no friend of mine buy from me that red satin. Certain materials are going to be sought on the shelves of New Orleans—and that is one of them. That is why I preferred to burn it in the swamp. I could have sold it a dozen times, but—not I, m'sieu."

Except for the scarecrows that Lafitte had set up, which were fabricated of pure fiction, there was nothing essential in what he had said with which Monsieur Collard was not already familiar. Yet because it had been Lafitte's policy never to embarrass his buyers by references to the source of his wares, Collard had become accustomed to leaving certain things tacit. He did not break this custom by expression now.

One question he was forced to ask. "Is this, m'sieu, then, the end of your importations?" There was the hint of a deep financial sorrow in the merchant's voice.

"No," said Lafitte. "This will not be for long. Only, I urge you to wait for my word. This you may assure yourself: when I again bring you samples it will be with the certainty that any risk involved is mine, and mine alone. I think you know, now, that you can depend on me, m'sieu. One does not burn satin—unless one values certain other things more. . . ."

Well, the work was done. When Lafitte had urged that his words to Collard be kept in strictest confidence he went his way with the complete assurance that before the next morning all New Orleans would be smoking with confused rumours of a new and impressive danger to purchasers of Baratarian goods. As a last resort he had turned a new intangible weapon against René Beluche.

No cart from M. Collard met Beluche's lugger that night on the lower levee road.

Chapter XV

1

"BY GOD," said Manault at Northrup's elbow, "the luck's holding! That brig is a fool!" He lowered his telescope and thrust it into his skipper's hands. "Another quarter hour—"

Since dawn Northrup's eye had been upon that sail whose course was converging with their own. She was but two miles off now, standing northwest by north on their port bow, and coming on very fast.

"A Spanish brig, Havana to Pensacola," Manault declared. "Laden with arms and provisions, most likely; carrying money certainly. A piece of luck."

They had now been six weeks out of Barataria Bay. In the matter of obtaining Cartagenan privateering commissions for Lafitte, they had failed, though through no fault of their own; upon their arrival in Aux Cayes, Gutierrez was not to be found, nor indeed any decisive news of the insurrection. They lay a week in Aux Cayes Bay, in hope that the envoy from the revolted province would come; but when at last a vessel from Cartagena dropped anchor it brought word only that there was as yet no revolt and that the restive situation on the Spanish mainland was little changed.

The situation was one partly covered in Lafitte's instructions. "If for any reason you are unable to meet Gutierrez, return." That was all. Northrup, however, was beginning to think he understood this Lafitte. More than once he had availed himself of opportunity to observe, with reactions of mingled admiration and contempt, the manner in which Lafitte systematically kept clear his own skirts, leaving upon others the liability for such illegalities as the trade demanded. It took no very long thought for Northrup to decide that Lafitte's instructions to him were designed with that requirement in view. A careful rereading of the letters to Gutierrez and other papers which he carried convinced him that this was the case. Not a line, not a phrase, was so couched as to implicate Lafitte in a hostile project of any sort, or, indeed, to convict him of so much as guilty knowledge of an anti-Spanish conspiracy.

Lafitte's own letter to Gutierrez, for example: "I have, my dear friend, asked my Captain Northrup to call at St. Johns, in the hope that you still reside there, and that he may convey to you this expression of my continued esteem. Any local information you can give him, of a commercial nature such as might interest the conservative mercantile concerns which I represent . . ."

"Hell," said Northrup. Even the name of his destination was incorrectly stated, so that no one into whose hands those documents might fall would learn so much as the intended location of Gutierrez.

The Yankee regretted now that in his long conversation with Lafitte the present situation had been inadequately discussed. As to the use of the men and guns, Lafitte had been sufficiently clear: "Not the fairest prize must be attacked under any circumstances. . . ." But, Northrup recalled, Lafitte had each time added (with a certain air of vagueness, Northrup thought in retrospect): "For that would constitute a delay."

Since his mission had failed, Northrup supposed delays were now of less consequence. There had been, he thought, a certain amount of intent between Lafitte's lines. And there were those extra men Lafitte had foisted upon him; a heavy fighting crew, hard to keep under discipline, and serving no purpose, unless. . . .

"Northeast through the windward passage," he had told Manault on the eve of their sailing from Aux Cayes. "Thence northwest through the Bahama Channel and into the straits of Florida. If we don't pick up Spanish merchant sail in the Narrow Seas, then there are no Spanish merchant sail."

Round Cape Dame Marie they had sailed, in fair light weather, northward past Cape Maysi, then northwest by west through the narrow waters between Cuba and the Great Bahama Bank. They schooned by night through the then treacherous narrows by Cay Cruz, Manault fighting so shy of the breakers on Minerva Bank that he scared himself half out of his wits by grazing Lobos Cay; then northward by the broad Santaren Channel until the Dog Rocks of Cay Sal told them that they were in the straits of Florida at last. That took them two weeks, yet in all that time they sighted no sail of interest other than a single Spanish frigate, from which they easily slipped away in the dark.

And so on westward, still without raising anything that looked like a prize; until, just south of the Dry Tortugas, seventeen days from Aux Cayes, a bright dawn came out of the sea in time to show them a great wallowing Spanish brig but three miles across the water upon a converging track.

2

Now the vivid blue-green of the warm sea was splashed at its wave tips with the gold of the rising sun. In the west a deep violet haze hung upon the edge of the world; and against this the high-piled canvas of the two-master, no more than a mile away, reared flat and golden, sublimely tall.

She was standing northwest by north across the wind; and the red-yellow-red of the Spanish ensign that had fluttered to her peak told them that if she was not out of Havana bound for the Spanish port of Pensacola, then no man could say who she might be.

"There's money in that brig," said Pironeau to Northrup from the side of his mouth. His eyes glittered. "Every one knows Pensacola's governor has been crying for money these many months. There sails the whole support of a colonial government, right across our nose!"

Northrup said nothing. What the mate said seemed true; but he was not prepared yet to believe his luck. He handed the glass to Manault.

"She shortens sail!" said the big Frenchman after a moment. "She's trying to give us sea room to cross her bow."

After a moment Job Northrup nodded; then called over his shoulder to the men at the four-foot travelling wheel: "Bring her square before."

For a few moments there was heave and haul and stamping feet as the topmen under Pironeau reset the schooner's sail; and for five minutes the *Two Brothers* cut through the stinging cross-chop less steadily, for she hated to run before the wind. Then: "She cracks on, again," said Northrup; "she'll try to cross before us, by God! Bring her to the quarter."

Once more the easy haul of many hands upon the sheets, to the shouts of Pironeau and the pick-up cries of bosun's mates in four tongues. And again the *Two Brothers* picked up her stride and drove heeling and plunging through the heavy cross-chop of the sea. Over the lee rail a man lay retching, miserably sick with the broken heave of the racing ship; and so deep did the vessel heel that the man's hand almost trailed in the sea.

"There's no judgment in her," said Pironeau. "If there was she'd pay off, now, and go before."

"It'll pretty quick be too late for her to try that," said Manault. "Another bell and I'll rake her to hell with the bow swivel if she wears."

"She's well in hand," said Northrup. He raised his eyes to the dizzily dipping crosstrees of the main, where the lookout stood, lashed to the mast, for comfort, by his own heavy belt. Far out at the peak of the gaff crackled the gold-and-crimson Spanish ensign that the privateer had sent up in answer to the signal from the brig.

"Well, you in the lookout?" His voice boomed and carried like a foghorn, easily heard over the shock and wet hiss of the turned seas, the drone of the rigging, and the myriad small plaints of straining cordage.

"No sail, sar!"

"There better not be! Never you mind the Spaniard; it's other sail I want from you. By God, if any cry sail before you, I'll keel haul you till your ribs are bare!"

For all the drive of the privateer and the steady angling press of the Spanish brig, it seemed that for hours the two stood still.

"Take the ship," said Northrup to Pironeau.

Quiet and cool, but with a queer rasping quiver in him just the same, he went down the ladder to see if what he had ordered had been done.

In the semigloom below decks there sounded more audibly the deep, satisfying bass moaning of the schooner's hull, and the hissing steamlike race of the waters under her keel. The officers' quarters, comprising the whole of the narrow skylighted stern, had been perfunctorily rigged as an operating room. Over the table where the officers customarily fed were looped great straps, for there were no anaesthetics, and the straps must serve in their place.

No one was there, but the dirty old man that had stood aside at the companionway to let him pass now followed him down. It was the ship's carpenter, who said he had studied medicine once.

"Is there hot water?" said Northrup.

"In the galley, sir." The old man lied, for he thought cold water upon the wounded good enough and heating it a sissy trick.

From the officers' quarters opened the only entrance to the magazine, a small stuffy hole. The door stood open and here by the light of a horn-glassed lantern a swarthy man was hastily stuffing linen cannon cartridges with powder from a keg, in evident haste to finish and have a look on deck.

Northrup returned to the deck and went aft to the travelling wheel on the flush deck poop. The brig was perceptibly nearer now. His eye ran up and down the deck of his privateer, searching for something to do, eager for work where none was to be found. Forward of skylight and mainmast stood the main swivel, so close to the booby hatch amidships that the muzzle of the seven-foot nine-pounder swung over the hatch itself. The gun was loaded and primed, almost pointed; but it was still covered by its unlashed tarpaulin, that its outline might be disguised: a probably futile measure. Against the waiting gun stood its gunner, a square-set man named Johanness, brother to the Captain Johanness of sea-raid fame; in his hand was the long, drooping, cordlike match, smouldering at the end, its tenuous smoke torn streaking away forward by the wind. At the waist of Johanness swung a black powder horn mounted in silver, looking heavy and bulky, like the man himself.

This gun the men called by various pet names of women, but mostly by the name Ma'm'selle Chérie.

Forward, between the foremast and the runty little windlass, waited Manault's bow swivel, called Long Tom by a tradition drawn from American privateers. This was a long nine in every respect similar to that of Johanness. These two comprised the whole armament of the privateer, the ridiculously small tonnage of the *Two Brothers* permitting not even a stern chaser nor broadside carronades.

On either side of the foremast stood rough wooden cases in which the cylindrical powder cartridges were stacked. Both the forecastle companionway and the booby hatch amidships were battened down; and nailed upon each of these hatches was a rough gridlike rack upon whose slots and pockets the four-inch round shot, greased and polished, lay piled in unnecessary quantity. By the rails were fire buckets, in which the heeling of the ship permitted a little sloshing water; but the open rum keg lashed below the mainmast fife rail was dry. At either rail, opposite fore and main, lay coiled the heavy grappling lines; the thirty-pound, three-pronged grapples now hung by their own hooks upon the rails, to prevent fouling. The most powerful men in the ship were chosen to sling those hooks over the enemy's rail.

But these were details that must be sought by the eye; for the striking impression of the scene was one of innumerable men. There were but fifty-odd, barring officers, but on that little one-hundred-and-ten-foot ship they seemed a massed horde. All along the weather rail they sprawled, their back to the bulwark, their legs before them on the deck. Among them were men of all nations, broad-faced Dutchmen, bird-faced Portuguese, white-headed Swedes, bullet-headed black free-men; men for the most part unwashed and unshaved, with about them the reek of the packed forecastle in which they slept, when the deck was wet, in layered tiers—a smell of spoiled sweat and the peculiar slimy odour of bilge. They were naked to the waist and barefooted, and their heads were bound in handkerchiefs, supposedly to keep their lank hair out of their eyes. Here and there gleamed a bright brass earring, or the dull white stroke of a scar.

In fair weather the sprawling bodies of these men so cluttered the decks that the topmen of the night watches continually stumbled over them, drawing curses and bitter threats. The *Two Brothers* under Northrup was a clean ship as privateers went; but the Yankee never was able to accustom himself to the topheavy mass of her crew. He was used to the hot smother of the tropics in which a portion of any ship's company was always diseased; and he was inured to such minor hardships as the tropic foulness of the waterbutts, which, though freshly watered at Aux Cayes, were already thick with the long white filaments of a peculiar slime and particles of a spongy brown-green scum. But he never quite shook off the feeling of too many men about him, of being pressed in a floating mob.

In the belts of the privateersmen swung heavy pistols and long knives; and their hands fiddled with the short heavy boarding hangers that were to the privateers what the bayonet is to shock troops to-day. Here and there was an ugly long-handled ax; but there were no boarding pikes, for those were defensive weapons, unsuited for coming to close quarters. Only the bosun's mates were standing or allowed to stand. Of these there were no less than eight, nearly one for every six men; privileged bullies who in the forecastle occupied red-painted bunks farthest from the ladder and were permitted the use of knotted rope ends for the enforcement of orders. They were picked fighting men; had there been a ninth outstanding bully in the crew he would have had to be made bosun's mate also.

All others were forced to keep below the level of the weather rail; for though the heel of the ship exposed them to the Spaniard's glasses it was considered important that but few be seen outlined against the sky and the sea. Yet every eye was upon the canvas of the brig. The men were silent, mostly, with a bright glaze of the eye induced by the triple ration of grog, and with flushed faces; yet when they spoke it was merrily and with a waiting eagerness.

It seemed that the two vessels sailed for hours, slowly converging; but the sun was hardly clear of the sea, and at the pace they were making it could not have been long. The brig, after her single effort to let the *Two Brothers* cross her bows, made no further attempt to evade the approach.

"This is a queer thing," said Pironeau.

"Shut your head," said Northrup.

Later Pironeau said suddenly, "Sweet Jesus, how we drag! She'll put us astern! Do you want the spinnaker? Do you want the spinnaker?"

"No," said Northrup disgustedly; and Manault laughed in Pironeau's face.

"As we board," said Northrup, "hold your whole starboard watch on the grapples; Manault will board with the port watch and the gunners. When the lashings are fast, board with your port watch, and not before. Can you remember that?"

"Am I crazy?" snapped Pironeau.

Slowly, slowly, for all her speed, the *Two Brothers* closed in. The sails of the brig grew from flat gold against the sky to great rounded bulges. They could see figures upon her and the curl of the foam from her teeth. She was only a quarter mile away; she was three hundred yards. . . . Manault looked along the line of the privateersmen. A fine pack of wolves to loose, and an easy kill ahead.

"This will be easy, with that fool," said Manault.

Northrup said nothing; there was in him a queer grim dread. He knew that by now the crew of the *Two Brothers* must be visible to the Spaniard's glasses, though they were well below the line of the rail. Yet steadily the Spanish brig stood on.

"Lay her to!"

3

MANAULT LEAPED FORWARD to his bow swivel and hurled the tarpaulin aside. With a great wrenching heave he roughly trained the long nine and stabbed the vent hole with his smouldering match. With a terrific concussion the Long Tom spoke.

The whole length of the *Two Brothers* seemed to jerk with the force of the discharged gun. A sulphurous whisk of smoke blew kiting forward with the wind, and a hundred yards in front of the brig a white spout sprang up, higher than the Spaniard's reaching sprit.

Down from the privateer's peak ran the Spanish ensign, and up ran the French tricolour. All along the weather rail the Baratarians surged up with a great roaring cheer. Manault's gun crew sprang forward; a frenzy of energy made up in part for what they lacked in systematic drill. Without orders they leaped at their work. It seemed that the charge had hardly left the muzzle before the sponge was slammed into it; the vent hole of the gun snorted smoke as the sponge rammed home. Quick hands clapped a powder cartridge into the muzzle as the sponge came out; somebody thrust forward a circular wad, and a huge black shoved in the metal after it—chain shot this time, two of the four-inch iron shot joined with heavy links. No less than four men flung themselves upon the rammer to drive home the charge.

"Easy, you fools!" bellowed Manault. He jammed his priming iron down the vent to break the cartridge and tapped an overdose of powder into the vent from his powder horn; then laboriously swung the creaking turntable to sight upon the mainmast of the brig and stood by.

"By God, she don't strike!" he cried. "Stand clear! If I don't jump the sticks out of that—"

Northrup caught Manault's match arm. "Wait a minute. She sets her mains'l aback, I think."

Pironeau was gibbering at his elbow. "Shall I shorten? Shall I—"

"Hell, no," said the Yankee. "She'll near go aback as we weather and hook. What— *For God's sake get down!*"

Already Northrup had delayed his helm command until it seemed as if the *Two Brothers* would ram. Now below the bulwarks of the brig four gun ports opened like slowly waking eyes, eyes rimmed with paint as red as blood. One after another there were run out the stubby muzzles of the Spaniard's unsuspected carronades.

From the side of the brig a ragged thunderbolt broke, four concussions that for a moment hid her to her yards in a roll of smoke. Under their feet the deck of the *Two Brothers* jumped as if she had grounded on stone, and she reeled to the shock. From the bow went up a hideous outcry, and a great yell, "Stand from under!" came too late for a warning as the foremast crashed in a great dragging wreck of snarled rigging.

"A masked corvette, by the good God!" screamed Pironeau. "Down helm! Cross her stern and rake her with grape!"

"Starn hell!" roared Northrup, leaping aft to the wheel. Swinging as he leaped he sent the weather wheelman spinning, and himself put hard up the helm. "Down under the lee rail! Down, God damn you! Blow down those men!"

With bitter curses and lashing ropes the bosun's mates drove the Baratarians to the deck; and in the next instant a hundred heads showed along the rail of the brig, and there burst from her a great ripping crackle of small arms. The lee wheelman beside Northrup strangled and went down. Three bosun's mates dropped sprawling, and two of the gun crew of Manault.

Slowly the *Two Brothers* swung, so slowly, that it seemed she would ram the Spaniard's quarter; then she slurred, spilled, and lost way as she wheeled at last. A whistle blew upon the brig, and there were shouted commands, and a great rumble of running feet; evidently she had signalled boarders away, for the awaited second shock of the carronades never came.

Now the swivels of Manault and Johanness roared almost together, splintering the high Spanish rail; and from her came the ghastly cry of torn men. Over the din the Baratarians heard Northrup's great voice as he left the now useless wheel: "Stand to board! Grapplers clear! Out hooks! Out hooks!"

Amidships with drawn hanger Northrup leaped upon the rail as the brig towered over them. The driving leeway of the schooner brought her against the side of the brig with an impact that hurled men from their feet. Afterward Northrup thought that he had sprung for the high rail of the brig alone; but in that he had underestimated his men. With the shock of the collision the *Two Brothers* spewed onto the deck of the Spaniard a score of boarders; and of these Manault, at least, was before him.

The leaders of the *Two Brothers*' assault found themselves at grips with a great press of men. At first the defenders, unbalanced by the collision of the ships, were flung back by the sheer shock of the attack; and the murderous pikes, that should have made boarding next to impossible, were never brought into play. For a moment or two the twenty from the pirate covered the decks with the blood of unready and retreating men. Then the numbers closed in, and the Baratarians fought desperately for a moment more to hold their lives against a crush of foes.

What numbers there were against them the fighters could not estimate, though afterward they named a number high enough. But in the sudden give and take in which the battle was to be won or lost it seemed at first as if the men of the *Two Brothers* were defeated. Then Pironeau, fighting like a fiend, sprang into the struggle with twenty-five men more, and the Spaniards gave back.

For three minutes then the men of the Spanish brig fought stubbornly against men gone mad. Slabber-mouthed and mad-eyed, mouthing inarticulate snarls, fighting with an insanity of rage, the men of Barataria swept the Spanish deck. . . .

4

MADELAINE—FRANÇOISE—CÉLESTE. . . . By the light of the near tropic stars the *Two Brothers* limped westward over a still sea.

Far off somewhere toward Havana, lost in the dark, stood the gutted Spanish brig, nursing her dishonour and her wounds. Off there, too, somewhere under the slow-moving hills of salt, nine Baratarians rested with Davy Jones under the sea—if the dead can be said to rest in the company of scavenger sharks and squid. But on the ballast in the *Two Brothers'* shallow hold were stowed eighty cases of Spanish wine, forty heads of Cuban rum, and a great miscellany of boxes and bales such as had appeared, on short examination, to be worth more than their natural bulk. And in Northrup's cabin there were thirty thousand dollars, at a rough estimate, in Spanish gold.

Behind him as he leaned upon the taffrail the cabin skylight existed only in prongs of shattered trash. The foremast was a stump; and the main topmast was gone, snapped off by its own stay when the foremast went by the board. The free run of grog following the looting of the brig left the crew sprawled in windrows all over the full length of the deck; the night was restive with their slobbering snores and with the muttering of wounded men. A man whose leg the ship's carpenter had amputated on the mess table gibbered steadily in the low thick voice of delirium, speaking obscenities half understood. Yet Northrup in his weariness remained detached, as if he had been far away.

He was thinking of Madelon; almost he could see her dark eyes and feel the light soft touch of her fingers upon the stubble of his cheek. Somehow that dark-eyed girl immured in the far swamp was able to reach across all those leagues of sea to make Northrup a stranger to himself, a man to whom all things had turned as freshly new as fields of clover after a Northern rain.

He saw her slender figure against a half-hidden jungle tapestry of blues and greens; the blues as living as peacock sapphires, the greens as lucent as emeralds. Or he saw her in an atmosphere of gay lights that shone through the repose of subtropic nights, with still-lying waters reflecting those lights. Slowly, as slow as the motion of the crippled ship, the bloodshot heat subsided in his eyes, and the pulse in his brain turned cool.

Chapter XVI

1

𝒯HE WEEKS FOLLOWING the departure of the Yankee dragged through the September heat and into October, and as they passed, Jean Lafitte watched his fortunes slowly fade. They were hard weeks upon Beluche, as well: Lafitte's enemy, having at last sold a few bills of goods for the rebellious privateersmen, found himself unable to collect. Against Jean Lafitte's steady campaign of obstructionism Beluche worked patiently, apparently a stranger to discouragement; his perpetual refrain droned or unchanged, keeping his comrades in line: "We have the goods; we have the niggers; no one can beat our price."

The handful of men at the Temple grew to four hundred, to five hundred, to six; few departed, and every week brought in more. A dozen ships now lay idle in the anchorage at Grand Isle. Yet, so far as Jean Lafitte could see, Beluche remained unperturbed. Lafitte's occasional visits to the Temple accomplished nothing. The former boss of Barataria was beginning to understand that after all he had not materials at hand with which to master those dour, obstinate men. It was a grim and soured Jean Lafitte who, in the middle of October, made yet another trip to the Temple through the Bayou des Familles. All this time Lafitte had avoided Madame de Verniat. His passages between

New Orleans and the Temple were now infrequent; and though he still left his horse at the plantation, he had each time gone striding from stable to landing without approaching the house. Twice Madame had sent servants running after him with invitations to coffee, which Lafitte gracefully declined. But, on the occasion of his October journey, Jean's luck failed him in this as it had in all other things, and Madame de Verniat cornered him at last.

"Ah, Captain Lafitte! How fortunate that I happened to be walking on the path! You have neglected us shamefully. I have been so hoping that you would stop in. And now you *must* stop for coffee, since I have caught you slipping past us again!"

"My dear madame," said Lafitte, "nothing would please me more. It is my extreme misfortune that I am needed at the Temple at once. I seriously doubt if there is a moment to spare. I am sure you will understand— matters of business, you know—and you'll forgive me, won't you? And now if you will excuse me—"

"But," Madame de Verniat wailed, "it is so necessary that I talk to you! I am in the most urgent need of your advice!"

Lafitte, who was in no position to have his purse drawn upon, thought he had a good idea of what kind of advice Madame needed. He doubled his efforts to escape.

"Only too happy, madame, to give you the benefit of my trifling experience. But, unfortunately, just at this moment an important ship—" He had already worked past her and was backing away. It was his not very resourceful strategy in a case like this to talk himself practically out of hailing distance, then make a bolt, with a graceful wave of the hand to cover his retreat.

"It's about Madelon," Madame interjected. "Captain, the most frightful difficulties have arisen. You never would have guessed it! I am in despair!"

Lafitte was checked. "What's happened?" he demanded.

"But surely, Captain, here on the path—"

He gave up and walked beside her to the house, while in his ears whimpered the preparatory laments of Madame.

"I hardly know how to speak of it," she told him when coffee cups were at last in their hands. "I am humiliated—but I must have advice. And who am I to turn to but you, our dear friend? *Madelon is in love!*"

Lafitte started. For a moment he held the flattering hypothesis that he must himself be the object of the girl's affection; but he recognized at once that if this were true he would be the last one to whom Madame would turn.

"Well, well," he commented with a deprecating gesture. "I wouldn't take it too seriously. Who is the fortunate young man?"

"I can hardly bring myself to tell you! Such an impossible person. A *Yankee!*"

Lafitte maintained an unbroken polite gravity. "Yes, yes. And which one?"

"The only one I know of," said Madame. "Just to think, I suppose there was only one such person in Louisiana—yet she should pick that one! That abominable Captain Northrup!"

"Dear me," said Lafitte. "I *am* surprised. Well, in that case, I think I should advise—"

"It is half the doing of that terrible little friar," Madame de Verniat rushed on. "Would you believe it, he encourages the atrocious affair in every way. He has hardly given me any peace; between the two of them I shall be driven frantic. He has said the most awful things to me. He has tried to make it a point of religion. He assures me that the Yankee's soul is at stake, that because I show some sense I am trying to destroy an immortal soul. Did you ever hear anything so impossible?"

"No," said Lafitte.

"That is the kind of nonsense I must listen to night and day. Sometimes I think I can hold out no longer. But I will never give in, never!"

Lafitte set down his coffee cup and rose, his hat held inconspicuously in his hand. "I'm very glad you spoke of this," he told her. "I shall see to it that this—uh—undesirable suitor removes himself. You will deny him the house, of course, if he comes back? I really think you will have no real cause for distress. After all, Northrup has been gone for some time; I've no doubt the whole thing would have blown over before this if Père Miguel had not concerned himself. Discourage his coming here, if you can. Or, I can take care of that, too, if you wish."

His manner was deprecatory and reassuring. The profound irritation within him he was able to conceal. There was only a minimum of sentiment in his attachment for Madelon, but he was susceptible to jealousy, nevertheless. That Madelon's attention should turn to the Yankee when Lafitte himself was available was in itself a ground for sufficient annoyance. However, he had other things to think of than Madame's hysterics. He was already reabsorbed in the problem of self-extrication.

"But—" the tears sprang to Madame's eyes at the prospect of being so readily deserted, and she dabbed at them with her handkerchief—"you have not heard all! That is only the beginning."

Lafitte hesitated, resigned himself, and sat down provisionally on the edge of his chair.

"Madelon—Madelon—how can I say it?—she has compromised herself!"

This time Lafitte sat staring at her, while Madame, with a great flutter of handkerchief and smelling salts, burst into tears.

"Compromised?" he repeated at last in a casual voice.

His calmness exasperated her but could not check her burst of words. "Père Miguel has seen her in—in the Yankee's arms!"

Jean gnawed his moustache. His eyes, which she avoided, bored into her. "Anything further?" he asked clinically.

"Good Father in heaven! What are you asking? No."

Absorbed in her own woes she did not perceive that Lafitte was reddening with anger. Although he did not see the matter in the same lurid light as did Madame, he could not prevent the values of the times from colouring his own reactions, and he had invisibly marked Madelon as his own. If another daughter of a family so eligible had been available to him he could have thrust Madelon out of his plans; but it recurred to him now with some force that there was not. She was a necessary material to his ultimate arrangements. It was intolerable that this girl whom he had chosen to bear the name of Lafitte was being pawed over by a Yankee adventurer.

Madame was raving hysterically. "It can't be! I shan't let it be! I shall die first!"

"What is it you want me to do?" demanded Lafitte, his voice full of exasperation.

Madame de Verniat made one of her astonishing turns from the hysterical to the practical: "You have often spoken of arranging to send Madelon abroad. I thought—what time could be more opportune?—I thought, if only—"

The impotent wrath was rising to Jean's head again. He recognized that this of all moments was an expedient one in which to send Madelon to France for the distinguished schooling he wished his wife to possess. Yet that was one more project closed to him by the grit of Beluche. Still—

"I'll see what can be done," he conceded dourly.

Madame poured forth again. "Ah, I knew you wouldn't fail us! You've been like a father to her! What would we do without you! How can I—"

Lafitte got to his feet abruptly.

"And will you speak to her? Tell me only that you will do this one thing more, that you will talk to this foolish girl?"

Lafitte gnawed his moustache for a moment or two more, and he was still able to simulate that reflective air that was his gift.

"Send her here," he decided.

"I'll call her at once!"

"Of course, madame, I'll wish to speak to her alone."

"But—unchaperoned—"

"I think your squeamishness about chaperonage comes late," he told her. "Sit in that window there, if you wish."

"Yes, that is it!" She bustled off.

2

JEAN LAFITTE was aware that his brother Pierre had been unlocatable the night before in New Orleans. What he did not know was that Pierre had been to the De Verniats', and there talked with Madelon.

It was a curious and ironic circumstance that in those days of intense chaperonage and in the face of Madame's open dislike Pierre of all men was the one who had most often contrived to be alone with Madelon. Pierre was at the moment infatuated with Madelon in an unhoping and pained sort of way that would have reduced a more accountable man to the status of a convenience. Madame, for whose society he cared no more than she for his, would have none of him; but Pierre had a bold, haphazard ingenuity of his own.

He had once made Madelon a present of a bird he called the bugler, a magpie-like creature from an equatorial jungle. It had a single whistling refrain of three notes, singularly accurate in chromatic scale. The song always started slowly, as if the bird were testing the pitch; then ran faster and faster, silvery and true, until the bird ran short of breath and ended in an off-key squawk. The bugler had escaped. For a time it had remained near, whistling less and less often, and sometimes at night; until at last Madelon had found it dead. Pierre, after that, had adopted its whistle as his own.

Madelon had heard Pierre come through the dark whistling that refrain perhaps half a dozen times; and she was always struck with the accuracy of the notes, as if the ghost of the bird had returned, and were calling to something that could never respond. Pierre somehow gave the simple notes a mournful inflection, impellingly suggestive of the fore-written, half-defeated destiny of the man himself. In answer to the song of the vanished bird Madelon usually came to her window, and once or twice had even boldly descended alone to the garden.

Upon this night Madelon, hounded almost to distraction by her mother's nagging, had been sitting by her open window in the dark, trying to bring the features of the Yankee close to her again, and hardly able to repress her tears. The inopportune opening and closing of the dining-room door on the day of Northrup's visit had permitted Père Miguel to see that which astounded him, and he had in due course reported his discovery to Madame. Poor vacant-headed Madame de Verniat was given something to occupy her mind at last. As the days stretched into weeks and the weeks into months, the old woman's grievance grew and grew. Her daughter's indiscretion—which was the mildest word she could find for Madelon's submission to Northrup's embrace—seemed to magnify itself in Madame's eyes as it receded into the dimmer focus of the past. Her first hysteria passed in the course of a few days; but it left in its place a routine of importunity that was nearly as bad.

If Madelon could have said, "Yes, I will give him up," life would have been an easier experience in those sultry weeks. But an unexpectedly tough fibre was displaying itself in the girl, who was clinging to her dream with her whole strength. At first she had felt that it would have been disloyal to the Yankee to have denied him, even in expedience; and afterward resistance had hardened into a habit, gathering the full strength of an intrenched defense.

But there were times when the persistent raking fire of her mother's obsession was almost more than Madelon could endure. She longed to run away, to lose herself forever in the friendly muck of the swamp. Every day she watched for the Yankee's return, scanning Smuggler's Bight from the upper windows, listening for the down-rattle of a lugsail at the landing. She had no knowledge of sailing distances or the speed of ships; Northrup had hardly weighed anchor when she had begun looking for his return. But the long weeks had dragged by without any word.

On this night, in which she sat dry-eyed in the dark, it seemed to her that life as it was could hardly go on. She could not remember when food had seemed palatable, or when any daily routine act had seemed worth while.

As she sat by the window she was trying to imagine Job's arms about her, hard and knotty as peeled cypress; as she had imagined them a thousand times since he had left. Those moments with him had been so few, her memories of him were so meagre, hardly glimpsed; and they were getting threadbare now, fragile elusive things, less a satisfaction than a taunt.

Then, as she sat there alone, she heard the whistle of Pierre Lafitte, its cool tinkling notes coming through the trees from the Bayou des Familles.

She heard him coming a long way, whistling at intervals; until presently the tropic refrain sounded directly beneath in the dark. She called down to him in an exaggerated whisper, secure in the knowledge that her mother's windows were shut and swathed.

"Hello!"

"Can—can you come on down?"

She hesitated. Lately she had become somewhat afraid of this big, lurching figure. There was too much repressed, unhappy energy in the man. She had the well-founded idea that some day he was likely to grab hold of her, and she could not stand the thought of that angular cross-eyed face boring in upon her own. It was this very possibility that had made him perversely exciting, before the appearance of the Yankee. Beyond that their surreptitious but unprogressing friendship was based, on her side, upon her warm sympathy for his uncertainties and his bitter consciousness of his crossed eyes. To-night he was a heaven-sent diversion; anything was better than the loneliness of the dark.

Of the two Lafittes Pierre was the man of direct

action. He was the seaman, the cruiser; a good sailing master and a good leader in a fight. On the sea, and there only, he was completely at home; for on the deck of his own ship he could justify himself by dragging into open fight any man who looked queerly at his crossed eyes. In the restraint of shore society he believed himself the object of constant ridicule; and the genius of diplomacy was not in him.

What Pierre did have, and what few ever gave him credit for, was all of Jean's determined energy, with physical force thrown in. His spare angular frame with its awkward lunging stride was capable of a brilliant fighting activity; and with his inclination toward direct action added to this, Pierre was preciously near to being a first-class cutthroat. And yet, in spite of all this, Pierre was a better candidate for the discipline of domesticity than his brother could ever be. In the hands of women he was clay. It is significant that in the end Pierre became a settled married burgher of New Orleans, and was, in fact, raising five children in poverty at the time that Jean Lafitte died in a far place.

Whenever Pierre was with Madelon he was assailed by all conceivable doubts of himself. Even her liberality in coming out to talk with him alone in the dark, which any other man would have dangerously interpreted, he could only explain to himself as a pitying condescension: as if he were not to be considered as other men but more like an impersonal animal. He remained silent for long periods, while Madelon talked in informal monologues, like a child; or else he expostulated with her, trying to get her to see him as he would wish to be seen but could not see himself. At these times his words came in gaspy, broken spurts, huskily whispered, while his fists gestured stiffly about her shoulders, longing to seize her but not daring.

He began such a demonstration as she presently appeared before him in the garden. "You—you—"

"Hello, Pierre."

"Hello. You—you didn't want to see me. If you had wanted to see me you would have said so. Written a note. Why should you want to see me? you say. Who is Pierre? Jean's brother. Crazy-looking brother of that smart Jean Lafitte."

"But—you never write to me, Pierre. I never thought of such a thing. You never wrote to me in your life."

"Why should I write to you? How could I? What would I say? You know what I have to say. You have heard it all. I love you. You knew that before. You have heard it a million times. But I should write you—I should put it down. All right. When I go back I will write it. Much good may it do me. Yes, I know. If it were Jean it would be different, heh?"

"Pierre, you know I don't care anything about Captain—"

"That smart Jean," Pierre insisted. "But let me tell you something. His smartness looks good, but where is it? It will all come to nothing. You'll see what it comes to. And that before long. Men aren't to be fooled always. They're tired of his smartness. He's at the end of his string. I know him. I wiped his nose for him before he could walk. And it'll be me that's buying his dinners pretty soon. I'm different. No, I'm not the smart

234

Jean. But I'm something else—"

"But I tell you—" Madelon tried to put in.

"Something else," declared Pierre, "not so smart and so pretty, but something that will be good when he's gone. You always see me in these frippery clothes. I can't wear clothes, I know that. But I wish you could see—I wish—if only sometimes you were on a— Look here! See this arm. It can break a man's back over a rail. It can, so help me God!"

"Pierre!"

"Oh, I know. That's not what ladies want. A man that can twist a wheel in a gale, somebody men get out of the way of—that is nothing to you. I know. But look— I don't say what I mean. Look here—I can do things. I can get things done. Jean gets rich quick, but I'll live to toss him pennies. Look— take my name, and I'll show you who can whip the world for you! Cartagena is up. Well—Admiral of Cartagena—how does that sound? Cartagena will be a new country, free of Spain. Already in Haiti the commissions are out. I'm going to get out of this and go. I love you. Remember what I say."

Haiti! Her mind, already wandering from that gusty, broken monologue of his, caught the name she had heard the Yankee speak. She hardly knew what it was or where, but it was the place to which her lover had gone. What had happened to him in Haiti? All her discouragement and her longing welled up in a rush. She hardly knew that Pierre was talking, until presently he paused.

Her hands suddenly caught hold of the front of his coat. Instantly his own hand came up and gripped hers.

He leaned toward her, as if the spell that had prevented his touching her was broken, and he could take her in his arms at last. She was startled, but her question rushed out nevertheless.

"What is Captain Northrup doing in Haiti? What's keeping him there? Why doesn't he come back?"

He peered down at her a moment in the dark, then dropped her hands, "Northrup?" he said thickly, as if he had not understood.

She said, "I've watched for him so long; it seems a hundred years."

Pierre slumped. He was not a diplomatist, but he was not a dullard. He saw instantly that through all his passionate discourse her mind had not once listened save in politeness; that a *Yanqui perdu,* not Jean, had beaten him and was possessing all her thoughts. He slumped, humiliated and despairing. But up through the despair his savage anger struck like a knife from under a coat.

"That Yankee?" he said slowly. His voice was curiously like his brother's when anger put all that stuttering and stumbling aside: cool, almost audibly calculating like Jean's. "That Yankee. I suppose he is exactly where he is said to be, exactly where you would expect one of those, a *Yanqu' perdu:* lying around Haiti in a sack with a yellow wench!"

He wheeled his shoulder slowly, meaning to turn his back upon her and walk off like a hurt bull; but the gasp that was torn out of Madelon made him check a little, in surprise. As his face swung toward her she struck him across the mouth with all her strength; then turned and went running toward the house.

The sting of the blow brought him to his senses. He called after her: "Madelon! Madelon!"

She was gone, and he blamed himself. Yet he knew that in a truer sense she had never been with him at all, not even when she had stood before him with those slender thin hands almost broken in his fist.

He plodded slowly toward the landing. Down there among the cypresses he whistled that tropic bugle bird refrain once more, a mournful sort of finale, whistling himself out of her life; and he hoped that she had heard.

3

THE CAPTAIN wished to speak to me?" Madelon stood with hands folded before her in an attitude of resignation. But there was a sulky smoulder of obstinacy in her eyes, none the less. She remained unreassured by the gallant deference of Jean Lafitte's bow.

Jean knew that Madame was listening eagerly behind the pane of the window at his elbow. "Shan't we take a little stroll under the trees?" he smiled; and they sauntered down the steps. If there was a disgruntled movement of the window curtain neither of them looked to see.

Lafitte approached the subject in hand with his typical indirection. No one could have appeared more kindly, more suave. It was the inherent strategy of Lafitte to work by dissimulations; he liked to draw an enemy into compromise by masked skirmishes, and sorties from misleading directions. To oppose a man, he wished first to appear that man's ally.

"I've had a very bad half hour," he said, as if in an intimate burst of confidence. "Your mother is an extraordinarily fine woman, talented in every way, but a little—excitable, don't you think?"

Madelon glanced at him but offered no reply.

He seemed to expect none. He took her arm for a moment, but, finding that unsatisfactory, crossed his hands behind him.

"I can't tell you how much I sympathize with your situation," he went on. "She's told me everything, you understand. I wouldn't want her to know I said this, of course: but I wish to say that I think you are quite right in taking the position that you do."

She looked at him curiously, and found that his face, which was not turned toward her, fairly radiated a sort of serious, wide-eyed innocence. Oddly, this childlike expression, instead of making him look silly, gave him an appearance of extraordinary competence and youthful sincerity.

"You are quite old enough to know your own mind," Lafitte assured her confidentially. "It is absurd that this little discredited friar—and your own mother, for that matter—should persist in treating you like a child. I think you have a most remarkable fortitude to bear up under it at all."

Madelon, in receipt of the first intelligent sympathy she had heard since the Yankee sailed, walked in a daze; it was only that daze, perhaps, that restrained the tears.

"I want you to know," said Lafitte, "that I am your friend. I've tried to—to mollify your mother somewhat: didn't make much impression, I'm afraid, but you can be sure I'll do everything possible to make things easier for you here."

He paused to pick up a twig, which he began tearing to pieces with that slightly exaggerated elegance of gesture that he loved to affect. It sometimes gave him a slightly factitious appearance, like that of a man not quite himself—until those clear gray eyes struck over, creating reality.

"As for Northrup," he went on, "I do not know him well; but I try always to think the best of a man. Especially," he put in, as if impulsively, "since learning of your opinion. I absolutely disagree with some of the other captains that he is unnecessarily treacherous and cruel. Believe me, there are exigencies in his profession, which would undoubtedly explain everything; I wouldn't think anything at all about that side of it. You know him well enough, I take it, to trust that his practices were justified under the circumstances, however they may have looked; there is no need to listen to a lot of miscellaneous captains no better than hims—no better than they should be."

She seemed about to utter a question, but he pushed ahead.

"As for those abominable stories about past affairs, which these people have been dinging at you, you are absolutely right to ignore them. For my part I think they are mostly gossip—purely the evil gossip of old women, and men who think like old women. In any case, the past is past and deserves forgetting. Really—you probably haven't had the chance to observe this, that I have; I should hope you hadn't—the very best families of New Orleans have more skeletons in their closets than you could believe. If I should tell you some of the things I know about the very men that head those families you couldn't possibly believe me. But what am I saying? Such things cannot be spoken of in decency."

He tore at the twig, timing his next remark to intercept hers.

"And as for this story that has just now got about, brought back from Haiti—I want you to know that I discredit it. It's true that his letters have not been perfectly adequate in explaining his long delay"—he depended on her ignorance of sailing distances—"but I have no doubt that he can explain it when he returns. Certainly the delay is nobody's business more than mine, for it is costing me money, and if I am satisfied, I think the rest would do well to keep their mouths shut." Here he allowed a slight look of puzzled uncertainty to come into his face. "I can't imagine why such a story should attach to a man so seemingly—uh—upright in every appearance. Of course, I have known men to make up these tales for their own amusement. Well, in any case—" He appeared to falter.

"What story?" The question came like a cry that she had tried to suppress.

Lafitte looked appalled. "What—what story? What do you mean?"

"What is it? What is keeping him in Haiti?"

"But—but surely—do you mean to say—has no one said—"

"No one has told me anything! Tell me! What is it?"

It was of course beyond Lafitte's power to turn pale;

but his lineaments accurately simulated those of a man who had done so. "My dear girl—if I had for a moment dreamed—if I had suspected—"

"What is it? What has he done?" she insisted in a panic. She had passionately refused to let herself believe Pierre's accusation, but now his words were ringing in her ears. Nothing further from Jean was necessary; he had said enough and more than enough.

Next to his impressive tall force, Jean Lafitte had no asset like his plausibility. He had a genius to delude and deceive; and he used that flair over and over in the exalting of his fortunes by his wits. He had seen men turn back from easily won goals, falter even in certain knowledge that they possessed, before the plausibility of his address; and these encounters delighted him, were the spice of his life.

But for this once, perhaps for the only time in his life, Lafitte found himself appalled by the effectiveness of his own device. The eyes of the white-faced girl were looking at him like eyes of a frightened ghost. Suddenly, as if he had not seen her before, he perceived her slenderness, her frailty; he towered over her as if in truth she were a child. He was swept with a sense of shame. His own words droned back at him—"cannot be spoken in decency—" and in this reaction was a sense of amazement, as if he had been attacked suddenly and treacherously from an unsuspected quarter. The devious method he had used had seemed a logical one to him, and his purpose justified. He had only, after all, set out to eliminate a bit of immature and dangerous foolishness, for the best interests of the girl as well as himself.

But now Lafitte, who was accustomed to the circum-
venting of able and determined men, felt that he had
turned his artillery to the beating down of a child. He
attempted to modify the devastation he had achieved.

"Remember, I am only telling you that nothing need
be believed—that there is nothing in this affair which I
believe myself, or that I attach any importance to. Be
assured, it will all come out for the best. I will leave no
stone unturned—"

He saw that she was not hearing him. Obviously she
did not even notice at what point his voice trailed off
into silence. It was as if she had fainted upon her feet,
with those great dark eyes fixed terribly upon his face.
He bit his moustache reflectively, yet studying her
white face, until he felt it impossible for him to stand
before her an instant longer.

"You'll excuse me now," he mumbled cravenly; "I
must hurry away, for now." He half turned to go
striding off to his waiting lugger. Then he turned back.

"Listen! Listen to me!" He gripped her shoulders and
shook her a little until he thought she was understanding what he said. "Remember this: I am your
friend. There's nothing I'll not do for you. Only depend
on me and everything will be all right in the end."

He took her into the house before he left, cursing
silently the circumstances that had let him into such a
situation. After all, he was able to tell himself, this girl
was only going through one of the disillusions of youth
necessary to all. He could almost regard himself as the
casual passive instrument of an inevitable experience.
For this he savagely blamed Madame de Verniat.

He surveyed the poor lady with a gruff distaste as, just before he left, she tried to learn from him what he had said and what had been the effect.

"Listen to me," he had told her angrily. "I blame nobody but you for this whole affair. I want no more such things happening here. The girl is not to blame, so mind you don't go taking it out on her, either."

It was the first time she had ever heard his voice discourteous. "Oh, good Father in heaven, what are you saying!"

"Mind you listen and find out what I'm saying," he told her shortly. "If you want my help you're going to have to do what I say. You've driven this child beside herself with your silly rantings, you and that scow-bottomed little carrion crow of a friar. I want no more of that, do you hear?"

"Merciful Mother of God, Captain Lafitte—"

"Listen to me! You're going to regret it if I find that you haven't done as I—advise," he said, bearing down ironically on the last word. "I want you to treat this girl decently for a change. And if that half-frocked little scapegrace comes here have him kicked off the place. A fine comfort to her you have been. But now you're going to be kind to her, d'you hear? K-I-N-D, kind. If you know how to be."

He went off in an angry fighting mood, but on the whole feeling a great deal better.

Chapter XVII

1

T HE MILD DUSK was closing down as Lafitte walked into his blacksmith shop on Bourbon Street, but the three negroes still laboured at the forge. The half-naked smiths were visible only as darker, more solid blocks of shadow intercepting the light of the forge fire. A flurry of ostentatious effort was perceivable in their obscure movements as Lafitte came in.

The smithy slaves of the Lafittes were good picked men, skilled artisans of their craft. They made no horse-shoes or wagon tires; only those fragile-appearing trac-eries of iron that still decorate close-leaning balconies in the old quarter of New Orleans. There was, however, no money in this affair—people would pay nothing, those who had nothing to pay setting the price fashion for the rest. And those negro smiths, good and skilled as they were, were deathly slow.

Lafitte hardly glanced at them as he went striding through the shop, picking his way through disordered junk with practised step, and went into the little room at the rear that was the brothers' office. Pierre was standing at the open window, looking out into the little courtyard behind; he looked fixed and dusty, like the few plain chairs, the heavy desk, and the little cabinet that held the drinks. Even the drinking water in the pail on the floor showed a dusty surface where it caught a glint of the sky. Pierre more than anyone else hated that dust, which always reappeared no matter how many times a day the place was cleaned; it had a harsh gritty feel, like the ash-tracked floor underfoot, as if it were the sharp dust of the iron itself.

Pierre glanced over his shoulder.

"Oh, it's you. Accomplish anything?"

"No."

"Knew you wouldn't." Pierre returned to staring into the courtyard. In front of the low plaster-walled slave quarters, a few yards away, a shapeless old negress was peeling potatoes. He seemed to study her with imponderable gloom.

Jean was fumbling with flint and steel, trying to get a spark with materials worn too smooth. As the candle swelled into light Pierre said, "Desnoyers was here this morning."

Jean stared expectantly. "Well?"

"Well what? He's been here about every day. You know what he says. You've heard his song before."

Jean's hands moved again, laying aside the tinder box, placing the bottle in which the candle was stuck. "How long can you hold the ring?"

"Who, me? Hoonh! How long can you? Not a minute. The fools are holding themselves. It's beginning to soak in that it isn't prices we're holding off for. They know, or can guess pretty close, why the hell we can't deliver. And another thing. That clean-up rumour you started has exploded in our hands. A fine piece of work you've done! First you send the *Two Brothers* to get privateering commissions from a nation that doesn't exist.

What do you do then? Start a rumour that the United States has named the uncommissioned privateers pirates and is going to prosecute the receivers of their goods as procurers of piracy. Drivel! The last thing you ever tell is the truth: that the United States wants to overlook the rendezvous at Barataria because it inconveniences Spain. Procurers of piracy, for Christ's sake!

"And how did the rumour work, my smart Jean? They're saying now that it's not the privateering nor the smuggling that Governor Claiborne is so hipped on. They say it's you, and that when the governor's crowd get you cornered you'll pull half the ring into the soup with you. You did a fine thing when you got funny with Claiborne. Half our buyers will feel safer the day you're out of business. And you can thank yourself!"

"If that's so, it's because you've bungled it."

"Bungled? Me? Don't talk to me about bungling. You started that crazy rumour. And you sent our best crew on a goose chase. You—"

"Beluche get his money from Epinay?"

"No. And maybe he won't, and what of it? It's only a matter of days until Beluche gets together with Desnoyers. The whole batch is a bunch of thickheads on both sides, or they'd have got together long ago. But they will. And when they do you're through."

"I? Both of us."

"Me, I'll be glad when it's over. I belong on the sea. We'll soon have an end to sending damned Yankees out in a ship as much mine as yours!"

"You're a fool, Pierre."

"Hoonh! I'm your brother!" Pierre's chief eye stared

back mockingly. The other eye was looking out the window: it peered across the gaze of its mate as if straining to see around a corner, in stealthy alarm.

Jean fiddled with the flint and steel. "That damned Yank," he said, "has been gone nearly seven weeks."

"Yes," Pierre jeered, "I expect he has! And if we see the ship again we're lucky! My God, with what a crew, at that! They'll have him overboard some nice night. I know those bastards. He'll——"

"Romain Very is back. And a fine nasty temper he's in."

"Any prizes?"

"No. He was beaten off by a brig no bigger than himself. A lucky shot knocked down his mizzen. . . . That makes more than seven hundred men in Barataria, nearly all of them at the Temple. They burned that warehouse of ours the other night."

"Anything in it?"

"You know damned well there wasn't. A few kegs of rum. Lucky there was. Otherwise there wouldn't be a stick left standing."

"Well, what are you going to do? Three months without any business! You'll look good when I give you a mate's berth on a privateer. Good and seasick. What are you going to do?"

Jean shrugged. The candlelight gave his skin a weary, sallow cast. He was thinking of that growing angry mob at the Temple, among whom he could no longer appear without genuine physical danger. Lately he had more than once made overtures to Beluche: overtures, that is to say in the Lafitte vein. Jean could be magnanimous, or pretend to be; but it was not in him to admit defeat. To have made the concessions Beluche required was impossible; but he had advanced halfway. Once, for example, he had gone to Beluche with an expression of sympathetic distress on his features: "Look, Beluche, I hear that some of your mob are down to salt horse and suchlike pickings. You and I are opposed, and all that, but I have a sort of duty to these men as well as you. Let me make you a temporary loan for provisions. Or—I'll tell you—I'll take that cloth off your hands—I can get enough for it to stock you up for a while, and next month we'll talk about some arrangement."

"Go to hell," said Beluche.

Nor could he obtain a foothold with the lesser captains, among whom, since Dominique You had left, he no longer had a sincere supporter. There were two or three who pretended to be working with him, but—that everlasting monologue of Beluche's had at last got in its work: "We have the goods, we have the niggers. Nobody can beat our price. Do you think the speculators will go broke to please Lafitte? Hold fast, and we'll soon see where the money has gone!" And now Beluche had added another string to his bow, a monologue like the other, hammered in by endless repetition: "Lafitte is working against us. He pulls strings, he spreads lies. If you starve here it'll be Lafitte's doing. But stick with me—I'll wipe the laugh off his face. And we'll soon see where the money . . ." Those who wavered, he taunted before their friends: "Go on, go lick the boots of Lafitte! That's what he wants—bootlicking dogs who'll cruise for nothing. But mark me!—

soon there'll be no more room for boot lickers here."

Meantime, the goods at the Temple had piled up incredibly; the loot of more than half a dozen merchant ships was stored on that one spit in the swamp. And the crews were piling up with the goods. Captains coming in with their prizes had been unable to put to sea again without money to refit; or else they feared to leave their prize goods unprotected and their interests unwatched. The rising enmity for Lafitte had unified them but could not make them trustful of each other. Where formerly the crews of one or two boats had rested between cruises the crews of ten now seethed and fretted, blaming Lafitte. They quarrelled and brawled among themselves, swearing that somebody was going to answer.

Beluche was close pressed. That refrain of his had done its work, but it could not feed men or manage men unfed. He knew better than anybody else that his leadership had not far to go. Yet he held on; and it was beginning to look as if, after all, he could not fail. The delay Lafitte had caused by intercepting the buyers at the Temple had worked immeasurable damage upon Beluche's cause. But now it was Beluche that held the Temple. The slackness of summer trade, in combination with the wily tactics of Lafitte, had made the disposition of contraband impossible; but that was over. The cotton crop was on the rivers, trade was taking on new life. The speculators were hungry to get back to their profit-taking—and they knew, now, that at the Temple cheap wealth was waiting. The day was close at hand when Jean's subterfuges could keep privateersmen and speculators apart no more.

Lafitte settled deep into his chair, his tongue wandering slowly about his lips, his eyes heavy. He was thinking, "This is the battle of my life. Win this and the other years will surrender." But it seemed to him that he had been saying that since his earliest youth.

"Master mind now in deep thought," Pierre sneered.

Jean's fingers had been puttering about the top of the desk, arranging a couple of dozen gun flints in senseless patterns, but now he struck them aside. The leap of the flints suggested that they could no better have resisted his fingers had they weighed ten pounds a piece.

He said in a reverberant voice, "I'm getting old, Pierre."

"You sure as hell are, Jean," Pierre, chortled. "You just find that out?"

"But not so old as you," added Jean. "You're older."

"Older and tougher," agreed Pierre. "But not so damned smart. I was old when I was twenty-one, and won't be any older when I die. But look at you—you're coming to pieces. Too damned smart, that's your trouble. Look what it's got you."

A dark angry smoke came into Jean's eyes, but he did not reply. Over their silence sounded the dull complaint of hot iron crushed by the hammer's wallop, and the clearer bell note of the anvil.

"What's these papers here?" Jean demanded, rummaging in a drawer.

"That's lists of what's at the Temple. That's what that is." He suddenly came whipping around the table in a couple of big lurching strides. "There's that silk prize. Waldren'll pay a dollar the pound, and glad for it. There's these wool bales—" He went clamouring down the list, naming prices obtainable for items now mildewing in the swamp. "A hundred thousand dollars' profit on those sheets! But you had to dictate to better men than you, the men that brought the stuff in. Where are you now? No place, that's where you are, so damned smart!"

"Be careful who you're talking to," Lafitte growled, his face reddening.

"Who, me?" Pierre shoved Jean's head sideways with a big hand and then went striding and lurching around to the liquor cabinet. "Who am I talking to?" He went off into that irritating falsetto laughter. "A smart fellow, huh?" He poured something into a glass, his hands shaking with his senseless merriment. "Here, have a drink—while it lasts!"

Lafitte did not decline.

2

THAT NIGHT Lafitte walked in black mood about the streets of New Orleans. Over the open sewer gutters hung those lovely balconies from the forge of the Lafitte's, overreaching from either side the narrow streets so that they nearly shut off the sky. Beneath, in the dense shadow, great carriage arches and battened shutters stood lightless, as if everywhere the man were shut out.

He was one of those occasional men to whom even

the suggestion of a restraint was intolerable; a sense of liberty and power were as essential to his peace of mind as to a shark or a gull.

When years before he had arrived in America a penniless adventurer, a new world had opened to him, new in spirit as well as in actuality. Behind him, far behind now, was the peaceful ancient village in which his youth had been spent: a village set in mountain defiles, a small old town that was a centre for shepherds and small farmers. Things were static there. A boy learned the work of his father and lived exactly as his father had lived until he died. None rose from the estate to which he had been born; none hoped to rise.

But the map of the Western Hemisphere was in the making. No boundary had a meaning of any permanence. Nations sent their colours across vast wilderness domains, flung out new frontiers; sometimes to be thrust back, losing a thousand miles of earth in the exigencies of a moment. It was the day of filibusters, adventurers, and dreamers who had no scheme so wild that there was not hope for its consummation. Burr had tried to wrest an empire out of the Mississippi valley, Long and Perry had their eyes on Mexico, a land almost as vast as the whole of Europe. A black man who had been a slave was emperor of Haiti. It was a new earth to whip, a world in which titles and backgrounds were at a discount.

It was Lafitte's tragedy that, having imagination to grasp possibilities and common sense to recognize the absurd, he yet had reached either too high or not high enough—and thus had fallen between two stools. He had a political genius, a dominant and impressive façade, and a shrewd ability to handle men. And he had belief in himself amounting to a passionate arrogance. Yet he never quite shook off the memory that he was a country boy from an obscure mountain defile, of a race that had worked with their hands to little advantage and humble ends. He could have been Governor of Louisiana or sat in the Senate of the United States.

Perhaps he had something of that sort in view. He sought, in any case, the security of eminence, social as well as financial. It was his concealed desire to be looked up to, respected, everywhere desired and received. With sound insight he sought first to amass a personal fortune, believing on rather good grounds that whatever else he desired could be purchased. Unhappily, he overestimated the wealth necessary to his ends. Had he retired from his illegal activities at the end of 1808, and devoted himself to political pursuits, there would have been a different story of Lafitte. But he plunged ahead, seeking to double and triple his gains. In the interim between the days of the embargo and the days of the irregular privateers, he turned to the smuggling of slaves; and thus acquired the unacceptable odour of the blackbirder, which was to cling to him the rest of his days.

He saw his mistake too late. But he was not ready yet to admit his defeat. More wealth, greater wealth, such wealth as could buy and sell the town: that was the means he sought to the old end. Of one thing the embargo of 1808 had convinced him: there was no man in Louisiana who could so skilfully turn a situation to his own profit as Jean Lafitte.

But now even that assurance was leaving him. His resources and his organization were crumbling, and a stubborn bitter sea captain seemed certain to replace him as boss of Barataria. Lafitte was slowly but irresistibly being forced off the board. A sense of helplessness was driving him savage. All he needed, he told himself as he walked the dark New Orleans banquettes, was a touch-off match; any happening from which he could stir up a great factitious dust and smoke. Only let there be confusion once more, and he was willing to gamble that out of it, when the smoke cleared, Lafitte would be found to have emerged dominant. . . .

Presently he was attracted by the singing of fiddles and the rhythmic tread of dancing feet. Jean turned into a carriageway that was open and lighted and climbed the circling stair to the hall above. Whether the dance was private or public he did not know; the saffron lackey at the door, in either case, bowed and let him pass.

The broad hall was a thick pattern of figures, a tapestry that moved and changed. The light from the myriad candles was the colour of champagne; it permeated everywhere, but softly, so that there were no deep contrasting shadows nor bright high lights. The ballroom was a live pastel in which soft patches of colour shifted—apricot, Chinese blue, misty white, and jade.

In the amber light the women were beautiful. Their gowns hung suavely straight from their high waists, making them look more slender than some of them were. Bright filets of silk were twisted into their hair, the darkness of which so contrasted with the satiny paleness of their shoulders; and their eyes were deep and warm, eyes that seemed to murmur through their veiling lashes when they looked into those of a man.

And the men—the shoulders of their coats were darker blocks of rich colour, bottle-green, oxblood, mulberry, or marine blue; but their faces, to Jean Lafitte, were those of common men, such as he had out-witted and mastered many times before. There was no one here that Lafitte deferred to as more intelligent, more suave, or more powerful than himself. He was acquainted with nearly all. Yet they nodded to him coolly, and none came forward to greet him or to engage in trivial conversation. Their eyes wandered away, rather, as if they were looking for someone else.

They were a smug lot as seen through the eyes of Jean Lafitte, valuing out of all proportion their petty social and commercial interests and contemptuously depre-cating the privateers. There were not two among them who could envision the terrorism, the mad valour, and the bloody brute methods that brought them their cheap goods out of gun smoke and the breath of hurricanes. They had not seen, or had forgotten how to picture, the ridiculously small ships of the raiders plunging in the heave of the seas; they never comprehended that on some of the silks they purchased lay invisible blood.

Between Jean Lafitte and these men a barrier stood, as if they were of a different and more valued flesh than he. There were men here who had talked eagerly with him in that dusty room behind the forge, men who had asked favours and who had been glad to offer them.

Sometimes they stopped him on the streets to chat of this or that, glad to know this adventurer Lafitte. Yet here they seemed to feel that they walked upon another plane, as if silk knee breeches could make them different men. He detected an embarrassment in them as they conferred those cool restricted nods: an embarrassment not that they must speak to him but that they could do no more, lest the Baratarian force a presentation to their daughters and their wives.

Lafitte, hypersensitive in the blackness of his mood, felt himself snubbed and flaunted by men whom he held in contempt. He said to himself: "By God, some day I'll make these bastards come fawning." But he no longer believed.

The banks of candles in the chandeliers were burning short. Soon the ball would thin out and end. The fiddles were singing a sadly ringing old royalist song, half begging for battle, half mourning in defeat. He did not know why a mournful tune should make him think of Madelon, who would now perhaps never grace a great New Orleans house in his name. The sense of beaten helplessness became unendurable. Yet externally he remained cool and suave. There was a gleam of an ironic smile in his eyes as he leaned, tall and imposing, against the side of the door; as if it were Lafitte himself who had put that intangible barrier up, because he could not bring himself to be bothered by the thin amusements of these lesser folk.

Afterward he walked, lagging uncertainly, in the neighbourhood of the cathedral. Under the deep arches the ironbound doors were closed; but through the wicket he could see the sprinkled pinpoint lights of tapers before the altar of the Virgin, some yellow, some crimson, as they burned in their glasses. A life-size figure of the crucified Christ hung upon a pillar, silhouetted against the quiet points of flame. Lafitte desired to pray, to cross himself, to kneel; but he could not. It was not consolation that he wanted, but victory, the power to crush, the green light of envy. He turned his back upon the cathedral, wandering off into the graying mist of the Place d'Armes.

Chapter XVIII

1

IT HARDLY SEEMED that Jean could stave off defeat a day longer; yet another week passed without material change before the Yankee returned.

Jacques Durossac's little one-gun *Culebra* came to anchor at Grand Isle two days before Northrup's *Two Brothers*. In the other days Lafitte would have been apprised of the distant sighting of the *Culebra*'s sail as quickly as wind and muscle could bring him word; but so lackadaisical had become the shame-faced remnants of his organization that Durossac was at the Temple before Lafitte knew that the *Culebra* had returned at all.

Jean had been in New Orleans, engaged, as usual now, in the desperate effort to stand off the speculators who had once formed his ring, but who were now ready, even anxious, to trade with Beluche. Upon hearing that Durossac had returned, Lafitte instantly set out for the Temple, meaning by hook or crook to find what news the *Culebra* had brought back from Southern waters.

Jacques Durossac, meantime, having waited a day at the Temple for Beluche to appear, had already set out for New Orleans in search of him. Due to Lafitte's practice of going by horse to the De Verniats' before taking to his lugger, Lafitte failed to meet Durossac, who went all the way by boat. Thus Jean arrived at the Temple to find that his bird had flown; and, having spent an uneasy night on the island, started back to New Orleans by the first light of morning.

All this managed a considerable delay, so that Northrup, of whose arrival at Grand Isle Lafitte had not even heard, set foot on the soggy ground of the Temple scarcely a quarter of an hour after Lafitte had shoved off.

Northrup took no more than five minutes to learn by what a narrow margin he had missed Lafitte. He immediately threw the best of his men back into his longboat and set out in pursuit. The hard-driven oarsmen of the longboat pulled into Mosquito Reach just as Lafitte's lugger was leaving it to the east; and Northrup, by pistol-signalling across the quarter mile of water, induced Lafitte to lay to while he came up.

Lafitte's astonishment at sight of Job Northrup, whom he should have desired to see above all men, was matched by his annoyance at being taken by surprise. What he had learned of the Yankee from Madame de Verniat, too, had its chilling effect; he had indeed already made certain plans for the banishment of Northrup from Barataria, as soon as he had used the Yankee to the best advantage. He therefore had no difficulty in hailing Northrup with the air of a man who has learned of an expected blunder rather than one newly exposed to a possible rescue.

If Northrup found anything lacking in Lafitte's greeting, he was not deterred. He abruptly took charge of both boats, to the poorly hidden amusement of some of the oarsmen.

"SHIP them oars!" he roared as his boat came boiling up. "GET 'em out o' that, you fools, you want 'em sheared?"

Lafitte's port oars were snatched out of the water as if they had touched something hot, and the gunwale of the Yank's longboat came grinding along that of the lugger. Northrup, stepping into the lugger's stern sheets, went on with his own arrangements as if Lafitte had been luggage misshipped in transit. He instantly picked a little spidery man as a weak spot in Lafitte's crew and chose to replace the man with one of his own.

"Here, you Portugee! Get over into my boat. Take his oar, nigger!"

The Portuguese rose half decided, not clear as to what was wanted of him, and an enormous black from the Yank's boat came piling over, half flinging the Portuguese into the longboat with one backward shove of his hand.

"What do you mean, sir?" demanded Lafitte, the blood coming quickly into his face.

"Sure," said the Yankee obscurely. "We got to get

back to the Temple. Snatch your boat out o' there, you! Now, STARB' OARS! Lay into it!" He took the tiller which Lafitte held without so much as glancing at the man, and with one hand forced it down hard. The slim little lugger heeled as she swung about. "Now, all hands! Make 'er jump, now! Here, you, aft' oar, come on with that stroke—you hump-backed?"

"You seem to have taken things in charge," Lafitte commented, managing a dry chuckle.

"Listen," said the Yankee, lowering his voice. "Listen. What I've got to say will take only a minute. Then if you don't want to come back to the Temple for half an hour you can turn and go on and I'll go back in my longboat. Otherwise we'll save time, and at this end it's needed."

Jean Lafitte's eyes lay heavily and coldly upon Northrup; yet he managed a minimum of expression. If the Yankee was prepared to ignore those who might overhear Lafitte was not. He waited in silence for further information.

"I've got prize money here," said the Yankee. "I'm dividing it this morning at the Temple. Ordinarily I would have made the division aboard ship. But you know how these fellows are. Paid off and gone, that's them. I wanted certain materials brought up to the Temple, to turn over to you, before the crew got away. So I held their money up. Now I'm ready to divide, and I'd have done that without you; but when I found out you had only just left and could be overtook I figured you'd want to be in at the final count. That's all."

"Prize money?" said Lafitte almost inaudibly. His

face was still expressionless; if there was a hint of anger in the words it was only in their repression.

"The *San Agustin*, Havana to Pensacola, was our meat," Northrup told him. "Not as rich as I had hoped on sighting her, but well worth the voyage, more than worth the voyage, I should say. There's more specie than cargo; such cargo as there is will be easy to dispose of. The men will wait for their cargo split; it's the specie I'm dividing now. Right now the Temple is asleep. If we look sharp we can have our business over with before the mob comes to life. Personally, I don't like a mob like that watching money passed out. My God, they're lying all over that island like dressed hogs in a half deck!"

"Yes?" said Lafitte.

"You'll want to be in at the split—am I right?"

Lafitte nodded but his lips were pale. So great an anger quivered in his throat that he could not trust himself to speak for a little while. "And the—man you went to see?"

"No luck," said the Yankee. "He ain't there."

"You failed in your mission completely?"

"I didn't fail at anything," Northrup declared. "He wasn't there, that's all. What you figured would happen didn't happen. You missed your guess, that's how it was."

Lafitte's anger choked him, and he turned away his face as the blood returned to his head. Job Northrup was continuing his report.

"I let go anchor at Grand Isle yesterday morning, after standing off and on half the night. But what with finding luggers and transshipping to them I didn't get away from there until pretty near noon and couldn't make the Temple last night. I beached ten miles below, where there's a little dry land, at the edge of the salt marsh, and give the men a rest. This morning we come on before daylight. . . ."

Jean Lafitte was but half listening. A curious transmutation of emotions was taking place within the man; his features seemed to harden like a drying mask drawn slightly off true. His first anger at Northrup's disobedience in attacking a prize when everything might perhaps depend upon the speed of the *Two Brothers* was swiftly lost in a mightier but more impotent wrath as he learned that the Yankee's mission had failed.

Had Northrup obtained privateering commissions of Cartagena success would still have been in the hazard; but Lafitte had looked to that even as a possible turning point in his struggle for Baratarian supremacy. The legalizing of the work of the privateers and the news of open war in the Caribbean were not so unimportant that he could not have magnified them to suit his needs. A hogshead of rum broached before his hut at the Temple, money tossed to the crew of the *Two Brothers* in full view of the camp, fifty drunken bullies shouting, "Lafitte and Cartagena! Lafitte and free gunpowder! Up with Cartagena!" And out of the excitement and confusion Lafitte had hoped to draw such advantages as he needed for the overthrow of Beluche.

That hope was gone. In its place it left—nothing; nothing but the slow dragging days of the deadlock, with Beluche triumphant in the end.

He said to himself: "There is no longer anything for which to wait." If he was to save the situation now, he knew that it must be by his wits alone. Every day, every hour, weakened his position and strengthened the hands of Beluche. At any moment his last hold upon the rich revenues of Barataria might slip from his grasp. His anger faded, and with a sense of desperation he searched his mind for materials with which to work.

"You've been gone a long time, my friend," he said to Northrup; "a long time for a man that has failed."

"Poor wind," said the Yankee. "The *Two Brothers* is faster than I thought and did well to make it so soon. Half the time we had following winds; and she won't run before, not even as good as most schooners. It's her lines. Starting with the first day out . . ."

He went into a compact discourse concerning the sailing aspects of his voyage. His terse descriptions were soon over.

"To-day," Lafitte was saying to himself. "Now. This is the time." But the words were meaningless to him. His problem was a hardened sphere into which he could not set his teeth. The oarsmen were rowing steadily, but the Temple was still fifteen minutes away.

"Where did you overhaul your prize?" asked Lafitte aloud. He was not interested, but under the Yankee's drawl he hoped to find cover for his own turbid thoughts.

Northrup's eyes gleamed. Not even the crew of the *Two Brothers* knew that the capture of the *San Agustin* had been the Yankee's first action at sea. The details were clear in his mind. He could see the *San Agustin*'s pale canvas, only half visible against a dark western sky as the dawn came up to give her away. In his ears was the hiss of the spray as the *Two Brothers* drove heeling through the long rollers. He could hear the blast of the Spaniard's guns and feel the shock of the *Two Brothers* as the unexpected broadside smashed home. By the shattered bulwark were smears and runnels of red. . . . The Yankee's account said nothing of such details.

"We cast her adrift off Loggerhead Key," he concluded, "and she was bearing south-sou'east at dark."

The first direct rays of the sunrise were striking across the Baratarian swamp, throwing curious glimpses of rich colour—blue, green, and red-gold— into a tapestry woven deep behind the cypress trunks. Three hundred yards away, down the ribbon of still water, Lafitte could now see the lugger landing at the Temple. Figures moved there, the forms of Northrup's men. Against the sombre sun-shot tangle the figures appeared in delicately nuanced grays, as if made fragilely of the mist that still hung in torn scarfs over the water.

Lafitte knew that hundreds were quartered in the silence of the wooded island beyond. As many more depended upon such sustenance as they could receive here. A crawling swarm, unmanageable, dangerous, unaccountable; the pack for whose leadership he struggled with Beluche. He stared bleakly ahead, his eyes piercing the growths to where the ancient shell heaps rose gray behind the trees.

"Starn all," growled the Yankee. The port oarsmen shipped their dripping sweeps and fended off the rotten pilings with their hands.

Along the edge of the crude wharf shouldered a score of ragged seamen, silent in the moroseness of early morning. They were not tall men; but, seen from the stern sheets of the lugger below, they appeared to tower enormous, a race of giants, ugly eyed and sullen.

"Gangway," snarled Job Northrup. "WHAT you doin' with them oars?"

The figure of Jean Lafitte stiffened imperceptibly, and his eyes half closed. He had suddenly recognized the weapon that he must use against Beluche. There it lay, ready to his hand—a weapon difficult to wield, as dangerous to the man behind as to those in front.

2

LAFITTE'S ARM was across Northrup's shoulder as they strolled toward Jean's hut, and he was speaking in a low voice into the Yankee's ear. An amiable, heads-together conference it must have appeared to those seamen of the *Two Brothers* who drew back to let them pass.

"Listen carefully," Lafitte was saying to Northrup. "You've gone exactly contrary to my orders. But I won't speak of that now that it's done. Things have happened here since you sailed that have changed everything. I have no time to go into that now. I can tell you only this: I will have need of your persistent help during the next twenty-four hours. If you give it to me without question you are a made man. If you don't, you are finished here—and perhaps I am also."

The Yankee considered, and would have remained silent had he not seen that Lafitte was awaiting a reply. "I'll take a chance," he offered tentatively.

"How much hard specie did you take with the *San Agustin*?"

"Thirty thousand pesos, a little short. Other than that, forty-two kegs of rum; eighty-odd cases of fair wine; two boxes of watches; fourteen cases of—"

"Thirty thousand. Less than I had hoped. Still, with fifteen thousand as the owner's share— You already have it all here, at the Temple?"

"All but the leather and the arms. The *San Agustin*'s swivel guns, of course, I left aboard the *Two Brothers*; the musketry—"

"What I am going to ask you to do," Lafitte went on, "will some of it be difficult, and most of it will seem without any meaning; but bear this in mind: it must be carried out without question. There is no time to be lost; least of all time for explanations. Do you understand?"

"What kind of ruction is this?" the Yankee wanted to know.

"First," said Lafitte, "there must be no division of the *Two Brothers*' money until I'm ready. That will be some time to-night. In the meantime, the money must be turned over to me."

The Yankee turned a hard eye upon him. "Not by a damned sight," said Northrup with conviction.

"I give you my word," Lafitte said, "that I'll not leave the Temple until the division is made. You have sixty men here, I have none. Let them know who has the money, if you wish. In the meantime, we can see that they're liquored enough to be content with the delay. You can say to them that I am awaiting for word from New Orleans in the hope of giving them cargo money also."

"I'll think about it," said Northrup after a pause. "Next?"

"Have you any friends at the Temple? Men, I mean, with whom you would be likely to exchange news?"

"There may be some or there may not. I don't know who's here."

"If you speak to any let this be known: I, Lafitte, have reached an agreement with Beluche. To-night every man in Barataria who has an interest in a prize will receive advance money upon that prize."

"Is this true?" Northrup demanded.

Lafitte looked him in the eye and lied. "Yes. As it happens you are the first to know."

Job Northrup thought he detected a gleam in Lafitte's eye that told him all was not what it seemed; yet he had no logical reason to believe that Lafitte had not told the truth.

"But mark this," Jean went on: "Do not let this out as coming from me. Say only that you are certain that it is true; that money will arrive here under heavy guard and be paid out to-night. Do you understand?"

"Yes," said the Yankee uncertainly.

"There is a bald-headed man asleep in a lugger at the lower landing; his name is Manza. Bring him to me at once. Get your longboat crew at their oars and have a jury sail rigged; they will start at a moment's notice for New Orleans, and two men whom I shall name will go with them. If you have a man you trust—Manault? Pironeau?—bring both to my hut."

Northrup had not proceeded ten strides toward the lower landing before the Baratarian called him back.

"As to that longboat crew that is going to New Orleans," Lafitte said: "send in it only men that you distrust."

"Distrust?" the Yankee repeated.

"How many of your sixty men from the *Two Brothers* would stand with you if there were general fighting on this island to-night?"

"Not fifteen," said the Yankee with a grim smile; "But perhaps those could swing the rest."

"See that those fifteen do not leave the Temple for any reason whatsoever."

"You mean—?"

"Perhaps. Père Miguel would tell you that we are in the hands of God."

A new light came into Northrup's eyes. "This is going to cost you extra," he told Lafitte.

Chapter XIX

1

DUROSSAC AND BELUCHE were alone as they piloted their sluggish craft through the starlit dark of the Bayou des Familles. Durossac, who had reached New Orleans from the Temple only the evening before, had not expected to return so soon, for his cruise had made him hungry for the town. Beluche, too, was undertaking the present journey reluctantly, but for another reason.

In the course of the past few weeks Beluche had been able to dispose of a certain amount of the prize goods that had accumulated in the hands of the privateers—to find that collecting the money was another matter. Day after day he fumed about New Orleans, exerting himself to no result. The business side of the illegal trade, he was learning, was one for which he had neither training nor natural aptitude.

Little knots of empty-pocketed privateersmen had begun to appear on the streets of New Orleans, blustering for free meals and drinks; it was impossible for the captains to keep their crews out of the city, just as it had previously been impossible to keep them on the coast at Grand Isle. These penniless and not too civilized arrivals had begun to attract the attention of the citizens even on a water front which had already been made one of the toughest in the world by American flatboatmen and the spindrift of the seas.

Meantime, the remaining captains at the Temple—there were now fourteen of them, each commanding from forty to ninety men—kept sending Beluche increasingly urgent demands. Latterly some of the captains themselves had appeared in the city, all too obviously seeking an accounting from Beluche. And the old sea dog had been reduced to the ignominious dodging of men properly subordinate to his leadership. Day by day he more bitterly despised the position into which he had worked himself.

Yet he was not discouraged. His everlasting monologue had first of all convinced himself. And he still believed that if he could but keep in hand for a little longer that growing swarm of malcontents in the swamp, victory would be his. Above all, he was hating Lafitte.

Thus matters had stood with Beluche on the afternoon that Durossac found him drinking alone in the back room of a bar. Beluche had been inclined to be taciturn, but Durossac soon brought him out of that. "What's this?" Durossac had demanded. "You've come to an agreement with Lafitte?"

"Not in a thousand years," Beluche replied.

"Then what's this rumour?" Durossac demanded. "The crews are leaving the city like rats out of a fire ship. Six boatloads have started for the Temple to my knowledge. The word is that there will be a division at the Temple to-night."

"Impossible," declared Beluche.

"The rumour is everywhere," Jacques Durossac insisted. "It's being talked openly in the Exchange. Even the captains at the Temple believe it."

"What makes you think that? When you left the Temple yesterday—"

"I heard nothing about it then," Durossac told him. "But there's a man on the water front from Nez Coupé. Nez Coupé has called his men in for a pay-off!"

"That fool—" Beluche raved—"that fool—"

"You'll have to make good," Durossac warned him. "I'm only just in from the sea, but I can tell you this: the crews are in no mood for foolishness. Nor the captains either, for the matter of that. You and I may as well start back for the Temple, Papa Beluche."

"Impossible," declared Beluche again. "I can't toss them a dollar, not a picayune! At least, not to-night."

"Then you give up the fight, you mean?"

"No, by God!"

"It looks mightily," said Durossac, "as if you have your choice. There will be seven hundred men—maybe more, maybe a thousand—at the Temple to-night. What will the captains say to them, with them drunk and wanting money—or trouble—or both? You can't leave us adrift now. Not if you mean to go on. . . ."

They had talked there an hour, Beluche cursing the ill turn of his luck.

"Jean Lafitte is at the Temple," Beluche pointed out at one time during their discussion. "He went there yesterday looking for you; I happen to know that he has not returned. Let him deny the rumour and let him answer for the result."

"I have seen a bosun's mate, fresh from the Temple," said Durossac. "He says he challenged Lafitte with the rumour to his face, and that Jean did not give it the lie."

"Who was that man?" Beluche demanded suddenly. "Manza, the old one with the bald head," said Durossac. "And there were four or five others—"

Beluche slapped the table so that the glasses jumped. "Runners for Lafitte!" he raged. "Manza? I know that man! A snivel-nosed wretch that runs back and forth for Jean Lafitte, bearing tales! I see it now!"

"If you mean he started the rumour himself," said Durossac, "you're down by the head, Papa Beluche. This Lafitte is at the Temple. Would he risk his hide and

271

money in a game like that? No, not him!"

So the argument had gone, Beluche ranting, Durossac happily detached and inclined to be amused. And in the end Beluche had been forced to concede that they must go to the Temple, face the music at all costs.

2

IT WAS NOT SURPRISING to Durossac, under the circumstances, that Beluche was in a black and ugly mood as the lugger slowly yawed her way down the Bayou des Familles. The boat seemed holding back, unwilling to complete her journey; and in the same way, it was obvious, the spirit of Beluche was holding back, uneager to reach the Temple, dreading what the night ahead might hold. Beluche was a brave man who had led more than one close-matched fight upon the sea; but he now found himself at a disadvantage he thought mystifying and unfair.

As for Jacques Durossac—that man was of another mind. He had a happy habit of closing his mind to such unpleasant circumstances as were beyond his control. His inability to liquidate what few prizes he owned did not disturb him. And he optimistically believed that the whole trouble with Lafitte would presently work out into something extremely fortunate for them all, without effort of his own.

The *Culebra* had not enjoyed a thoroughly successful cruise. Off Cape San Antonio she had chased aground one little tub of a Spanish brig and swarmed over her without fight. From this insignificant vessel, which its owners must have supposed beneath the notice of privateers, Durossac took something over four hundred pesos in cash and as large a cargo of cornmeal and salt pork as the *Culebra* could carry away.

In addition to the brig, the *Culebra* had picked up one fishing boat in the Gulf of Gonave. The code of the privateers, as it happened, prohibited the molesting of fishermen; but Durossac made his own codes. From this unfortunate shallop the privateer took ten free negroes of the republic of Haiti, under the pretext that they were illegal slaves. Durossac distributed the negroes among his crew at the rate of one negro to each four men, each four being charged with the duty of keeping their slave busy at useful tasks. Before reaching Aux Cayes one of the negroes had died of certain experiments performed upon him by his four bosses and a second had jumped overboard at sea as a result of misunderstandings not clearly reported. These losses were considered a great joke upon those left slaveless.

However, there had been no mishaps except of a humorous nature; and, with every man of the crew waited on hand and foot by the remaining negroes, they had made Aux Cayes on only the second trial, the first stab at the shore happening to land them in Jacmel Bay. At Aux Cayes Durossac had divided the four hundred odd pesos among his crew—it came out about ten to the man—and they had all got drunk, Durossac with the rest.

Durossac, as was usual, no matter what his fortunes, was well pleased with himself. His men were discontented and getting troublesome about money matters, but, since he had already decided to pay them nothing more, this bothered him very little. He had the fastest boat in a light wind that he had ever seen, and enough powder, salt pork, and cornmeal for one more cruise. He blandly twiddled his good-looking moustache, sucked his teeth, and thought highly of Durossac.

It was almost nine o'clock, and there had fallen a heavy darkness hardly modified by the winding belt of stars above the bayou, when the lugger came into that reach which touched the De Verniat landing. Durossac, straining his eyes through the swamp growth, thought he caught a gleam of candlelight from the house. He was afflicted with a sudden caprice, partly, perhaps, because he was not altogether eager for the moment when he must stand with Beluche before the disappointed crews; but partly, too, because for three days he had been thinking about the girl with whom he had once sat in a tree, upon the De Verniats' swamp plantation.

He was of the opinion, after going over his unique experience perhaps twenty times, that he had neglected a worthwhile possibility here. As he remembered Madelon, it seemed to him that she had combined a certain appearance of invitation with such evidences of good birth and such perfect freshness as he had never found available to him. He was feeling a little annoyed with himself over his failure to follow the matter up. And it was typical of his manner of thought that when he suddenly decided the moment to be opportune for his second call upon the De Verniats he felt no compunction over leaving Beluche idly waiting for him in the lugger at the mercy of the mosquitoes.

He flipped free the snub of the brace, spilling the lazy sail, and went clambering over the thwarts to the bow.

"Be back in just a minute," he said shortly as he sprang to the landing.

"Make it fast," said Beluche. He was savagely trying to imagine what he would say to those waiting men. Busy with his mental acrobatics, he failed to ask what might be Durossac's business here; nor indeed wondered until half an hour later he became conscious that Durossac had not returned.

3

JACQUES DUROSSAC walked leisurely up the path, glad to remember, since he did not get along well with dogs, that there were none at the De Verniats'. A faint fog lay under the trees, so that the substance of the house he approached was at first invisible in the dark air; the lighted windows appeared independent of support, like flat golden screens hung in the mist. Then, as he came nearer, the building took on a black bulk, and the lighted windows began to show a delicately valued depth of detail. Durossac hooked his thumbs into his heavy belt and paused, unwilling to climb the steps to the gallery without a better knowledge of what lay ahead. Then he turned and began to circle the house cautiously, with the hope of ascertaining the exact situation within.

The first figure brought into view, as he strolled,

peering at the windows, was that of Madame de Verniat. She was sitting very stiff and straight upon the edge of her chair; and he saw at once that her attitude was rigidly, stubbornly forbidding. This he considered to be strictly in character, in so far as he knew Madame de Verniat—which he esteemed to be plenty far enough. Here Durossac again wavered, almost ready to withdraw from any situation in which the old dragon was a factor; but on second consideration he strolled on, eager for a glimpse of the girl he had come to see.

He continued his cool reconnaissance; and, as he circled, the interior of the room slid slowly past the window through which he stared, as if the figures, the excessive ornaments, and the heavy furniture were painted on a rolling panorama. Thus there presently came into view a second seated figure, this time that of Père Miguel.

The little friar sat hunched over his knees, chewing his finger nails distractedly. From time to time he rolled his eyes to one side and spoke a few nervous words to some third person not visible to Durossac. A touch of genuine compassion stirred the privateersman as he perceived Père Miguel's uncomfortable situation. After his own single experience with Madame Durossac was prepared to sympathize with anyone so unfortunate as to find himself in that lady's presence.

Sauntering on, Durossac now brought the third member of that inner circle into sight; and he brought up short as he instantly recognized Job Northrup. He had not been aware that the *Two Brothers* had reached port so close behind him, and his first reaction was one of annoyance at finding a disliked rival already on the ground. This momentary exasperation was transmuted into a keen amusement as he studied the Yankee's pose.

Northrup sat braced back in his chair, head forward and hands locked between his thighs. In comparison with the two small people in the same room he looked enormous, a great rocky figure like a gaunt lion, dwarfing even the massive chair in which he sat. But the thing that struck Durossac was the dogged obstinacy that showed in every line of the Yank's lean frame. He might have looked the same had he been clinging to the helm in a hailstorm; even his hair seemed raked back from his face, as if the man were hanging on by his teeth. The caprice of Durossac's shallow temperament found humour in the surface aspects of many things; and now a glitter of mordant delight was in his eyes.

"The expression—on—his—face!" he whispered to himself, and swung a hand to slap his thigh, only swerving the blow at the last instant as he remembered that silence was appropriate to him here. He craned his neck to glimpse Madame de Verniat again. "Give the big bastard hell," he breathed. Still hoping for a glimpse of Madelon somewhere within the room, he wandered on around the corner of the house.

A slim white figure was visible in the shadows ahead. Durossac checked in mid-stride, badly startled; for a moment he was not at all sure that he was not looking at a ghost. Then with a slow disbelief he realized his luck. Madelon was not behind those shut windows, after all, but outdoors, alone in the dark; reconnoitering, pcrhaps like himself.

He stepped back a few paces and began whistling lightly through his teeth, that she might not be startled by his approach. Then he sauntered toward her, his whistle disarmingly casual, too soft to be heard within. He did not permit his gaze to rest upon her steadily, lest she be frightened and run away; instead he glanced idly about him, at the darkness, at the windows, reassuringly at her, as if they were meeting by daylight on a thronged street.

4

HE COULD HAVE SPARED his pains. Madelon was as insensible to the significance of his presence as if she had been drugged. She was staring wide eyed through the window, her gaze fastened upon the Yankee's face. By the dim suffused candlelight from beyond the panes the privateersman thought he perceived a touch of wildness in her eyes. It put him momentarily at a loss.

"Hello," he said at last.

Madelon turned her face slowly. For a moment her eyes looked vaguely puzzled, as if she did not recognize him at once. But she appeared to be without comprehension that it was extraordinary for Durossac to materialize out of the dark, that it mattered whether he was a man or a plant. She half turned away from the window, as if she would walk away, but her eyes were drawn back to it again.

His own glance followed her, and he saw that Père Miguel was now looking out the window, apparently staring directly at him. For an instant he thought that he was observed; then he saw that there was no seeing intelligence in Miguel's eyes. His confidence in the darkness, Durossac assured himself, was justified. Nevertheless, that direct unseeing gaze gave him a queer sensation, as if the eyes of a dead man were upon him; or as if he were himself a ghost through which Miguel unconsciously looked. He remained motionless until the friar looked away, then he grasped Madelon's arm and drew her out of the faint shaft of light.

She let him lead her away with an indifference of which he approved, though it puzzled him so thoroughly that when she stumbled he wondered if by any chance the De Verniats drank much wine. He lowered his head to peer into her face, but in the misty dark he could see only its whiteness, marked by her dark eyes.

They were a little way from the house when she stiffened and swayed dizzily. He threw a steadying arm about her, and she let him support her weight. Suddenly she cried out in a harsh, choked voice, "I hate him! I hate him!"

"That's all right, honey child," he answered. "I ain't very crazy about him myself."

He realized that she did not hear him. Suddenly her shoulders contracted and shook, her hands hid her face, and she began to weep convulsively, silent except for the spasmodic catch of her breath.

"Now, now," he started to say, and was silent, giving it up. He took her in his arms, and she buried her wet distorted face in the ruffle of his shirt. Durossac let one hand stroke her shoulders; then he braced his legs more comfortably, gazed about him, and waited philosophically for the storm to pass.

How long they stood there in that way, Durossac could not tell; but to him, who after all was only biding his time, it seemed that hours passed before her body began to relax and droop in his arms. Her passionate weeping subsided at last, and she stood inert against him, breathing irregularly, her head resting on the damp front of his shirt.

"Now this is too bad," he said consolingly. "Somebody gets swiped in a heap for this, I give you my word for it."

What he said meant nothing to her. He was as removed from her situation and her troubles as if he had been of another world. She could not look to him for help in her grief, nor for so much as a glimmer of understanding. Yet there was a soothing quality in the husky timbre of his voice.

The week that had passed since the separate visits of the two Lafittes had been to Madelon a chaotic nightmare in which she had walked bewildered through a disordered world. The factors of her environment had been simple—inadequate, indeed, to her needs. Nothing in her experience had possessed the significance of her oddly incomplete relationship to the Yankee—a relationship no more than begun but weighted with unknown promise. Almost her every thought since Job's departure had been built around him, for him, or of him. If her new conception of life was distorted and incomplete, it was because her conception of the Yankee was based on insufficient acquaintance with fact. Overnight he had become the pillar supporting her world—a pillar now destroyed.

She hated him with the fury of a swamp animal trapped. Yet when she had heard his voice at the door of their house and realized that he was again near her in the flesh she had forgotten everything in the great leap of her heart, and had run through the house to fling herself into his arms. Her mother had prevented that; and after she had been turned back the chilling memory of what the Lafittes had told her returned. She believed that she wished never to see this man again; yet she had been drawn irresistibly to walk outside that window, unable to deny herself an effort to see once more what he really looked like.

Then she had stood trembling in the cool of the mist, watching his candlelit face. At that moment Job Northrup's expression was grave, and his face was rocky hard, not as if he meant it to be, but as if that were his bred nature, to be cold and hard as Northern rock. She watched his level eyes unconsciously breaking down her mother's hostile gaze, and saw them flick aside at the little friar, not scorning him, but only half considering that he was there. And she felt that this was a man who could not be turned or swerved a hair's-breadth by these people, or by the Lafittes, or by anybody else, that no resistance to him could even rouse him to knowledge that resistance was there.

As she stood there, separated from him by the width of the room, and the darkness, and the panes of glass, she recognized that she loved him still; she thought that she would always love him, that life without him would be bleak beyond all endurance. Yet, even as she knew that, she was recognizing that this face was not quite the same as the improvement upon it that she had carried in her dreams, that this man was one she did not understand and could never understand, a being of a different race and blood, hard and cold and unaccountable. And even while she wanted to be taken in his arms again she believed that what the Lafittes said of him was true, and that she could never belong to him or see him again.

Durossac, appearing out of the dark, had been of no more significance to her than a chair or a tree, against which she leaned while grief convulsed her as if hands from within were tearing her slender muscles apart.

The inner storm that twisted her throat exhausted itself, leaving her limp, and bleak of mind in her despair. She became conscious of Durossac then, and of his arms about her. But she did not tear herself away because it seemed to her that she no longer cared where she was or what became of her. She rested in his arms, comforted by the warmth of his body and his caressing voice. Her only desire was to forget the Yankee, the thought of whom was bringing her an infinite aching weariness and recurring pain. She did not resist when Durossac turned her face upward and kissed her mouth.

This Durossac was a man of certain valuable attributes of his own. The worst possible view of him could not ignore the fact that physically he was the perfect human animal, supple and strong. His warm animal magnetism was as palpable as if an electric force emanated from his sound flesh. Madelon could sense that subtle tingling force impinging upon her own racked exhaustion, like an augury of spring making itself felt in a winter swamp.

It soothed her, seeming to bring back a part of her strength and her desire to live. The fibre of her youth remained hot and demanding; even in her exhaustion a complete resignation was not possible to her. She submitted to his lips, hungrily seeking to draw from them a new enlivenment, a living defense from sorrow and despair.

Presently, when Madame's bleating voice sang out from the window at the side of the house—"Madelon! Mad-e-LON!"—neither of them started, for it came to them dimly, an irrelevant noise in another sphere, until, sounding over and over in the night, it conveyed an insistence not to be ignored.

Durossac was exasperated. He was of the opinion that in this hour, unmolested, he could possess Madelon body and soul. Still, he considered philosophically, that could wait. Perhaps, after all, the interruption was for the best; Papa Beluche could be expected to come storming up from the landing any minute now, and he knew that a loud discussion in the yard would betray Madelon to her mother.

He kissed her once more, long and leisurely; then extricated himself and moved at a trot toward the landing.

Chapter XX

1

THE YANKEE STOOD gazing down at Madame de Verniat, conscious, even in his embarrassment, that Madame looked like a haughtily ruffled hen. That he was painfully unwelcome here was obvious; but he had prepared himself for that. He was glad to be inside the house at all. He was in because the friar had unintentionally admitted him; and the friar himself had got in because Madame de Verniat did not know just how to exclude him.

"I may as well say at once, Captain Northrup," said Madame, "that I have learned of your—your intentions. You are no longer welcome here."

Northrup stood looking at her steadily with a troubled forbearance. When he was tired, as he was to-night, his head hung forward a little, giving it an effect of massy weight, as if it were cut out of rock. It made him resemble a mild-tempered bull, staring at something he could not clearly distinguish.

"So," said Madame uneasily, her cheeks quivering a trifle, "you may as well go."

There was another pause, while Madame fidgeted under that steady stare. Then he said, "Sit down, madame."

It was a politely spoken suggestion, but delivered with such assured expectation of compliance that Madame seated herself before she realized what was done.

Then, instantly, she was on her feet again, hurrying to one of the tall white doors that led to the back of the house. Beyond that door they had both heard Madelon's quick step running toward them over the bare floorings of the anterior rooms. The Yankee thrilled at the sound of those quick footfalls, and took half a step toward the door after Madame; but the door shut in his face. He had the feeling that in another moment Madelon would have been in his arms again and that, whatever might have followed, all would have been well.

He heard the barely distinguishable murmur of Madelon's voice as she answered her mother, and he almost rushed to the door, overwhelmed by the unsuspected strength of his hunger to see her once more. But he remained stiffly immobile, standing his ground. He was a man whose instinct was to build soundly, preferring to break down and crush opposition rather than to overleap or evade it, leaving it alive to attack him again, perhaps from behind. So he stood still, waiting like a foredoomed bull, while his moment of opportunity passed. He recalled that moment afterward, recognizing it for what it was; but not even hindsight could show him that he was born too courageous—or else not courageous enough.

Madame de Verniat returned, of course, alone. What she had said to Madelon the Yankee never knew, but it had evidently been sufficient to its purpose. The Yankee indicated a chair where he wished her to sit; and when he had himself sat down, she hesitantly followed his example. She perched on the extreme edge of a small chair with slender gilt legs; her dumpy figure looked insecure there, as if the bandy-legged contrivance were expected at any moment to collapse. The hovering friar, apparently unable to remove himself, timidly sat down a little distance away.

"I think," said Northrup, "that I don't understand you, altogether."

"One has a right," said Madame, "to choose the people one receives in one's home."

He said, "That's not what I meant."

And she replied, "I think, however, that you understood perfectly what *I* meant."

They were silent again, Madame glaring more and more nervously back into the Yankee's slow gaze. She was approaching the aspect of a frightened terrier who is prepared to die in something or other's defense. These silences were upsetting to her in the extreme. She was glad when Père Miguel, himself appalled by the deadlocked quiet, broke in with amicatory suggestions.

"I think, Madame de Verniat, I think what Captain Northrup is trying to say is, his intentions here were most honourable, most thoroughly so."

The Yankee shot him an inconsequent glance. "That's naturally taken for granted," he said. "I recognize that you don't like me, madame, and I'm sorry to find this to be so. But what I want to say is that Madelon does, and I think she is the one to be considered in this."

Madame drew a breath to destroy this absurdity, but let it pass. "My daughter has had a complete change of heart," she told him. "Other plans are being completed for her. It should not be necessary to say anything further. But if it is necessary I will say that these plans have been carried too far to be altered now, even if I wished them altered."

Another silence, gruelling for Miguel and Madame, which Madame ended by rising abruptly. "It seems to me there is nothing further to be said."

"Sit down," said the Yankee absently. His eyes were in her direction but not focussed upon her, as if he were looking through her at something behind. He was indeed trying to see through to things behind not her figure but her mind, the things behind the situation in which he found himself. It gave him a curiously unperceiving and implacable aspect, as if he were now intrenched in his chair and were not by any resource to be blasted out. Madame would have got up and left him, but she feared that he would then successfully seek out Madelon. She uncertainly sat down.

Within the Yankee was stirring an odd uneasiness, a sense of dread. The statements of Madame de Verniat, whom he thought valueless as a source of truth, had nothing to do with it. It was a sensation that had been growing within him during the last days of the voyage from Aux Cayes. Under it he had become crotchety, uncertain of temper, and hard to please. As it happened this had made easier for him his handling of the tough motley crew of the *Two Brothers*. To those sea-fighters, accustomed to consider themselves part owners in the fortunes of the ship, one hard-driving Yankee bucko was nothing to worry about; but this man they found to be a capricious explosive. They admired him for this, and it made them tractable. The Yankee, unaware of the difficulties of his job, and with his mind only half on his work, recognized no change in himself, but only thought that the strong-headedness of the Baratarian crews had been greatly overrated.

The uneasy dread of an unknown mishap had increased gradually with the days. He had paced the after deck of the *Two Brothers* more watches than his own, swearing at the weather and spitting disgustedly over the rail. Madelon had been forever in his mind. He worried about the influence of the ubiquitous friar and worked himself up over imaginary transgressions by the Lafittes. He was becoming aware that for the first time in his life he possessed something he was afraid to lose.

He had been glad when he had stood before the hostile Madame de Verniat again, in a position at last to come to grips with the obstacles that stood in his way. Madame he did not fear; in the last analysis she presented a barrier that he could, at worst, ignore. Yet, as he sat before her, trying to find ways to show her that she was in the wrong, that uneasy dread was increasing from moment to moment, making him settle more obstinately into his chair, with sullenly tightening muscles. He blamed his growing disquiet upon the nervousness of Père Miguel, who was almost frantically chewing his nails.

"Stop your fidgeting!" he commanded; and the friar's hand dropped from his mouth as if it had been struck.

"I think you're making a mistake," said Northrup to Madame. "I can tell you that my prospects are of the best. I can't see what objection you are finding to this. It may very well be to your best advantage."

"I am the judge of that, Captain Northrup," said Madame frigidly.

"Perhaps you don't know," said he, "that I am the owner of a seaworthy ship. You probably don't; I've concealed that. As it happens, I own the brig *Charles*. She's lying in the port of New Orleans. You don't believe me? I can show you the papers. . . ."

Thus it went, without progress, the Yankee trying slowly to work down the hostility of Madame de Verniat and Madame using her every ingenuity to get rid of this man in any way she could.

And Père Miguel—he was there because he could not bring himself to go away. There was an itching curiosity in this little man, an avidity for the affairs of others which his peripatetic experiences had only served to whet. Nevertheless, those tight silences were becoming more than he could bear. The room was stifling, every window being shut against the mist and the mosquitoes; and there was in addition a sulphurous quality in the silences themselves that made him long for the outer air.

This was his situation when he turned his eyes to the window for that moment in which Durossac, unseen out there in the dark, had looked into his vacant face. Père Miguel had indeed not seen Durossac, but he had seen something else. He had caught a glimpse of Madelon's white dress, wraithlike in the dark mist; and, like Durossac, after a moment's doubt as to the earthly wholesomeness of what he saw, he had recognized it for what it was.

His nervousness increased to a quiver, and once more

he began gnawing his finger tips, the Yankee's command forgotten. Miguel was experiencing one of his rare flashes of insight; for a moment he partly understood what sort of emotion drove that slight fragile girl to prowl in the dark damp under the trees. He wanted to rush out to her, to assure her that he was handling the situation nobly and that everything would be well.

When Miguel looked again, she had moved away, and a new doubt attacked him. Suppose, he thought, that she were in truth distraught and should go wandering off to be lost in the swamp or be dragged under by the suck of the floating prairie? He sat there a long time more, after that, watching the slow meaningless sparring between Madame and the big Yank, until he could endure his imaginings no longer.

"Excuse me!" he blurted out at last and fairly dashed out of the room by the door at the front of the house.

Madame de Verniat and the Yankee looked after him questioningly for a moment, as if they stared at the wake of an unaccounted minor phenomenon; then immediately forgot him.

The Yankee had by this time wrenched the fruitless argument into a discussion of Jean Lafitte.

"I'm not questioning your prospects," he said bluntly. "You know the plantation is worthless as well as I do. Anyone can see that. And you know New Orleans is bankrupt. Now you talk about investments. You ring in the name of Lafitte. All right. I know something about that, too. I don't have ears for nothing. Investments with Lafitte! Yet you say you don't want your daughter matched with Lafitte. Let me tell you something:

Lafitte gets all he pays for and more. What do you think he's buying with these hundred-per-cent. returns on your investment? What do you think you have that he wants?

"I'll tell you what. It's Madelon that he wants. And it's Madelon that he'll get. Except for me. I won't have it. Let me tell you what you're doing with these 'investments' with Lafitte. You're selling your own flesh and blood just like she was a nigger. Just like a stolen nigger, sold by the pound!

"You say I offer nothing. Let me tell you something: Northern men don't buy their women. And they don't stand by and watch their women sold. This girl is mine because she promised me she is. Of her own free will, because she herself wanted it that way. But you want to sell her to this water-front boss because he pays a good price. I won't have it—you hear? I'll put a sticker through this Lafitte before ever I see her come into his hands. . . ."

Jerky sentences, in a dull voice, monotoned by repression. All the emotion of that long voyage was leaking out of him in those short-coupled words, on and on as if inexhaustibly; for if the outlet was small and slow the press of his sullen anger was not the less for that.

He paused at last, passed a hand over his eyes, and looked about him. For a moment, as if he had just come out of sleep, he perceived the paradoxical nature of his surroundings. The French-patterned furniture, the intricately cut and polished brasses, the embroidered antimacassars, were artifacts of another race than his own.

They bore no relationship to his background or the materials of his life. Among them he was as out of place, far more out of place, than he could have been in a grass hut in Burma or in a Singapore seraglio. Job Northrup, product of a far harsh coast, sat in a subtropic swamp, telling a distraught Frenchwoman what he would or would not stand for in the management of her family! Yet there remained clear in his mind the small fragile face of Madelon. . . .

Madame de Verniat sat aghast, hardly able to believe her ears. What she heard was fantastic, incredible. Insult upon insult, crudely delivered—while this out-lander sat unexcited, ungesticulating, with only a surly dark gleam in his eye to indicate that he realized what he said. . . . She was trying to gather herself to spring to her feet, to drive this intruder from her house with such a blast of disdainful imprecation as would be resistless. But she was without words or breath; almost the room swam about her in indignation.

Then suddenly she was whipped out of her daze by a shock of terror that came as the climax to an outrageous nightmare. At the window behind her sounded a sudden violent scrabbling, a fumbling and scratching noise that rattled the pane: and simultaneously the Yankee leaped to his feet.

Père Miguel was at the window; his face was a dim moon lighted vaguely by the candlelight from within and distorted by the vagaries of the glass. They could see that he was wide eyed with some emotion; he gesticulated, beckoning to Northrup, apparently urging him to haste.

Job reached the window in three strides and wrenched it open. It swung outward with a shuddering complaint, almost striking the friar's face. Père Miguel was gesticulating again, vibrating a finger against his lips. Mysteriously, with almost a comic sincerity, his gestures urged the Yankee to silence and at the same time begged him to come forth. Northrup stepped outside.

Miguel seized the Yankee's wrist, and, when they had descended from the gallery, set off headlong into the dark.

"What—" Northrup began.

"Be still!" the friar spat at him. He slowed his pace as they rounded the corner of the house; his feet were silent on the damp loam. He was leading the way cautiously now, to a ragged wall of some rank growth, a great reedy row of sugar cane, or something like. With one hand he gently bent some of the stems and pointed through.

Northrup saw a gray blur of white a little way beyond, a dim brush stroke in the dark, and knew instantly that Madelon was there. At first his eyes made out nothing more, and he would have pushed through the canes to go to her; but the intensity of Miguel's grip upon his wrist warned him of something else and so held him back.

At first his eyes, unadjusted to the dark, made out only that Madelon's upright figure was partially and irregularly obscured; this puzzled him, so that he squinted and swayed his head. Then suddenly he caught the outlines, and instantly what he had not before seen was clear to his eyes. It was like the materialization of some big protectively coloured animal in dusk—one moment an invisible nothingness, the next moment distinct, complete.

Sickened with shock, he saw Madelon's hand, looking white in the darkness, creep up the shoulder of Durossac's coat, and cling. . . .

From that instant a madness filled him; there was a roaring of the sea in his ears, and within him a muddled surge of unknown emotions, as inchoate as an insane gibbering in a score of tongues. As if the poignant memories of things that had never happened were lancing upward at him from the soil. As if old wraiths of apelike ancestors merged their ghosts with his body, struggling with each other for control of it, swaying and twisting it without being able to impart to the flesh messages that were themselves chaos unknown.

He was not in that moment conscious of the environment in which he stood; yet long afterward certain odours, certain sounds and aspects of night shadows could bring back to him the vivid memory of that night as if he were looking back through a chink between the years. There was the faint odour of Père Miguel's beads, which were pressed of rose leaves, fragrant in the damp. It was an odour he had not noticed, and he could never recall its source; but a long time later, in a fit of unexplained wrath, he flung such a rosary into the sea.

And there was the heavy wet-loam-and-cabbage-palm smell of the swamp, the land that was not land and the water that was not water: the mother swamp of soft darkness and dank heat, motionless, lush, prolific; and heavy with an unnamed madness that worked within the body and was strong enough to put the Yankee's woman into another's arms.

He could never endure the bayou country again; the offshore wind never brought him the smell of it across salt water without giving him the sickening sense of being dragged down by muck, unclean. He could not have so hated it if the muck itself had closed over his head, marking him with the fear of death. . . .

Behind him, from the open window around the corner of the house, Madame de Verniat's voice pealed out over and over: "Madelon! Mad-e-LON!"—a grotesque, bleating obbligato to an evil dream. The Yankee saw Durossac kiss Madelon once more, then step away, speaking to her gently before he trotted off into the dark. Northrup recognized Durossac's springy step, and thus for the first time knew who the man was.

He snapped his wrist free from Miguel's grasp, struck the canes aside, and walked unsteadily to Madelon; and for a moment or two he stood looking down at her with a face as blank as if he had gone completely mad. And poor Madelon stood wide eyed, meeting his gaze, the back of her hand pressed against her mouth. He swayed toward her, and she thought that his fist would smash her face. Her hand dropped limp away from her mouth. But he only turned and walked away. His step swished uncertainly for a few moments in the grass; and he was gone, his figure taken by the dark.

The Yankee heard her cry out: "Job! *Je t'aime, Jobee!*" And he increased his stride, seeking the water like a stricken rat.

His rowers were gone, and his boat; but he found a pirogue with a paddle in it; and with this he set out for the Temple, driving it with ragged bubbling strokes.

Chapter XXI

1

𝔉OR AN HOUR a steady booming like that of a devil drum had sounded in the far end of the Temple clearing; from the door of his hut Lafitte could see, two hundred yards away, black shuttling figures about a fire among the live oaks. The free negroes of the crew were drunk, tramping in circles, and hammering an overturned pirogue to flinders with a capstan bar.

But more impressive to Lafitte than the dance of the negroes, which he considered to be foolishness without meaning, was the great number of privateersmen in view from where he stood. All afternoon they had been straggling in, and more were expected before the night was out. From within his shanty where he had sat issuing orders, carefully sending out the rumours and counter-rumours that were to be the undoing of Beluche, he had heard shuffling feet, the mutter of voices, occasional shouts or fragments of song; and he had kept an accurate check upon the number of incoming privateers. Yet the actual sight of them thrust itself upon him with a curious sense of impact.

Perhaps eight hundred men were there, gathered in a

space twice the size of the New Orleans Place d'Armes. The eye could look nowhere without finding them in knots and clusters and drifts, here a dozen, there a score, until it seemed to Lafitte that the island in the swamp was crawling with the crews of the privateers. A shuffling reef of them were scattered in a half moon before the shack of Beluche, where the captains were gathered in conference. Less conspicuously, knots of them hung about his own shanty, there a half dozen in the shadow, there ten lounging in a clutter under a tree. A swarm of them still shifted about the now empty whisky barrels, held by the smell of liquor, like flies; the light of a fire near the barrels high-lighted unshaven faces, red shirts, muscular shoulders wet with sweat. They were everywhere, they were inescapable; they were waiting for something that they were perhaps not going to get.

A small figure stepped out of the shadows and chucked Lafitte's elbow with an importunate thumb.

"I seen to it, Cap'n." A husky whisper.

"What did he say?"

"He looked suspicious as hell."

Lafitte looked down into the little man's face—the ill-proportioned face of a runt, a face too-bright-eyed, a big-nosed face made of yellow oilskin, which excitement had now contorted as if by the drawing of inner strings.

"Did you roll those whisky casks into the mud?"

"Aye, Cap'n! Aye, Cap'n!" The man was too unctuous, too eager to please, of a type at once violent, irresponsible, and servile. He was a tool, though, that

Lafitte could use now, because he fitted the work.

"Anybody see you?"

"No—oh, no, sir!"

"Well, be ready to roll them out again, but not until I tell you. See that you're ready when I want you."

"Aye, Cap'n!"

Lafitte forgot him. That chant of the drums, which he held in contempt, nevertheless had an effect of attrition, beating upon veneers until they fell away like battered bark and let old angers and old desires lie open and dangerous. Thus Jean Lafitte was unconsciously made to think of Madelon, a figurehead of his ambition as incongruously delicate as the carved female figures that decorated the prows of certain ships, their serene rondures bashed by the sea. He thought of her as a possession. A supreme and precious possession, decorating and ordering those other chattels that he was striving to wrest from the illegal trade.

His mood was savage as he stood flicking his glance about this dank unlighted rendezvous in the swamp. Here and there among those waiting ruffians he recognized figures that he knew: Jerron, of Beluche's crew, lank, crooked-faced, with a back so heavily muscled that he looked stoop-shouldered; Sauniac, a one-time leader deposed by his own worthlessness, with a bloated face like a great unclean cat; Joab Saunders, a little Cockney Englishman, so lean that his ribs showed just below his collar bones; and, strolling about alone, a big negro named Mars, with the features of a white man and a skin the colour of a seal.

The servile little man of violence spoke at his elbow:

"Wha' say, Cap'n?"

"Has anyone gone in or out of Beluche's house?"

"No, sir, Cap'n, not as I know of. Well, Cap'n Gambio, he went out a while ago."

Lafitte grunted. He was trying to think how he was going to gain admittance to that conference of the hostile captains; but he was distracted by the consciousness that a hundred or so of the privateersmen were watching him from the dark, curious to see what he was going to do. They were men of nearly a dozen nations and mixtures of those nations; yet no man of those hundreds was a fair example of what his race could produce. Most of them were undersized and ratty siftings from the waterfront riffraff of the world. In common they possessed a single trait necessary to their trade: a recklessness sired by the desire to get something for nothing.

There were few from among those idle crews missing from the Temple to-night. Those who had elected to live by their wits in New Orleans, or those who had straggled off through the bayou country to hunt and fish, were assembled now. A dozen cat's-paws like the little unsavoury man at Lafitte's elbow had seen to that. And the whisky that Lafitte had caused to be poured among them had put them in an inflammable mood.

These were the men with whom he had to deal. Or, rather, with the leaders of these men, the captains now in council in the shanty of Beluche, a hundred yards away. Captains as ugly and inflammable of mood as the men, but more determined, more intelligent, and at least equally reckless. Captains in a dangerous and unstable situation now brought to a climax by the rumours of

Lafitte. It was curious that Lafitte, as he stood looking over that mob, was thinking of the face of Madelon, of a richly furnished house with a gardened patio, and of gentlemen in white stocks.

The tom-tom beat suddenly ceased, for no accountable reason, and the Temple seemed utterly silent. For a moment the living stillness of the swamp crowded in, pressing leaning walls above the scattered throng of men; until into the stillness smaller sounds began to rise again, like the recovery of trodden grass.

The scene took on a new drab reality, the reality of clods of dirt and pistol flints. And suddenly it was borne in upon Lafitte's mind that this gathering of hundreds of fighting men in the swamp rendezvous was extraordinary beyond comprehension. Within a few miles of the city itself was gathered an army of reckless nondescripts strong enough to take the town; an army of scum, a drunken mass of armed men who lived by cannon and battle; while Lafitte, the gentleman, stood here among them, planning to juggle this lethal mob to a merchant's profit, computable in dollars and cents!

He coolly realized that he might never leave this place alive; and he could not deny to himself that he was afraid, that more than any other thing he wanted to leave the Temple, to get his own body clear of the explosion that perhaps he himself could not prevent.

2

OVER NEAR THE SHANTY of Beluche Lafitte perceived a movement among the lounging privateersmen, a sulky shifting aside, as when something moves in deep grass. He saw that Gambio was walking through the crowd before Beluche's shakedown.

Lafitte, eager for a chance to get through Beluche's barred door, went swinging across the clearing, hurrying his stride. He was close at hand as Gambio spoke a word with his mouth pressed to the crack of the door; and as the Italian was admitted Lafitte stuck his foot into the quickly closed opening. Instantly he set his shoulder to the planks, hurled the door open with a quick heave, and stepped inside.

The shanty of Beluche was small, merely intended for sleeping quarters overnight. In a Northern climate it would have been hardly more than a bunk with a door, but the subtropic need for air made people build their rooms larger than otherwise necessary, so that there was room for a table, a number of chests, and places to sit. The floor was of hard trampled earth; the walls were wattled of woven reeds, plastered outside with mud that pressed through in ragged gray gouts, making the walls scabrous. There was no ceiling other than some crooked poles through which the palmetto roof dropped dust and bits of sticks whenever vermin stirred in the thatch.

But it was the men that Lafitte saw, not the room. There were eight of them there, counting Beluche, who sat at the table as if he were the chairman of a board. The rest were disposed about the walls, lounging on the bunks and chests. So small was the room that their feet almost tangled in the middle as they sprawled. They made the den seem crowded, packed; and their bodies heated it, filling it with a hot sweaty reek, thickened by smoke and the odour of chewed cigars.

Lafitte's flicking glance took in the burly figure of Cochrane topped with a head like a rough-squared block, and thick flat cheeks covered with peppery bristle; the broad-mouthed and moustached face of Ducoing, with eyes too bright in deep-shadowed hollows, like a death's head; the great shapeless black beard of Spanish Dick, over which the nose seemed suspended loosely from between hard merry eyes; and the flat face of De Verge, a saffron triangle suspended in the farthest shadows. La Maison was there, sitting somewhat to the left of Beluche on a box; his hands worked at the weaving of a Turk's head at the end of a bit of rope, and he kept studying the job obscurely, with bent head, so that only his prominent nose was visible, like a bit of broken blade.

Lafitte missed three captains that he had expected here; and where the great number of mates and sailing masters were he could only surmise. Some, he supposed, were out there circulating among the sea fighters and wharf scum, hoping either to control a part of them in the event of a crisis or to join whatever faction should gain the upper hand. Some, perhaps, had not been reached, or had been too far away. And a few, he knew, who were hated for having more wits than courage, would have departed by this time, not caring to take the very likely chance of a knife in the back in a general scrimmage.

Lafitte jammed the door shut, dropped the bar, and stood with his back against it, dusting his clothes. He looked ruffled and slightly red in his face.

"You fellows made a bad mistake," he declared before any of the others had gathered themselves to speak, "by setting your gangs to looting my whisky. My God, you ought to know these crews by this time! A few gallons more whisky under their belts and they won't be manageable by you or anybody else."

Cochrane smiled wryly. "Manageable, he says. Manageable, for Christ's sake!"

"You talk like *we* set 'em at it," said La Maison belligerently.

"I've got a pretty good idea about that," said Lafitte, shooting a glance at Nez Coupé.

"We've got a pretty good idea about that ourselves," said Beluche, locking eyes with Lafitte.

Lafitte glared back. "Who started this rumour that I was going to pay off the crews?" he demanded.

Beluche unexpectedly found himself on the defensive. "Who started it?" he repeated.

"Your crews are streaming in here from every direction. What are you going to say to them? What do you expect *me* to say? There's some of you going to sweat for this damned foolishness."

"You bet there are," said Cochrane, "and if you think you—"

"What did you expect to gain by it?" Lafitte continued, directly questioning Beluche. "Oh, I see your game, all right! You wanted a chance to make something by sacking Jean Lafitte. You knew the *Two Brothers* is paying off, so you build up a general riot. Fine, clean-cut strategy! Stir up a general row and hope to pull something out of the confusion!"

"We know nothing about your pay-offs, and we don't give a hoot, either," said Beluche. "What we do know is—"

"Well," Lafitte bore him down, "your game is back-flashing through the pan, isn't it? Let me tell you something: there's men of you here that will never get off this island alive. That mob knows who's here and who is accountable to them. You've put off their divisions until half of them think you've pocketed the money yourselves—you fixed that for yourselves when you smuggled all those bales to New Orleans. You hold them off until they're at the riot point, and all they need is to be got together and a match touched to them.

"Then what do you do? You pass out word they're to be paid off. Without a cent in your pockets, you get them here on a pretext like that. And you set them to stealing my whisky and get them brawling drunk!"

"Who the hell asked you in here?" De Verge demanded unexpectedly from his extreme corner, and there was a general stir and mutter among the captains.

"Shut your head," Beluche tossed at De Verge. He looked grayly tired, but among these lesser captains he retained an appearance of reliability and austerity. It was surprising, Lafitte thought, how capable and sound the man could look.

He spoke in a bitterly menacing voice to Lafitte. "There's a hundred ears within fifty feet. If you're making a play to the mob by coming in here and shouting to be heard all over the camp I know a damned fine cure for that."

Lafitte glanced over his shoulder at the door, pretending that he had forgotten the men outside, which was by no means the truth; he had hoped it would be the others who would forget. He lowered his voice, but went on talking in a hard monotone, directly at Beluche.

"You expect to turn the blame for this off on me. You expect to turn these crews onto me, give them the idea that Lafitte is the one that's held out. You could have got rid of me easier by a knife in the dark any time you wanted to. But the situation has become too much for you, hasn't it? You thought by throwing Lafitte to the wolves the edge would be taken off this mob you can't handle. Well, you spoiled that game by carrying it too far. Why did you tell your men Lafitte had brought money to pay off? They're out there loading up on whisky from my stores. You even told them the liquor was a gift from Lafitte! What maybe you don't know is that they're drinking to the name of Lafitte and ready money. You want to ask yourselves how many of that mob are going to turn on you after I'm down.

"I've got a few thousand dollars here. You know how far that will go in a scramble. I'm just as well organized as you are here. The crew of the *Two Brothers* is out there with the Yankee at their head. Those are men that know me and know my brother; they've never missed prompt division and prompt pay. What will happen when sixty men begin yelling, 'Beluche has looted the division money?' You know."

He shot a glance about. "'Get Ducoing! Hook De Verge!' You can hear them already!"

There had been talking and shifting among the captains while Lafitte spoke, but his low voice had been cutting through the minor buzz. As he paused there was silence. Before Lafitte had forced his way in, the conference had been divided in opinion, some thinking that the rumour of reconciliation and ready money had been spontaneous, others correctly thinking that Lafitte was at the bottom. Beluche had arrived at the Temple far too late to spike the false news that had sent the mob roaring drunk. By then the harm had already been done; and he found Nez Coupé and Jean Ducoing, who fraternized their men, eager to brush over the fact that they had elatedly drunk with the crews, joining in cheers that linked the names of Lafitte and Beluche.

Never had the name of Lafitte been greater anathema than in that conference of captains. They saw now that they should have withdrawn from the Temple early in the day, but they also recognized that the time for retreat was past.

They hesitated, confused by the whiteness of Lafitte's face, and by his two admissions—that he had brought a sum of money to the Temple which he stood to lose, and that he was now in as tight a fix as they.

Lafitte gave a final turn of the screw. "Do you think you can get away from here? You'd like to leave me holding the sack, but you can't. Three or four of you might get clear—and leave the rest to answer. That might be the best plan for you."

A dozen plans for extricating themselves were in the minds of the captains. What they lacked was a knowledge of Lafitte's preparations. They would have been surprised at nothing; for all they knew, Lafitte had an attacking party stationed near the shanty, or ambushed rifles covering the luggers at the landing.

In the momentary interval of silence they could hear the devil drum booming again at the island's end. Beluche turned to Ducoing. "Why isn't Durossac here?"

"He said he was coming," said Gambio. "I tried to haul him in, but—"

"Go out and get him," said Beluche, and Jean Ducoing went out with the grim face and forced step of a man threading through quicksands.

Lafitte clamped a cigar in his teeth and lighted it from the candle by Beluche's elbow; he did not dare trust the steadiness of his hands to raise the flame. Nez Coupé, whose mind worked in simple ways, entertained the hope that he was going to bash out the light, and watched him steadily until he stood back again.

"Look here," Lafitte said; "this boycott nonsense has hurt us all. I've lost the most money by it, but you haven't made anything from it, either. If you want to know what the men think about it, stick your head out the door. I'll call it square if you will. Give me bills of sale on your stuff. I'll pay out to this mob of tarbacks by percentage, as far as I can to-night, and give you notes for the balance. I guarantee you a good price. If you want a way out of this, there it is, and we can go about our business again. You should have learned by this time I'm the only man in New Orleans responsible for cash on the hammer."

"He's wasting our time," growled La Maison, fiddling with the Turk's head.

"I've had your stuff listed for three months," said Lafitte. "I know what each of you has here, and what I can pay for it. Bills of sale for most of it have been ready for weeks. There won't be fifteen minutes' delay after you decide to call off the boycott. I know roughly what each of your crews has coming. Give me your warrant lists and I'll get this thing over in two hours. What about getting back on the sea again? You can't stay here forever."

A curious expression which Lafitte could not explain was in Beluche's eyes as the man at the table studied him. The truth was that Beluche was the only man there who completely understood Lafitte's game. Yet Lafitte recognized clearly that in Beluche lay his chance for success—a more slender one, it now appeared, than he had hoped.

Cochrane broke the silence. "Look here, this son of a bitch stands here trying to make monkeys out of us all. You know what he has the guts to want? He wants to cheat us out of the stuff that better men than him fought for on the high seas. I'm sick of it. I think he started this whole damn business himself. All right, let him finish it. He says he has money. Let him pay it out pro rata, far's it'll go. But if I have my way he gets not a stick or thread of prize goods from me or anybody else!"

"What do you do after that?" Lafitte asked. "I lose about nine thousand dollars split up among your mob. That isn't twenty per cent. of the expectancy of your crews. When are you going to pay the balance, and with what? What will your New Orleans buyers do when they learn that I brought nine thousand dollars to the Temple to advance on goods and was robbed of it? Where are you going? How are you going to shake loose from these crews you've cheated?"

Beluche said, "What we need is time. The first thing is to loosen this jam."

"Your jam is no jam at all," Bill Cochrane insisted. "Stick a gun in his back and stand him up in the door. He has a dozen flunkies within call. Let him send one of them after the money. He can turn it over to us, and we'll pay it out as we damned see fit."

Lafitte sought to ignore Cochrane, playing his next card before, he hoped, the American's suggestion would have time to take hold. His voice instantly sliced through the voices of those who sought to advocate Cochrane's plan.

"I'll do better than that," he said, "to show you that I hold no grudges and play fair with you all. You have no ship now," he said directly to Gambio. "I need a captain for the *Two Brothers*. I'll give you command of her on the usual shares, with the privilege of buying out my share of the first fast vessel that you take."

There was a moment's lull while the captains attempted to evaluate this new proposition from Lafitte, each from the standpoint of his own interest solely. Gambio appeared dumbfounded. "This Yankee—" he began.

"I have other work for the Yankee," Lafitte lied. "Your men are the most fractious and unmanageable out there, because they have no hope of pay and damned little of employment. Well, you take out the

Two Brothers for me, and I'll advance ten dollars to each man to-night, to be taken out of their shares on your first prize."

Gambio stared, nonplussed by Lafitte's apparent change of ground. What stopped his mental processes, what confused them all, was the apparent businesslike nonchalance of Lafitte. Except for the faint grayness of his face the man did not seem to comprehend that he stood in a position of hazard, that they all were in a precarious place. He seemed dealing as he always dealt, in terms of dollars and cents, with no other factors in his mind. They were men avid for those same dollars and cents, accustomed to risk their lives for profit, but they were not built to understand the cool preoccupation of Lafitte.

De Verge pushed his sallow, broad face forward into the light.

"You sell us out now," he growled across at Gambio, "and, by God—"

Other voices were striking in, dominated by Cochrane's heavy bass: "There ain't any problem here, you damned fools; this bastard stands here unarmed, trying to dictate what we do and what we don't. What are you, a lot of old women? Stick a gun in his back."

Afterward Lafitte remembered that moment in terms of insignificant and disconnected things: the liquid course of a drop of grease, twisting down the bottle in which the candle was stuck; the obscene waving legs of a centipede three inches long that fell on its back beside Beluche's hand from the poles above. Minute details fixed themselves in his mind with unnatural clarity, while the dimly lighted faces remained vague; and as if the walls were the ghosts of walls he was acutely aware of sounds and movements outside, as if the eight hundred without were each of them tangibly represented in his consciousness.

It was Lafitte, not Cochrane, who was ignored. They had been too long under strain without action; the course of direct result appealed to them as a release.

Beluche rasped, "Make up your minds. You haven't got all night." And over the voices Cochrane roared, "You yellow swamp puppies, what are you waiting for?"

Nez Coupé leaped to his feet, jerking his pistol out of his sash; it swung heavy in his hand, half as long as his arm. And as he rose five others came to their feet. Their shadows surged up the walls behind them, as if each candlelit figure were backed by a dark ghostly djinn three times the size of himself.

Nez Coupé stepped so close to Lafitte that he almost trod on the tall man's boots and jammed the long pistol into Lafitte's side.

"You get that money here," said Bill Cochrane to Lafitte. "We'll open that door, and you'll stand in it. Say what you please to who you please. Nez Coupé, give him the gun in his back. The first off-colour word he says blow his spine in two. You, Lafitte, we'd as soon see you dead as not. Sooner, by God! Think of that with the iron against the back of your pretty coat. All right! Somebody open the door!"

Lafitte was white to the lips. The jab of Nez Coupé's gun muzzle sent a reflex jerk over his whole body, but he did not shift his weight.

"Don't trouble yourselves," he said. "You'll get nothing on a basis like that."

De Verge snarled, "We'll see if we won't! Let him have the butt if he wants it!"

"Turn him to face the door," said La Maison.

Lafitte, without unhooking his thumbs from the arm-holes of his vest, let his head droop sideways as if in a weariness of contempt. He saw that Cochrane was half checked, made uncertain by Lafitte's lack of reaction.

"How about a knife?" Nez demanded of Cochrane. "An inch of steel—"

Lafitte dropped his eyes to Nez Coupé's gun. He seemed to smile drily. "Put a flint in that, you little fool."

Nez Coupé dropped back, disconcerted, for they could all see that the flint was gone. Spanish Dick, who had risen with the others, now chuckled and sat down.

"That's the class of brains that's been talking here," said Lafitte. "Are you going to let yourselves be stampeded by rabbit-heads like that? I'm talking to you, Beluche, and you, Gambio. You ran Barataria before the others came. You know better than this. You, Dick, you know better, too. You're the ones I'm talking to. You want to hear the *Two Brothers'* devil yell? You think you can smother me so quick I can't get it off? You couldn't last in here a quarter of an hour: this brush heap would go up like a torch, with you in it and the *Two Brothers'* pikes outside."

"Your sixty men would be whelmed in two minutes," said Cochrane.

"By whom?" said Lafitte. "I doubt if you could win a pitched fight among your own men if mine stood aside!"

"He isn't going to yell," said Cochrane. "He ain't got the guts nor the beginning of the guts!"

"You think I won't?" Lafitte demanded, staring into the face of Beluche; and Beluche dropped his eyes. Lafitte's ears were ringing; his teeth showed under his moustache in what may have been meant for a grin. He swayed slightly forward, as if drunk; and there was a glazed light in his eye that they were afraid represented an unreckoning madness. "You think I won't? You think I won't?"

There was a moment's pause. "Shall I try the knife?" said Nez Coupé.

"Don't start something you can't end," Beluche said.

The strain slackened, and one or two eased themselves down onto their haunches again.

"Here is the proposition I came here with," said Lafitte, "and this is my last: I suggest we form a board for the disposal of prize goods. Three men—Beluche, Gambio, and myself. Let those three decide what are fair prices and fair profit for the work I do in getting rid of the stuff. I can't go farther than that."

"What's all this?" mumbled La Maison after a moment; and Lafitte went over it again.

There was a silence, while they looked to Beluche.

Outside the thud of the improvised drum fluttered and stopped, leaving a curious silence through which something seemed falling, falling from far above. Then they heard the pad and scuffle of running feet, and a new increased flurry of raised voices, scattered, insistent. Under these sounds they sensed something else; a general movement throughout the camp, a movement unexplained and threatening but without voice.

"What's out there?" demanded Nez Coupé suddenly. They had all lifted their heads, listening motionless.

"Open the door and see," said Beluche.

There was a general movement forward as Nez flipped the heavy bar out, but Cochrane and Beluche signalled them back. "Stay where you are, the rest! One man."

Nez Coupé flipped up the heavy bar and leaned far out, gripping the door jamb with one hand as if the hut were sanctuary. In a moment he stepped back.

"Couple bucks having a fight," he explained. The group relaxed.

"We'll have to come to an answer," said Lafitte. "We haven't got all night."

"We've got to know more about this," said La Maison, fidgeting, his chin in his chest.

"There is no more," said Lafitte. "I'll take the goods and pay the men of the captains that will leave prices and handling to Beluche and Gambio and myself."

"I'll not give him an inch," said Cochrane, spitting.

"I'm not asking you," Lafitte answered.

Neither Beluche nor Gambio lifted his eyes. "Do you want that? No?" Lafitte harried them.

When it seemed the silence could last no longer, Beluche spoke slowly.

"I'll do as Gambio decides."

Their eyes shifted to Gambio's sulky bulldog head.

Cochrane muttered, hardly above a whisper, "If you sell us out—"

They waited; and Lafitte knew that Gambio alone would have wished, in consideration of the *Two Brothers*, to accept. But he was surrounded by men who hated Lafitte, and his own bitterness was undiminished. Lafitte, sensing what passed in Gambio's mind, suddenly knew that the Italian would refuse. Beyond that, chaos; with no scheme ready or way out.

Then behind Lafitte the door rattled, and after a quick glance at the others Nez Coupé stepped over to lift the bar. The candle flame, stifled and small, flared brightly for a moment as Ducoing thrust himself inside.

"Where's Durossac?" Beluche demanded instantly.

Ducoing stopped biting his moustache to clip out, "He's out there fighting."

"Fighting?" Nez Coupé echoed.

"Him and that damned Yank is fighting," said Ducoing. "Just them two, with their knives. You can't get near. . . ."

The crowd in the shanty was on its feet. La Maison cried, " 'Rossac'll kill that damned—"

"It won't last long, with knives," said Beluche, his voice sounding far away.

"Who's carrying it?" demanded Nez Coupé avidly.

"The Yank's bleeding," said Ducoing. "He rushes in like a crazy man. 'Rossac'll be ripped if he don't look out."

Nez Coupé sprang for the door and disappeared as if snatched by a rope. There was a general push foreward.

"To the luggers!" De Verge cried out in a queer voice.

315

"This is our chance to get clear o' this."

"Leave 'Rossac to the mob?" said Beluche savagely. "The man that runs now will never set foot in Barataria again!"

Spanish Dick laughed, a raucous guffaw, and flung De Verge backward with the heel of his hand as he went thrusting toward the door. They crowded out, Beluche last; except for Lafitte, who stepped out behind them all.

Chapter XXII

AHEAD OF JOB NORTHRUP'S PIROGUE the bayou unwound endlessly, wandering and bending through the swamp. From the plantation of the De Verniats to the shell heaps called the Temple was a long way, long enough to cool the tempers of a man who paddled it alone. But something besides temper had the Yankee by the throat; and it did not relax its grip as he slowly put the turns of the bayou behind, and the slow far stars wheeled across the belt of sky above the bayou, marking the hours. Over the narrow water the unseen jungle bent close, hiding the surface in its own blackness; and, in that dark, Northrup's eyes kept seeing Madelon's hand creeping up the shoulder of Durossac's coat, clinging to the shoulder of the privateer.

The cords of his wrists tired, and his lips were dry and cold; he paddled steadily and efficiently, unhurrying. It seemed to him that he had no choice; that there was only one thing left to him to do. He was sickened by an unaccountable sense of shame, as if his skin were covered with the swamp scum and the muck. Only the inevitable work ahead of him could free him from his consciousness of bitter loss, of sickening disgust.

It was nearly midnight when he climbed onto the Temple landing, kicking the pirogue from under his feet.

From far away the boom of the negroes' devil drum had told him that the situation at the Temple remained unchanged. He could see, as he strode through the trees into the clearing, the same thronging figures that he had left behind when he had drawn away to visit Madelon. The same groups were squatting on their heels, lounging, arguing, waiting; and in all things the place was unchanged, almost exactly as he had left it at dusk. Yet it seemed to the Yankee that he had been gone a hundred years, that these must be other men, gathered now for other reasons, waiting for other things. He gripped the shoulder of the first man he reached.

"Jacques Durossac—has he been here? Where is he?"

A group no more than sixty yards away, a little to one side near the fire, was pointed out to him. A few mates and bosuns loitered there about a case of bottles, privately obtained, no doubt, from the spoils of the *Two Brothers*. Durossac stood erect, a bottle in his hand; he was talking in a jovial mood, rallying the others, and Northrup could see that they grinned.

After that his eyes did not turn from Durossac's figure. He walked straight ahead, unhurriedly, toward the firelit group; and as he walked he flung aside his shirt, leaving himself naked to the waist. A little nearer he paused to draw a long seaman's knife from one of his boots, and kicked the footgear away.

At twenty yards he called out warningly, "Durossac!" and eyes turned toward him.

"Look out!" said someone: "What's this here?" The squatting figures came to their feet.

Durossac stood looking at the Yankee, his face surprised; and Job Northrup came on. The Yankee was at five yards before three or four men interposed.

"Stand aside!" Northrup snarled.

They seized his arms and were almost lifted from the ground as the Yankee sought to fling them off, too late. No one mistook Northrup's intention now.

"Give him a chance!" someone growled in Northrup's ear. "Can't ye wait until he gets off his boots?"

"Oh, so that's the tune, is it?" said Durossac. He took a last mouthful from the bottle and flung it down. It dribbled and gurgled its liquid upon the sandy ground, and somebody snatched it up. Durossac, the surprise gone from his face, made his preparations with businesslike alacrity. Almost the man seemed pleased. "What about a knife?"

Four or five were offered him at once. He chose one with a ball pommel curiously carved of brass, and examined the set of the blade. Then, when he had tested the footing with his bare feet, he motioned them to turn the Yankee loose.

Out of the arms of those that had held him, before they could half release their grips, the Yankee burst like a thing from a catapault, and a shout went up as Northrup's mad rush drove Durossac back eight yards before he could recover his balance or break clear. A quick stream of red appeared along the length of Durossac's upper arm, and startled anger instantly blazed in his face. His knife slashed twice as he sprang into the air and aside; then he dropped low to the ground, bracing himself, and his blade darted out as the Yankee was upon him.

Men were now running from all parts of the camp. Their dim-lit figures bobbed like driven leaves that caught and drifted in a vortex about the fighting men. The devil drum off there in the trees fell silent as if the drummers had been struck down, and a long straggle of blacks joined the running men. Shouts were going up, inquiries, comments, scattered cheers.

"Who is it?" "How'd it start?" "Go into him!" "Go into him!"

Under the turmoil those of the inner circle heard Durossac's voice, gasping and desperate, for the man was very hard pressed: "For God's sake, bring a light!"

The cry was passed back through the crowd: "Lights here! Get torches!" And in a few moments half a dozen men came shouldering through the press, bearing aloft flaming bundles of sticks and rags that scattered sparks and hot fragments upon the shoulders of the crowd.

In Job Northrup bitter disappointment and scalding wrath had exploded in a rush of fighting passion that was half whip driven and half an insane, savage joy. The balls of his feet were light upon the packed loam, his muscles were living steel, and a pure battle lust was surging up through the anger that pounded in his head like the silenced drum. A thousand years fell away from him, and he was the hunting animal, his prey cornered before him and fighting for its life. He rushed and rushed again, trying to close with the light-footed figure that protected itself with quick hands and darting knife, slipping from under the stroke of his blade. The Yankee's teeth bared in an insane grin as a long red runnel sprang into sight upon the shoulder to which Madelon's hand had clung.

And Durossac—he was unaware of what had set the Yankee upon him. He had read at first glance the lethal wrath in Northrup's eyes; he had not needed the flash of the Yankee's knife to tell him that he was confronted by no ordinary weapon pass, but a rough-and-tumble without rules, in which he must quickly put the Yankee down if he were to save his hide.

He was a man smaller than the Yankee by inches, but he had fought from his earliest youth and was accustomed never to think of size as either a handicap or an advantage. Combat to him was the lightning placement of a weapon, the swift flickering tricks of feint and thrust, deceptive evasions, and the unexpected flash of the rush when the opponent had been made unready. He was an instinctive fighter, loving combat as men love women. In the hazards of battle he attained the high keynotes of his life, those instants of almost unendurable intensity which reduce the remainder of life to half living, a dormid hibernation of faculties unused.

His favourite weapon, in which he had perpetually sought to improve himself, was the épée, the light, balanced foil of thrust and parry. He was holding his knife like such a weapon now, the pommel in his palm, the blade extended like a continuation of his arm. The steel flickered in and out, flashing yellow light, and the supple wrist evaded the clutch of the Yankee's left hand.

And still Northrup rushed and rushed, striking aside the skilled defense, trying to close and end the battle with a single stroke. There was blood in his eyes; it was on his arms and running down his chest; but still he followed Durossac without respite, so that the Frenchman's ability could turn to nothing but a continual desperate defense.

About them the circle of the mob pressed close, those in front forced forward by those behind so that less than fifteen feet of clear ground was left to the fighting men; the circle was forced to shift repeatedly, opening new lanes to make way for the Yankee's hard, stubborn rushes, closing again about them as the mob pressed in behind. And with each rush and shift the pack of privateersmen yelled and seethed, swaying, shouldering, struggling for place.

Here shouted the roughage of all nations: French, Italian, Portuguese, American, faces unshaved, faces brown, black, or yellow, high-lighted by the torches; twisted faces, with yelling mouths brutal and loose, with eyes avidly gleeful. Every cord of consciousness knotted in that tight shifting ring; a hundred tensed wills struggled there, hovering over the bodies of the two. Behind them the swamp had ceased to exist, as if the world for this quarter hour centred in a single spectacle, glorious and macabre.

Of the eight hundred men of the privateers, perhaps a quarter knew and hated Durossac, fearing his ability, and hating him because they were ashamed of that fear; yet those men were cheering him now. They had not believed that the captain of the *Culebra* could be beaten in single fight; and now as they saw him close pressed, fighting for his life, they loved him because he was turned to a common man again, human and defeatable like themselves. They roared his name, begging him to stand and fight, shouting to him their advice. To them the Yankee was an outlander, powerful and unknown; and their wills projected themselves into the ring, trying to stem the Yankee's rushes and bear him down.

The fight was changing now. The Yankee's mad rushes were shortening, slowing down; yet the tightening of the ring about them blocked the dancing evasions of Durossac, so that now he was forced to come to grips. Over and over now Durossac matched his lithe strength against the Yankee's iron, because there no longer was any escape; and as they locked together, gripping each other's wrists, struggling to free their blades, Durossac seemed to become smeared with the blood he had drawn from Northrup with his own darting point; so that the watchers could no longer tell who was hurt or how seriously.

That shifting avid ring of men was watching a spectacle that was to them rare and precious: the struggle of two captains, the leaders that they feared and resented, fighting for each other's lives. Slim, quick Frenchman, dare-devil, master of weapons and the art of fence, and mad Yankee bucko skipper, with the knife arm of a harpooner and a charging attack like a crazed bull—those hundreds had seen no such show before and would not again. . . .

The voice of the mob, steady as the growl of breakers, now rose to a continuous roar, the roar of a prize-fight crowd coming to its feet for a knock-out: the voice of the pack, yelling without knowing that it yells, begging for the kill. Words slashed through that chaos like words coming through wind and rain: "Gut him, 'Rossac!" "Overhand!" "Stom*ee!*"—pleading, blood-hungry voices, quickly lost again, drowned in the storm.

In the vortex, in the heart of sound, the two half-naked men fought silently, backs straining, locked like pit bulls, while long moments passed; then once more—the wrench free, the quick single slash of knives, the shift of the ring as the Yankee rushed, the grip of the clinch again; and again the long straining moments of muscle against muscle, weight against weight, while the sweat marked their backs with twisting rivulets that glinted in the little light. The Yankee was the stronger man, but the long miles by paddle were counting against him now.

Durossac's breath was whistling through his teeth, close to the Yankee's ear, "Are you crazy? What—"

"You son of a bitch!" gasped Northrup. They were the last words the Temple ever heard him say.

They lost their grips, hands slippery with sweat, and Durossac leaped away, white faced. He spoke once more, and though the voice of the crowd drowned his words Northrup read his lips by the light of the smoky flames:

"If it's that damned wench—"

By the fresh blaze of hatred in Northrup's eyes as he rushed Durossac learned his answer. As they clinched again the Frenchman felt a tremor in the muscles of the big Yank, and he laughed in Northrup's face.

Those on the outskirts saw Durossac's knife hand, the wrist clenched in the Yankee's grip, rise above the heads of those in front. The long blade quivered and swayed, upright in the torch smoke. Then they saw Durossac's hand wrench free and fall, and a great seething bellow went up from the ranks in front.

"What is it? What happened?" clamoured those behind, craning and struggling among themselves for a view. In the vortex of the pack Job Northrup was down.

. . .

Before his eyes swam darkness; and his ears were numb to the roar of the mob. He was clutching for his enemy with his free hand as the floor of the island struck upward, filling his mouth with dust. His racked chest heaved convulsively as he struggled for fresh breath. Every muscle of his body, every cell of his brain seemed drained of blood. Underneath, somewhere, a spark detached from all the rest, the fighting instinct lived, a fragment of unquenched hate. Blindly he got to his hands and knees and drew one foot under him, seeking to rise. His muscles would not answer; he had no muscles, nothing but an overwhelming weariness of weight and pain. The wills of the eight hundred hung heavily upon his back, holding him down.

He raised his eyes straining to see; and so made out the white face of Durossac and a heaving blood-streaked chest—only that much gleaming faintly in the torchlight, afloat in a swimming blackness. The fighting hatred blazed, and he surged to his feet and once more rushed.

Something was gone in his left arm; it dangled useless before him as he came in, head low. Durossac was thrown back by the impact, but he kept his feet, and struck. And once more Northrup was down.

The roaring died, giving place to the querulous clamour of those behind. Durossac stepped backward uncertainly. He looked curiously for a moment at his enemy, limp and grotesque at his feet, like a disused thing.

Durossac raised his head and rolled his eyes slowly about the circle of faces, yellow, red, oyster white, and brown. He said in a strong voice: "Is there anyone else wants some of the same?"

Then suddenly he turned and walked unsteadily away, his knife still gripped in his hand. A lane opened to let him pass; then instantly closed about him again as he was seen to stagger. A dozen arms caught him as he fell.

Chapter XXIII

1

IN THE DISORDERED SHUFFLING of the mob Lafitte was unable able to see what became of either Durossac or

Job Northrup. He knew that the Yankee had been the first to go down; but he did not learn until afterward that the bleeding body of Northrup had been carried away by Père Miguel, Manault of the *Two Brothers*, and a Spanish luggerman called Mendez.

There are men who cannot see others fight without wishing to plunge into battle themselves. Hundreds of that type were among the dozen crews concentrated at the Temple. The mob that had been a unified mass, held unconscious of itself by a single vivid centre of interest, instantly became a seething swarm as that centre was removed. A hundred or so trailed after those who carried Durossac to a hut at the far end of the little island, but the greater number of the privateersmen continued to weave among themselves in the clearing where the fight had been. New fights were already in progress. A hatchet-faced mulatto, drunken and belligerent, had struck down a man who supposedly had trod on his bare foot with the heel of a boot. This man lay where he fell. Three men had instantly leaped upon the mulatto. One of these had staggered a little way out of the mêlée to drop in a huddle on the trampled ground; and the mulatto in turn had been dragged down. The single fight had become four, then six; it promised to become a general action. Eight men from the *Two Brothers* were cautiously closing in on a little knot from the *Lucia*; the *Lucia* knives were already out, and those who had drawn were urging the others to come on.

Above the clamour new cries were ringing: certain men in that disordered pack still remembered that fighting could be put to use. "Pay or fight! Pay or fight!" Grim faced under the threat of that cry, Beluche was trying to gather a squad of his men about him; but they were scattered, and their attentions were otherwise engaged. Gambio, making a like effort, had already run into trouble; he was forced to ignore insolence from men upon whom he had depended, and was glad to stalk out of the crowd without drawing his own seamen upon him. The moment for which Lafitte had schemed was at hand.

A long table, improvised of casks and planks, now stood before Jean Lafitte's hut. Pierre Lafitte, arrived from New Orleans in response to his brother's call, had planted himself behind that table, a heavy flintlock pistol in his hand and a strongbox between his feet. It was rumoured that what few thousands the Lafittes could still raise were in that box, together with such moneys as the *Two Brothers* had brought in. In the doorway behind Pierre the barrels of muskets glinted.

Jean Lafitte sprang upon the table. "The *Two Brothers* pays off!"

He repeated it three times, in a great bellow that partly stilled the camp; and from all quarters of the Temple the men of the *Two Brothers* came on the run, forgetting their quarrels at the call of pay. With them, converging upon the hut of Lafitte, there came more slowly a great ragtag and bobtail of other crews, drawn by the call that was not for them. A straggling, turbulent line of men formed before the table, shoved and shouted into position by bosuns' mates. The thonged "colts," or knotted rope ends, with which the bosun and his mates kept discipline at sea, were not in evidence now; but, by main force of bellowing, some sort of order was established before the pay station of the Lafittes.

Jean Lafitte leaped down from the table, his hands full of papers. He went shouldering roughly through the crowd, ignoring the risk of a shot in the back. At one side he found De Verge, in consultation with Jean Ducoing and Spanish Dick. He drew the saffron-faced captain aside.

"I have lists of your prize goods here. If you want to get out of this mess I'll give your men stop-gap money at the rate of one dollar to every ten they have coming."

"The other captains—" De Verge began.

"I can't do this for everyone," Lafitte told him shortly. "If you don't take this chance it's on your own head. There are more than enough of you eager for my money now." He started to turn away.

"Wait!" said De Verge. "I'm your man."

In a few moments a great ragged cheer went up as a second announcement was shouted from the table before the hut of Lafitte: "The *Gay Marie* pays off!"

Ducoing and Spanish Dick sprang forward, angry of feature, to demand of De Verge what he had done; but the captain of the *Gay Marie* had thrust his way through the crowd and was out of their reach.

"What kind of favouritism is this?" Spanish Dick demanded of Jean Lafitte. "Why should that yellow-bellied—"

"I can still make the same offer to two or three more," said Jean. He extricated a bill of sale from the sheaf of papers that filled his hands, and held it low, so that the light of a near-by fire fell upon its face. "Do you want to sign that?" It was a bill of sale for such merchantable properties as Spanish Dick controlled.

The bearded man bent low for a moment; then raised himself and spat. "Your price is too low by half."

"Under these conditions it is all that I can pay. If you don't want it—"

"I'll take it," said Spanish Dick, spitting again. He wiped his beard with the back of his hand.

"You mean to say—" Jean Ducoing demanded, his moustache quivering.

"Take care of your own hide," said Spanish Dick with a grin. "I'm taking care of mine." He leaned close to Ducoing as Lafitte walked away. "His price was a third better than Beluche offered, and half again better than I would have been glad to take. I'm not running a charity game, my friend."

Another ragged cheer as the shout came from the torchlit pay table: "The *Baracuda* pays off!"

Jean Lafitte was talking to Gambio. The ugly head of the Italian swung lower than ever; from his lips trailed a half-audible stream of slow oaths.

"Your friends are running for cover," Jean told him. "In fifteen minutes you will be absolutely alone. I haven't money enough for all. Ten dollars to the man, advance pay, if you want to take the *Two Brothers* out. If you do, speak now."

"Beluche will have something to say," Gambio growled.

"Beluche can do nothing for you. You'll find he's going to be glad to do something for himself. The advance I am offering you is something I can't very well afford. If you don't want it I'll give it to Jean Ducoing as first money on his prize goods, and the *Two Brothers* goes to Manault."

As Gambio hesitated a short man with grizzled hair about his ears nudged Lafitte's arm.

"Jacques Durossac can't speak," he said, his voice low and worried. "I got your message and I'll answer for him: Go ahead."

Jean Lafitte half turned, and shouted across the crowd to Pierre: "Pay the *Culebra*!"

And the answering shout from under the torches said: "The *Culebra* pays off!"

"You don't want the *Two Brothers*?" said Lafitte to Gambio. "It's all right with me. You see how things are going and it's on your own head."

"This is every man for himself," said Gambio. Then the words seemed wrenched out of him: "I'll take—your damned—ship."

An hour passed before Jean approached Beluche, who stood apart, dour and alone. In the interval new kegs of rum had been opened, rolled out of the mud of the swamp where Jean had caused them to be hid; and about the fresh liquor groups of men, of a different temper now, were shouting snatches of song. Nine of the eleven rebellious captains had accepted the overtures of Lafitte.

A new rumour had swept the mob; everybody had it at once. It was that commissions were on the way from Cartagena, that they were all to sail under a new flag. The crews were set aflame by wild hopes of a change of luck. "Cartagena!" they yelled. "Up with Cartagena!" And the men that Jean had planted roared, "Lafitte and free gunpowder! Lafitte and free grog!"

"You're a good man, Jean," said Beluche wearily. "With any sort of backing I could have beat you. But these yellow-bellied skunks—"

"How's Durossac?"

"Badly hurt, I heard. You got rid of him handily. Oh, I know your ways by now. I'd like to know how you set the Yankee on him; but anybody can see that's what you did. It cost you a good man, though—that big Yank—"

"I knew nothing about it," said Lafitte truthfully. "As for the man it cost me, I had no use for him."

Beluche shot a glance at him from under his brows but did not reply.

"You should have taken my suggestion for a board of three," said Lafitte.

"If it's open," said Beluche, "I'll take it now."

"It isn't," said Lafitte with finality. "One thing is: I'll take over all your assets and liabilities and pay your men as I'm paying the rest—first money now and the rest when it can be raised."

Beluche did not answer.

"Oh, I supposed you'd refuse," said Lafitte. "Well— good luck to you, René—"

"Refuse?" said Beluche. "I am like hell. Pay 'em off, and, by God, we'll try this flag of Cartagena. . . ."

Barataria belonged to Jean Lafitte once more.

The lines of men waiting for pay shifted and writhed, shortening slowly, foot by foot. And by the rum kegs the increasing crowd of those who had been paid were laying the foundations for complete debauch. Men staggered away from the liquor to sing, wrestle, fight clumsily with their fists; seven games of chance were already redistributing the pay by the little light of torches and ships' lanterns.

An elderly charlatan, whose high opinion of himself had made him an inadequate bosun, decided that public speaking was in order. With maudlin tears running into his beard he climbed upon the head of an empty barrel and sent his voice thundering over the crowd:

"Men-n of CartaGENA! MEN-N-N of Cartagena! WE-E are about to—"

Somebody blew a loud trombone-like blast through his lips, and the old simpleton, howling with rage, hurled himself into the crowd with drawn hanger, to be smothered and disarmed by a dozen hands.

Jean Lafitte went to the table behind which his brother, with armed men at his back, toiled over lists and stacks of coin. He bent close to Pierre's ear.

"Is it coming out all right?"

Pierre rolled a slow eye at him and held up a bill of sale for Jean to see.

"What's the matter with it?" said Jean.

"It's all right—very much all right. Only—I thought we had agreed to pay La Maison—"

"At the last moment," said Jean, his lips hardly moving, "seeing the confusion, I reduced all offers ten per cent. . . . To pay our expenses, as it were. . . ."

In the middle of brawling and disorder, where safety was assured to none, Jean Lafitte had been thinking about his profit in dollars and cents and had taken time to change a figure here and there on those sheets he carried in his hands!

That was the man who, a long time later, was gratuitously called the Pirate of the Gulf. He never in his life won a success by the command of any ship or fleet; the few raids he led in person were inconspicuous and mostly futile. But, perhaps, after all, he was just as hard, as courageous, as game in his own interests as the cruisers from whom he drew his wealth—and his unearned bad name. . . .

2

IN A HUT at the far end of the island Durossac lay; they had laid him on the rude bunk that was almost the cabin's only furnishing, with under him a wet stained blanket and loose straw. His head and shoulders were propped up by a roll of varicoloured rags; and about his naked torso were dirty bandages that had once been white but were already soaked through with great blotches of red. They had not taken time to wash the drying smears from his shoulders and his face.

He lay with his hands across his stomach, one on top of the other; at first he had drawn up his knees, but they had slipped down again now, and one leg trailed off the bunk, so that the bare foot rested upon the floor. And he was perfectly still; so still that not even his breathing was perceptible. That he was badly hurt, Durossac knew. He saved himself, not spending by so much as the lift of a finger the energy that remained to his body, and waited for what was ahead. Only his eyes rolled a little, from time to time, in an expressionless face, then returned to staring directly above him at the dusty poles.

By the small light of a single candle stuck in its own grease upon a jutting board he could see that he was alone. The men who had carried him here were not only gone, but by this time had forgotten him, among events of more personal interest to themselves. The short man with the grizzled hair, who was the first mate of the *Culebra*, had been the last to go; but the message from Lafitte had called him away, and he had not returned.

The candle flickered, and a figure entered, timorously, stealthily, almost. Durossac's eyes turned sideways once and then returned to their contemplation of the poles above. The one who had come in was black of face, very gaunt and skinny, and dressed in a ragged apron that passed for a dress. It was a negress called Zanty, who had remained at the Temple a long time, simply because no one had offered to buy. Durossac, in his one sidewise glance, saw that she was big with child. Whose child it would be, on an island thronging with the scum of the sea, perhaps no one would ever know or care. But Durossac, who had an instinctive loathing for the creature, knew that it was not his.

That it was not was no fault of hers. Upon Durossac she had repeatedly tried to thrust her attentions, following him like a dog, worshipping him like a dog, bringing him stolen bottles of wine, trinkets, bits of food. He had more than once driven her away with blows of a stick; he could not help himself now.

The negress brought with her a pan of water and a

piece of sponge. As she leaned over Durossac he found her face hideous as never before. But her eyes were kind, still soft and pleading, like a dog's. He closed his eyes to shut out the sight of her face; and he did not open them again as she slowly bathed the blood from his head, his breast, and his arms. It took a long time, for she moved carefully, knowing the clumsiness of her clawlike black hands.

At last, when it was done, she felt of his skin and found it cold. She drew a rough blanket over him, up to his chin; and gently lifted the foot that had fallen from the bunk and laid it beside its mate. Then she squatted on her heels at one side, silent, waiting for a time to come when there might be something she could do.

When he thought she was gone he opened his eyes and once more let them wander around the scabrous walls of the hut in which he lay. He seemed listening, for the voices of the drunken crews were coming more and more dimly here, as if the rest of the island had weighed anchor and were slowly drifting away.

Durossac's lips moved, and the negress sprang up to lean close over him, trying to find out what he asked for or what he said. The walls and the candlelight had blurred out of Durossac's sight; but perhaps he was able to see that despised black face, hovering above his own. With a writhing effort he turned his head, face to the wall, and coughed once, explosively; and into his throat came a sound between a strangle and a snore.

The negress jerked upright and threw a frightened glance about the hut; hesitantly she stepped back, biting her knuckles. She had heard the death rattle before and knew it for what it was. Suddenly she became aware that she was alone; or, rather, that into the hut with her and the wounded man had come a third entity, terrible, unseen. As the rattle sounded once more in Durossac's throat the negress turned and rushed out into the night.

The candle wavered, almost went out, then burned clear and steady again, a point of yellow flame. The form upon the bunk was motionless and seemed diminished, as if under the blanket hardly anything was there; and a rat ran across the yellowed face.

Chapter XXIV

1

As THE WEEKS PASSED Job Northrup slowly recovered As his strength; his cabin in the stern of the brig *Charles*, whose ownership he no longer denied, was a familiar home, and the effects of his night of madness in the swamp wore away. Agents ashore had obtained a cargo for the brig; lighters were alongside, loading her for her return to the sea.

One day Northrup's bosun thrust in a shaggy head: "Sir, there's a priest or somethin', one o' these bathrobe clergymen, up here on deck, aimin' to see you."

And Northrup said, "Send him down."

As the Yankee had expected, it was Père Miguel, the Capuchin friar, who presented himself. It seemed to Northrup that the little man had a look of easily scared humility, as if he were in a constant faint distress.

"Ah, my son," said Père Miguel, "I fear you have found Louisiana unkind."

His voice was so low that Northrup did not quite catch the words. "Seems possible," the Yankee answered amiably. "Have a seat."

Père Miguel looked at him curiously and lowered himself to the edge of a bunk; and there was a long silence, made awkward by the humped, painful attitude of the friar.

"I thought," said Père Miguel diffidently, at last, "that you might wish the consolation of religious counsel."

"Consolation? For what?"

Père Miguel was stopped again. "I—I just thought you might require it," he said almost pathetically. It was plain that he considered himself, not the amenities of religion, to have been rebuffed. Yet, despite the patient woefulness of his face he seemed somehow to welcome the rebuff, as if it were a needed trial. There was another long pause.

Père Miguel was baffled by Northrup's collectedness, his palpable self-sufficiency under circumstances which Père Miguel thought he understood in every detail. He sought to approach abstractly the subject that was on his mind.

"Women are curious," he suggested in that mild voice of his; "indeed, one may say that they are a perpetual mystery. One—"

"Mystery?" said Northrup. "How?"

"You mean to say," demanded Miguel, appalled, "you—you understand women?"

"Certainly," Northrup assured him. "You fellows are

337

always trumping up some folderol about nothing. What do you expect? Women bear children, don't they? That keeps them at home, doesn't it? So they don't get a chance to get hold of any facts. But a head has to fill up with something, so, for lack of facts, a woman's head fills up with notions. That's all there is to your mystery. Simple."

Père Miguel looked patient. "You think well of yourself, don't you?"

"I don't understand you."

"I would have thought," said the little friar, fumbling at the scraggle of his beard, "that your misfortunes would have—uh—somewhat broken your spirit, may I say? There are forms of humbleness—"

"What do you want me to do, cry? I'm not dead, am I? Maybe next time things will go different. . . . Just the same," he added, "I'm free to admit this business has been a lesson to me."

"My son! I am glad to hear you say that."

"The next time I brawl with a crack duellist," Northrup went on to explain, "it won't be with blades, I can tell you that much! There's something in this épée de combat practice, after all. I tell you, hanger play will be a different thing in these waters when every manjack of the crews is made to practise with the épée. I've learned something."

The light that had come into Père Miguel's face died away. Another of those stilted silences followed; but if there was an awkwardness between them the Yankee did not notice it. To Northrup's mind nothing essential to a pleasant afternoon of conversation was lacking here. His cigar filled the stuffy little stateroom with opalescent swirls; and if Miguel's lips were dry for lack of a drop of wine Northrup did not perceive that, either.

The little friar sat teetering gently on the edge of the bed, regarding the Yank with oyster-like eyes. In the poor light the Yank's head appeared to Miguel to be badly hewn out of wood. But Northrup's crudities had served to turn the friar from his own thoughts only momentarily. Père Miguel was an introspective man, much interested in the expression of his own beliefs. Beginning with a few abstract philosophic statements to which the Yankee could not very well reply, Père Miguel wandered back, through long digressions, to his chosen subject.

The Yankee did not mind: he was not listening. He was staring comfortably through a porthole at the rain, absorbed in his own wool gatherings. It was quite a while before a slight emphasis of the friar's voice regained Northrup's attention. Père Miguel had risen and was pacing what space remained for that purpose when two were in the room. But even in his preoccupation his humility seemed to bear him down, so that the Yankee conceived him to be limping with both feet.

"And thus," Miguel was saying, "we come to accept such failings of women as God has deemed fitting; and at the same time we come to expect certain—uh—uh— embellishments which God has judged proper. And—"

Northrup felt the assurance of this humble man to be incongruous. "At least," he mumbled, "you seem to know exactly where God stands on this thing."

Père Miguel didn't catch it. He turned a vague blank

gaze upon the Yankee, but his words hardly faltered. "Women," he went on in his pulpit manner, "are supposed to have the strength of character, the cool heads. Men, the warmth, the tenderness, the fervour."

The Yankee's mouth opened. He was appalled by such an idiotic concept. But the friar was rambling on in an effort to prove his tenet. "Perceive the virtue of chastity," he urged mildly, "a virtue of coldness, of strength. Where do we expect to find it? In women, not in men. Consider . . ."

Northrup closed his mouth. He esteemed it hopeless to set right anyone as far off the course as Père Miguel. Yet, though he smiled, he could not avoid the comparison of his own turbulent past with the lives of the languorous, close-chaperoned Creole girls. He was of a breed distinguished by its flat practicality, its coolness of head. And yet . . .

He was thinking of scenes halfway round the world, beyond far seas. He saw again queerly ornamented Siamese girls; they moved like puppets before a background that had become in memory a blurred jumble of warm colour blocks, dazzling slashes of sunlight, and shadows unnaturally deep; a background in which rococo temples, grotesque gods, and thronging toast-coloured faces wove and shifted in patterns painted on mist. He remembered odd uneasy incenses, half pleasing, half warning, and the perpetual tinkle of bells.

But the Siamese girls, with their faces like tinted porcelain under their intricate headdresses—they were intimate and real. Their breasts were like old ivory bowls inverted; the skin of their backs was like warm living satin. . . .

The friar, it appeared, had brought his philosophies and allusions to bear upon someone specific. "Such a woman," he said, "is a dangerous fire, a flame. All evil, I can tell you, begins with such a one."

Suddenly Northrup said loudly, "I wouldn't give a hoot for any other kind."

Père Miguel sat down on the bunk disconsolate. He saw now what he would have seen long ago, if he had not been misled by that unworldly looking curly blond hair: that Northrup was only a hopeless dunce; no better, in fact, than the barbarian he was supposed to be—*un Yanqui perdu.* . . .

2

JOB NORTHRUP made no move to seek out Madelon until he had ascertained that the girl and her mother were once more at their town house. The weather had turned cold and raw, putting a harsh twingy stiffness into his wounds, very suggestive of rheumatism, so that a slow threading of chilled bayous offered no attraction to him; and he was one who knew how to wait. The delay was not a long one. Before the brig was ready to sail he heard in the coffee shops that they were in New Orleans.

He walked to their house slowly along the banquettes which the gunwales of broken-up flat boats prevented from tumbling into the brimming gutters. His bearing was straighter and stiffer than ever, but he carried his left wrist, slingless, against his stomach. It was raining again; indeed, for ten days the sky had not cleared. The clammy drops touched his face with weeping fingers, trickled down the yellow folds of his oilskins. Yet it was not the stinging rain of the North, but edgeless, a softened thing; a Southern rain, gentle and clean and cool, like the bleak tears of nuns. It seemed to cling about human figures as if seeking warmth. He disliked this kind of enveloping wetness, which made him feel ill-conditioned, like a man standing in a swamp; he would rather have had the raking downpour of his own rough Northern coast, rain that was a drenching scourge and a whip for the wind.

The house of the De Verniats was small, smooth-stuccoed to protect the crumbliness of the available brick. It stood on a corner of the Rue Ursuline, its one-story walls rising sheer from the banquette like those of its close-shouldering neighbours. The three low steps that led to its door jutted out into the banquette, a stumble trap for late parties who had been festively inclined.

Yet, in spite of its immediacy to the street the little square house maintained an air of most thorough privacy. Its low-hipped roof clamped down over it protectively like a turtle shell, and the peepholed batten blinds were always tight shut, as if the dwelling were facing inward upon its own courtyard, with no regard for the street against which it braced its back.

Northrup walked slowly along the high wall, which separated the De Verniat courtyard from the Rue Ursuline, to the heavy cypress door. He was cool and steady within as the rain; his years on the sea had well accustomed him to disappointment. When the Creoles reached out for a desired thing they thrilled with the expectancy of grasping it. The Yankee, used to a success that was never granted until compelled by repeated assault, looked upon the attainment of even a casual meeting as problematical, hardly to be expected in one attempt.

But in spite of his coolness he found that some hidden temerity had made him drift past the obvious front door and turn the corner to the courtyard gate. Like a reconnoitering soldier he tried the heavy door in the wall. It unexpectedly yielded, and he stepped inside.

His glance swept the little court, taking in the paving of irregular bricks and flags; the two-celled cottage for servants at the back; and a great lopping banana plant that rested its arms on the wall top in one corner, looking very dejected in the cold. And he found himself sheepish, hesitant to rap upon the door.

Madelon, moving in the rear of the house, heard his uncertain step upon the paving of the court and looked out to see him standing there as if he were lost. Her fingers went to her lips, and she reached for the door latch, to call him in. Then she checked herself; and, flinging a long cape about her, she went out to him instead. He turned at the sound of the door, turned slowly, so that by the time he saw her she was standing under the edge of the kitchen shelter, looking pale and sorrowful, her clasped hands relaxed before her.

At the sight of her he was momentarily disordered and confused; but this time the blood did not rise to his head as it had once before, and the next instant found him contained and cool again, with that static balance of his that made him misunderstood. He waited for her to say something; but she did not; only her eyes wavered and dropped.

"Well," he said, "do you want to explain yourself?"

His voice was too rocky, too cold, its irony, meant to be mild, too blunt and harsh. His voice always had a kind of nasal zing to it, never heard in the Southern born. Her eyes rose, flickered against his, then held steady. He was impressed again with the dark largeness of her eyes; her triangular face, completely quiet, seemed even more frail than he had remembered it. He could not force her eyes down again. They were sorrowful, beaten, resigned; yet with something in them that he could not bend—a base-rock strength, a visible life. That quality in her, now at its lowest ebb, was still recognizable as the one that made her vividness inescapable to him.

His own face was cool as the laving rain, and mildly stern; but with a spark of humour behind it like a flick of snow; as if his easy irony rebuked an unruly child.

Then, although her sorrowful gaze did not change, he thought that at first he had misread it. Her eyes still seemed hopeless and resigned; but in their murky depths was a sultriness that he had not at once seen, burning darkly. And suddenly he recognized it as a desire, a hopeless desire, a desire that stood unclothed before him in the depths of her eyes. A twinge of his Puritan blood urged him to drop his eyes from it, as from a thing at once too specific and too grave; but he could not. He found himself tremulously disturbed, deeply moved by that dark warmth that still lived under the frankness of her resignation and defeat; a warmth that inevitably drew his mind to the beauty of her body under her clothes.

It melted the ice of his own eyes; and when she saw that softening, tears welled into her own. She suddenly came forward into the rain, took his lapels in her small hands, and hid her face in the frill of his shirt. There was an unhealed wound bandaged under that frill, but the stab of pain that shot into his chest was welcome to him now.

A faint puffy rattle of the rear windows told them that somewhere a door—probably the front one—had opened and shut. Madelon tossed a little startled glance at the house; then, slowly, yet somehow as if acting on an impulse, she pulled open the heavy door in the wall and went into the street, drawing Northrup after her. The sudden sense of assured companionship that swept the Yankee as she did this brought a wavering smile to his lips.

They walked toward the river between rows of Old World French houses that compressed the street between walls gray with the soak of the rain. The ditches beside the banquette brimmed with sluggish water; beneath its rain-prickled surface little cumulus clouds of mud drifted as through a strip of sky. The gutters were inhabited; dozens of minute brown minnows flicked and wriggled through the small mud clouds, living a world of their own.

Two little barefooted girls trotted past them, their hands holding hooded capes tight about their throats; otherwise the street was deserted. Northrup and

Madelon strolled in silence, close together, past the partial shelter of the balconies to the open rain of the levee itself.

He said suddenly, "I want to show you the ship I'm taking you away on Thursday morning."

At first she seemed not to have heard him, so that he was about to repeat himself. Then she gave him a quick upward glance, partly startled, partly uncomprehending. They tramped up the levee's muddy ridge. Below them lay a wharf boat, a great flat scow, empty and deserted. One end of it was warped cock-bowed, so that it seemed to be lifting itself up, as if the river might be rising uncomfortably under it, and it was trying to climb out into the saturated land.

Beyond, the great waste of water might have been a sea, a currented, massively moving sea pouring itself over the edge of the world somewhere in the fog beyond. The rain fretted its drifting surface with a million disappearing, reappearing pocks, each backed with a touch of tarnished silver that flickered an instant under the eye and was gone. Behind the weaving veil of rain dark ghost ships rode, their spars indistinct. Their bowsprits reached up stream toward the amorphous sky; and against their bows the current purled as if they travelled perpetually yet were locked motionless by a spell. The Yankee pointed to one of them, a narrow brig, tall masted and low in the waist. To Northrup she never looked quite right; too much lift to the nose, perhaps, as if she were not all in one piece. A game, solid craft, just the same.

"You see that one? That's my brig, the *Charles*. Our

ship. They're loading her now—you can see the lighter alongside when the fog rifts. They'll batten hatches tomorrow afternoon, some time, at the latest. And the next morning we'll weigh her hook." She still said nothing, and he stirred uneasily.

Along the crest of the levee a group of American flatboatmen tramped past, hunched and grimly sullen in the rain. Their boots squnched, their shapeless felt hats poured water in condensed glinting streams. They hulked along like giants, those rivermen, alien men here, tall as the Yankee. The mist gathered them into itself, gradually diminishing them into a shifting shadowy blur.

She suddenly said in French, "Do you mean it?" Her voice was small, and trembling with a suppressed emotion.

"I most certainly do," he said gravely. They were silent again. He said hesitantly, "Do you think you can be happy, leaving your land behind?"

She drew a deep breath, and he felt her stiffen beside him. Suddenly she burst out, "I hate this place! I hate everything in it, and around it, and under it, and over it!"

She turned on her heels, quick as a bird, to face that small wet town, huddling so close over its brimming streets. She was even paler than before; her nostrils quivered, her eyes were angry black fire, and from her lips a torrent of defiant invective poured. He could not catch many of the rapid French words. He smiled, stirred by her spitfire vivacity, even while he was thinking, "She'll turn on me like that some day."

The fire went out of her; the tears appeared in her eyes again, and he saw that she was shivering. Her flimsy heelless slippers were soaked and spoiled by the mud. He threw open his oilskins to cast the wing of them about her, and drew her against his unwounded side. She leaned heavily against him, her face hidden. Her weight set his wounds to throbbing again, but there was a keen pulse of happiness in him, keeping pace with the pain. He smiled somewhat grimly across the water at his ship. About the *Charles* the cold vapours were rising, rolling slowly up current under the slanting whip of the rain, as if a horde of ghosts were dragging themselves out of the waste of sea before it plunged over the edge of the world. . . .

He was thinking that for the first time in his life he seemed to know what it was to stand against the world not alone.

Chapter XXV

IN THE ROOM behind the forge Jean Lafitte sat; his arms were on his desk, that desk that perpetually gathered a gray film gritty to the touch, like the sharp dust of iron. Days had passed since Madelon and Job Northrup had stood together on the misty levee, but the weather was unchanged. In the little courtyard behind, now bleak and cheerless, Lafitte could hear the continuous dripping of the rain.

His hands were turning over a trinket of small value:

it was a locket enamelled with a representation of a flower basket—a cheap thing with a flimsy chain. It had been brought to him early one morning, a few days before; about it had been wrapped a brief note that said only, "In friendship—M." What puzzled him was that the locket was one he had given Madelon himself— through her mother, of course. She could not have returned it to him for that reason, however; there were other things that she had received from him—some of which, because of their greater intrinsic value, Lafitte would rather have regained.

Puzzled, he decided that the thing was just what it pretended to be—a gesture of friendship, or of gratitude, perhaps. It was curious that she should have selected for that purpose an article that he had given her; but, come to think of it, the De Verniats had not in recent years possessed much of anything that had not come, in one way or another, from the beneficences of Lafitte. He could not understand why she should have sent him anything at all; or why such a gesture should have been possibly her last act before her departure with Job Northrup in the brig.

After the elopement of Madelon, Lafitte had done what he could to help the poor, distraught Madame de Verniat present an effective dissimulation to the Louisiana world. It was Lafitte who had evolved the ingenious lie explaining Madelon's unexpected absence. They had given out a story that Madelon had at the last moment been placed aboard the clipper ship *Daniel Walker* at the Balize, and was bound for France in the charge of a Madame Récamier, who was taking her own daughter to Paris, too. The falsehood, for the present, was plausible enough; and the very few who knew its untruth were people who in no way counted. In time, of course, the lie would be exposed; but perhaps some other ruse could be devised to serve the purpose then. . . .

Now that Madelon was gone, Jean Lafitte of course deceived himself that he cared for her more than he had known. He had been able, however, to smother his first impulse to send Gambio in the schooner *Two Brothers* to hunt down the Yankee's slow brig. After all, he recalled, Madelon could be of no value to him now; and under the circumstances it was just as convenient to let the girl and the brig disappear from the port forever.

By means of information from more than one source Lafitte was able to piece together the complete story of the departure of the Yankee and the girl. He could even reproduce in his mind the scene on the levee when Madelon and Job Northrup had stood together in the shrouding rain, the Northerner's oilskins flung about the shoulders of the girl.

He could go farther than that. His imaginative mind could picture for him the years ahead of those two people who had in common no memory, no background, no single habit of thought. And his anger at the loss to his own arrangements was clouded and diminished by a pity that filled him for that girl, now no better than a waif upon a sea whose rough power she had never before seen. He could see her in the unkind and unfamiliar background of the brig's cabin, or lonely in a cottage upon a raw Northern coast. But in her future he could conceive of no ameliorating light or warmth; but only an increasing wretchedness in the company of a man who could never hope to understand any part of those backgrounds that had made Madelon what she was.

He wondered if, on that levee in the rain, Madelon could have glimpsed, even dimly, the world of disillusionments, dismayed discoveries, and frantic, caged despairs that must lie ahead. He both hoped and believed that she had not. And he wondered, too, if those unguarded ones would ever find their way back to the knowledge that they were, after all, two human beings very much alike in necessities and in flesh, in spite of the irreconcilable backgrounds they had known. And if, by any chance, they might some time find a way to apply that philosophy of Job Northrup's—that in a haphazard world, whose purpose they could not know, they might as well make themselves—each other—at home; and so learn, in the end, to help each other through. . . .

He sat staring at the trinket she had sent him, twirling the chain about his forefinger, untwirling it again. It was valueless, not worth selling at all; yet she had taken the trouble to send it, and he did not like to throw it away. Presently he kicked open a chest and flung the locket in a corner of it, among some odds and ends of his things.

Long afterward, it happened, that forgotten locket was found among certain seized possessions of the Lafittes. The clipper ship *Daniel Walker*, upon which Madelon was erroneously supposed to have sailed, had been unaccountably lost at sea, giving rise to conclusions unfavourable to Baratarians and uncommissioned privateers in general. And thus by a curious irony that trivial locket, bearing the name "Madelaine Françoise Céleste," became the only evidence of lethal piracy that ever stood against the name of Jean Lafitte.

Center Point Publishing
600 Brooks Road ● PO Box 1
Thorndike ME 04986-0001 USA

(207) 568-3717

US & Canada:
1 800 929-9108